SPARK OF PASSION

"How could I trust you?" Sheridan asked. "I barely know you."

"Then we must get better acquainted, so you will know I'm a man of my word." A spark flared in his eyes, and he brushed her cheek with his fingertips, slipping them into her hair to cup her face in his hand. He traced her lips with the edge of his thumb, sending waves of pleasure rippling through her body.

"Sheridan." The word was a caress, spoken softly and soothingly. "The beauty of your name is only surpassed by the one who bears it."

She knew she should turn away, but there was no force on earth strong enough to pull her from his power. Amber eyes locked onto blue as he slowly bent down to her upturned face. . . .

Other Leisure books by Sharon Gillenwater:

UNWILLING HEART

HIGHLAND WHISPERS

SHARON GILLENWATER

Book Margins, Inc.

A BMI Edition

Published by special arrangement with Dorchester Publishing

Printed in the United States of America.

To Mama and Papa, for your unselfish love and belief in me. Thanks for teaching me how to dream.

Chapter 1

Scotland, 1790

" 'Tis good to have ye with us again, m'lady. Been a long time since ye passed through on yer way south." The innkeeper caught the eye of a young serving girl and held up four fingers to signify the room number. "The lass will stoke up the fire in yer room. It'll take a wee bit to heat up." He glanced down at the newest names in his guest register. "Would ye and Mrs. Gannon care to eat down here with the rest of the guests?"

Lady Sheridan Sinclair hesitated for a moment. In addition to her friend, Kyla Gannon, only Sheridan's coachman and guard traveled with her. It would be wise to keep the lack of an escort their secret.

Sheridan shrugged a delicate burgundy clad shoulder. No doubt, it would be only a matter of minutes until the innkeeper spread the news himself. The fragrant aroma of Cock-a-Leekie stew mingled with the musical Scotch-

English flowing from the dining room helped to make up her mind. After being in England for four years, the enticement to surround herself with the sounds, smells and people of her homeland was too strong.

"The dining room will be fine, Mr. Jennings," she said, with a brief nod of her dark curls. Sheridan quelled a tiny spark of anxiety and waited for the proprietor to walk around from behind his desk.

A fire burned brightly in the huge brick fireplace, combining its lights with that of candles on the tables and in sconces on the walls. The soft light flickered off the white-washed walls and soot-blackened beams to give a homey welcome to the occupants, mostly local townfolk.

Ignoring Kyla's frown, Sheridan followed the innkeeper into the dining area. Kyla tagged along reluctantly, her frown deepening to a scowl by the time they were seated in the center of the room. "This was a mistake," she said softly, squirming a little in her hard chair.

With her head slightly lowered, Sheridan glanced behind Kyla, uncomfortably aware of the total silence, which now engulfed the room, and of the stares from the leering men surrounding them. Someone coughed; another made a lewd comment in a loud stage whisper; a snicker rippled across the silence. Suddenly, an excited hum ricocheted around the room as it became obvious the two lovely young women were alone.

"You're right," Sheridan said quickly, "let's go upstairs." She picked up her knotting-bag and pushed the chair away from the table. The room grew silent once again, and her blue eyes shot up, widening in apprehension at the drunken giant bearing down on their table. "We're too late, Ky," she whispered, controlling her urge to run.

The man stumbled to a halt beside the table and gave

a slightly lopsided bow. " 'Tis been many a day since we had the pleasure o' such beauty in our humble village. Where be ye fair lassies goin'? Mayhap ye'd like to keep ol' Davy company tonight, eh?"

"We have no intention of keeping anyone company tonight. Now, please leave us alone." Near London, Lady Sheridan's icy command would have produced obedient results instantly, but at this lonely country inn, her words had the opposite effect.

Moving with a speed surprising for one in his condition, the attentive drunk grabbed Sheridan's arm and jerked her to her feet, knocking her white beaver hat to the floor. "Ye're a bit uppity, ain't ye now. Mayhap ol' Davy'll have to teach ye some manners."

Sheridan jerked her arm free. " 'Tis you who need some manners, you cloddish oaf." She swung her arm wide, gave him a resounding slap across the face, then brought her heel down sharply on his toes.

"Why, ye little slut." He raised his hand to strike her, but Sheridan ducked under his uplifted arm and ran toward the stairs. She would have made good her escape except for the foot that one of Davy's cronies inconsiderately stuck in her path. She tripped over the muddy boot and was catapulted across the room in a scrambling tangle of skirt and limbs. The floor loomed ominously before her, and her eyelids snapped shut as she braced herself for the bone-jarring impact.

The painful collision never came. Two strong hands grabbed her beneath the arms, lifting and swinging her until her feet flew off the floor, only to touch it again a few seconds later. Instead of the rough, unyielding wood beneath her cheek, her skin rested against the cool smoothness of silk covering a taut but yielding cushion of muscle.

Sheridan gave a little push against the man's chest, and a small space appeared between them, much smaller than she intended, since his hands still held her firmly. Her startled gaze traveled up a brown and buff striped silk coat, cream silk waistcoat and neatly knotted cravat, continuing upward to crash head-on with stunning amber eyes. She was so lost in their searching depths that she was only vaguely aware of his question.

"Are you hurt, m'lady?" he asked quietly.

"No." She cleared her throat and said in a stronger voice, "He didn't hurt me."

As Davy lumbered toward them, the gentleman swung around, removing his right hand from her side, but letting the left slide down to rest at Sheridan's waist.

Davy swayed to a stop in front of them. "Take yer hands off my wensh. I saw 'er first."

The gentleman cocked a sandy eyebrow at Davy. "There seems to be some mistake here since the lady is with me." He looked down at Sheridan with twinkling eyes. "Did you give this man a reason to think you were his wench, my sweet?"

Sheridan straightened and tried to pull away, but his fingers tightened subtly at her waist as he held her firmly against him. Shock and disbelief lit up her deep sapphire eyes, now shimmering with renewed spirit. "Of course not!"

"I just wanted to be sure." He winked and gave her a roguish grin before resolutely pushing her around behind him.

"Please, Mr. Mackenzie," whined the innkeeper, twisting his hands nervously, "dunna' fight with him. I just replaced the furniture Davy broke last week."

Jeremy Mackenzie smiled amiably at the drunk. "Cracked a few heads, did you?"

"Aye, and I'll crack yers if ye dunna' hand her over to me."

"Now, Davy, surely you must realize, even in your

muddled state, that I can't do that. I'll fight you if I have to, although it would be foolish to come to blows over a simple mistake. If the innkeeper had shown the ladies to the private dining room as I requested, none of this would have happened.'' He sent an accusing glare in the proprietor's direction.

"But, Mr. Mackenzie, I—I—'' The innkeeper's sputtering reply died on his lips as Kyla tried to edge her way around the drunk, stopping abruptly when he turned in her direction.

Davy's wide mouth spread in a toothless grin while he surveyed her tiny five-foot frame. "Ye dunna' need two lassies. I'll just take this one here.''

"You touch her and I'll break every bone in your body,'' rumbled a deep bass voice.

Sheridan swerved her head around to stare at the newcomer, who had silently stepped up beside them. Though the same height as Mackenzie, a little over six feet, his fashionably cut jacket did little to hide the build of a gladiator.

His dark brown eyes flickered from Davy back to Kyla, his fierce expression fading to one of tenderness. "Come here, little one,'' he said, his voice rolling around the room like distant thunder.

Kyla skirted quickly around Davy and followed his command, thrusting Sheridan's knotting-bag and hat into her hands when she reached the trio.

Davy eyed the newcomer angrily, his brain growing more numb from his many pints of ale. "I 'pose she's with ye.'' His hands clenched into fists. He stared first at Mackenzie and then at Sheridan standing defiantly behind him. For a moment, it appeared he wouldn't back down. Then his gaze shifted to his other massive, dark-skinned opponent.

"I wouldna' want the lads to think I'm selfish. Ye can

have 'em. I worked hard all day and want a lass willin' to please, no' one I have to tie down." He leaned over to look around Mackenzie, bracing his hand on a table to keep from toppling over. "She's too skinny anyways."

He scratched his chin and looked toward Kyla, blinking to clear his vision. "And she's such a wee thing, I'd squish 'er." With a loud guffaw, he staggered a few steps and fell into a vacant chair. Grabbing a pint of ale out of another fellow's hand, he downed it in one long drink, wiping his mouth on his sleeve, and tossing the empty pewter container on the table.

Mackenzie turned quickly and gripped Sheridan's arm gently. "Now, my sweet, we'll just follow Mr. Jennings to the private dining room."

"But Mr. Mackenzie, I dunna' have a private dinin' room," said the innkeeper.

"Then your stableboy is addled, sir, since he told me you could arrange a private meal for us."

"It'll have to be in yer room, sir."

"Very well, if it's the best you can do. Come along, sweet, we'll get you settled and then enjoy a long, pleasant dinner." His grip tightened as he propelled Sheridan across the entryway and started up the stairs.

"Mr. Mackenzie," Sheridan said under her breath, "I have no intention of dining with you in your room. I can certainly get to my room on my own."

"Don't spoil our little drama, my dear. If the others guess you truly aren't with me, we will be hard-pressed to protect you against these ruffians."

Sheridan glanced behind them to see Kyla following with her rescuer, her hand tucked contentedly through the curve of his arm, a look of total adoration lighting up her hazel eyes. When they rounded the corner to the second floor, Sheridan pulled her arm free and slowed her rapid pace.

"You don't have to manhandle me, Mr. Mackenzie. Take care or I'll be putting you in the same category as the drunk downstairs."

"I apologize, madam. I didn't mean to treat you roughly. I only felt it expedient to make a rapid retreat." A lazy grin spread across his ruggedly handsome face, doing strange things to Sheridan's pulse. "You must admit I'm cleaner than dear Davy."

Sheridan lifted a daintily arched brow and ran her gaze over him. Even his dust-covered clothes did nothing to take away from his manliness. Lean, hard, tan and so very confident. Nothing like the delicate aristocrats of London society. Goose bumps rippled across her skin as his warm gaze flickered over her, copying her own bold glance.

"Only a wee bit," she muttered.

They drew to a halt in front of the ladies' bedroom. Mackenzie slapped the wide brim of his beaver hat against his breeches leg, rousing a cloud of dust. "At least I don't smell like stale ale and leeks," he said with a grin, running a hand over his reddish-blond hair.

Or a year's worth of sweat, thought Sheridan. "No, I must give you that much. I have yet to thank you for rescuing me. I fear I would have been a mass of scrapes and bruises if you had not caught me."

"Or worse," he said grimly. "Do you have any idea what would have happened to you if that drunk had caught you? Not one person down there would have come to your aid. You two have no business traveling by yourselves, Lady—" Suddenly, he smiled, the little lines at the corners of his eyes crinkling in a way that said it was a frequent occurrence. "I don't even know your name. How can I give you a scold when we haven't been properly introduced?"

Sheridan laughed. "Perhaps I shouldn't tell you. Then you wouldn't be able to scold me."

"I'd do it anyway." He clicked his heels together in a military manner and brought her hand to his lips in a brief, formal kiss. "Jeremy Mackenzie of Boston, m'lady."

Sheridan gave a shallow curtsy. "Lady Sheridan Sinclair. I couldn't quite place the accent, but I thought you might be an American."

"Does that make me a monster of some sort?"

She carefully pulled her hand from his. "Of course not. Although I don't fully understand why the Colonies would wish to be free of the mother country, I respect those who are willing to fight for what they believe in."

"Someday, when we have more time, I'll explain the reasons we strove to become an independent country." He glanced at his friend and Kyla, who were deep in their own conversation. He motioned his hand toward the other man. "Lady Sinclair, may I present my friend, Patrick Hagen."

Sheridan and Patrick exchanged greetings, then Sheridan introduced Kyla to Jeremy. "Mr. Mackenzie, this is my friend, Mrs. Kyla Gannon." Seeing the men exchange a quick look of surprise at the mention of Kyla's marriage, Sheridan hastened to add, "Kyla is a widow. She went with me four years ago when I moved to London to live with my grandmother. I don't know what I'd do without her."

Kyla smiled. "You'd probably get into even more scrapes, and I wouldna' be around to help get you out of them."

Patrick chuckled. "If tonight's incident is an indication of the kind of adventures you get into, you'd better hire a bigger bodyguard."

"Just what are you two doing traipsing around the countryside by yourselves?" asked Jeremy, his smile vanishing.

"We are not traveling by ourselves. We have a coachman and a rather large guard accompanying us."

"Where were they tonight?"

"Seeing to the coach and horses, I suppose. It really is not your concern, Mr. Mackenzie. We have had no other problems on our journey, and I'm sure the rest will go smoothly."

"I wish I could be as certain, Lady Sinclair. Obviously, you have not stayed at inns all the way from London. Otherwise you would have had trouble before now."

He let his gaze drift slowly over her. Davy might think she was skinny, but that was only because he was too drunk to see better. Of medium height, Sheridan Sinclair had just the right amount of fullness in just the right places to set a man's blood to churning. Add a pile of dark, silken curls, large sapphire eyes with incredible golden glints and soft rosy lips that begged to be kissed, and even a mythical god would be lost.

Sheridan tried to calm her racing heart. She was used to men looking at her; she had been courted by practically every available male member of London society and ogled by all the rest. None of them had ever aroused more than her irritation, and most had been simply boring. But not so Jeremy Mackenzie. His blazing appraisal stirred something unknown and frightening. A warmth spread over her, and breathing became a conscious act. She knew she should reply to his comment, but speech was impossible; even if her lips formed the words, no sound would come. Blast him, she thought, I haven't suffered from my affliction for years. I won't let him trigger it now.

Jeremy lifted his gaze from that enticing mouth, noting her flushed cheeks and a spark of panic in her eye. His brows creased into a frown, and he wondered if he had imagined her fear as her chin lifted in determination, daring him to do battle.

He turned his head quickly, pretending to be interested in the other couple's conversation. The last thing he needed was to get mixed up with a woman on this trip. A few choice words ran through his mind, none of which he could speak in mixed company. He stole a look at the beauty beside him and stifled a groan. He was no god—just a man who felt more mortal with each passing minute.

Kyla had not missed the strained silence building between Sheridan and Jeremy, and sought a way to draw them into the conversation. "Sheridan, Mr. Hagen was just tellin' me his middle name is Growling Bear." She smiled up at him, thinking that the name was appropriate, considering his size and deep voice. "I dunna' think I have ever heard of anyone named Growling Bear before."

"My mother is Oneida Indian, Mrs. Gannon. Although married to a white man, she was determined I would learn as much about her heritage as I would my father's, so when I was born, she named me Sleeping Bear. About the time I became an adult, my grandfather decided it should be changed." He grinned. "I'm just glad he didn't decide to call me Snoring Bear."

"I dunna' blame you," said Kyla with a laugh. "Did you live near your mother's people?"

"They lived in central New York, so they weren't too far away, and we visited them often. During the Revolution, the Oneida tribe sided with the Americans, so we were in even closer contact then."

"Your mother must be a very special woman to be willin' to leave her people."

"Indeed she is, madam. She is a woman of grace and dignity. Perhaps I'll have another opportunity to tell you more about her, but now, you must make yourselves comfortable. I hear Mrs. Jennings coming up the stairs with your meal."

Sheridan looked at him in amazement. She certainly couldn't hear anyone coming up the stairs.

Jeremy smiled. "One of Patrick's great assets is his uncanny hearing. I suppose it comes from spending much of his time with his Indian grandfather. At any rate, it has proven most valuable in certain circumstances."

His twinkling eyes made Sheridan wonder just what those circumstances might have been.

He took her hand in his and brought it gently to his lips, brushing first her gloved knuckles, then briefly touching the skin of her wrist just above the glove, sending a jolt surging through her. He detained her hand in his and leaned forward to speak quietly. "We will be across the hall, Lady Sinclair. If you have need of anything, please let us know."

He tarried for a moment, mesmerized by the star bursts in her eyes. "Lock your door and open it only for a voice you recognize. Davy and his friends are no doubt gaining greater courage from their drink, and I fear it may make them too brave. If you hear anyone outside your door during the night, call out, and we'll come at once."

Sheridan lowered her gaze and gently withdrew her trembling fingers from his. "Thank you for your kindness, Mr. Mackenzie. It's very comforting to know we shall have help if we need it." She looked up with a brilliant smile. "Mr. Hagen does indeed have marvelous hearing. Here comes Mrs. Jennings with our dinner."

Jeremy returned her smile with a winsome one. "Remember, if you require our assistance, call out." He paused, his gaze racing over her, his silky baritone voice dropping low. "Will you join me for breakfast in the morning, m'lady? I doubt if the inn will be crowded early in the day. I fear I will not sleep a wink unless I have your assurance that I will see you again.''

''I would be happy to join you for breakfast, sir, as a means of showing my appreciation for your intervention this evening.'' Sheridan opened the door to her room and swept inside, followed by Kyla. Mrs. Jennings bustled in, huffing and puffing from her climb up the stairs, and placed the food on a small table near a smoke-covered window.

''There ye be, ladies. Meggie will be up in a bit with some water so ye can freshen up.''

''Thank you for the food, madam. It smells wonderful. I apologize for the disturbance we caused downstairs.'' Sheridan followed the landlady to the door, thanking her again. When she moved to push the door closed, she noticed Jeremy standing in his doorway directly across the hall.

''Good night, Lady Sinclair.'' His head dipped slightly as he acknowledged her.

''Good night, Mr. Mackenzie.'' She pushed the door closed and turned the key in the lock. Only then did she hear her avowed protector retire to his own room.

''Ach, Sheridan, did you ever see two finer men?'' Kyla collapsed on a small chair at the table and stared wistfully toward the portal. ''I have no' met a man since my Angus who sent me into such a flutter.''

Sheridan sat down opposite her and attacked her Cock-a-Leekie, a savory stew of chicken and leeks, flavored with prunes. ''You're in a flutter because we were accosted by that nasty man. It was enough to make anyone jittery.'' Snapping her fingers to bring her comrade out of her daydreaming, she picked up a spoon and poked it into Kyla's hand. ''Here, maybe you can think better when you have some food in you.''

Kyla stirred the stew for a moment, laid the spoon

down and rested her chin in her hand, her elbow leaning on the table. " 'Tis no' food I'm a hungerin' for."

"Kyla! We just met him and you're ready to . . . to crawl between his sheets. Whatever will they think of us? You've never behaved this way before. You act like a naive chambermaid, not someone old enough to know better."

Kyla smiled at Sheridan with patient indulgence. "I'm only seven-and-twenty, Sher, no' ancient. I still have feelin's, desires, but I've no' met a man who ever came close to my Angus until tonight. Dunna' get yourself in a dither. I've no intention of scandalizin' myself for Mr. Hagen's pleasure. I have somethin' more permanent in mind."

Reading the look of total bemusement on her friend's face, her voice softened. "You've never had a man to call your own. You dunna' know what 'tis like to be loved and have that love taken away. When Patrick looked at me tonight and took my hand in his, I felt whole. He's the one I've been lookin' for, and I think he knows it."

"Oh, Kyla, I just don't want you to be hurt. They'll leave in the morning, and we'll never see them again."

"We'll see them again, mark my words." She watched hopefulness drift across Sheridan's face to be replaced quickly by indifference. "He's no' like the fops you left blubberin' in London, is he? Your Mr. Mackenzie is the kind of man you need—one who can keep you in line and satisfied. 'Twas no accident we met them tonight. 'Twas meant to be. We've no' seen the last of those two."

"I'm perfectly satisfied with my life as it is, and he's not my Mr. Mackenzie." Sheridan threw the spoon down on the table to emphasize her point, glaring at it when it bounced onto the floor. With a noise something akin to a growl, she bent down and picked up the utensil, setting it on the table with a sound thunk.

"You need a husband."

"I don't want a husband."

"A lover, then."

"No!" Her vehemence shocked them both. Subdued, Sheridan said quietly, "I don't need anyone. I like running my own life."

"How well I know," Kyla chuckled.

Sheridan pushed her chair away from the table and paced the room a few times, pausing beside the window.

Kyla stepped up beside her and ran a finger across the murky pane. As she rubbed the smudge from her finger, she said quietly, "The right man wouldna' try to control you; he'd work with you to accomplish your dreams."

Kyla studied her friend out of the corner of her eye. For a split second, Sheridan's face mirrored her unhappiness, but her feelings were quickly covered by the mask of indifference that was so familiar. Kyla had known Sheridan since she was born and had lived with her these last four years, first as her dresser, then also as her companion as their friendship grew. She frowned, realizing she had stumbled upon something Sheridan had kept hidden even from her.

"Dunna' be afraid to love, Sher."

Sheridan wrapped her arms around her middle, hugging herself tightly to ease the ache in her heart, an ache so great it was an actual physical pain. "I'll not be hurt again," she whispered fervently.

"You're hurtin' now."

"Don't you see how much worse it could be? I loved my parents and they left me. When they died, loving them only brought me pain. I saw how you were when Angus died. It took you months to overcome your grief. You loved him desperately, and for what? He's gone and you have nothing."

"I have my memories. They're stored in my heart for a lifetime."

Sheridan squeezed her eyelids tightly shut. Her head dropped slowly, her chin resting against her chest. She curled forward, her agonized whisper piercing Kyla's soft heart. "I remember so little about them. The few memories I have are so jumbled, I might as well have nothing at all."

A moment later she straightened slightly and said quietly, "Kyla, to know love and then lose it would be the far greater pain. I couldn't bear the hurt or the emptiness."

Kyla drew her friend into her arms, her light auburn hair resting against Sheridan's dark curls. Tears poured down her cheeks. No one had discovered that Sheridan could not remember her parents. They knew she had forgotten the fire that took them, but they always considered the lack of that memory a blessing. Now, she realized the few times Sheridan had mentioned her mother and father, she talked about things one would have gleaned from looking at a picture or from hearing others discuss them.

When she was able, Kyla pulled away and wiped the tears from Sheridan's cheeks. "Sher, you were only five when your parents died. A wee bairn would no' remember as much as an adult. You must no' determine the course of your life by what happened then. You must no' shut out the chance for love. I promise you, the rewards are much greater than any heartache it could bring." She straightened a stray curl and smiled. "If God gives you the opportunity, do no' turn away. I think Jeremy Mackenzie has touched a part of you no man has reached before."

Sheridan squared her shoulders and gave her dear friend a wobbly smile. "He certainly makes me feel things I've never felt. When he looks at me, I get all quivery inside and feel as if I'm burning with a fever."

Kyla giggled, determined to lighten her friend's

mood. "That's called desire, my dear, and believe me, it gets worse."

"I'm not sure I want to be infected with this malady."

"Ach, but the cure! The cure is wonderful."

Sheridan smiled, but shook her head and walked across the room to answer a knock at the door. A soft voice called from the hallway, "I've brought ye some hot water to freshen up, m'lady." Sheridan opened the door, stepping aside to allow the young girl to carry in the steaming bucket of water.

"Thank you very much."

"Ye're welcome, mum. Are ye through with dinner? Ye have no' eaten much."

When Kyla nodded her head, Sheridan replied, "Yes, we've finished. The stew is very good, but I fear all the excitement has taken away our appetites. You may take the dishes."

"Very well, m'lady. Have a good rest." The girl gathered up the dishes and left the room quietly.

After shutting and again locking the door, Sheridan removed her clothing and poured some of the water in a basin near the bed. Using a small piece of soft cotton cloth, she washed the travel grime from her body, then slipped into a soft linen nightshift cut fashionably low over her bosom. She poured the water into a chamber pot in the corner, and crawled tiredly into bed.

Kyla moved quietly about the room, getting ready for bed as Sheridan had done. She laid out the things they would need in the morning and put their soiled clothing away. Lastly, she banked the fire so the room wouldn't get too chilled during the cool night, and blew out the candle before going to bed.

Sheridan was so exhausted, she fell asleep in a few minutes, dreaming of a smiling face and intense amber eyes. Suddenly, she sat straight up in bed, unaware of what woke her, but alert to danger. For a moment she could only hear the rowdy laughter drifting up from the pub below, but soon her ears picked up a shuffling sound coming from outside her door. Someone rattled the latch quietly, as if testing it.

"We'll have to break open the door. Wait until ye hear the lads laughin' and then heave again it."

"Ye can have the dark-haired wensh. I got me eyes on the little bit o' fluff that be with her."

Sheridan slipped from the bed and pulled on her deep blue satin robe, tying the sash quickly. Opening her mouth to scream, she was dismayed to find no sound would come out, her throat constricted with fear. She crept across the pitch black room, groping her way around the wall to the table. Picking up a chair, she moved back to the portal, using the thin sliver of light shining underneath it as her guide. She tilted the chair on its back legs and braced it against the door. Continuing to feel her way around the room, she found the wooden water bucket, empty but still heavy, and picked it up before making her way back to the door. Unsteadily, she stepped to the side of the doorway and waited.

There was a burst of loud laughter from below, and Sheridan raised her weapon over her head. The latch rattled and the hinges groaned as the two scoundrels pushed against the door.

The laughter died down, and Jeremy's stern, low voice cut through the quiet night. "Pardon me, gents, but you seem to have picked the wrong room. I think the ladies made it clear they did not desire your company."

He was answered by the slurred speech of a drunk. "I aim to teash that high-minded wensh a lesson. Ye dunna' make a fool out o' me and get away with it."

"Now, you know we're not going to let you through

the door. Why don't you run along like a good boy and sleep it off.''

"I dunna' like ye tellin' me what to do, and I willna' stand fer it.''

"Then you can sit.''

There were sounds of shuffling feet and indiscernible grumblings, followed by a sharp crack as fist connected to jaw. Someone stumbled away quickly, then all was quiet.

Sheridan set the bucket down and moved the chair away, scraping it against the wooden floor.

"Is that you, m'lady?''

With a struggle, Sheridan answered in a low, raspy voice, "Yes.''

" 'Tis over now, Sheridan. They won't be bothering you again.''

Sheridan unlocked the door and slowly opened it, catching a glimpse of Patrick as he carried the unconscious Davy down the stairs. She stepped into the hallway and turned toward Jeremy. Struck with the sensual impact of the man, her breath caught in her throat. Clad only in buckskin breeches, the muscles in his broad shoulders and thick arms flexed when he shifted his weight to lean against the wall. Her first impression had been correct. Lean and hard without an ounce of fat, his wide chest tapered down to a slim waist. In the flickering candlelight of the hall, the fine mat of blond hair on his chest and arms glistened against his dark skin.

His sparkling gaze poured over her like warm, fragrant oil, skimming her frightened face and sleep-mussed hair, which cascaded wildly to her waist. His gaze slowed as it moved back up the soft curves of her body and came to rest on her face.

Trembling beneath his fiery look, Sheridan sagged against the wall and pulled the door partly closed. She broke eye contact, looking down at his chest before frantically averting her eyes and turning her head away from him.

"Why didn't you cry out, sweet?" he asked gently.

"I was so frightened I couldn't scream. I tried, but I couldn't make a sound. It is an affliction I suffered as a child. Whenever I became upset or frightened, speech would leave me. I thought I had long outgrown it, but now I'm not so sure."

"I wouldn't worry about it. I suspect many people would have reacted the same way. You wouldn't have been so frightened if you had trusted me. I told you I would be here to help you."

Sheridan's expression was troubled when she looked back at him. "How could I trust you? I barely know you."

"Then we must get better acquainted, so you will know I'm a man of my word." A spark flared in his eyes, and he brushed her cheek with his fingertips, slipping them into her hair to cup her face in his hand. He traced her lips with the edge of his thumb, sending showers of pleasure rippling through her body. "Sheridan." The word was a caress, spoken softly and soothingly. "The beauty of your name is only surpassed by the one who bears it."

She knew she should turn away, but there was no force on earth strong enough to pull her from his power. Amber eyes locked onto blue as he slowly bent down to her upturned face. As his visage blurred, she closed her eyes in expectation and was rewarded by the tender brush of his lips against hers. Her response was hesitant and unsure, but filled with longing.

Jeremy sensed her need. His kiss deepened as he placed his arm around her waist to draw her closer. His other hand remained against her jaw, his fingers tangled in her hair, his thumb tenderly stroking the sensitive skin of her throat.

Her lips parted at his coaxing; her senses reeled under the gentleness of his touch. The kiss seemed to last forever, slowly etching an imperceptible crack in the wall she had so carefully built around her heart. It was her first real kiss; she had never allowed anyone to even come close before.

He pulled his lips from hers, brushing them across one eyelid, then the other, nuzzling the soft skin of her throat as he filled his nostrils with the sweetness of roses.

"Jeremy."

A breathless sigh—almost a plea—her voice stirred him as nothing else had. His mouth sought hers hungrily, ignoring her innocence, teaching her the depth of a man's need. Her legs turned to jelly, and she raised her hands to his chest to keep from falling. The warmth of his skin beneath her fingers shocked her back into reality. Pushing weakly, she broke away from his kiss, her head drooping against his chest.

Jeremy eased his hold, but would not set her free. He buried his face in her hair, whispering in a ragged breath, "Ah, Sheridan, you're so lovely, so passionate. You almost make me forget I'm a gentleman."

The candle closest to them flared, then sputtered out in a silent trail of smoke, leaving them sheltered in the shadows. He sensed, rather than saw, the tear that slid down her cheek.

"I should not have allowed this," she whispered. "I shouldn't have let you kiss me."

He brushed away the tear with his thumb and gently stroked the line of her cheekbone, lifting her chin so that she looked at him. "You could not have stopped me."

"You're too sure of yourself, Mr. Mackenzie." She tried to pull away, mortified by her wanton behavior and angry at the husky tremble in her voice, but he resisted, gently showing that she was no match for him.

" 'Tis a Mackenzie trait. When we see something we want, we go after it. Usually get it, too."

Shame and anger flooded Sheridan's face. "I'm not a thing or an it. Don't waste your time." She shoved hard, and he released her.

"I can see I'm going to have to choose my words more carefully," he said, grinning. "I didn't mean to offend you, Sheridan."

"This whole sordid scene offends me. I don't want to see you again, you . . . you rake." She spun around, reaching for the door handle.

Jeremy grabbed her around the waist and pulled her back against him, the heat of his lean body penetrating through her clothing to set her aflame.

"What we just shared was not sordid, nor offensive." He nuzzled her hair aside and sprinkled kisses along the nape of her neck and behind her ear, smiling when she shivered against him. "Don't run from the magic—believe in it." Suddenly, he released her and quietly opened the door to her room so she could slip through. "I *will* see you in the morning."

Sheridan shut the door quickly, a sob breaking from her throat. She leaned against the cold wood and cried softly, muffling the sound against the back of her hand. What was he doing to her? How could he completely wipe away her defenses with a simple kiss? She shook her head. It wasn't a simple kiss. She was certain none of her other admirers would kiss her the way he had, nor would their touch set off such a violent reaction. Just the memory of that touch sent a new heat spiraling through her, evoking a longing and need she didn't understand.

Finally, the coldness of the room forced her to seek the bed. She wiped her tears on the sleeve of her robe and took a slow, deep breath. Latching the door, she propped the chair against it for good measure. She shook her head when she heard Kyla's deep, even breathing. "At least one of us will get some sleep tonight," she muttered.

Jeremy waited in the hall until Sheridan locked the door, smiling slightly when he heard her push the chair against it. Was she trying to keep out the drunk or him? He heard her crying and was sorely tempted to push open the door, sweep her up in his arms and carry her back to his room to kiss away her fear and anger. But he didn't. Instead he went back to his room alone and tried to block out the memory of her soft, pliant body in his arms.

When Patrick came in a few minutes later, Jeremy was staring gloomily out the window at the stars. "What did you do with him?" he asked, not moving.

"Dumped him in the stables."

"With the pigs?"

"No, it was too much trouble to get to them. I just threw him in a pile of hay next to a cow."

"Suitable companionship," chuckled Jeremy, turning back from the window.

Patrick stretched out on the bed, resting his head against the wooden headboard. "Are you in a hurry to get to your aunt's?"

"Not anymore."

"Good. I think it would be a good idea if we ride along with the ladies until they reach their destination. Somebody has to keep an eye on the little fools."

"They're not hard to keep an eye on. I could look at Sheridan all day."

"And all night."

"Aye, especially all night." Jeremy grimaced and lay down on his side of the bed. "I may have spoiled our chances of going with them. She's angry with me right now.''

"Shocked her sensibilities?" asked Patrick with a wry smile.

"Aye. As beautiful as she is, I don't think she'd ever been kissed, at least not like a woman should be." Jeremy smiled, staring up at the ceiling, his eyes shining with the memory of her innocence, then flaring at the thought of her naturally passionate response. "I think I unleashed a tiger she never knew existed."

"Well, even if Sheridan sends you packing, I intend to get to know Kyla." Patrick paused, rising to strip off his breeches and pull back the covers. "I may even court her."

"I knew we were in for trouble when I saw the way you looked at her tonight." Jeremy hopped up and stripped down to his drawers quickly, blowing out the candle as he crawled into bed. "She'll have you wrapped around her tiny little finger in no time."

Patrick laughed. "Perhaps she already has. She's so delicate and fragile, I feel compelled to protect her. She's mighty pretty to look at, too, with those big hazel eyes and that soft, light auburn hair. Being a widow, she's no innocent. She'll know how to please; I can see it in her eyes."

Jeremy groaned, pounded on his pillow and decided it was filled with bricks. "It's going to be a long night."

Chapter 2

For Sheridan, too, rest came fitfully with dreams of strong arms and long, intoxicating kisses. More than once in the night she awoke, her young body taunted by sensations she had been unaware of previously. In the early hours of the morning, she gave up trying to sleep at all. She huddled under the covers and attempted to focus her mind on the things she wished to accomplish when she reached her home. Since her twenty-first birthday, half of the estate belonged to her, and she had a great many plans for what had been her father's land.

Unfortunately, even those things she had dreamed of for months could not displace Jeremy Mackenzie from her thoughts. Try as hard as she might, the memory of his arms around her and his lips against hers intermingled with thoughts of tilled fields, moors and noisy sheep.

The first pink rays of sunlight were filtering through the murky window when she heard the sounds of Mrs.

Jennings moving around below. Sheridan rose quietly from the bed, slipped into her robe and washed her face in the remnants of the water in the basin. She threw a few pieces of wood on the fire and lit a candle on the table before gently shaking Kyla.

"Wake up, you lazy maid. Morning's here and we'll soon be on our way."

Kyla groaned and pulled the blanket up over her head, but Sheridan pulled it back down again with a laugh. By now the sun struggled to shine brightly through the dirty windowpanes. Relenting to the excitement in her friend's voice, Kyla dragged herself out of bed to follow Sheridan's steps of throwing on her robe and washing her face in the cold water.

"Ohhh!" she gasped as the water hit her face. "That must be penance for our sins, whatever they be." She stood before the now blazing fire and lifted the hem of her robe and nightshift a tiny bit to allow the warm air to flow underneath.

"That's what you get for missing all the excitement last night," said Sheridan with a giggle.

"What do you mean, miss the excitement? I had enough excitement last evenin' to last me a long while." She peered at Sheridan closely. "Oh, no. What did I sleep through now?"

Sheridan related the events during the middle of the night, including seeing Patrick carry the unconscious man down the stairs. However, she left out the scene she and Jeremy played in the hallway, praying no one would ever find out about that episode. It would be hard enough to face him after she had been so willing to let him kiss her. She also realized, somewhat wryly, it would be even harder not to see him this morning.

The women dressed hurriedly and packed away their night things. Sheridan sat down on the chair to let Kyla comb her hair, which she smoothed into a simple chignon at the nape of her neck. The front and sides were left in soft, loose curls around her face. When she was satisfied with her mistress's hair, Kyla carefully attached a cocked straw hat at the top of her head. A band of bright lemon ribbon trimmed the hat, and a matching ribbon rosette adorned one side. Three pale yellow ostrich feathers bowed gracefully over the other.

Her gown was made of white and lemon striped silk with the long, full overskirt puffed out in back over a false rump. In the front, the white lace edges of the overskirt formed a perfect frame for the lemon silk petticoat.

Sheridan adjusted the white muslin neckerchief, tucking it in the low décolletage of her gown so the billowy fabric quite effectively hid her charms. "Well, what do you think?" She stood, smoothed her white sash and looked expectantly at Kyla.

"You look stunnin', Sheridan. I've a notion you'd like to impress someone special this mornin'. Be there a reason your eyes have a wee bit more sparkle than usual, lass? Did you be forgettin' to tell me somethin' about last night?"

Sheridan could feel the hot color rush to her face and smiled mildly as she nonchalantly picked up her small silk bag. "No, I didn't forget anything."

Kyla quickly pulled her hair back into a chignon similar to Sheridan's and smoothed her peach-colored muslin gown. Her cloak of golden brown wool was not trimmed with fur like her lady's, but it was made of a fine weave of cloth and kept her nicely warm.

When the two women reached the bottom of the stairs, the Americans were waiting for them. Patrick took Kyla's hand and tucked it through the crook of his arm.

"Good morning, little one. You look very beautiful this morning and well rested."

Kyla laughed softly, casting a glance at the other couple as Patrick steered her toward the dining room. "Thank you, sir. I must be the only one who slept well. I understand there was quite a ruckus outside our room last night."

"You heard nothing?"

"Nothin'. Unfortunately, once I go to sleep, it takes the roof fallin' in to wake me up."

Patrick held out the chair for her and pushed it carefully forward when she sat down. Bending over her, he said softly, "I can think of much more pleasant ways to wake up."

Kyla flushed slightly, but met his eyes without hesitation. "So can I," she whispered.

Jeremy waited until the others stepped away before speaking to Sheridan. "Good morning, m'lady. Did you rest well?"

Sheridan braced herself against the rich, melodious tones of his voice, tones that wrapped around her, stroking, soothing, flowing with the possessive emphasis of his words. She took a deep breath and carefully avoided eye contact. "I slept very well once I knew the drunk was taken care of."

Jeremy leaned over, his face only inches from hers. "You're very beautiful, even with dark smudges beneath your eyes. If it's any consolation, I spent a restless night, too."

Sheridan raised her eyes to his, thinking of crisply murmuring some platitude about bedbugs, but quickly changed her mind. With his handsome face so close to hers, she had to stick to the most mundane of topics to remain cool.

"My coachman is waiting, Mr. Mackenzie. If you would kindly step aside, I would like to eat my breakfast."

Jeremy moved back, allowing her to pass into the

dining room. She congratulated herself on a small victory, but would have been thoroughly disconcerted had she turned and caught the predatory gleam in his eye as he followed her to the table.

Other than exchanging pleasantries with Patrick, Sheridan spoke hardly a word during the whole meal. In any other circumstance, she would have enjoyed the Scots Eggs, boiled eggs wrapped with sausage, but the spicy meat only served to singe her already uneasy stomach. The oat bannocks tasted like parchment smothered in orange marmalade. She forced herself to eat everything, however, since she had eaten practically nothing the night before.

As they rose from the table, Jeremy took Sheridan's arm to escort her out to her waiting carriage. "M'lady, Patrick and I would like to accompany you to your destination to make certain you arrive safely."

Sheridan gritted her teeth, trying to stifle the happiness those words brought. When she looked at him, her impersonal facade revealed nothing of the excitement she felt. "You are very kind to offer, Mr. Mackenzie, but I'm certain it is not necessary. We have only two days travel left. Surely nothing will happen so near to my home. We have never had any problems in the past."

"I beg to disagree with you, madam. The innkeeper was telling me earlier of highwaymen who have been roaming the area. A single coach with only one guard would be an irresistible prize. I must insist that we join you."

"Do you even know which way we are traveling, sir?"

"No, but it doesn't matter. We will go entirely out of our way if necessary to insure your well-being." They stopped in front of the coach, and Jeremy turned to face her, his hands resting lightly on her upper arms. "I won't let you simply ride away. You will not be rid of me so easily."

Touched more than she wanted to be by his words, Sheridan ventured a glance at his face, a spontaneous warm smile softening her cool facade. She was practically being devoured by those amber eyes, which glistened brightly in the early morning sun. His gaze moved repeatedly from her eyes to her lips and back again, rousing an almost uncontrollable desire to curl her fingers in his hair and urge his mouth down to hers.

Heart pounding and almost in a panic, Sheridan spoke quickly, her voice not quite steady and not nearly as commanding as she would have liked. "It is a public road, sir; there is no reason you could not travel along with us. However, I would suggest you ride somewhat ahead of the coach; otherwise you will be choking on our dust all day."

"Very well," said Jeremy calmly. It was not what he had hoped for, but he would accept these conditions for the moment. "Which road do we take?"

"My home is on Loch Earn. We travel to Callander today, by way of Stirling."

Jeremy's face broke into a broad grin. "Wonderful!"

"Wonderful?"

"Aye, m'lady, wonderful. We, too, are traveling to Loch Earn. My aunt has recently married again, and it is her new home. Perhaps you know her husband, Lord Balfour Maclaren."

Sheridan's eyes grew wide, excitement battling with dismay inside her chest. "I know him very well. His estate lies next to my uncle's, or rather next to my portion, now."

Jeremy threw back his head, his happy laugh startling a nearby woodpigeon into its clattering flight, the broad white bar on its wing flashing in the sunlight. "Destiny has truly smiled on me, my sweet. Now I know you shall be mine."

"Your arrogance is overwhelming, sir." Sheridan turned quickly and climbed into the carriage, jerking her arm away when he tried to assist her.

"The English are arrogant," Jeremy said with a smile. "Americans are just confident." He tipped his hat jovially and sauntered across the yard to his horse, his top boots crunching on the small stones. "I've been banished," he called to Patrick, "but she might be persuaded to allow you in the coach."

Patrick looked down at Kyla, still wondering at their instant understanding of each other. The attraction was easy to comprehend, but this feeling of having known her forever was beyond his experience. "I suppose I should keep my troublemaking friend company."

Kyla sighed. "Yes, it would be better. I'll see if I can convince Sher to ask you to ride in the coach later." She lowered her voice. "I dunna' really know why she's so upset, but I can venture a guess. She does no' quite know how to handle Mr. Mackenzie."

Patrick helped Kyla into the coach, took her hand after she was settled, then kissed it lingeringly. "I'll see you at lunch, little one." At her smiling nod, he released her hand, strode quickly across to his horse and mounted smoothly.

They traveled for almost two hours before Kyla mentioned Jeremy and Patrick. "You're no' very talkative today, Sher. I think we should ask the gentlemen to ride in the carriage with us the next time we stop. At least then I would have someone to talk to."

Sheridan continued to gaze out at the passing scenery. Under normal circumstances, the early summer pink of the heather moors would bring a peaceful contentment, but today nothing seemed to alleviate her restlessness and irritability.

"I don't particularly want to listen to a lot of meaningless chatter. They're doing fine on their horses; let them ride on without us for all I care." She belied her apparent disinterest by adding, "Besides, I haven't seen them for quite a while. They must have tired of our slower pace and gone on ahead."

Kyla chuckled, even at the risk of incurring her companion's anger. "They've only gone ahead a little way. I saw them no' ten minutes ago, and I'm sure you did, too."

Sheridan shot Kyla a frown. "I am not overly concerned with their whereabouts."

"Of course no'. Ach, we're pullin' into Stirlin'. I suspect they'll be waitin' at the inn where we water the horses."

Sheridan unconsciously smoothed her hair and skirt, attempting to glance surreptitiously out the window. As Kyla predicted, the two Americans stood beside the inn when the coach drew up.

Patrick swung open the door and lowered the steps before the guard could disembark. "Good morning, ladies. Would you care to take a walk while the animals are being tended to?"

"Of course," declared Kyla. "The road is even worse than the last time we traveled through. Oscar did his best, but some of the potholes were almost big enough to swallow the carriage."

"Don't exaggerate," snapped Sheridan, purposely forgetting the times during the morning when she actually envied Jeremy's ability to dodge the washed-out places.

Kyla blissfully ignored her, strolling off across the grounds with Patrick.

"I don't believe the trip is improving your mood, m'lady." Jeremy grinned from the doorway. "Why don't we take a little walk, too, and see if it can revive your spirits. You can give me a history lesson about the castle on yonder hill.''

Sheridan wrinkled her nose. "I am blue-deviled today."

"Lack of sleep will do that."

She glared at him. "I would prefer not to be reminded of last evening, Mr. Mackenzie."

"Jeremy."

She climbed down from the coach, accepting his assistance without thinking. "Do you want a history lesson or not, Mr. Mackenzie?"

"Only if you promise not to act like headmaster. I expect to feel the rod crack across my backside at any moment."

"What a pleasant thought."

Jeremy took her arm and guided her to where they had a better view of Stirling Castle. "Now I'm beginning to understand why you aren't married," he said cordially. "Beneath that enchanting exterior lies an educated fishwife."

She turned toward him angrily. "I am not a fishwife."

"No," he said thoughtfully, "perhaps a termagant is a better word."

"Not better, only longer," she said sullenly.

Jeremy very patiently counted out the letters of each word on his fingers. "Only one letter longer. Does that make it more intellectual?"

She looked up at him, expecting to find his expression mocking and disdainful. Instead, those beautiful eyes sparkled down at her, his most charming smile lighting up his face. "Come, tutor, I'm ready for my lesson."

Sheridan smiled and slipped her arm through his, somewhat amazed at the simple pleasure of his company when she relaxed her guard. "As I suspect you already know, Stirling Castle is the sight of Bannockburn. This is where Robert Bruce finally gained Scotland's independence from England in 1314.''

They strolled along the pathway, and Sheridan related the events of Scotland's greatest victory. By the time they turned back toward the coach, she was certain he had known the story as well as she did.

''I would have liked fighting with Bruce. What a courageous knight!'' Jeremy declared fiercely.

Envisioning Jeremy in a suit of armor, Sheridan decided he would have been a very handsome knight and probably as brave as Robert Bruce.

''How long were you in England?'' he asked, interrupting her daydream.

''The last four years. I went to London to live with my grandmother, so she could present me to London society.''

''From the inflection of your voice, I assume you didn't care too much for London society.''

''Not really. Generally, they waste an awful lot of time and money on frivolous things.''

''Ah, your Scottish frugality takes precedent. Is your grandmother English?''

''She was. She died six months ago. My mother was English, my father was Scottish.''

''Was?'' Jeremy asked gently.

''My parents both died when I was a child. My uncle, my father's brother, raised me at the family estate on Loch Earn.''

''You mentioned earlier that my aunt and uncle's property borders on yours. I take it you have recently come into an inheritance?'' At her sharp glance, he continued, ''Don't worry, I'm not looking for a rich heiress. I have plenty of money.'' He grinned impishly. ''I'm just trying to figure out how old you are, and it wouldn't be polite to ask.''

Sheridan laughed. "I'm one-and-twenty, and yes, I recently inherited by father's share of the property." She gave him a mischievous grin of her own. "And you?"

"The ancient age of thirty, and since my father is still alive, I haven't actually inherited anything yet." His smile faded as his expression grew serious. "But I will."

Jeremy helped Sheridan into the coach. "Will you be riding with us, Mr. Mackenzie?" asked Kyla.

"Not right away, Mrs. Gannon. I saw the way your carriage bounced along the ruts, and I'd prefer my horse for the time being. It looks like rain, so we'll probably take you up on the offer a little later." He smiled and turned abruptly, jerking his head for Patrick to follow.

The two men mounted and kicked their horses to a gallop ahead of the coach. The incline grew steeper as the road led upward into the Highlands. The heather grew upon the hills, giving them the appearance of an endless pink and purple sea; a crisp breeze blew down from the distant mountains, forewarning of the building storm. A flock of lapwings flew overhead, their white bellies looking like a puffy, white cloud.

"Sheridan seemed in a better mood. Why didn't you want to ride in the coach?" asked Patrick.

"I didn't want to push my luck. I'll let her spend some time thinking about my innumerable good qualities."

Patrick laughed, slowing his horse a bit. "She'll have to think hard, but I hope she comes up with something. From the looks of those clouds, we'll be stopping them soon and begging a ride."

If Jeremy could have been privy to Sheridan's thoughts at that particular moment, he would have declared her magnanimous. She had just reached the conclusion that Jeremy Mackenzie would make the perfect match for her. He was certainly the most attractive man she had ever met, as well as intelligent, witty, charming and presumably wealthy. His courage and chivalry were unquestionable. On the other hand, he was stubborn, presumptive, and at times over-whelmingly arrogant. Still, he was the best she had met since her comeout—if one were in the market for a husband.

Sheridan did not even entertain the idea of taking him as a lover, though there were several long, delicious thoughts of just how proficient he would be. For a young woman of her position and upbringing, it was un-thinkable.

She had been greatly disappointed when he did not join her in the coach, and it surprised her. For the first time, the aspect of spending a lifetime alone was depressing, even bleak.

She could not deny her attraction to the American, but was mere physical desire enough for marriage? Many of her peers married only for wealth or a title. She needed either. Her Uncle Galvin, Earl Sinclair, had invested her inheritance wisely, making her a very rich woman. According to Scottish law, since she was the last of the family line, the title would pass to her upon his death and she would become Countess Sinclair.

A wry smile flickered across her face. Here she was, thinking about marriage, and she didn't even know if Jeremy would want her for a wife. Despite Kyla's encouragement, Sheridan did not think she would ever be able to truly love anyone. Life with Jeremy would probably never be dull, not with his quick mind and fiery passion. Companionship was enough for her, but would it be enough for him? She sincerely doubted it.

Don't run from the magic—believe in it. Sheridan swallowed the quick lump that formed in her throat. *I want to, but I'm afraid.* Staring off at the cloud-shrouded mountains, she subconsciously prayed for rain.

The ascent into the Highlands was gradual, the road winding slowly up the brae, only to drop down occasionally into a quiet, wide valley. Spring was all around them. The heather hummed with bees darting in and out the tiny, bell-shaped pink flowers as they captured the fragrant nectar for honey. A red deer bounded across the road in front of the coach, disappearing through a line of silver birch to hide in a grove of towering oak trees just beyond.

They were halfway between Stirling and the village of Doune when a small door behind the driver's seat flew open, and Henry, the guard, peered into the coach. Even before he spoke, the coachman's loud cry and crack of the whip warned of trouble.

"Riders comin', m'lady. They be ridin' too hard to be friendly."

"Do you see Mr. Mackenzie, Henry?"

"Nay, m'lady." Henry grabbed the coach rail as it tipped precariously going around a corner. "Too many curves and boulders."

"We'll do what we can to help." Sheridan shifted across the coach to sit by Kyla, lifting the seat cushion she had just vacated. Beneath the seat were several muskets and a large quantity of ammunition. Both women grabbed a musket and began loading it. Tearing the end off a paper powder cartridge with her teeth, Sheridan poured a little powder into the flintlock pan and the rest down the barrel. She rammed the ball and paper from the cartridge down the barrel as several bullets sang past the side of the coach. Opening a long, narrow window behind the back seat, she took careful aim, pulled back the cock and squeezed the trigger. Her shot missed its mark, but she took the loaded musket from Kyla and aimed again.

Jeremy and Patrick turned back at the sound of the first shot. Moments before they drew even with the coach, the thunderous boom of a musket sounded above the clatter of the horses and wheels. Jeremy watched one of the thieves fall to the ground to breathe no more. Henry was raising his musket to fire, so Jeremy knew the shot had come from inside the carriage. As the vehicle careened past, Sheridan's pale face and wide eyes were visible for a moment.

Both men fired, taking out two of the highwaymen, before riding after the carriage. Jeremy rode up alongside and called to the coachman, "Oscar, there's a clearing just beyond some rocks after the next curve. Pull the carriage in behind them."

The coachman nodded and began to slow the horses, swinging the team and coach around the corner and across the heath to the protection of the cluster of large boulders.

Before he had the team fully stopped, Jeremy pulled the carriage door open. He held out his hand, and Sheridan grabbed hold of it with both of hers so he could swing her to the ground. Kyla followed in the same manner. "Get behind those rocks," he commanded. Scooping up the muskets and ammunition, he raced behind them to shelter.

The coachman and guard scampered down from atop the coach. As Oscar led the team farther back from the road, Henry took up a position behind a large rock, shooting the first highwayman to ride up.

"You two load as fast as you can," Patrick ordered, taking careful aim as the robbers came into view. Both Jeremy and Patrick were crack shots, and when four more of their henchmen fell from the saddle, the other members of the band turned and fled.

"Ladies, you amaze me," Jeremy said, turning

toward the women. His smile faded when he saw the hem of Sheridan's skirt disappear around another boulder. Handing his gun to Patrick, he followed quietly behind.

Sheridan got as far away from the others as she could before her stomach heaved and she lost her breakfast. She took a few steps and sank down on a sun-warmed rock, her shaking legs refusing to hold her up anymore.

Jeremy sat down nearby and handed her his handkerchief, then a flask of wine. "Take a small sip. It will settle your stomach."

Sheridan doubted whether anything would soothe her stomach, but she welcomed a sip of just about anything to clear her mouth of its foul taste. She took a drink, replaced the lid with trembling fingers and handed the flask back to him.

"It's never easy to kill a man, but the first time is the hardest," Jeremy said quietly.

"I could never bear even to go hunting; I always practiced with targets. To shoot a man . . ." Her voice trailed off as she took a shuddering breath.

"It was your life or his, sweet. You had no choice. He knew the chance he was taking when he rode after the coach."

"Are they all dead?"

"I don't know. Patrick is checking, but they probably are."

Sheridan stood up and held out her hand to Jeremy. His warm fingers closed around her cold ones as he rose. "Mr. Mackenzie, thank you for insisting on riding with us. I have been very foolish, not only in traveling without a larger guard, but in spurning your help." Feeling suddenly shy, she turned away from his warm regard and took a deep breath of chilly air. "It's going to rain any minute. I would be honored if you and Mr. Hagen would ride with us in the coach. It isn't far to

Doune, but it would be a shame if you were soaking wet when you got there.''

Jeremy squeezed her fingers. "I'll ride in the coach on one condition." Her gaze met his.

"What?" she asked, half afraid and half hoping that he would demand a kiss.

"Call me Jeremy, and give me permission to call you Sheridan." His twinkling eyes told her he had guessed what she expected him to say. "Considering the way I feel about you, I find calling you Lady Sinclair far too formal, almost hypocritical."

She was being drawn into his whimsy, and she was thankful for it. "How so, my lord?"

He raised a sandy eyebrow. "My lord?"

"My pardon, sir. I forgot Americans don't use the term."

"It has some merit, as in lord and master." She couldn't quite stop the frown that wrinkled her forehead. "Ah, but you wouldn't want a master, would you? You have a mind of your own and would want free rein."

Sheridan didn't like the turn of the conversation and started back to the coach at a leisurely pace. "You were going to tell me why acknowledging my title is hypo-critical."

"The title has certain merit, depending upon the way it is said. *M'lady* is of no use to me, but *my* lady has a completely different connotation." He drew her to a halt, turning her to face him. "Now, I ask you, which sounds better: Lady Sinclair, I adore you; or Sheridan, my sweet, I adore you?"

His words were said playfully, but there was an underlying tone in his voice, a sensual thread weaving back and forth between them. Her gaze dropped to his lips, then to his chest, which rose and fell with slightly increased rhythm, a tempo that matched her own quickened breathing. She wanted . . . what? These desires, these emotions were all too new. She had to resist now or make a complete cake of herself.

She smiled up at him and lowered her eyelashes slowly, startling him with her coquettishness. "They both sound wonderful," she said softly, "but a bit outrageous."

Jeremy smiled. "Nothing I do is outrageous, *my lady*."

"That's only your opinion, Jeremy," she said, laughing, not even realizing she called him by his first name.

Jeremy silently applauded his small victory and wisely said nothing.

They sobered quickly when they met Patrick back at the coach. The highwaymen had made sure only the dead were left behind. Oscar and Henry dragged two of the bodies over to the side of the road with the others, where it was decided to leave them for the authorities.

An hour later, the carriage pulled into the village of Doune, and the magistrate was notified of the attempted robbery and subsequent deaths. At the inn, the ladies were fussed over and shown to a room where they could rest for a while. The solicitous innkeeper clucked sympathetically when none of the travellers had an appetite, and obligingly served the ladies tea.

While they were in the Blue Boar Inn, the rain began, large pounding drops that soon saturated the ground and left muddy pools in every low spot. When they emerged an hour later, it was still a veritable downpour.

Oscar pulled the coach as close to the door as possible, but there was still a large puddle of water to wade through. Kyla and Patrick stepped from the inn first, standing on the stoop to survey the pond that lay before them. Patrick gave a loud whoop, swung Kyla up in his arms and crossed the water in four long strides.

They disappeared in the coach, Kyla's ringing laughter filling the air.

Before Sheridan could say anything, Jeremy picked her up likewise and promptly deposited her in the carriage. Seconds later, he climbed in and shut the door.

She looked down at her cloak. It was hardly wet from the pounding rain. She watched him brush a few drops of water from the cape of his great coat, then smiled when he looked up at her. "How did you manage to keep us from getting wet?"

"I ran between the raindrops." He grinned and leaned back in the seat as Sheridan laughed. The coach lurched into motion, the wheels slipping a little in the mud as the driver turned it around.

"What business are you in, Jeremy?" Sheridan asked.

"Patrick and I own several ships, although for now, we have elected to be the captains of none of them. We came to England on one of our vessels, which we left in Portsmouth for unloading and the taking on of more freight. I had several stops throughout the country to make for my father, so we chose to come by horseback. Our ship will be arriving in Leith in a few weeks to take on more cargo, including sheep and cattle from my aunt for my father's estate."

"Were you born in America?"

"Yes, my father and mother moved to Boston three years before I was born. My father was an adventurer, having captained a grand vessel between the Colonies and England for five years before he met Mother and decided to settle down. He was visiting some friends in Ireland, where he met his lovely, red-haired colleen. He made one more trip to the Colonies without her." He smiled, his affection for his family evident. "The next time they went as man and wife. He bought land in Boston, and along with Patrick's father, developed a fine shipbuilding business, which they will one day turn over to us. Fortunately, my father believed in making me work hard; therefore, I was able to acquire a modest fortune on my own regardless of any inheritance I may someday receive.''

He moved his arm so it rested across the back of the seat, his fingers softly brushing the nape of her neck. "Until now, I never cherished idle time. In fact, I loathed it, but at present I can see where it might be beneficial not to spend ten months of the year aboard ship. Perhaps it's time for a long delayed dry-dock."

She wiggled away from his caressing fingers and smoothed the chignon, fussing needlessly with her hat. "I'm sure our paths will cross, Jeremy. Though the country social life doesn't compare with the endless activities of London, there are plenty of dinner parties and other gatherings to keep one busy."

"Tell me, my dear, now that you have become a lady of property, what do you intend to do with it? You said you planned to make Scotland your home; do you not wish to go back to London?"

"I really don't care for London. The parties bore me, as well as the people. Few persons who frequented my path are genuine friends. I find them shallow, with no purpose in life." She looked toward him again. "I sold the townhouse I inherited from grandmother, but did keep a small estate in the country. 'Tis old and needs a lot of work, but it was one of my favorite places. Unfortunately, grandmother preferred London, so the country cottage was not maintained as it should have been. As for Scotland, I intend to raise sheep."

His eyebrows rose in surprise. "I assume you have some experience, or at least have done some studying?" Seeing her rising irritation, he hastened to add, "Now, Sheridan, don't misunderstand. I'm not being critical. I'm just curious as to what measures you have taken to prepare for this endeavor.'' He gave her a lopsided smile, melting her aggravation.

''I've done a large amount of studying, from both books and visits to prosperous farming estates in England. I realize conditions are different in the Highlands, but I have read much about the progress that has been made there. Indeed, your new uncle has been one of those who has accomplished a great deal in salvaging the land.'' She shook her head regretfully. ''Unfortunately, Uncle Galvin does not care for farming and has not implemented any of the newer techniques that have been introduced in Scotland in the last thirty years. The few tenants who remain with him only manage to eke out an existence, instead of making the land really productive.''

''Are the tenants part of your clan?''

''No, most of our clan live on the northeast coast. These lands came through the family from my greatgrandmother's side. The tenants who live on the estate are from various clans that were broken up after the Forty-five.'' Jeremy only nodded, but she knew from the brief anger flickering across his face that his family, too, had been touched by the harsh hand of the English after Bonnie Prince Charlie's defeat in early 1746.

Turning slightly to look at him, her face earnest, she said, ''I think . . . no, I know, I can change that. The land is good, it's no different from Lord Maclaren's or Macveagh's on the other side, and both estates are profitable.'' Her eyes sparkled with excitement. ''I've already begun the change. I sent several of the lighter English plows up a few months ago to my tenants, and I'm very anxious to see if they have helped them.''

''If your enthusiasm is contagious, there'll be no stopping them.''

''At my direction, the tenants are already taking measures to drain the marsh and to bring in lime to further enrich the soil. I am hopeful we can plant a test field this spring."

"It sounds as though you have everything well in hand already. However, you must make me a promise, my lovely."

"And what might it be, sir?" She smiled at him prettily, tipping her head to the side.

Her smile was returned with a roguish one, and he captured her silk-gloved hand, his thumb moving in lazy, thrilling circles inside her palm. "Promise me you will not stay out in the sun until you bake your lovely skin and become as parched as a desert, nor that you will only visit my aunt's in order to discuss farming with my new uncle."

"I do have an aversion to wearing hats when I'm out-doors, I'm afraid, but I'll try to remember to shade my face at least part of the time. I'm not anxious to become a wrinkled prune. No doubt, Lord Maclaren will have a great deal of advice to give me on recapturing my land; however, I will make an effort to curtail my interest whenever I'm invited to visit. Do you have any knowledge of farming, Jeremy? Perhaps you could be the one to give me advice."

For the first time in his life, he regretted preferring the sea to land. "Alas, I know very little about agriculture. Most of my life has been spent around ships, so reluctantly, I will have to allow you some time in the presence of Uncle Balfour."

Sheridan gently slipped her hand from his with a wry smile and shake of her head. She shifted in the seat so she could lean against the corner between the red velvet cushion and the wall. Now, she could face him directly while putting her hand out of his reach.

"You said earlier that it is never easy to kill a man. Have you killed many?"

A sadness crept across his face, and she wished for a

moment she hadn't mentioned it. "Some. In the war, mostly; a few on the trade route when we were attacked."

"Did you fight in the revolution, Jeremy?"

"Aye, I did. I joined the Continental Army in '78 and served under Lafayette, along with Patrick. A few years later my father presented us with our first ship and a mission. We went to France and brought back part of the supplies the French had provided for our country. Unfortunately, we couldn't carry all of the provisions, so many of the muskets and much clothing remained in France. Our country just didn't have enough ships to carry it all to the States. After we returned to Boston, we were commissioned as privateers by the Continental Congress."

"Oh. You were a pirate."

"Not a pirate, my sweet. A privateer is very different. We helped our cause by commandeering rich English ships and 'borrowing' their cargo for the Republic. It had been done for years by both sides, and since the English had most ports effectively blocked, it was our only means of clothing our men."

"And you made a nice profit in the meantime."

"Nay, not really. True, many did and were indeed little more than pirates; but Patrick and I were young and patriotic. We did it for the cause and only kept enough profit to provide for our men and the ship. We proved quite good at our job. Most American privateers were captured and rotted away in English jails."

Sheridan couldn't quite suppress a shiver at the thought of him in an English jail. Few who entered those hellholes ever came out.

"I really can't be too critical of you," she said. "Sir Humphrey has educated me on world affairs to some extent, and I'm fully aware that such 'aid to the cause' existed on the English side as well."

Jeremy felt a twinge of jealousy. From the softness of her voice when she spoke of him, the gentleman mentioned meant something special to her. "Who's Sir Humphrey?" he asked casually.

"A very dear friend." She watched him beneath her lashes, strangely pleased when his eyes narrowed slightly and his lips pressed ever so minutely tighter. "I suppose I should say a very dear and very old friend. He was courting my grandmother when she died."

Jeremy relaxed visibly. "Courting your grandmother?"

"Aye. They had been friends forever and talked about marriage off and on for the last five years."

"Never could quite bring themselves to make a commitment?" The corner of his lip quirked in amusement.

"No, at least Grandmother couldn't. I think poor Sir Humphrey proposed once a month, but Grandmother always turned him down. She loved him in her own way, I think, but she was a very independent woman. Sir Humphrey was accompanying us to Scotland, but he had an attack of gout on the way. We left him in the care of his sister."

"I'm surprised he allowed you to continue the journey alone."

"The decision was not his to make," Sheridan said quietly. "The carriage and horses are mine, and although Oscar and Henry will work for him when they return to England, for the present they are still in my service."

"I see you inherited your grandmother's independent streak."

Sheridan ignored him. "Tell me of Lafayette. Is he truly as marvelous as the gossips would have us believe?"

"He is a most remarkable man. In '77, he arrived in

America with his own ship and supplies, ready and more than willing to fight for liberty. He was adventurous and young, receiving a major general's commission by the Congress a month before his twentieth birthday. In fact, he slipped out of France secretly in order to come to the States. It seems his father-in-law didn't like the idea of his leaving his young bride to fight in another country's war.''

"I think I might agree with the father-in-law. What did Lafayette's wife think of such behavior? I don't believe I would have been too pleased.''

Jeremy shrugged. "I don't know what she thought. He never said, although after a while he seemed to feel guilty about leaving her so hurriedly. I never have understood arranged marriages. Whenever I wed, it will be because I love the woman, not because my family picked her for her bloodlines.'' He stared at her thoughtfully for a long moment, then looked away.

And would she have to love you? The words almost tumbled out. Flustered, Sheridan looked down, picking at the ribbons of her knotting-bag. When she regained control of her expression and wayward thoughts, she glanced back up at him. He was watching her intently, his brows drawn into a slight frown.

She gave him a warm smile. "Didn't Lafayette persuade the French to send your countrymen the supplies?''

His frown faded, being replaced by a twinkle in his eye. "Yes, he did. The French court was flattered by the attention and admiration he received in America, so he played an important role in obtaining help from them.''

"If I remember correctly, he convinced the French king to send an expeditionary force to help out Washington at Yorktown.''

He grinned at her. "How is it you are so informed

about the revolution? You aren't hiding a bluestocking behind that lovely face, are you?''

She shifted uncomfortably. Her grandmother was probably turning over in her grave. She had frowned upon Sheridan reading anything heavier than a novel, admonishing her over and over that a man didn't want an intelligent wife, but one who complimented him by her beauty and biddable manner. To that dear old lady, any gentlewoman who could be called a bluestocking was an insult to her class. Sheridan shrugged her shoulders and looked him square in the eye, daring him to make fun of her.

''I must admit I am an avid reader and found studying about your rebellion intriguing. Sir Humphrey encouraged me to study history and science and the classics. He is of the opinion a woman should not simply concern herself with parties and stitchwork, and I'm prone to agree. I detest too much of both.''

''Sir Humphrey sounds like a very wise man.'' He smiled kindly, pleased to see her relax at his words. ''What do you enjoy besides reading?''

''I love to ride, work in the garden and generally do things that increase my knowledge or experience.'' But most of all, she thought, I enjoyed being in your arms last night and knowing the wonder of your kiss.

Her face betrayed her as deep crimson crept up from her neck to her cheeks at those unchaste thoughts. Jeremy chuckled and leaned across the coach to whisper softly, ''I enjoyed it, too.'' He sank back into his corner of the seat, laughing silently at her dismay.

Sheridan decided it was a good time for a long silence, and shifted so she could look out the window. There wasn't much to see. The mist cloaked the woods and completely hid the mountains. She looked forward to her first sight of Uamh Bheag, but knew she would be fortunate if she could even see the mount the next day.

The sleepless night, stressful morning and swaying of the coach began to take their toll on Sheridan. It wasn't long before she was asleep, her head leaning against the corner wall of the carriage, her hat pushed over at an angle. In her sleep, she was remotely aware of the chill seeping into the air and pulled her cloak tighter around her. She was in a deep sleep, however, when Jeremy pulled her over to rest against him, and was unaware of his arm comfortably lying around her shoulders.

There was only one problem with this cozy arrangement. An ostrich plume on Sheridan's hat was strategically positioned to brush ticklishly against the tip of Jeremy's nose. Kyla and Patrick held their sides in fits of smothered laughter as Jeremy tried to outmaneuver the attacking feather. Finally in desperation, and with a great show of dexterity, he carefully removed the hat and placed it on the seat beside her. Having successfully won the skirmish, he gave his laughing companions a self-satisfied smile and closed his eyes for some much needed sleep. In a short while, the only sound inside the vehicle was the steady, relaxed breathing of the dozing passengers.

Chapter 3

Much later, Sheridan stirred in the warmth that surrounded her. A brush of butterfly wings whispered against her lips, and she snuggled deeper into the strong arms that held her. The butterfly fluttered along her brow and across her forehead. A quiet, wonderfully deep, masculine voice said, "Wake up, sleepyhead. We'll be in Callander soon."

She opened her eyes slowly and tried to discern her surroundings. Through the muddled haze of sleep, she realized she was lying on the seat, her torso stretched across Jeremy as he cradled her in his arms.

It was dusk, the inside of the coach dim and filled with shadows. Slowly, her eyes adjusted to the faint light, so she could easily make out the ruggedly attractive face smiling down at her.

"Good evening, my sweet. Are you warm enough?"

His coat was wrapped around them both, and one large hand had found its way beneath her own cloak to settle with burning possessiveness against her hip. His other arm supported her weight as her head rested in the crook of his elbow.

"Aye, I'm warm." Too warm, she thought, meeting his seductive gaze. "You've placed me in an awkward position."

He smiled lazily. "You needed the sleep, and you didn't look at all comfortable with your head bouncing against the side of the coach every time we hit a pothole. You didn't sleep well last night, did you?"

"Of course I did. I slept very well, thank you." She gave a little push, trying to sit up, but he held her fast. At the disbelieving lift of his eyebrow, she relented. "You know I slept miserably, and I hope you did, too."

"Ah, in truth, what little sleep I obtained was far from peaceful. It was filled with dreams of a soft temptress in my arms; of a body so lush, I shuddered at the very thought of touching it; of kisses so sweet, I was sure I would drown in their nectar."

"You're a prodigious liar, Jeremy Mackenzie. Let me up," she said, trying to ignore the huskiness of her voice and her cartwheeling emotions.

"Not just yet. And I never lie." She started to move again, but the look on his face stopped her. Vulnerability was something she had never expected to see on his well-sculptured features. "I've never known a woman as beautiful as you," he whispered. "I've never wanted a woman the way I want you."

Brushing each corner of her mouth with his lips, he meant to kiss her with great care, to show her gentleness and ease her fear, but when her lips sought his, gentleness took a backward slide and hunger prevailed. She was softness and beauty, goodness and innocence, storm and lightning. Nothing else mattered—the others in the coach, her gentle breeding, the fact that he had known her for less than a day—those were things of another time, another place. For this endless moment, she was his, and she wanted him.

Beneath his caressing fingers, strength and security swirled with excitement and need. Some primitive beast sprang to life within her, an unfamiliar being that answered kiss for kiss, touch for touch. She pushed her hands beneath his waistcoat, through superfine and silk to caress the hard, rolling muscles of his back, only to be frustrated by a barrier of soft linen.

This was what she longed for, to be in his arms, to know the meaning of being a woman. He could be her fortress and her haven, her joy—or her misery. The old fear flashed through her, even more intense than before. Dare she allow herself to care even a little?

Jeremy smoothed his hand along the curve of her hip, and felt her stiffen. He moved it quickly up her side, holding her rigid body against him. Shaken by what had passed between them, he was angry with himself for not maintaining more control. "I'm sorry. I should not have taken such liberties." His voice was hoarse and strained.

"You . . . you ill use me, sir," Sheridan whispered, more frightened by her behavior than ashamed.

"Nay, Sheridan, nay." There was a hint of desperation in his voice. "I meant you no harm, no disrespect." He very gently raised her to an upright position. As she swung her legs around to the floor, he ran a hand distractedly through his hair, clearly searching for the words to explain. He shifted away from her, leaning against the corner of the coach to put some distance between them.

Sheridan glanced across the carriage at their companions, relieved to see that they were still asleep. Her relief was short-lived when she realized Kyla was curled up against Patrick, her head resting against his chest, his arms wrapped securely around her. She groaned inwardly. Oh, Lord, what they must think of us!

Jeremy smiled ruefully. "It seems that when you're in my arms, I lose my usually stoic control." His face sobered, and he drew a deep breath, then released it slowly. "Sheridan, I have greatly overstepped the bounds. I should not have treated you as I just did, nor as I did last night. I truly only meant to hold you so that you might sleep more comfortably." He chuckled, but his soft laughter held a hollow ring.

"I even dozed a little myself, but for the most part I sat here for the last two hours watching you, absorbing your beauty as a freezing man soaks up heat from a blazing fire. The longer I looked at you, the more I remembered how it felt to have you in my arms last night. I thought if I could kiss you once more, it would be enough, but I was wrong. It will never be enough—for either of us."

Sheridan gasped at his plain speaking; the color that had slowly begun to fade from her flushed cheeks returned instantly. She could not deny his words; they were true. Nor could she lay the blame on him alone. She had wanted him as desperately as he had wanted her.

She stared at the dark floor of the carriage, unconsciously biting her lower lip. Finally, she looked up at him. "Are you always so blunt?"

"No." The corner of his lip lifted, forming a very endearing lopsided smile. "Usually, I'm known for my tactfulness. I'm a cautious fellow, thinking everything through thoroughly before I act, especially when a woman is concerned." He didn't miss the slight lift of her eyebrow and irritation in her eyes. So, she was a little jealous. He found it immensely pleasing.

"You, however, seem to dislodge all the social niceties my parents drilled into my head, giving room for my baser instincts to take over." The twinkle disappeared from his eyes, and his countenance grew serious. "I'll make a great effort to behave in the proper manner, Sheridan. It's your right to expect it, but I can't promise that I will be completely successful. You are Circe, sweet, forever pulling me to you."

Her lively imagination depicted Odysseus and his companions after the enchantress worked her magic, and Sheridan laughed wryly, shaking her head. At his miffed expression, she said, "No one has ever called me Circe before. Keep your distance, sailor, or I shall turn you into a swine."

He bowed his head in mock surrender. "I am pleased, m'lady, you do not already consider me one."

The next afternoon, the coach passed through the village of Lochearnhead and started down the edge of Loch Earn just as the sun broke through the clouds. In a few minutes the sky began to clear, and Sheridan tugged impatiently on Jeremy's sleeve, interrupting Patrick's description of a Virginia plantation he had recently visited.

"You can see Ben Vorlich." She pointed at the majestic mountain to the south. "It's the one with snow on top. There is a marvelous view of it from Lord Maclaren's home. In his drawing room he has a large window that frames the mountain perfectly."

"Have you ever climbed to the top?"

"No, but I've thought about what it must be like. There's snow much of the year, so I think it would be difficult. Just imagine the view from up there."

Jeremy lowered his lashes slightly to hide the sparkle in his eyes. "Oh, I don't think it would be much of a view. There's nothing around here but a loch or two, and lots of heather."

"Not much of a view! How can you say that? There's

nothing more beautiful than the Highlands. They're mysterious and ever changing. I've always thought of the mountains as brooding giants. When the sun shines on them, their craggy tops are blue and majestic, but if a storm is brewing, they're gloomy and threatening.

"And the moors, how can you see the endless waves of heather, the acres and acres of pink blooms in the sunshine, and not be moved? All you have to do is breathe deeply, and you're surrounded by the sweetest fragrance God ever made."

Jeremy smiled indulgently. There was one other fragrance he preferred: the scent of roses rising from her soft, smooth skin.

Her voice grew hushed, her gaze fixed on the shimmering turquoise water of Loch Earn. "Even in the winter, when the buds on the heather are long gone, the silence and tranquility will still be here, covering the countryside like a mantle of peace."

Jeremy knew now why she had come home. It was the peace she sought, the tranquility she clung to even now. He wondered what haunted her and felt a strong desire to shelter and protect her, to drive away whatever brought such a sad, melancholy look to her eyes.

She smiled and said just a little too brightly, "Even the eagles are friendly. For some of us, they soar down from their nest high in the cliffs or the pine trees, screeching their welcome."

"More like a warning."

"No, not to me. They were my friends. It sounds silly, doesn't it, but when I was a girl we shared some kind of kinship. I don't know, perhaps they were warning me to stay away, but it always seemed like a friendly cry."

"You've missed the Highlands very much."

"Yes, I have. 'Tis said a Scot loves Scotland even more when away from it, and it must be true. Somehow, there's something about this country that becomes a part of your soul, and when you're away, your heart is ever longing for home."

Jeremy watched silently as she blinked hard, barely keeping back the tears that suddenly stung her eyes. He slipped her his handkerchief secretively and whispered in her ear, "Don't you dare cry."

She sniffed. "I wouldn't think of it."

Jeremy turned to Kyla. "It seems you're just as anxious to be home as Sheridan. Is someone special expecting you?"

"Aye, someone very special indeed." A smile danced at the corners of her mouth.

"Not a suitor, I hope. I fear Patrick will be sorely unhappy if that is the case. There'll be no living with him."

"Nay, no' a suitor, but my best friend. My father is Lord Sinclair's coachman and bodyguard. I was born at the manor and lived there all my life until I was married. Angus worked for his lordship, and we lived on the estate until he was killed."

"Then you moved to London to live with Sheridan?"

"Aye. I had always known her; even though she is six years younger, we had always been friends. Lord Sinclair suggested the move, thinkin' the change would help heal my grief." She glanced at Patrick. "I loved my husband very much. It took a long time to get used to his bein' gone."

"What is your father like?"

Sheridan spoke up. "I think you'll like him. When I was a child and heard the story of David and Goliath, I always pictured Waverly as Goliath. He is taller than you are and built like Patrick. He and Cookie have a running battle to see who can tell the most outlandish tales. I think he was born on the estate, too, at least he has worked for my family since he was a boy. He is fiercely loyal to my uncle. I have no doubt he would willingly give his life for him if the need arose.''

Abruptly, Sheridan rapped her knuckles on the small door behind the driver. It opened instantly to reveal Henry's smiling face. "Yes, m'lady?"

"Tell Oscar I'd like to walk the rest of the way, Henry. The gate to the manor is just down the road.''

Henry nodded and closed the door, passing on the message to the coachman. In just a few moments, the coach slowed to a halt, and Henry hopped down to lower the steps and open the door.

"Kyla, tell Uncle Galvin that I'll be along in a few minutes. He'll understand. He knows I like to walk over the moor from here.''

"I'll tell him. You dunna' mind if I ride on in the coach, do you? My shoes are no' made for walkin' very far.''

"Of course not.'' Sheridan climbed down from the coach and smiled at Jeremy. "Would you like to walk the last half mile, Jeremy? It might give you a better appreciation of the heath's beauty.''

"Of course, sweet.'' Jeremy jumped down from the top step and said softly, "Though it willna' be the moor's beauty I be admirin'.''

Sheridan laughed at the sudden appearance of a thick Scottish brogue. "I think we may convert ye yet, Mackenzie.''

Jeremy swung Sheridan over the hedgerow as the others resumed their journey. She ran up the slight brae, laughing delightedly, and stopped at the top of the hill. To the left was a small glen, secluded all around by small green hills. To the right was another larger rise. Sheridan raced up it, flinging her arms wide and twirling around.

"I'm home,'' she cried happily, and took a deep breath. "At last, I'm home.'' Jeremy paused a few feet down the brae, watching as she slowly turned in a complete circle, soaking up the scenery, absorbing the silence and tranquility. Suddenly, an eagle soared overhead, gliding in a lazy circle around them. He flapped his massive wings once, gave his screeching cry, and dove toward the waters of Loch Earn. Sheridan turned to Jeremy triumphantly. "See, I told you they were my friends."

He smiled, not really able to deny her assessment. He stood with one foot on a low rock, knee bent, arm resting casually across his thigh. Wanting her had become a familiar ache gnawing at his insides, but the feeling that intrigued him for the moment was contentment. A warm contentment that came from being with her, watching her smile, hearing her laugh, knowing she had let down her guard to allow him to share this very private homecoming.

His smile widened in a grin when she clapped her hands and spun around once more. "My, my, such exuberance. Whatever would your grandmother say?"

Sheridan stood very still, her back poker straight, hands folded primly in front of her. Tilting her head so her chin lifted and her nose was turned up, she assumed the proper haughty expression. "My dear child," she said in a crisp English accent dripping with arrogance, "you are no longer a wild Scottish hoyden. You are a very proper English lady, and I expect you to act like one. You must strive to control the pagan blood in your veins and remember that you are half English, thank God."

Jeremy threw back his head and laughed, a beautiful sound. He had left his hat in the coach, and the sun glistened off his hair like sparks from a fire.

Sheridan liked his deep, rich laugh. It matched the warmth of his voice and reminded her of the moments she had heard its velvet timbre low and husky with passion. His face was deeply tanned from long hours at sea; his lean muscular body was well at ease walking through the countryside. The Highlands suit him, she decided. He was no more a city person than she was. Fighting the urge to run down the slope and fling herself into his arms, Sheridan decided then and there that he would learn to love these Highlands as much as she did. He had to.

"Was she really so bad?"

"No, not quite. As often as not after such a lecture, she would suggest I go for a brisk ride."

"English ladies don't go for brisk rides. They parade around Hyde Park at a walk."

"Ah, so you have been there. However, there are a few other trails where one may ride at a good clip, if you go early enough. It was grandmother's one deviation from propriety. She so wanted to see me marry a good, staid English earl, although I think she favored a marquess or duke. She never forgave herself for allowing my mother to marry a Scotsman. It was her contention that if she had forbidden the marriage, my mother would still be alive."

"What happened to your parents, Sheridan?" he inquired gently.

She dropped her gaze to the ground in front of her, then looked up across the heath, not meeting his eyes. "They were killed in a fire when I was five. We had been in our new home for only a year when it burned. I don't remember anything about it, although from things I have overheard I was there. I don't remember much of my life before the fire, or even what happened for a time afterwards. Occasionally, there are flashes of memories, like my mother's laugh or smile, and my father giving me a horsey ride across the grass, but I don't feel as if I ever knew them. I find that the hardest thing to bear. If

I only had some memories to treasure, but it's as if even those have been taken from me."

Jeremy quietly stepped up beside her and drew her into his arms. Words seemed unnecessary; she needed to touch him, to feel the reassurance that comes from contact with another person. He held her gently, running a hand slowly and soothingly up and down her back. In just a moment, she took a deep breath and straightened. The ghosts were laid to rest for the moment.

"Good lord, is that Sinclair Castle?" Jeremy released her, letting his arms drop to his sides.

Sheridan giggled and swung her arm toward the four towers of the baronial keep with a flourish. "My humble home, sir."

"Humble? It's incredible." The hundred-foot stone tower walls were at least fourteen feet thick. Surrounding the bailey was a twenty-foot tall stone wall, complete with drawbridge and moat. A flag of Scotland flew alongside one of England atop a front turret. From the ramparts of the other tower, the Sinclair banner waved proudly in the breeze. Jeremy rubbed his chin thoughtfully. "I half expect to see your uncle ride out in full armor to meet us."

"Ten years ago, he would have, but since the plaid is no longer outlawed, it's more likely he'll meet us in a kilt and tartan."

"I suppose you have claymores crossed over the fireplace?"

"Aye, along with pikes and targes our ancestors used at Bannockburn. You won't find any relics from Culloden. The Sinclairs stayed out of that fight."

"Cowards."

"No," she said, a brief smile flitting across her face. "We had mixed loyalties, so we tried to remain neutral, although there is a family legend that a large supply of Sinclair goods found its way into Prince Charlie's camp.''

They started walking down the brae while Jeremy studied the castle. His gaze moved slowly from the narrow slits, which served as windows in the towers, down once again to the moat. "Are there monsters in your moat?"

"Only trout and salmon at certain seasons. Uncle Galvin had the stream diverted so it runs through the moat. Actually, it's been filled in on the back side of the castle so you can go out the back door and up across the moor. Grandfather had it filled in when he grew tired of having to go out the front every time he wanted to go hunting.''

"What happened when the castle was under attack? Wasn't there a back way out before he filled in the moat?"

"Yes, but I think it was built to encourage fighting to the last man. There is an escape slide down into the moat. I assume the idea was to swim across the slimy water to a clump of trees on the other side. Unfortunately, when there has been a lot of rain, the end of the slide is underwater."

Jeremy caught her around the waist and lifted her down a slight cliff. "No wonder you love it here. It's beautiful and, ah, interesting."

She laughed. "I think you mean eccentric."

"Well, it did cross my mind. I even thought I heard bagpipes a minute ago."

Sheridan laughed and grabbed his hand, leading him down the slope. The thrilling sound of the pipes drifted to them from across the glen, gradually filling the valley with its mournful wail. Stricken, Sheridan jerked to a halt, her fingers clenching Jeremy's hand until her knuckles turned white.

"Sher, what's wrong?"

"It's a funeral," she whispered. A cold knot of fear congealed in the pit of her stomach, slowly spreading its icy tentacles through her body. She could barely hear for the thunder in her ears, slowly realizing the pounding was the beat of her frightened heart.

Jeremy's gaze followed hers as she turned her head toward a small church, several hundred yards from the castle. A group of people stood outside and on the steps of the kirk, apparently an overflow crowd from the small building.

"It's the Sinclair lament."

The dread in her trembling voice sent a shiver down his spine. He tugged gently on her hand. "Come on, Sher, we'll find out who it is."

Sheridan was paralyzed with terror. Jeremy once again gently pulled on her hand. "No," she whimpered, and drew back.

Jeremy put his arm around her shoulders. "We'll go down and face it together. It may be one of the servants or one of the tenants. Whatever has happened, Sheridan, I'm here and I'll stay with you."

The nod of her head was barely perceptible but enough to let him know she understood. They moved down the rest of the slope, quickly reaching the churchyard. When they approached, a stunned murmur rushed through the crowd milling around outside, and a path cleared for them up the worn stone steps and into the church building.

One look at the well-dressed figures lining the pews confirmed Sheridan's worst fears. She slowly walked to the front of the church, unconscious of Jeremy's warm hand at her waist. In the distance, she heard soft murmurs and comments as they passed by, but the words were a blur along with the haze of faces surrounding them.

When they reached the altar, Albert, her uncle's long-time butler, stepped out to meet her. There were others behind him, but her eyes could only focus on his face. Pain dulled her mind and body; it seemed to seep from her pores only to return with each indrawn breath. She stared at her old friend, watching a tear as it welled up in his eye and slid slowly down a timeworn crevice in his wrinkled cheek.

He bowed his head, and her eyes dropped to his hands, watching in dazed amazement as he twisted and crumpled his best hat. I'll have to buy him a new one, she thought.

When the servant lifted his head, he was startled to find her smiling kindly at him. He swallowed hard and cleared his throat. " 'Tis yer uncle, m'lady. He was shot in a robbery two nights past."

"At the castle?" Her polite, carefully controlled voice brought a frown to Jeremy's forehead, and his arm tightened around her waist.

"Nay, m'lady. His coach was attacked on the way home from the mayor's dinner party."

"Highwaymen?"

"Aye, mum. They must have known his lordship was comin' because they felled a tree across the road. There was no way Andrew could keep from hittin' it."

"Was anyone else hurt?" She waited patiently for his answer, thinking how silly she had been to be afraid. There was no pain; the numbness hid it all. Grandmother had been right. A proper English lady could control her emotions at all times. She must always command respect, especially in front of the servants.

"Andrew hit his head when he was thrown from the coach, but he's healin' up. Waverly was shot, too, but Maisie thinks he'll pull through. He's a strong one."

"I see. Thank you, Albert. I'll buy you a new hat next time I'm in the village."

Jeremy searched the faces of those around them until his gaze met his aunt's. The alarm on her face mirrored his own as Sheridan turned to Lord Balfour and thanked him for coming to the funeral.

She expressed her thanks to the mayor and a few others whose faces she did not even see. Then, she stood before the closed casket. Sheridan decided she was in a dream. None of it was real. In a moment she would wake up and talk with Kyla about her nightmare.

She touched the wood, running her fingers along its smoothness until she came to a nail holding the lid shut. It was real. She stared at the row of effigies lining the wall of the kirk. Her grandparents, her parents, and now . . . Her vision tunneled, transfixed on the gaping hole next to her parents' crypt. In her mind's eye, it became three open tombs neatly stacked on top of each other. Two other caskets were shoved inside, and the stones honoring her parents slid into place. *They are going to put Uncle Galvin in that dark, black hole and never let him out again, just like they did Mama and Papa.*

Oh, dear God, it's real! The only father she had ever known was gone, never to laugh or tease or play his beloved bagpipes again. Suddenly, the pain crashed over her in sweeping waves of torment that tore away her breath, molded her heart into stone and then shattered it into a thousand pieces.

Sheridan threw back her head and screamed, "Nooooo!" Her keening cry swirled around the vaulted stone ceiling in a mocking echo. She could not bear such pain. She did not feel Jeremy's arms as they closed around her, nor know that he gathered her close. Everything slowly faded, all sound, all sight, all feeling. The blessed numbness returned, and then slowly, so very slowly, she closed her eyes and allowed the blackness to cover everything.

Jeremy felt her go limp against him, and he scooped

her up in his arms. "Reverend, do you have an office here where she might lie down?"

"Nay, unfortunately no'. My kirk is in Lochearnhead. This one has no' been used for years except for funerals and tenant weddings."

Jeremy's aunt stepped forward, Lord Balfour Maclaren at her side. "You'll have to carry her to the castle, Jeremy. We all walked down."

Jeremy nodded grimly and turned toward the door.

A large, blond-haired young man spoke up. "I'll go with ye, m'lord, and help carry her if ye need it."

"Thank you." Jeremy noticed a large bruise and cut on the man's forehead. "You're Andrew?"

"Aye, m'lord."

"Are you up to carrying her?" Andrew nodded his head. "Very well. Come along. For now you can clear a path through the crowd."

Andrew moved through the door, his determined gait clearing the way.

When Jeremy reached the bottom of the steps, he found Sheridan's carriage waiting for them. Oscar sat in the driver's seat, reins in hand, while Henry stood solemnly beside the open door.

"When we 'eard what 'appened, we thought our lady might 'ave need o' us," said Henry sadly.

"You're good men. Thank you." Jeremy placed Sheridan on the seat and climbed in, lifting her into his lap after he sat down. Lord and Lady Maclaren joined them.

Jeremy spoke to Andrew through the open coach window. "Will you come with us?"

"Nay, m'lord. My father needs me here. We'll be along shortly."

Reverend Ainsley looked at Sheridan through the window. "Ach, 'tis sad she had to arrive during the funeral. Poor lass, such a terrible shock to her. I'll finish the services and then check at the castle to see if there is anything I can do.''

Jeremy nodded his appreciation, turning to smile sadly at his aunt's curious stare when the coach began to move. '' 'Tis good to see you Aunt Genna. I assume, sir, you are my new uncle?''

"Of course this is Balfour, Jeremy. But, what in the world are you doing here with Lady Sheridan? I wasn't aware that you two were acquainted.''

"We weren't until a few days ago." Jeremy gazed down at the unconscious beauty in his arms, a look of such tenderness sweeping across his face that his aunt and uncle exchanged a surprised but knowing glance. He shifted her a little in his arms in an effort to make her more comfortable, silently reminding himself she probably wasn't aware of comfort or discomfort.

"I met her at the inn in Falkirk. She asked Patrick and me to ride with them yesterday after their coach was attacked.''

Lord Maclaren spoke up. "They were alone? I understood Sir Humphrey was to accompany the lassies.''

"Evidently, he traveled with them for a while, but he became ill and had to stay behind with his sister. I suspect Sheridan was too impatient to wait until he recovered.''

Lord Maclaren smiled fondly at Sheridan. "Patience was no' the lass's strong point.''

The carriage rattled across the drawbridge to stop in the courtyard in front of the castle. Henry swung open the door, and Lord Balfour disembarked first, turning to give his hand to Lady Genna. Jeremy gently laid Sheridan on the seat, climbed down from the coach and carefully lifted her out.

As they walked up the castle steps, the great, arched oak door was flung open by the housekeeper, Maisie, who was also Albert's wife. "Ach, my poor wee bairn, just look at ye.'' The tears gushed down the older woman's round cheeks as she clasped Sheridan's cold, clammy hand in her own. ''Bring her upstairs, sir. I knew my wee bairn could no' bear such a shock.''

Maisie absently pushed a graying blond strand of hair under her mob cap and rushed her portly figure up the stone staircase ahead of Jeremy. The stairs were built into the thick walls of the castle, leading upward in a steep, narrow spiral, the stones worn from centuries of footsteps. The housekeeper opened another arched door leading into a withdrawing room. At some point in time, the room had been divided to provide a library at the opposite end.

They crossed the drawing room to go through yet another door, again arched, but this time so low that Jeremy had to bend almost double to enter the bedroom. With great concern, he placed Sheridan on the smooth sheets of her canopied bed. A small fire blazed in the fireplace, taking away the chill, which seeped through the stone walls even in June. The peacock blue curtain on the side of the bed opposite the fire had been drawn to capture the heat and shade the bed from the window.

''I'll be in the drawing room, madam, if you need any assistance. I would greatly appreciate it if you would let me know when she is dressed and tucked into bed. I intend to sit with her for a while in the event she awakens.''

Maisie's eyes grew wide. ''Ach, sir, that willna' be necessary. My daughter Dora and I can take turns sittin' with the mistress. There's no need to be troublin' yerself.'' Disapproval was written all over her face.

''Madam, I intend to stay with her, for a while at least. I would be obliged, however, if one of you ladies would sit with her also.''

Maisie released a heavy, troubled sigh. ''Very well,

m'lord. I'll call ye when we have her settled. She'll no doubt need a wide shoulder to cry on."

Jeremy met Patrick and Kyla in the drawing room, noting out of the corner of his eye the young girl who quickly entered Sheridan's bedroom. One look at Kyla's tear-reddened eyes and pale face told him she was still in a state of shock, too. "How is your father, Kyla?" he asked gently.

"He's hurt very badly, but Patrick agrees with Maisie that he should pull through. He woke up for a moment when we came home, but he is so terribly weak." Tears sprang afresh as she sank down on a rose brocade settee. A shudder rolled through her small frame. "I've ne'er even seen him sick, much less hoverin' at death's door."

"He'll make it, little one. He's strong and he'll fight." Patrick put his arm around her. "How's Sheridan?"

"She fainted. At first she seemed completely in control, too much in control; then it hit her." He sat down on a dark gray velvet chair, leaning his head tiredly against the back. "I'll never forget that scream or the agony on her face for as long as I live. After she cried out, she seemed to just fold into herself. I don't think she was aware of anything going on around her. She just grew very, very still and slowly closed her eyes, fainting dead away." He stood up and paced the floor in front of a long narrow window. "She should have regained consciousness by now."

The housekeeper closed Sheridan's door and stood a few steps into the drawing room, sobbing. The other three ran to her side. "Maisie, what is it?" cried Kyla.

Maisie wiped her tears on her apron. "She's closed herself off from us, Kyla. I used the vinegarette to wake her. She jerked her head away from the bottle and opened her eyes, so I know she's conscious, but lookin' at her is like lookin' at a dead woman. 'Tis like it was before; she does no' see anythin' or hear anythin' or—"

"Or speak," whispered Kyla. "Oh, dear God, no' again."

"What do you mean? This has happened before?" asked Jeremy, dread creeping over him.

"Aye," said Maisie. "The night her parents were killed, we found her curled up in a wee ball, lyin' on the grass. She was just like she is now, eyes glassy, barely blinkin'. She stayed curled up in that tight, wee knot the whole night, no' movin' so much as a finger until mornin'."

"She began to respond to us in the mornin'," said Kyla. "She would follow us with her eyes and soon she was movin' around, but it was months before she ever said a word."

"Months?"

"Aye. One day we were out for a walk, and she spotted the eagles. She started talkin' about them. Her words came slowly at first, but within a day she was talkin' normal again. Afterwards, whenever she would be frightened or upset, speech would grow difficult again."

"Is she still awake?"

"She was when I left, sir."

Jeremy pushed open the door and ducked through it, followed by a silent Kyla and Patrick. Maisie stood just outside the door, clucking and shaking her head.

Jeremy pulled a chair up beside the bed and took Sheridan's hand in his. It still felt cold, and he rubbed it gently with his thumb. She lay flat in the bed, her head resting on the pillow, her face turned upward, eyes open and unseeing.

"Sheridan, how do you feel?" he asked softly. No response. He waved a hand in front of her face, but her eyes did not follow the movement. "Sheridan, do you hear me?'' He squeezed her hand tightly, almost to the point where it would cause her pain. Nothing. Her eyes fluttered and drifted closed, her breathing even and slow.

Jeremy released her hand and stood up, deep lines of concern etched on his face. ''She's asleep now. It's probably what she needs most at the moment. I'll come back in the morning.''

Maisie put her arm around Kyla and ushered her toward her room. ''Ye need some rest yerself, lass. I'll sit awhile with yer father, and Dora can stay with the mistress.''

''Just for a little while, Maisie. Call me in a few hours and I'll sit with him.'' She craned her neck around to look at Patrick. ''Will you come back tomorrow?''

''Of course, little one. You only need to send word, and I'll come sooner if you need me.''

''Thank you. Good-bye.''

The warmth of their exchange was not lost on the old servant. She eyed the two of them speculatively, wondering what was brewing between them. Her eyes darted to Jeremy standing tensely by the window, a thoughtful and troubled expression on his handsome face. Anyone could see he had deep feelings for the mistress; did Lady Sheridan feel the same? Suddenly, Maisie almost smiled. Her mistress would recover, she could just feel it. This braw lad would no' let Lady Sheridan stay the way she was. If he loved her enough, he'd figure out some way to bring her back to them. She glanced over her shoulder as Jeremy straightened and moved toward the stairs, his jaw set in a determined, almost fierce line. Maisie let the tiny little smile lift her lips and her spirit. He loved her enough.

Chapter 4

Sheridan slept for almost two days. When Jeremy finally shook her awake, her eyes opened, but she still did not respond to anyone in any other way.

Jeremy dropped her cold, strengthless hand onto the quilt and jumped to his feet. "Maisie, I'm going to take Lady Sheridan outside. Dress her in a warm robe. I'll also need a light quilt to wrap her in. It's not cold out, but I don't want to take a chance of her taking a chill."

Maisie frowned, wanting to trust him, but concern for her mistress weighed heavily on her mind. "Do ye truly think 'tis wise to take her out, sir?"

"I don't believe it will hurt her. I saw men react this way in battle. If they didn't snap out of their shock within a few days, they rarely came out of it at all. She loves this country very much; hopefully, it can reach her when we can't. I'm going downstairs to get some wine and bread. I'll be back up in the drawing room shortly. Call me when she is ready."

"Very well, sir."

Ten minutes later, Jeremy waited impatiently in the drawing room, a flask of wine and loaf of bread sitting in a bag on the table beside him. He was about to go knock on Sheridan's door when Maisie opened it.

"She be ready, sir. Poor lamb, she be awake but doesna' even know I'm here."

"I don't know how long we will be, Maisie. I'll bring her in before dark, and I promise not to let her get cold. While we're gone, I want you to go lie down for a while. Take advantage of the extra help Aunt Genna sent over. She did it for you and Kyla so you wouldn't get sick yourselves. Now, off with you, woman. Cookie will make certain dinner is served on time."

Maisie smiled gratefully, waiting until he had lifted Sheridan from the bed and she had tucked the quilt snugly around her mistress's blue velvet robe before retiring to her room.

Jeremy carefully made his way down the steep stairway. On more than one trip up and down the stone steps, he had marveled at the military ingenuity of its architect. The circular stairwell was built for security, enabling a right-handed defender to reach down and around the inner wall with his sword or pike, while using that same wall for protection. The attacking warrior was limited in the small area, unless he fought with his left hand, which was unusual.

There were many things he wondered about, curiosities here and there in the castle that had caught his eye, but most of all, he wanted to know about the woman herself. He wanted to hear her laughter, that joyful, musical sound, which had not come nearly enough times in their brief relationship. He wanted to know about places she had been, places she longed to go, books she had read, music she liked. Jeremy paused at the bottom of the stairs and held her close to his heart. Please, God, he prayed silently, let her come back to us.

He carried her out the back door and through a small gate in the wall, following a path on the hillside up to a small grove of birch trees. From there, they had a sweeping view of the castle and surrounding moors, as well as a breathtaking vantage of the gentle waves on Loch Earn.

Jeremy laid her on the ground and sat down beside her, lifting her across his lap. He leaned back against the trunk of the birch and took a minute to catch his breath, letting the silent beauty around him minister to his own troubled soul. The sunlight filtered through the delicate, lacy leaves overhead, making the open shelter comfortably warm.

Jeremy propped her head against his shoulder, noting that her eyes were closed. He let her sleep for a while before he gently shook her. When her eyes reluctantly opened, he began to speak.

"Do you feel the sunlight on your skin, sweet? Listen to the birds. I hear a skylark somewhere around, but I can't see him, he's so high." He paused as he heard a sharp hammering nearby. "There's a woodpecker. Just listen to him drumming on that tree. It's a good thing he doesn't look for food at night; nobody would ever get any sleep. Whose sad-sounding whistle is that? Hmmm, you must not know either."

Jeremy rested his head against the tree, glancing down to make sure her eyes were still open. He sat quietly for a while, hoping the chattering and singing of the birds would reach her. He shifted slightly so her head was angled toward the loch.

"Do you see the water, Sheridan? I do believe you're right. I don't think I've ever seen water that was a deeper turquoise. It looks so clear, we could probably see the fish if we were close enough. Look at the family of ducks floating around the edge.'' He chuckled softly. ''Do you see how the last little guy keeps going back to look at things? I'd wager he gets into all sorts of mischief.'' He took a deep breath. ''Ah, just smell the heather. You were almost right about that, too. There's only one other fragrance I prefer. If you'll move something, anything, just to let me know you hear me, I'll tell you what it is.''

Jeremy sighed, discouraged by her lack of response. He raised up one knee, letting her weight rest against it and easing a cramp in his arm. He was thankful he had left his cravat and frock coat behind, otherwise he would have been too hot. Closing his eyes, he allowed the warm sunshine and gentle hum of the bees in the nearby heather to lull him into a doze.

By mid-afternoon, Jeremy had almost given up. He had hoped she would sense the tranquillity surrounding her and that it would soothe her tortured mind. He had prayed the invisible bond tying her heart to this land would draw her back from her dark, unfeeling world.

He stared down at her beautiful face, remembering how she had slept in his arms in the coach and the special moment when she had awakened. It was fresh, clear, and poignant, as if it had been only a moment ago—the taste of her lips sweet upon his, sleepy sighs and a warm, contented smile, the passionate longing of a kiss that branded his very soul.

His helplessness rose up like a taunting warrior, mocking him, challenging him to do battle with an enemy he could not see nor touch, an enemy no cannon nor sword could conquer. He let his head drop back against the tree, hot tears stinging his eyelids and throat, pain and frustration searing his heart.

"Oh, Sheridan, my sweet, sweet Sher." He leaned down to touch her lips, unmindful of the tears trickling down his cheeks. He kissed her gently, lifted his head to look at her once more, and stroked a wispy curl at her temple. "What am I to do?" he whispered, his voice cracking.

Jeremy held her close, cradling her face near his heart, and wept silently. He bent his head to kiss her one last time, the saltiness of his heartache blending with the sweetness of her lips to fill him with bittersweet sadness.

Wait! Did she move? He jerked his head up and stared at her, trying to rouse her by the sheer force of his will. *No, it can't be . . . please, God, let it be.* With trembling fingers, he gently cupped her jaw. He eased his face toward hers, afraid to kiss her, more afraid not to. At last his lips touched hers, gently at first, then deepening their pressure in his desperate attempt to evoke a response. *There!* The fragile movement came again.

Jeremy pulled away, searching her face. Her eyes were closed, but to his utter joy, she whimpered slightly and snuggled against him.

"Sheridan, come back to me. Don't shut me out. Feel, sweet, feel. Let the sensations flood your body and mind. Don't be afraid of the pain. I'm here and I'll bear it with you."

Sheridan let the warm languor slowly drift through her. She felt safe and perfectly content wrapped securely in Jeremy's arms. His lips caressed hers. He teased. He enticed. She was helpless to resist him and wondered hazily why she was supposed to. He moved his hand over her, tenderly and with respect, not touching where he really shouldn't, but coming close enough to make her want the forbidden.

He's different than the last time, she thought. So

gentle, so patient, not demanding. How nice it was to lie in the heather with him. How wonderful it smelled, the sweet fragrance of the flowers and the whisper of his cologne. She smiled with contentment against his lips. *This is where we belong, Jeremy. Here on the moors with the birds and the sunshine, together.*

But why are we here? Her smile changed to a slight frown. *We shouldn't dawdle. Uncle Galvin will be expecting us.* Sheridan drew back, searching Jeremy's face, seeing the lines etched by weariness and worry. She tried to remember—there was something wrong with Uncle Galvin, but what was it? *He's been hurt—or did someone say he had been killed? No, oh no, dear God, it can't be true!* The pain was like a searing knife driving into her heart.

"Jeremy, Uncle Galvin, is . . . is it true?"

He nodded slowly. "He was killed three days ago."

Sheridan let out an agonized cry and buried her face against his shoulder, sobs wracking her body.

"Don't close your mind to it, Sheridan. I know it hurts, but don't leave me again," Jeremy pleaded. "Cry, scream, hit me, anything you need, but don't draw away."

Sheridan wept and wept, venting her grief, giving birth to the healing of her mind and soul. Gradually, the torment dimmed, leaving a dull ache and exhaustion. She lifted her head and raised her gaze to his face. Touching his cheek with her fingertips, she found them damp.

"Jeremy, you've been crying," she said in wonder.

"Nonsense, men don't cry." He attempted a wobbly smile, but failed completely. Pulling her tightly against him, he said roughly, "I hurt for you."

She let him hold her close for a few moments, then pushed away from his chest and gently wiped one side of his face with her hand. "Thank you."

He brushed his other cheek with the heel of his hand and looked out across the hills to Loch Earn, embarrassed by his unmanly display of emotion.

"When did we get home?"

"Two days ago."

"Two days!"

"You've been—asleep."

"For two days?"

"For most of the time. The rest of the time you were, well, beyond our reach. You didn't even know anyone was around. Do you remember coming home and going down to the funeral?"

"Yes, vaguely. It's like a dream." She leaned against him as a wave of pain swept over her. Sliding her arms around his waist, she whispered, "Hold me, Jeremy."

He held her close, until the fresh tears had been spent. Afterwards, she lay in his arms quietly, allowing the countryside to work its magic in her soul.

"Was anyone else hurt in the robbery? It was a robbery, wasn't it?"

"Aye, from what I understand, his lordship's coach was attacked by a band of highwaymen. Waverly was shot, too. He's in rough shape, but the fever broke yesterday, and he's regaining his strength slowly. He'll mend."

"What about Andrew? He's been driving the coach for the last year or so."

"The robbers dropped a tree across the road, and the coach crashed into it when they came around a corner. Andrew was thrown from the top and hit his head pretty hard. He says it's fine, but he was unconscious for a while. I think he's troubled because he couldn't help your uncle."

"Who helped Andrew and Waverly?"

"Your neighbor, Macveagh. Evidently, most of the gentry had been to a dinner party at the mayor's in Kingshouse. Lord Maclaren and Aunt Genna left a few minutes before Lord Sinclair. They didn't see any signs of the highwaymen and came on home. Macveagh came along a short time later and found the wrecked coach. He brought them to the castle and sent word to Lord Maclaren of what had happened. He had his men right the coach and bring it back."

"Where did it happen?"

"On the road between Kingshouse and Lochearnhead."

"How strange, we've never had trouble with highwaymen in this part of the country."

"Lord Maclaren, correction, Uncle Balfour, has sent to London for a Bow Street Runner to investigate the murder."

Sheridan raised her head. "Does he think there is more to it than just a robbery?"

"He's not sure. It does seem strange that no one saw anything, yet the murderers dragged the tree across the roadway just in time to stop your uncle's carriage. It's almost as if they knew someone would be coming along right then." He wiggled a little and discovered his backside had grown numb. "Enough of this supposition. The Runner will get to the bottom of it. For now, young lady, you need to eat and go back to the castle to rest."

"I am hungry and quite weak."

"You should be, considering how long it's been since you've eaten. I just happen to have a small bit of wine and bread. Perhaps it will tide you over until I can carry you back to the castle."

She smiled, a very welcome sight to Jeremy's eyes. "You think of everything, don't you?"

He nodded. "I do my best, my lady."

"Were you trying to seduce me?" She grinned as she reached for the flask of wine and took a long drink. Handing it back to Jeremy, she took the piece of bread he gave her and chewed slowly, waiting for his answer.

"I was desperate enough for about anything. I have to admit the thought did cross my mind, but I decided it wouldn't be fair since you weren't in any condition to really know what was happening. Besides, it's a lot more fun when you kiss me back." He tilted her chin up with his fingertips and kissed her lips lingeringly. "When I seduce you, you won't have to ask if I'm trying."

He chuckled and nudged her to the ground, gathering up the food and quilt. "There, I did succeed in bringing a little color to those pale cheeks." He pulled her carefully to her feet and wrapped the quilt around her. Planting a kiss on the tip of her nose, he swung her up in his arms and strolled down the brae to the castle, where she was showered with love and comfort by a very relieved household.

The next morning Oscar and Henry left on their return trip to England. After bidding them farewell, Sheridan slipped quietly into Waverly's room. When she sat down on the chair near his bed, the man opened his eyes. "Welcome home, Lady Sheridan," he said weakly. " 'Tis sad I be that I couldna' save Lord Sinclair. If I'd only paid more attention to the rumors about the highwaymen and hired more guards, mayhap it wouldna' ended like this. Forgive me, m'lady, for my failure."

Sheridan reached out to touch his hand. "Don't blame yourself, Waverly. I know you fought bravely and did your best. It will do no good worrying about what you think you should have done. I only care about your getting well. Please put your feelings of guilt away and concentrate on getting better. Kyla and I both need you; she as a father, and I as a friend and counselor."

"Thank ye, m'lady. It does help to know ye dunna' blame me for yer uncle's death." He closed his eyes and soon fell into a restful sleep.

Sheridan slowly regained her strength. Jeremy stopped by each afternoon for a short visit, taking care not to stay too long and tire her. Their shared laughter and conversations did much to dispel the gloom, which at other times settled over her spirit like a dark cloud.

During one of these visits, they strolled around the grounds, and Jeremy asked about some of the things he had been curious about.

"Whose armor is that in the great hall?" His eyes sparkled with merriment.

"The one with the dent in the helmet?"

"Aye."

"It belonged to an Englishman at Bannockburn." She returned his grin. "One of my ancestors whacked him on the head with his claymore. After the battle, he buried the knight and took the armor for a trophy."

Jeremy stopped and pointed up to the battered wall of the tower. "What's the story behind this?"

"Cromwell attacked in 1650. He had more firepower than anyone had ever seen here in Scotland and had destroyed many castles with his large cannon. The laird was given the option of walking away from the castle with his family and what possessions he could carry, or having it battered to a shambles. He chose to leave the stronghold and avoid its destruction, even though it meant forfeiture of the lands for several decades. I think it's why everyone has worked so hard to preserve the castle once it was returned to the family."

"I know something about losing the clan lands and then regaining them. My grandfather's property was taken by the Crown after the Forty-five. It was just returned to our family, reinstated in my father's name six years ago.'' He smiled broadly.

''Father is planning to return to Scotland to live, at least for part of the time. He is easing out of his part of the business so he and Mother will be free to travel. He is making the change quite slowly, so it'll be a year or two before they settle back on Loch Maree.'' They stopped to admire the blue hydrangeas and pink rhododendrons blooming in a small garden in the corner of the bailey. ''I have to go there soon to check on the condition of his estate.''

''Will you be gone long?''

''About two weeks. I won't leave for a few days yet. I want to make sure you're strong and well before I go.''

''I'm feeling much better. I'm going to look over my uncle's accounts tomorrow. He was a shrewd businessman, so I'm certain everything is in order. I just need to familiarize myself with my inheritance. I'm a little surprised I haven't heard from his solicitor, but it is a long way to Edinburgh from here.''

''Rest well tonight and don't try to take on too much in one day. I must be going, now. Aunt Genna is expecting guests, and I need time to change into more appropriate attire.''

''Thank you for stopping by. I hope you know how much your visits cheer me up.''

''It's why I come.'' He grabbed her hand and pulled her into the shadow of the wall. Cupping her face in both hands, he lowered his head toward hers, pausing just before their lips touched. ''I've missed this,'' he whispered, and let his head drop a fraction of an inch until they were no longer separated.

His lips clung to hers, feasting on her taste, touch and smell until the fire began to build. When he raised his head and dropped his hands, they were both breathing a little harder. "I don't think I'll be able to come by tomorrow. Uncle Balfour wants to go hunting grouse. Perhaps I can bag you a bird and get invited to dinner later in the week."

Sheridan smiled sweetly, locking her arm through his as they stepped into the sunshine. "You might be invited even if you don't bring the food."

He kissed her hand very properly and mounted the horse Andrew brought around from the stables. Jeremy frowned, noting the servant's lovesick gaze whenever he looked at Sheridan. Kicking his horse to gallop down the lane, Jeremy pushed back a little twinge of jealousy and concentrated instead on the very pleasant memories of the afternoon.

Along toward dusk, Sheridan decided to take a walk. She strolled contentedly across the moor, intending to intersect with the road and walk back up the lane.

A few moments before she reached the road, her eye caught a glimpse of a shiny object in the trees ahead. Squinting to see what it was, she was startled when the discharge of a musket barked through the quiet twilight. Sheridan fell to the ground, the musket ball zinging just overhead. She slid down the brae a few feet and flattened herself against the ground to hide behind a large clump of heather. A second shot hit the ground where she had dropped moments before.

Searching frantically for some other place to hide, she almost cried with relief when she heard Andrew yell.

"M'lady, stay down!" He paused at the top of the brae and fired his weapon in the direction of the gunman, but the musket ball only met with empty air. The thudding of a horse's hoofbeats faded in the distance as Andrew reached Sheridan's side.

"M'lady, are you hurt?" He dropped to his knees

beside her, laying his gun on the ground.

Sheridan pushed herself up, spit a blade of grass from her mouth, and brushed the dirt from her gown with trembling fingers. "No, I don't think so, not badly anyway. I scraped my hands a little when I fell, but that's all. Andrew, why would anyone try to shoot me?" she asked, her voice trembling.

Without thinking, Andrew put his arms around her and drew her close. "I dunna' know, m'lady. The sun was behind ye. Ye would have been outlined against the sky. There's no way a man could mistake ye for a deer." He brushed a strand of wayward hair from her cheek and suddenly realized how intimately he was holding his mistress. Straightening, he pulled away. "Can ye walk back, m'lady?"

"Yes, although I'd appreciate an arm to lean on. My legs are shaking rather badly."

"I'll carry ye if ye want."

"No, there's no need. Just stay with me."

"Ye can be sure I'll no' leave ye, m'lady. I'm only glad I was huntin' across the way."

After they reached the castle, Maisie insisted on Sheridan going right to bed, an order she obeyed willingly. Kyla brought up a tray for them both.

"Patrick said the Bow Street Runner should be here any day. You need to let Lord Maclaren know about what happened this afternoon. I'm beginnin' to wonder if your uncle's death was a result of the robbery, or if there is somethin' more to this whole thin'."

"I've been wondering about it, too. Why would anyone try to kill me? For that matter, why would anyone want to kill Uncle Galvin? I certainly don't have any enemies, and I can't imagine him having any."

"It does no' make a lot of sense, I'll admit, but neither does someone shootin' at you."

"No, and it's not something I'd like repeated."

Kyla gathered up the tray and empty dishes. "I'll ride over tomorrow morning and tell his lordship what happened."

Sheridan smiled at her friend and fluffed up her pillow. "You just want an excuse to see Patrick."

"I'll no' deny it."

"You two seem to be getting along quite well."

"Aye, we are, and though I've been tempted, I've no' hidden him under my bed—" she gave Sheridan a wink and grinned impishly "—yet."

From her high vantage point in the tower bedroom, Sheridan watched the tenants leave their cottages at first light and move along toward the fields. Andrew walked back from the area where the cow was tethered, carrying a bucket of milk. Dora meandered along behind him with fresh eggs from the henhouse.

Brooding will do no good, she thought. I must accept the challenges life has offered me and make the most of them. It will not help Uncle Galvin's memory if I sit idle. He would not want me to neglect his affairs; in truth, I can show my love and respect for him by tending well what has been left to me.

She dressed quickly, pulling out a simple black linen gown, buttoning it down the front from the low bosom to the hem of the long full skirt. It was one of several she had purchased after her grandmother's death and had only recently stopped wearing. Sheridan draped a black lace tippet around her shoulders and tied it in front to cover her bosom. She left her hair in its natural style, flowing freely down her back and framing her face in soft curls.

To Maisie's surprise, Sheridan stepped into the kitchen a few moments later. "Good morning," she said cheerfully. "I must be getting my appetite back; I'm famished. Will you prepare me a big breakfast, Cookie?"

The red-faced cook grinned from ear to ear. "That I will, m'lady. I'll cook ye enough to last ye until evenin'."

"Thank you," she said, returning his smile. "Maisie, I intend to look over uncle's accounts after breakfast. I don't want to be disturbed by anyone outside our household with the exception of Jeremy in case he comes to call." She sat down at the table and buttered a bannock while she talked.

"I'll just eat in here this morning. I'm not in the mood to sit in the dining room by myself. Oh, if Lord or Lady Maclaren stops by, I'll see them, but please tell any other callers I'm not receiving visitors today. I will call on them next week if they wish."

"Aye, m'lady. I'll guard yer privacy. It will like as no' be few who call today, since most of the neighbors have already paid their respects."

"I want to purchase some small gifts for the tenants, so I plan to make a trip to the village tomorrow. You might as well see if you need anything for the house."

"Aye, m'lady. There are a few things we need."

"I want you to accompany me when I do the shopping, so feel free to make any suggestions you think proper."

After breakfast, Sheridan secluded herself in the library, carefully going through her uncle's desk, studying ledgers and reading much of his business correspondence. By burying herself in the work, she pushed aside the nagging worry that someone had tried to kill her. Every so often, her thoughts would stray to the previous evening, but she purposefully did not allow herself to dwell on the shooting.

She discovered her uncle had been very wealthy, even more so than expected. She returned to her own room once to obtain her own stationery. On this delicate parchment, she wrote to her uncle's solicitor, advising him of the murder even though she was certain he was aware of the situation by now.

Sheridan assured him she had enough funds of her own to operate the manor successfully until the legal matters were settled. In fact, although she did not reveal this knowledge to the lawyer, she was almost as wealthy in her own right as her uncle had been. Her portion of the lands, as well as other funds belonging to her father, had been placed into a trust for her when he died. From this trust, she had received a generous monthly pension while living with her grandmother, but upon reaching her majority, her twenty-first birthday, she acquired full access to both the lands and the money.

In her letter to the solicitor, Sheridan confirmed her willingness to be responsible for all debts owed by her uncle, knowing there were few outstanding debts to be paid if his records were accurate.

Sheridan inquired if Mr. Smithson, the solicitor, would check on the progress of a ship being built for her uncle at the time of his death. According to correspondence filed in her uncle's desk, the vessel should be near completion and was expected to arrive in Leith soon. It was her intention to inspect the craft before it sailed from Leith and to meet the captain.

Her fingers thumped restlessly against the desk while she studied her note. She had knowledge of farming, since it was her interest, but little information about ships. She required expert assistance on this subject and decided to ask Jeremy to go to Edinburgh with her and inspect the vessel. If anyone could find any flaws in either the ship or its crew, he could.

Sheridan smiled at her own pretense, but convinced herself of its legitimacy. Even now, the simple thought of him increased her pulse rate, and a little shiver of expectation ran through her. She glanced out the window, and to her surprise, discovered it was almost dark. Disappointed because Jeremy wouldn't be visiting today, she closed the ledgers and made her way to the kitchen, rubbing her stiff neck.

"Will ye be eatin' in the dinin' room tonight, Lady Sheridan?" asked Maisie.

"No, I think not. I would like for us all to eat together here in the kitchen unless there are guests. I realize it's rather unusual, but I end up either dining alone or only with Kyla if we set the big table. I can't see any sense in doing so, nor do I really want to. 'Tis so much more pleasant here with all of you as my dinner companions."

"Aye, m'lady, if it be what ye wish, we'll be glad for yer company." She set another plate on the table and began to serve the food as Albert and Andrew came through the back door. The butler was a trifle taken aback to see his mistress sitting in the kitchen with the servants. She had done so many times as a child, but she was the lady of the manor now, and it did not seem proper. He drew a breath to object, but was stopped by her bright smile when she saw them.

"Oh, good, you've made it just in time. I was afraid Maisie was going to dish up before you got here." Directing her gaze to Andrew, she inquired, "Andrew, you've been to Edinburgh, haven't you?"

"Aye, m'lady. I've delivered many letters for Lord Sinclair and run other errands for him. Is there somethin' ye be wishin' me to do for ye?"

"Yes, there is. I have a letter I need carried to Mr. Smithson, Uncle Galvin's solicitor. Do you know where his office is?"

"Aye, m'lady. I've been there several times. I could leave at first light on the morrow, if it be pleasin' to ye."

"It would certainly be soon enough, Andrew. You'll probably have to stay a few days, for I've asked him to reply to some questions I feel are pressing. Would you be willing to do so? I would provide you with plenty of coin to pay for your expenses. I wouldn't expect you to simply sit in your room."

The young man shot a cautious look at his mother before answering. "I'd be willin' to stay, mum." He straightened his shoulders and stood a little taller. Daring to look directly at Sheridan, in spite of the awe he held for her beauty, he stated firmly, "I'll conduct myself with the most proper care, m'lady, so as no' to throw any hint of disgrace on the Sinclair name." Nor on ye, my lovely countess, he thought to himself.

Respecting his dignity, Sheridan replied warmly, "Thank you, Andrew. I'm gratified to know you are an honorable man and do not take the task lightly. Now, please, all of you sit down and let's enjoy our meal. It smells wonderful."

The others eagerly joined her and soon consumed the majority of the food. Sheridan scooted her chair away from the table, shaking her head when the cook sought to press another piece of fresh strawberry pie on her. "No, thank you, Cookie. I've already had my fill."

Directing her attention to Andrew, who was just finishing his second piece of the luscious pie, she spoke quietly. "Andrew, you seem to have a fine mind. I greatly appreciated hearing your insights into the tenants' plight during our conversation this evening." The blond lad blushed profusely at her praise, but she decided to pursue her course. "We had a good teacher here in the kirk when you were younger, didn't we?"

He looked at her in surprise. "Aye, milady. We learned to read and write and handle figures, and read Latin, although I have no' seen the value o' it."

Maisie spoke up. "Andrew was a good scholar, mum. He should have tried the university, but he dinna' want to leave the Highlands. He reads everythin' he can get his hands on."

"I hope you've taken advantage of the library here."

Andrew shifted uneasily. "I dinna' want to impose on his lordship. I ne'er asked to borrow any o' the books."

"Well, you don't have to ask. You may borrow any of them you like; you, too, Dora. Just return them to the proper place when you've finished them." She pushed back her chair. "Why don't you come pick out something now?"

Andrew followed her up to the library and stoked the fire to ward off the evening chill. His task completed, he stepped to the filled shelves and let his fingers graze lightly over the volumes there. "It will be a wondrous thing to read all o' these books, m'lady."

"You might not find all of them to your liking, but there is a great deal of knowledge and pleasure here." Sheridan moved across the room to stand in front of the blazing fire. "Andrew, there will be times when I'll need someone to handle the running of the estate for me. If my intuition is sound, you might be the person I would choose. You have a natural ability with the animals and the land, plus a sensitivity to the tenants. I would like my manager to have compassion for the farmers but a loyalty to me. I sense both in you. I will promise nothing, Andrew, for I know not what the future holds, but you can be assured that when the time comes, you will be considered for the position."

Andrew was dumbfounded. The highest goal he expected to achieve had been to be the coachman, a role which he already filled for the most part. He did not lack ambition, but to improve his lot in life would have meant leaving the Highlands and his family. It was something he simply could not do.

Andrew stared at her. Who would have ever thought his skinny playmate of years gone by would grow into this lovely creature? He could not forget how it felt to hold her in his arms, although he well knew she had clung to him only in fear and not as a man. Yet she seemed to genuinely care about his welfare. Dare he hope he could ever raise himself up to her level, to be her equal? He turned his head away, his eyes reflecting the pain of his answer.

No, he would never be her equal. Someday she might consider him a friend, but no matter how much he bettered himself, even if he made a fortune, he would never be a part of the aristocracy. It was lunacy to think she would ever give him a moment's notice as a man.

He took a volume of Shakespeare's *Macbeth* from the shelf. "Ye're very kind, m'lady. I'll do my best no' to disappoint ye and to be a help wherever I can."

"I know you will. Now, if you'll excuse me, I think I'll retire. My eyes are weary from reading the ledgers all day."

"Of course, m'lady." Andrew smiled and gave her a brief nod.

She returned his smile and left the library, walking through the drawing room to reach her bedroom. As she turned the doorknob, a knock sounded downstairs.

Albert opened the front door to admit Jeremy as Sheridan came down the stairs. "I had to come see for myself that you weren't hurt yesterday. We were already gone when Kyla came over today, and one of the new parlor maids misplaced the note she left." He took her hands in his and drew her into the great hall, anxiously searching for any visible signs of injury.

"I wasn't hurt at all, Jeremy, although I don't know what might have happened if Andrew had not been out on the moor. He would never admit it, but I think he was following me. No doubt Maisie told him to keep a watchful eye on me."

Jeremy silently thanked the good Lord for youthful infatuation and promised never to think ill of the lad again. "Did you see the man who shot at you?"

"No, all I saw was sunlight glinting off his musket. When I heard him fire, I dropped to the ground. I slid down the hill a little way and tried to hide. He fired again, hitting the exact spot where I first fell down. I suppose he might have mistaken me for a deer, but Andrew doesn't think it very likely."

"He'd have to be half blind to think you were an animal." Jeremy paced back and forth in front of the stone fireplace, covering its twelve foot width in four long strides. Coming to a sudden halt, he ran his fingers through his reddish-blond waves and put his other hand on his hip, pushing aside his blue frock coat in agitation. "Sheridan, what the deuce is going on here? Why would someone shoot at you?"

"I have no idea. The worst thing I've ever done was snub a few society matrons. I ruffled a few feathers, but even in their greatest wrath, those noble ladies would not deem it proper to hire a murderer."

Jeremy glared at her. "Don't be flippant. You should have sent Andrew over last night to tell us what happened. We would have scoured the countryside looking for him."

"It would have done no good. By the time we got back to the castle, it was dark, and he was long gone." She crossed the room and smoothed his wrinkled brow. "I didn't want to spoil Lady Maclaren's dinner party."

"Will you be serious about this?" he shouted.

"I am serious about it, but if I don't try to joke a little, I'll have the vapors."

Jeremy paced the floor a few more times, muttering under his breath, his fists clenching and unclenching at his side. "You aren't safe here. You should go back to England until this whole affair is cleared up."

"I will not."

"Then go to visit a cousin or someone in Edinburgh. Just get out of here."

"Jeremy, I'm not going anywhere. If someone wants to kill me, he isn't to quit trying simply because I go away. He'll follow me wherever I go."

"If you left secretively, how would he know where to follow you?"

"This isn't a big city. Every keeps track of everyone else, especially if something unusual has happened in the family. I couldn't get through the village without half the people noticing which way I went."

"You could borrow my uncle's coach and hide on the floor if you had to."

She threw up her hands and took his place in front of the fireplace, unknowingly copying his path back and forth. "This is ridiculous! I won't run away, and I don't want to hear any more about it," she said, her voice rising.

"Very well, madam, I won't mention it again, but don't expect me to mourn for you when you get your stubborn little head shot off." Jeremy grabbed his hat and stormed out the front door.

He stomped down the steps and snatched the reins from Andrew, muttering, "Stubborn, mule-headed wench." He swung up in the saddle and glanced down wearily. "I'll send some men over to help protect her. Make sure she doesn't go anywhere without an armed guard."

To Andrew's surprise, Jeremy held out his hand. "Thank you for looking out for her." The young servant hesitated for an instant before gripping the offered hand firmly. The handshake ended quickly. Jeremy swerved his steed around and headed down the lane, muttering, "Little fool . . . beautiful, independent little fool."

Sheridan listened to the sound of his horse clattering down the lane and fought to push aside the emptiness and fear closing around her heart. With a determined grimace, she straightened her shoulders and raised her head proudly, looking every inch the countess. "Go ahead and be angry, Jeremy Mackenzie, but you won't change my mind. I won't run away, not anymore."

Chapter 5

For the trip to Lochearnhead, Sheridan wore a simple black bombazine gown closed by lacing from bosom to waist. The overskirt fell open in a narrow gap to reveal the white silk petticoat. A snowy silk neckerchief filled in the low décolletage as was the fashion. Black shoes, short white gloves and a wide brimmed black silk hat trimmed with black and white ribbon completed her attire.

She stepped from the front door just as Albert brought the coach around. Although Andrew had already left on his mission to Edinburgh, leaving Albert to fill in as coachman, she was surprised to see one of the tenants sitting topside with him and two armed riders waiting behind the carriage.

"I asked Daniels to go along as guard, m'lady. Mr. Mackenzie sent these two over. They'll ride with us." He nodded to her left. "These two will stay here and keep an eye on the castle."

Sheridan smiled politely at each of Lord Maclaren's men as they doffed their hats. On the outside she appeared calm. Inwardly, she churned with a strange mixture of emotion; she was annoyed at Jeremy for trying to control her life, and relieved because he sent the men to protect her. Another feeling gradually overtook the others, a warm, pleased glow that came from knowing he cared.

"Thank you for coming to help us. Mr. Daniels, how is your family?"

The ruddy-faced man beamed with pride. "They be fine, m'lady. We've a new wee bairn, a lad just a month old. That gives the missus and me three wee ones under foot."

"And your wife? Is she doing well?"

"Aye, mum. She's a strong one, my Millie. When I left the hut this morn, she was a wipin' one wee one's nose, nursin' the babe and a yellin' at a goat in the garden all at the same time."

Sheridan smiled, shook her head in appropriate amazement and accepted Albert's assistance as she climbed into the carriage. Maisie climbed in afterwards, giggling like a girl at her husband's playful swat on her ample behind.

When they arrived at the village, they found the grassy village square transformed into a bustling open-air market. The traveling vendors called from their stalls, barking out the merits of their spices, cookware, beautifully woven Scottish plaids and even silver jewelry. Local farmers proudly displayed early season vegetables along with chickens, eggs, smoked hams and fresh salmon and trout from the nearby loch and streams. Market day brought a festive mood to the normally quiet village, and a chorus of voices filled the air with bartering and laughter.

The morning flew by as the women made their

purchases with Mr. Daniels following along behind at a respectable distance. There were five tenant families currently living on the estate, and Sheridan decided to provide at least one length of cloth for each family member. With Maisie's guidance as to how many people were now in each family, and whether they were male or female, large or small, she purchased the material. Bargaining shrewdly, she purchased enough for each woman and girl to have a dress, each boy and man to have a new shirt and pants. They arranged with the merchants for the goods to be delivered to the waiting carriage across the street.

They wandered farther down the row of open shops, purchasing spices, oils and nuts in one, a new pot in another and sampling the fried trout rolled in oats at still another. At last, having bought everything they could think of and having eaten their fill of the various treats, the women turned back toward the carriage. Mr. Daniels still followed behind, now loaded with packages and unshamedly sucking on a piece of taffy.

They were halfway to the coach when Sheridan took Maisie aside. "I'm going back to the little stall on the far end and buy that gown for Mr. Daniels's baby. It was so beautiful, I simply can't resist." Turning to her tenant, she said, "I forgot one small item. You two go on ahead. I'll just be a minute."

"I dunna' know, mum. Ye shouldna' be wanderin' about by yerself," said Mr. Daniels, peering between two boxes.

"Oh, 'tis not likely I'll come to harm. I could see the coach from the shop I need to visit, so you can keep an eye on me. It really won't take long."

"Well, if ye'll be careful, m'lady."

Sheridan speedily made her acquisition and wove her way through the throng of people toward the waiting carriage. As she stepped into the street, she checked for approaching traffic, then became preoccupied with tucking the paper around her present. She didn't want Mr. Daniels to guess what it was.

Hearing a noise and Albert's shout, she jerked her head up to find a terrified stallion bearing down on her, its rider sprawled in the dirt some distance down the road. Sheridan grabbed up her skirts and made a dash for the side of the street. Her hat flew off when she took one last desperate leap as the stallion skidded to a halt and reared beside her.

Instinctively, she threw up her arms to protect her face as she tried to dodge the flaying hooves. Two powerful hands snatched her from harm, the rescuer placing himself between the rearing horse and her. The dark animal snorted, slashing the air with his hooves.

Sheridan automatically buried her face in her guardian's coat, and he, just as instinctively, wrapped his arms protectively around her. A long minute later, the animal touched the ground again in a panicky gallop. The danger past, the gentleman reluctantly loosened his hold. She took a step back and slowly raised her head as he spoke.

"Are you hurt, m'lady? Thankfully, you had enough sense to run, otherwise you could have been badly—"

When Sheridan looked up at her rescuer, his color drained, leaving his skin ashen. He began to tremble as he stood transfixed, staring at her as if he had seen a ghost. "Alyson?" he choked.

"Nay, my lord," Sheridan said quickly, afraid he was going to faint. She had never seen anyone that particular shade of gray before. "Alyson was my mother. I'm Sheridan Sinclair."

His hands dropped to his sides, and he looked at her, still in a daze. "Sheridan? Her daughter?" He closed his eyes and rubbed his forehead with his fingers as if trying to erase some painful memory. When his gaze returned to her, he was regaining control, and his coloring slowly returned to normal. "Of course, I forgot about the daughter. You must forgive me, Sheridan. You look so much like your beloved mother that for a moment I was quite taken aback. I'm Lord Cameron Macveagh, your neighbor."

His face broke into a pleasant smile, which did not quite reach his icy gray eyes. Sheridan had the distinct impression nothing could erase the mixture of melancholy and torment she saw there.

"Thank you for pulling me to safety, my lord. You placed yourself in great danger to protect me. I am in your debt, sir."

"I fear it was more of a reaction than a conscious act of gallantry, but I know a way in which you can repay the debt, m'lady."

"How so, my lord?" She was almost afraid to ask from the blatant manner in which he was admiring her form.

"Dine with me tonight. My houseguest, Lady Grant, will be having some friends over for dinner. I would be most delighted to have you join us for the evening."

"I suppose it would not be considered improper if I accept your kind invitation, my lord, although I should be the one to entertain you and your friends to show my gratitude."

"Think nothing of it; my chef normally prepares enough to feed at least ten people in the hope that he may show off his talents. I'll send a coach for you around seven."

"There is no need to send a carriage, sir. Albert can take me."

"No, I must insist my carriage pick you up. I have many more men at my disposal, my dear. With the terrible events of these last weeks, I wish to make certain you are well protected. Please accept my deepest condolences on the death of your uncle. A tragedy, simply a tragedy."

"Thank you, my lord. Thank you, also, for helping Waverly as you did. If you had not rushed him to the keep, it is certain he would have died."

He gave a tiny, grave bow. "We only did what we could, my dear. Would that we had come along sooner, perhaps the whole sordid affair would have ended differently. How is Waverly? He will mend, I trust?"

They walked toward Albert and the carriage as they talked. Maisie hung her head out the coach window, her mouth gaping open.

"He is doing remarkably well," said Sheridan. "Maisie thinks he should be able to get out of bed for a short while tomorrow. He was in good health before the shooting, and that has helped greatly in his recovery."

Macveagh's hand touched her elbow as he helped her into the coach. Leaning against the open door, he said, "You must forgive me, Lady Sheridan, for no' visiting before now. If I had known of your arrival, I would have been over to pay my respects and extend my sympathy sooner. However, I have been in Edinburgh since shortly after the incident and have only returned this morning." He touched the rim of his beaver hat in salute. "Now, if you will excuse me, lovely lady, there are some business affairs that need to be put in order."

"Good day, my lord."

Albert picked up the shredded remains of her hat and handed it to her, closing the door with a snort. Wordlessly, he climbed up to the top of the coach, directing the horses through the crowded street.

Maisie cleared her throat, glanced at her mistress, then cleared her throat again. "Lady Sheridan, mind ye be careful of that one."

"Please explain what you mean, Maisie. I take it you don't care for Lord Macveagh."

"Well, I dunna' rightly know if I can explain, mum.

...I know is yer uncle dinna' care for the man. He said he dinna' trust him, and no' once was he ever invited to visit Sinclair Castle; at least no' since yer parents died, mum.''

"Yes, I had forgotten. I wondered about it occasionally before I went to London, but if I recall correctly, Lord Macveagh did not spend a great deal of time in the district anyway. How strange to be so unneighborly. 'Tis not like Uncle Galvin at all, is it? Was Lord Macveagh a friend of my parents, Maisie?''

"Aye, m'lady. He and yer uncle were close friends as lads since they were the same age.'' Her face crumpled as tears formed. "The poor laird. Five-and-forty is much too young to die.''

Sheridan squeezed the servant's hand and gave her a few minutes to compose herself before asking, "Do you know what destroyed their friendship?''

"Well, m'lady, beggin' yer pardon, but I think it had somethin' to do with yer dear mother.''

"My mother?'' Sheridan's eyes grew wide in surprise.

"Aye. Macveagh was away when she came to visit her friends in Balquhidder that summer. Ach, what a beauty she was. Ye look like her, ye know; in fact, there be times when the resemblance is most startlin'.'' The housekeeper studied her mistress for a moment, then shook her head, collecting her thoughts.

"Anyways, yer mother came to visit, and the menfolk for miles around practically fought over her. Yer father won her hand, and they were married in August.

"Lord Macveagh returned from the Continent a year later, a month or two after ye were born. He came around often, since he and yer uncle were such good friends. Everyone got along fine for several years, about four, I think, then somethin' happened, and yer uncle and Macveagh had a terrible argument.'' Maisie hesitated a moment. "I think Macveagh fancied himself in love with yer mum. He must have said or done somethin' yer menfolk dinna' approve of, because suddenly there was bad blood between the whole family and him. He never came back again, nor did any of yer folk ever set foot in his house afterwards.''

"Oh, my. That would explain why the poor man was so shocked when he first saw me. He even called me by mother's name.'' She stared at her gloves thoughtfully. In a few minutes, she looked up at Maisie.

"It seems like a good time to end this animosity. Since we can only guess at the cause, I see no reason for me to continue with it. After all, the man is my neighbor and probably saved my life. I at least owe him a dinner and a chance to get better acquainted. However, I'll be cautious and alert to anything that might warrant keeping my distance from Lord Macveagh. It may prove to be a very interesting evening.''

Albert drove the carriage slowly around the square, skillfully guiding the four-in-hand around a cart that had not pulled far enough over to the side of the road. In a few moments, they were travelling briskly down the road beside Loch Earn.

"Maisie, Lord Macveagh mentioned a houseguest, Lady Grant. Do you know anything about her?''

"Aye, a bit. Lady Melissa Grant has been a friend o' Macveagh's for years. Her family's from around Edinburgh, but she married an elderly English baron some ten years ago. She stays in Scotland most o' the year, but her husband ne'er leaves England. She's as pretty as they come and knows it, too. Got flamin' red hair and bright blue eyes.'' Maisie took a deep breath, pausing her effect. "Most folk think she and Macveagh are lovers.''

"Oh, dear. I'm sure it will be an interesting evening.''

There was a shout ahead of them, and the carriage slowed. Exchanging worried glances, Sheridan and

Maisie peered out the coach windows.

" 'Tis Mr. Mackenzie, mum. He's with Lord Maclaren, Mr. Hagen and another man."

Sheridan quickly smoothed her hair and skirt and licked her lips nervously, wondering if Jeremy would even speak to her.

Jeremy stopped his large bay stallion a few feet away from the coach, blocking from view the other men who were sitting on their mounts in the middle of the road. He jumped to the ground with the grace of a dancer and approached the coach window.

Sheridan tried not to stare, but he looked so achingly handsome she simply could not turn away. His gold-striped taffeta frock coat brought out the sparkling amber of his eyes and the golden glints in his hair. His buckskin breeches hugged the contours of his legs, giving a hint of his physical power.

She forced her fingers to unclench and raised her gaze to meet Jeremy's. Maisie nonchalantly rearranged the pile of packages, conveniently turning her back on her mistress in the process.

His gaze swept over her in a bold caress, taking her breath away. She moved her hand to the edge of the window, and he picked it up in his lean, brown one. Turning it over, he gently kissed the palm.

"How are you this morning, my dear? Obviously, you've been out spending your inheritance." He met her gaze directly, not willing to make an apology for his behavior the previous evening.

"Just a little of it." Sheridan studied his face briefly and decided not to mention their last conversation. "Thank you for sending the men over. I feel much better having them around."

"It was the least I could do."

She glanced at Lord Maclaren and the man at his side. Though fashionably dressed, his clothes were not cut from the expensive material of a gentleman, yet he emanated an unconscious air of authority and confidence. "Is he the Runner?"

"Aye, he arrived early this morning. Would you like to meet him?"

"Of course."

He waved to the others, and they moved their restless horses closer to the coach. "Lady Sinclair, may I make known to you Mr. James Biggs. Mr. Biggs, may I present the Countess Sinclair."

The Runner doffed his hat and bowed his head briefly. "Pleased to make your acquaintance, m'lady. I'll do my best to get to the bottom of this nasty business."

"My thanks, sir. Do you have any idea why my uncle was killed?"

"From what I've learned so far, no. It's always a possibility someone thought he might buy the estate cheap after his lordship died, assuming there were no relatives. Or, if they knew you might inherit, they figured you would sell. Lord Maclaren tells me you've been improving the land. Possibly someone might have wanted it."

"It's been in the Sinclair line for several generations and came into the family by marriage. I simply cannot believe anyone would want this estate badly enough to kill my uncle. It's not large or even greatly valuable."

"I didn't put much faith in the theory myself, m'lady." Biggs studied her closely for a moment. "Now, tell me who would have wanted your uncle dead. Did he have any enemies?"

"I can think of no one. Believe me, Mr. Biggs, I've tried. He was a quiet, gentle man. He got along with everyone." The conversation with Maisie ran through her mind. "Well, there is one person I'm told he didn't like."

"Who would that be, m'lady?"

"Maisie mentioned that Lord Macveagh and Uncle Galvin were once close friends, but something happened years ago to cause a rift in their relationship. I always knew they weren't particularly friendly, but I never sensed any real hatred between them. Perhaps you know something of their relationship, Lord Maclaren. Do you know what happened to dissolve their friendship?"

His lordship patted his horse's neck and shifted uneasily in the saddle. "Well, lass, your uncle had a falling out with Macveagh years ago over your mother. Macveagh became deeply infatuated with Lady Alyson. Galvin had an argument with him about his foolish behavior. Their friendship was ne'er the same afterwards, though the young buck seemed to settle down. I guess he hadna' realized how embarrassing his attentions were to Lady Alyson. It was no' long afterwards that your parents died. I ne'er knew there to be any hatred between Galvin and Macveagh. They just seemed to go their separate ways as they grew older. They were always civil whenever they met."

"Well, I'll check this Lord Macveagh out," said Biggs. "It don't pay to leave any stones unturned, so to speak. I heard about your run-in with the highwaymen on your trip from Edinburgh, m'lady. They were still talking about it at the inn in Callander. I saw the magistrate and learned they arrested some of the men. I talked to a couple of them, and it looks as if they weren't anywhere near here the night your uncle was murdered. Their story proves out. It would seem the band that held up your uncle wasn't from around here. A few of the local folk saw some strangers passing through along about the same time, but I haven't come up with any good leads yet. I assure you I'll keep looking, m'lady."

"I appreciate your thoroughness, Mr. Biggs." She

turned again to Lord Maclaren. "I thank you, too, my lord, for hiring the Runner. I must insist, however, that you defer his expenses to me. I would like for you to be in charge of the investigation, but I will gladly pay whatever costs are necessary."

"I willna' hear of it, lass. Galvin Sinclair was my dearest friend, and I'll find the vermin who killed him no matter what the cost." He turned his horse abruptly and moved around behind the coach. Patrick struck up a conversation with Biggs to allow his lordship a few minutes to himself.

Jeremy looked down at Sheridan's hand and smiled, realizing he had been holding it all the time. "Will you be home this evening? I have a grouse to bring over."

"Are you trying to wheedle a dinner invitation, Jeremy?" Sheridan laughed softly. At his grin and shrug of his shoulders, she continued, "I have an engagement this evening but will be home for tea. Could you stop by then?"

"I don't know. Uncle Balfour has some business on the other side of the loch, and he asked us to come along. He is to inspect some horses and wants our opinion of them. I'll do my best to get back." His smile lit up his eyes. "I won't have the grouse, though. You'll have to invite me again to get it."

"Such bribery, sir."

"Come, nephew. Quit flirtin' with the lass and mount up. We've got work to do." Lord Maclaren smiled affectionately at Sheridan and tipped his hat. "Good day to you, m'lady."

Having known him since she was a child, Sheridan was not annoyed or embarrassed by his teasing, but welcomed it as from a dear friend. She gave him a grin and waved. Jeremy still claimed her other hand in his and gave it a tiny squeeze before releasing it.

He swung up on his horse and turned the animal to

follow his uncle. Sheridan leaned out the window, watching him until he disappeared around a curve in the road, the moving coach stretching the distance between them.

In mid-afternoon, Jeremy and Patrick walked up the steps of Sinclair Castle only to have the door opened by Albert before they could knock. A soft peal of feminine laughter greeted Jeremy as he walked through the entrance.

"M'lady is in the kitchen helpin' Cook prepare sweets to take to the tenants on the morrow. He always did have a way of makin' her laugh at his tall tales." The twinkling in Albert's eyes belied his sober countenance. "I'll announce yer arrival, sir."

Jeremy quickly raised a hand to stop him. "Don't bother Lady Sheridan, Albert. I'll announce myself. I wouldn't want to disturb her merriment." Another laugh reached him from the kitchen, followed by a fit of giggles. He smiled at the butler. " 'Tis such a pleasant sound. Don't fret so, man. I'm not a stranger to a kitchen, and I'm not above taking my tea there, especially if I get to sample whatever it is that smells so good."

Albert watched Patrick head for the stairs. "Kyla is in Waverly's room, Mr. Hagen. I assume ye'll just go up?"

"That's right, Albert. I don't think either of them will mind."

"Aye, sir, I suppose ye're right; they'll both be happy to see ye."

Jeremy followed the sound of the giggles, with a dismayed Albert trailing along behind. Carefully, he pushed open the door to see Sheridan wiping her eyes on her apron as she tried to stop laughing. The door creaked when he pushed it wider, and Sheridan spun around.

"Do ye have a handout fer a poor starvin' man, m'lady?" he inquired, jokingly as he stepped into the kitchen.

Sheridan raised her hands to her face and smoothed back her hair, unknowingly leaving a dusting of flour behind.

Albert moved into the kitchen as soon as Jeremy had opened a path for him. "I'm sorry, m'lady. Mr. Mackenzie wouldna' let me tell ye he was here."

" 'Tis all right, Albert. If Mr. Mackenzie will not announce his presence, he'll just have to accept the fact that I'm not dressed for company. I've got flour up to my elbows."

"And on your face, too." Jeremy grinned, eyeing her loose-fitting gray muslin gown and long white apron. "You look lovely. Besides, I'm not company." His eyes sparkling mischievously, he closed the distance between them.

When he gently brushed the flour from one cheek, Albert disappeared out the door, and Cook faded into the pantry. Jeremy kissed the other cheek and made a face. "Flour tastes terrible without sugar. I'll have to sweeten things up a bit." Before she could protest his indiscretion, he lowered his lips to hers in a whisper of a touch. Then he stepped back a pace.

"Jeremy Mackenzie, where's your sense of propriety?" The scolding lacked the proper effect when what she wanted most was for him to take her in his arms and continue kissing her.

"But, my sweet little confection, there's no one here but us."

Sheridan glanced around the kitchen quickly and laughed. "You're a rake, Jeremy, but a charming one. Well, since you're here, you might as well have tea while I finish rolling out this dough."

Miraculously, Cook emerged from the pantry to prepare the tea, but he stopped in mid-stride when Jeremy calmly removed his coat and rolled up his sleeves. Sheridan, too, watched open-mouthed as Jeremy picked up an apron from the back of a chair and tied it around his firm midsection. He washed and dried his hands before dumping the shortbread dough out onto the floured board.

"You box up the candy, my dear, and I'll roll out the dough."

Sheridan shut her mouth and watched Jeremy mound half the dough into a ball, then press it with his hand into a large round. Picking it up, he put it on the baking sheet and pinched the edges together with finger and thumb in the traditional Scottish fashion. "Jeremy, you can't work in the kitchen. You're a gentleman."

"And you are a half-English lady, so you have no more social acceptance by being here than I do. Now, don't be so stuffy and let me enjoy myself. We're not so arrogant in the States; I often helped my mother with the baking." He reached out and pinched off a good-sized bite of the shortbread dough and popped it dramatically in his mouth. "But I do expect my just rewards, or should I say my just desserts?"

Sheridan groaned and sat down at the table to box the butterscotch and taffy.

Jeremy eyed the pastel candy greedily. "Is that Edinburgh Rock?"

"Yes. I assume you want a piece."

"Just a raspberry one." He grabbed the last pink taffy before she could pick it up. "Mmmmm, wonderful."

Sheridan shook her head and took a bite of shortbread dough. "Cookie, it looks as if you have two hungry helpers today. I hope you don't mind."

The ruddy-faced cook smiled. "No' so long as ye

leave enough to bake for the tenants. I'll no' have time to mix up any more today, mistress.''

Sheridan slapped Jeremy's hand playfully when he reached for another bite. ''We'll try to restrain ourselves.''

Jeremy scooped the other half of dough up into a ball, raising it threateningly in her direction. ''Perhaps m'lady would like another sample?''

She shrieked and jumped up from the table, running across the room. ''Jeremy, don't you dare waste that.'' Seeing the impish gleam in his eye as he slowly moved around the table, she pleaded, ''Jeremy, think of all the sweets the little ones could have if you don't throw it at me.''

He paused before lowering the ball back to the table. ''Well, I would hate for the wee ones to miss out. I'm very fond of children.'' He gave her a strange look, causing her heart to catch in her throat. Briskly, he said, ''Let's finish up here and go for a walk.''

They finished their self-appointed chores and drank a quick cup of tea, then left the castle by the back entry. Strolling across the glen, they reached a large patch of heather and bluebells painting the heath in a riot of color. Sheridan picked a bouquet while Jeremy stretched out on the ground, leaning on one elbow to watch her. She slowly expanded the distance between them, keeping her face turned away so he wouldn't see the mischievous gleam in her eye.

''I'll race you to the woods,'' she called over her shoulder. She took off in a run, skirts lifted to reveal a pretty show of ankle. Like her laughter, the flowers scattered in the breeze as she struggled to hang onto the bouquet and her skirts at the same time.

Grinning, Jeremy jumped to his feet and headed after her. He slowed his pace momentarily as he scooped up a sprig of heather, then trotted up the hill behind her.

Sheridan reached the grove of birch and oaks ahead of him and hid behind a large tree. Leaning one hand on the trunk, she peered around it, gazing down at Jeremy with a pitiful look. "You're so slow, Mr. Mackenzie. Are you getting old and decrepit?"

"I'll show you how decrepit I am when I catch you, wench." Then he ruined his fierce expression by grinning.

He came around the left side of the tree, and Sheridan dashed around the right side and across a small clearing. She peeked out at him from behind another oak, her face alight with mischief. As he moved closer, she inched away from the tree, tossing him a teasing smile.

"Best watch out for the fairies," she called in a soft, sing-song voice.

"They're off tormenting some other poor soul, but they left a wood nymph here to bedevil me." She edged a few more steps to the side and he shifted his course. He let his warm gaze roam over her slowly, and she stumbled over a small log but quickly regained her footing. Jeremy lunged and she dodged, scampering off with a trill of laughter to disappear in back of some thick bushes.

Sheridan peeped between the branches, but couldn't see him. She shifted her position and looked again, but there was no Jeremy in sight. Holding her breath, she listened closely, but could only hear the birds twittering and the breeze blowing softly through the leaves. Suddenly, his arms came around her from behind, and her breath came out in a shriek.

He spun her around, spread his big hands about her waist, and threw her over his shoulder like a sack of grain.

"Put me down," she cried, laughing and feebly pounding on his back.

"Certainly. All in good time, m'lady." Chuckling

and dodging her elbows as she swung her fists, he pushed his way out of the undergrowth into a flat, shady clearing. Bending over, he deposited her safely on the ground.

"How did you sneak up on me like that?"

"Age and cunning will win over youth and beauty every time." He grinned and flicked her beneath the chin with his index finger. "I spent a lot of time with Patrick's grandfather, too."

"Humph." Her lips puckered into a pout, but her eyes twinkled.

"Now, I'm the fearless warrior, and you're my slave. You must earn your freedom."

Sheridan looked up at him in mock horror. "What must I do? Start a fire?"

"Nope, don't need a fire."

"Feed your horse?"

"No." He chuckled.

"Grind your corn?" She smiled up at him in wide-eyed innocence.

"Don't have any corns, bunions either." He settled his arms around her and nudged her toward him until they touched. "The price of freedom is one hundred kisses."

"Don't you think that's a bit excessive?" She slid her hands up to rest on his shoulders.

"Well . . ." He cocked his head to one side and gave her a smile that made her insides melt. "I suppose ten good ones would do."

She considered the penalty for a moment, wrinkling her forehead and looking thoughtful. "Very well. That's fair. Go right ahead and begin anytime."

"No, no. You're the one who has to pay." He lowered his eyelids slightly, but they did not hide the flickering amber of his burning eyes. "You kiss me."

The crackling timbre of his low voice matched the look in his eyes.

"Oh."

"Go right ahead and begin anytime."

Her cheeks flushed a very becoming soft pink, and she gave him a peck on the mouth. He didn't move a muscle. She leaned back against his arms and looked up at him. He slowly shook his head.

"That wouldn't even count for practice. Try again. Put a little effort into it this time." Jeremy lowered his face toward hers, but left it up to her to close the remaining gap.

A small frown wrinkled her delicate brow, and she looked down at the white folds of his casually tied cravat. Sheridan suddenly felt shy and inept. When she raised her gaze back to his face, she found his expression had softened. The fearless warrior had disappeared, and an expectant, confident Jeremy was waiting.

He brought his hand around from behind her back and lifted the sprig of heather to his lips. He kissed the delicate petals, then brushed them against her lips.

A shiver raced up and down her spine, and a smile flickered across her face. Confidence was contagious.

She stretched that tiny distance and brushed her lips across his slowly, drawing back a fraction of an inch.

"Enough practice," he murmured. "Now, pay your debt." Still, he waited for her to come to him.

Sheridan slid her arms up around his neck and kissed him, her eyes drifting closed. She quickly forgot her shyness and put his past lessons to good use—one, two, and three.

Jeremy came up for air, then nuzzled the side of her neck, brushing aside the soft, lawn tucker to nibble on her collarbone. "You've got the hang of it, but go slower with the next ones. I don't want this delight to end too soon."

Neither did she. Sheridan drew him back and gave herself up completely to the kiss. He crushed her to him, taking her mouth with an urgency and intensity that made her tremble. All conscious thought flew from her mind. She was only aware of him, the places he caressed, the things he made her feel. She was so weak, she couldn't stand and clung to him for support.

He slowly sank to his knees, easing her down to kneel between them. Still he kissed her, scorching, demanding kisses that fulfilled the payment twice over. Her head dropped back as he moved to tease her throat with the tip of his tongue, sending one shudder after another through her body.

"I told you not to start a fire." His voice was deep and thick. He found her ankle and slid his hand along her smooth, cotton-covered calf, pushing her skirt up to her knee. "I want you. Oh, sweet lady, I want you. I've lost my senses."

The vague thought that she had lost hers, too, pricked her conscience, but she was beyond the point of caring. Caught in a magical web of desire, she was his and would gladly give up her innocence to please him.

He peppered kisses along her neck and shoulder as his hand inched above her knee. He toyed with the silk garter tied there, then brushed his fingertips along her skin above the garter, causing her to moan softly.

His lips touched her cheekbone and one corner of her mouth. "Sweet, sweet lady—I have to stop. Make me stop, Sher." His breath was coming in shallow gasps. "I can't dishonor you."

Honor Above All. Her family motto came to her mind with the force of a winter gale, followed by her uncle's stern proclamation on the eve of her first ball. "There has no' been a public scandal in this family for over six hundred years. I expect you to be worthy of your heritage, lass.''

She twisted away from him, falling backward on the ground, and rolled over, then scrambled to her knees. ''Stay away.'' Her breathing, too, was shallow and quick. ''Don't touch me.''

She watched Jeremy warily. He raised a shaky hand to his brow, shielding his downcast eyes. He drew in a deep, shivering breath. His other hand was clenched against the outside of his thigh, digging into the taut muscle.

Sheridan took a slow, deep breath, willing her mind to regain control over her trembling body. Conflicting emotions tormented her—desire and excitement, compassion and longing. And shame. It had been all her fault. She had led him on the chase. She had teased and tempted. She had blatantly encouraged him. Tears stung her eyes, yet she could not look away, for even now she wanted him. If he made the smallest move toward her, she knew she would fall willingly into his arms. Mortification filled her, and a small cry sounded in her throat. She raised her fist to her lips to bottle the agony up inside.

Jeremy dropped his hand and met her gaze. Pain and contempt filled his eyes. ''Go back to the castle, Sheridan.'' He spoke quietly, his voice strained.

''Jeremy—''

''Go back to the castle.'' Both hands curled into fists. ''Get away from me.''

Sheridan gasped at his clenched jaw and glittering eyes. Jumping to her feet, she raced down the brae toward the castle, convinced his disgust was directed at her. She slipped in through a side door and made her way to her bedroom undetected. Once there, she wept in humiliation. She could not blame him for loathing her. She had acted like a common strumpet. How she must have disgusted him! She pounded her pillow with her fists, frustrated because she had made a fool of herself, and angry because it mattered what he thought of her—it mattered very much.

It took all of Jeremy's willpower not to run after Sheridan when she left the woods. He knew he had wounded her, although unintentionally. He had seen the longing and hunger in her eyes, even when she told him not to touch her, and knew he was powerless to get up and walk away.

Once she was out of sight, he stood and turned to walk in the opposite direction. He hoped she would realize his contempt was directed at himself. Once again, he had proven he was no gentleman, in spite of his upbringing. Kicking a small stone with his boot, he swore angrily. How could he have been such an idiot? He had practically seduced her, and in the middle of the woods, for pity's sake.

Coming across a fat, woolly sheep, he glared at her wide-eyed stare. The ewe stood right in his path, and even though he could have easily walked around her, Jeremy stopped abruptly and growled. She blinked and backed up a step.

"I don't debauch innocent young women." The sheep bleated back.

"Don't you argue with me, or I'll have mutton for dinner." The cantankerous animal only shook her head and went back to nibbling the grass.

Jeremy let out a frustrated cry and jumped toward her with a snarl, waving his arms. The sheep ran several feet away, stopped and glared back with disdain.

"Very well, you can have that spot. I want this rock all to myself." Jeremy shook his head. He couldn't remember ever actually talking to a sheep. He sat down, going over the past hour in his mind. It wasn't long until the fuzzy animal wandered back to her favorite spot.

"She's driving me mad. I can't keep my hands off her." The sheep looked up. "What's wrong with me?" No answer.

About that time a ram came trotting majestically over the brae. He made a straight line for the ewe, stopping between her and Jeremy. With gentle nudges against her shoulder, he guided her away from the man. Once they were a safe distance from the intruder, the ram stopped and nuzzled her. Then, in a flash, he bounded down the hill, turning expectantly at the bottom. She followed leisurely behind.

Possession. Protection. Affection. Jeremy shook his head and smiled ruefully. Love. It was as simple as that small word, and as complicated. He stayed on the moor until dusk, sorting things out in his mind and coming to several decisions, one of them crucial. No matter how much he cared for Sheridan, he would settle for nothing less than a love match. He would not spend the remainder of his days with a wife who quickly tired of him.

He would pay court to her, play the gentleman—even if it drove him to distraction—and try to win her love. He would strive for patience, give her time to work through her grief and help her come to terms with her fears. He wasn't certain what haunted her, but knew instinctively it must be laid to rest before she would be free to love.

As Jeremy headed back toward the castle, he spotted an expensive carriage coming up the lane, flanked by several outriders. Disappointment welled up inside. He had forgotten Sheridan's dinner engagement.

He strode purposefully back down the brae. Since Cookie had not been busy preparing a meal for guests, he assumed Sheridan was going out. He frowned, watching the carriage, then relaxed. At least she would be well protected, wherever she was going. He slowed his pace, intentionally delaying his arrival until after her departure. Confident he could charm Maisie out of a meal, he planned to wait at Sinclair Castle until Sheridan returned. What he had to say to her couldn't wait until morning.

Chapter 6

Sheridan made her way down the stairs, the skirt of her elegant gown rustling softly. This time her gown and petticoat were both of black silk. A soft gray silk neckerchief was wrapped around her shoulders and across her bodice, then tied in a neat bow at her back. Other than tiny pearl earrings and a black velvet ribbon buckled at her throat, she wore no jewelry.

She gazed pensively out the window at the elaborate coach creeping up the drive, accompanied by four armed guards. "Kyla, I'm hesitant to place myself solely in Lord Macveagh's hands. I want to be able to leave if I need to. I doubt very much if there will be any problem, but since I don't really know the man, I need to be in as much control of the situation as possible. Would you please tell Albert to arrive at Lord Macveagh's at nine o'clock with my coach? That should give us plenty of time for dinner and pleasant neighborly conversation, and it would not appear rude if I chose to leave then."

"I'll make certain he arrives by nine, Sheridan. Do be alert tonight and very careful. I dunna' know what was between your kin and his lordship, but it was no' a good thing. I hope, as you do, this ill will can be put to rest."

Sheridan took her light woolen cloak from Albert and draped it around her shoulders, fastening the single clasp at the throat. "I'll be cautious. Hopefully, I can discover what the feud was about in the first place."

Albert opened the door for his mistress and stepped aside as she swept down the entry steps to the waiting vehicle. The footman held the door for her and assisted her into the carriage, while the guards exchanged looks of appreciation at her beauty.

Sheridan pushed aside a moment of apprehension when the coach wound up the long lane to Castle Cameron. In the twilight, it appeared dark and foreboding. She reminded herself that castles weren't really sinister, only people, and took a few deep breaths to slow her racing heart.

The carriage stopped in front of the stronghold, and Lord Macveagh strode proudly down the long column of steps to meet her. A handsome man, he cut a striking figure in his black satin breeches and gray and white waistcoat. The silver satin frock coat drew her attention to his eyes, those beautiful, haunted silver eyes. He opened the door for her personally and took her hand to assist her down the steps.

"You are very lovely tonight, my dear," he said quietly, lifting her hand for his kiss, a kiss that seemed to linger overlong. He turned smoothly and tucked her hand through his arm, escorting her up the steep stairway to the entry.

Although the outside of the castle looked its five hundred years, the inside had been remodeled and refurbished. It was apparent from the fine quality and coordination of the furniture and appointments that it had been decorated by an artist. In fact, several large, beautiful oil landscapes were the focal point in the massive entry, their vibrant colors a striking contrast to the gray marble floor and highly polished wood of a wide oak staircase in the center of the hall. Macveagh removed Sheridan's cloak, handed it to the waiting butler, and gave her a few minutes to admire the paintings before he escorted her up the great staircase, which spiraled majestically from the ground floor up four levels.

At the first landing, he drew her into a private drawing room. The ceiling was plastered in swags and ivy, with delicately painted panels in soft lavender color. The tiny flowers in the rug picked up the lavender, as well as the mint green of the satin chairs and sofa, and the soft rose of the heavy brocade draperies. There was nothing gaudy or overdone about the room, but it presented itself with a dignity that spoke quietly of the wealth of the master of the castle.

Sheridan strolled around the room, silently admiring the carefully selected furnishings. She stopped in front of the fireplace. In awe, she stared at a painting that spread the full width of the eight-foot hearth. The picture was of a small cove on Loch Earn, a secluded, quiet place where she had often gone as a child. She noted the signature in the corner and turned in surprise to Lord Macveagh.

"I was not aware you were such a magnificent artist, my lord. Your talent overwhelms me." At his pleased smile, she turned back to the picture. "It's so real, I feel I'm there. I can almost hear the gentle slosh of the waves against the shore and the gulls screeching overhead." She did not hear him move to stand behind her and was startled when he slipped his arm around her, his hand resting at her waist.

He spoke quietly and warmly. "I'm glad my meager talent pleases you, Lady Sinclair. Pick a scene you truly love, and I will paint it for you."

She carefully moved away, purposefully walking sedately across the room to inspect a smaller group of paintings. "Thank you, Lord Macveagh. I'll be very happy and honored to hang one of your creations in my home. Now, the only problem will be in deciding which scene for you to paint. There are many such lovely areas on my estate, all dear to my heart."

"Perhaps there will be time to paint them all, my dear," he said quietly.

Sheridan looked back over her shoulder. "Will Lady Grant be joining us soon?"

"Unfortunately, no. I arrived back home just a short while ago and found she had gone to visit a cousin who has been ill. She will not be returning for several days. I'm sure you can meet her another time."

"What of your other guests, sir?"

"It seems they took a small side trip on their journey from Edinburgh. That is why Melissa decided to visit her cousin now."

Sheridan turned to face him, her brow slightly wrinkled in a frown. "Then we will be dining alone, Lord Macveagh?"

"Call me Cameron, my dear. Yes, we will be dining alone. I trust you do not mind."

"It is not really proper, my lord. I'm sure you are quite aware of the scandal such an innocent dinner would cause in the minds of our neighbors, sir."

"There is no one to know. My servants are very discreet and will not mention it. I will certainly tell no one, and if you do not speak of it, no one will have cause to gossip."

"I do not like being put in such a position."

"Forgive me. I did not mean to cast a shadow on our evening. I saw no harm in neighbors spending a quiet evening together."

Before Sheridan could reply, the butler announced the dinner was ready. She reluctantly took Cameron's offered arm and joined him to walk into the dining room. Here, oak paneling was used extensively, accented with ornately carved swags and ivy to repeat the pattern in the drawing room.

The dinner was splendid, complete with turtle soup, roast duckling, smoked haddock, ham and a variety of fruits and vegetables, ending with a flaky pastry resting in a bed of clotted cream. The conversation during the meal was relaxed and casual, the topics ranging from the frivolity of London social life to the best turnips for planting for fodder for the sheep.

Sheridan was careful to only drink one small glass of wine with her meal and knew her relaxed state was not from the drink. As her companion strolled at her side back to the drawing room, she wondered about her comfort and ease in his presence. She felt as if she had known him for years.

Motioning toward the pianoforte, his lordship asked, "Do you play, Lady Sinclair?"

"My talents are tolerable." She smiled as her host drew out the bench and offered her a seat. Taking her place in front of the instrument, she began to play a fairly simple piece. Upon its conclusion, Lord Macveagh requested another song. She complied with one much more intricate and demanding of her skill.

When the last note of the melody faded into the quiet of the room, Cameron sat down on the bench next to Sheridan, facing her. "You make light of your talents, young lady. They are far from tolerable."

She laughed up at him, noting how his pleasure in her accomplishment had softened his face. "Just as you make light of yours, Cameron. Meager is not a word I would use to describe your artistry.''

A spark flared in his eyes, turning them to molten silver. He raised his finger to trace her cheekbone and jawline in a gesture similar to the gentle stroke of an artist's brush. "You're so beautiful," he whispered. "You have a child-woman quality about you that stirs a man's blood. Such fine lines as in a master's sculpture." A smile twitched at the corners of his mouth. "You have a penchant for sunshine on your face, and the freedom it symbolizes. The lips are soft and full, sensually begging for a man's touch. But the eyes, the eyes are the same artist's delight as your mother's. I want to live in their depths, my darling."

Sheridan was so fascinated in how he changed while he stared down at her she barely heard his words. Years fell away from a countenance that normally looked older than his age. His eyes were alive, sparkling with a mixture of happiness and desire. When he smiled, he became roguishly handsome. He lowered his face slowly toward hers, and she realized in dismay that he meant to kiss her.

She looked away quickly. "You flatter me, my lord." Cameron straightened, and when she looked back at him again, he smiled, but the sparkle had faded from his eyes. The desire smoldered, but the youthful look had fled from his face. Sheridan felt an odd twinge of regret that she had destroyed his joy of a few minutes before.

He stood up from the bench and took her hand. "Come with me, my child. There is something I want to show you."

She looked at him uncertainly, then stood and allowed him to retain hold of her hand. He led her out into the hall and farther up the staircase. "Do you realize how very much you look like your mother?" he asked when they reached the third floor landing.

"I've been told I favor her, but the only picture I have is a small miniature my grandmother had. It was painted about six months before she died, when she was four-and-twenty."

Fear swept over her as his fingers tightened on hers until they were almost painful. He strode purposefully down the long hall, dragging her with him. She resisted, lagging farther behind, and he slid his arm around her waist, half lifting her when she had to take two steps to one of his long ones.

"Lord Macveagh, where are you taking me?" she cried, struggling against his firm grip.

They neared the end of the hallway, and his steps slowed. He opened a door and drew her through the opening. "There is something I want you to see."

There was a strangeness about the room, a presence one gets when entering a church or temple. Candles illuminated the area in an eerie light, calling attention to a portrait standing in the center of the opposite wall.

When he released her, she was drawn across the room to the easel. The woman in the picture could easily have been her. Only the hair was different, a shade darker so as to actually be black instead of Sheridan's rich, chocolate brown.

"I painted it for her nineteenth birthday, not long after you were born. I fell in love with Alyson the minute I saw her. Unfortunately, she had married your father before we met."

Sheridan was struck by the bitterness in his voice. Unquestionably, he had loved her mother all these years and hated her father with equal passion.

She took a step closer to the painting, which obviously had been created with strokes of love. Without realizing it, she stretched out her hand to touch her mother's face. "She was so vibrant, so full of life." Her voice quaked with emotion. Sheridan was absorbed in the picture and gently traced her fingers across her mother's cheek, almost feeling the softness there. "Oh, Mother, I wish I could have known you. I wish I could remember you," she whispered sadly.

There was a choking sound behind her, and Cameron pulled her into his arms. He cradled her tenderly, each taking comfort from the other for the one they had lost. After a few moments, he led her across the room and through a door.

As the door swung closed behind them, Sheridan realized they had not gone out into the hallway, but apparently had entered Cameron's bedroom. A lone candle on the nightstand cast shadows across the room and lent greatly to the atmosphere of intimacy. Sheridan tried to move away from him, but he wrapped his arms around her, pulling her back to lean against his chest.

"Let me go!"

He answered with a quiet laugh, making her skin crawl. Brushing aside the cascade of curls with his cheek, he kissed the nape of her neck. She struggled and twisted, but he only tightened his hold.

"Nay, my love, do no' flee from me." His breath was hot and unwelcome against her ear, his voice raspy with deep emotion. "You're mine, mine alone. You were sent here by the Fates to replace the one who was lost." He spun her around to face him, his expression intense, his fervent gaze heightening her fear. "Dunna' you see, dearest, you belong to me. Stay with me, Sheridan, and give me the love I could never have."

She tried to turn away from his kiss, but he gripped her chin painfully, forcing her lips to meet his. His mouth slanted over hers in raw desire, twisting, painfully bruising, forcing her lips apart to be devoured by the strength of his ardor.

Sheridan grew terrified as the knowledge of his great strength hit her. If he chose to take her, there was no way she could fight him off. Certainly, no one in his household would come to her aid. She tried to keep calm, hoping rational communication would somehow convince him to let her go. She stood perfectly still, choking back a cry as his harsh kiss demanded a response.

He released her lips to stare down at her angrily. She spoke quickly, desperately trying to keep her voice soft, pretending concern for him. "I'm sorry, Cameron. I wish I could give you the love you need, to repay you for the hurt you've born all these years, but I can't."

"Do you love the one I saw you with this afternoon? The one you enticed into the woods so prettily." A savage snarl spread across his face. "Do you?"

"I don't know," she cried softly.

"Or is it just lust you feel?" He leered down at her, and his voice dropped low and smooth, almost hiding the undercurrent of menace. "Does he know your body well, or have you played the tease? Do his kisses make you burn and his touch make you tremble?" His hand moved over her, touching her with gentleness but in an intimate way that repulsed her. She could not hold back a shudder.

"Ah, you see, even I can make you tremble," he said softly. "I can set you aflame, little temptress." His caress grew rougher. "I can make you beg for my touch, beg to be mine."

"No!" A great flood of anger gave her strength, and she pushed on his chest with all her might. He gave in to her challenge and released her. He stepped back then, obviously admiring her snapping eyes and heightened color.

"How dare you try to force yourself on me! You're a fool if you think I would willingly go to bed with you. I will not stay in this house another minute."

His cold, callous laughter filled the room. "I'll make

you mine, willing or no', my dear. In a few days' time, you will become my wife, then you will have no choice but to yield to me. I will no' take you tonight, Sheridan, since you have such a high sense of honor.'' He nodded slightly in a mocking bow.

"I will never marry you, Macveagh,'' she said coldly. "I'm going to leave now and will never come here again.''

"You *will* be my wife. I'll see to it. As for leaving now, I must stop you. Unfortunately, my coach has been put away for the night, and the driver has gone to his home. No, I'll no' touch you tonight, my sweet, but here you'll stay. When word gets around that you stayed here with me in this house alone, indeed in my chambers, propriety will force you to marry me. You would be shunned by everyone if you did no', and shame the righteous name of Sinclair.''

"I thought your servants were discreet.''

"Ach, but they are, unless I tell them no' to be. They are very loyal to me, and will do as I bid with no questions asked.'' He stepped up to his dressing table and poured a small measure of brandy into a crystal glass. "Why dunna' you drink this, my dear. It will calm your nerves.''

She edged her way around toward the door while he poured the drink, placing herself between him and the threshold. When he handed her the glass, she raised it almost to her lips, but at the last second, threw the brandy in his face. With Macveagh momentarily blinded, she whirled around to open the door and race down the stairs, gaining a precious few seconds lead on him in her flight.

Sheridan swung open the front door and reached the steps as Cameron caught up to her, grabbing her arm above the elbow. She almost laughed in relief as Albert jumped down from the coach and came to meet her.

"It appears," she panted, "I won't have to try to outrun you after all." Jerking her arm free, she scurried down the steps with Albert right behind her. Climbing into the coach, she muttered to her servant, "Get up top and drive like the devil was after you."

"There's nothin' to be afraid of, m'lady. I brought along some help." He swiftly shut the door behind her and climbed up to the driver's seat, cracking the whip as he picked up the reins.

Dumbfounded, Macveagh stood on the stairs for a split second before he muttered an oath. Determining to go after her, he took a step down the stairway, but stopped when the carriage turned down the long driveway. A cloud slid out from in front of the moon, bathing the grounds in light. Four riders, muskets slung across their laps, took their places behind the coach. One of the guards stopped and spun his horse around to face the Scot, pointing his gun directly at his chest. Although he could not see the rider's face clearly, Macveagh knew instinctively it was the man Sheridan had been with on the moor.

A deep voice split the still night, calm and filled with unmistakable authority. "The only reason I don't shoot you now is because you saved her life today. If you've harmed her, or if you ever harm her in any way, I'll send you straight to hell." Jeremy turned his horse abruptly and galloped down the drive.

Macveagh returned to his castle, knowing he had just made a formidable enemy. Storming through the entryway, he let the door crash closed behind him. He slowed his step when Melissa Grant emerged from the library.

"It would appear, Cam dear, your affection was no' returned." The lovely red-haired woman handed him a drink and walked up the stairs beside him into the drawing room. "It would also seem the child has a protector. A lover, perhaps?"

Macveagh rubbed his hand across his forehead in a gesture that was all too familiar to Melissa. He threw the brandy down his throat before answering. "No, I dunna' think he is her lover yet. As for his protecting her, it was obvious." He paced back and forth in front of the fireplace, while his friend sat thoughtfully in an ornate chair near the fire.

Suddenly, he stopped and slammed his fist against the wooden mantle. "I will no' be denied. Her mother foresook me, disavowed her love and rejected mine." His voice was cold as death. "I was denied the mother, but I shall no' lose the daughter. The Fates have sent her to me, and she will be mine. Nothing will stand in my way."

"Now, Cam, dunna' do anything drastic. Perhaps I can be of help to you. Let me find out who he is before you make your move. Perhaps I can change the course of his affections. After all, am I no' lonely and beautiful, without a man to give me aid and comfort? Your new love might be more willing to turn to you if she found her sweetheart in another woman's arms." She pouted prettily. "Indeed, it will be difficult in this backward country area to find another man who knows how to please a lady."

Cameron eased his stance and leaned against the mantle. Melissa slowly began to untie her violet silk robe, revealing a voluptuous body long familiar to his touch.

"Am I beginning to bore you, Lissa?"

"Never, darling." She smiled, stood and let the robe drop to the floor, pausing as his appreciative gaze traveled slowly over her. When he looked back at her face, she stepped over the material and crossed the short distance between them. "I know your attentions are going to be directed elsewhere, and then I'll be bored."

"I'll no' be gentle tonight, Lissa."

"Just dunna' hurt me." Her breath quickened as she glanced up from beneath half-closed lids. "Close your eyes and pretend you're with her."

A short while later, she lay on the rug in front of the fireplace, staring into the crackling flames and cradling Cameron's head against her shoulder. Sated, but her body aching from the fury of his lovemaking, she wasn't sure whether she should envy the Sinclair chit or fear for her.

The carriage rolled to a stop in the bailey of Sinclair Castle. Sheridan waited for Albert to lower the steps and open the door, trying to calm down. Her body trembled; her emotions whirled in a confused jumble of fear, anger and relief. The door flew open, but it was Jeremy who stood beside the steps holding out his hand, not her servant.

"Did he hurt you?" His voice was low and intense. The lantern on the outside of the coach lit his scowling face with a flickering light.

"What are you doing here?" she asked in surprise.

"Trying to keep you safe. Did he hurt you?" he demanded, his frown deepening because his tone sounded harsher than he intended.

"No," she snapped, grudgingly taking his hand to climb down from the carriage. She was nearing the breaking point, and tears threatened to spill from her eyes any second. She took one look at him and concluded he was even more disgusted with her than before. He probably thought she got what she deserved; any young woman who dined alone with a man implied she was of low moral character simply by her actions. In her tired, confused state, it never occurred to her that Jeremy didn't know she had been alone with Macveagh.

"There's no need for you to stay, Jeremy. Go home."

"No, I want to talk to you," he said evenly. He gripped her arm firmly and propelled her into the castle, past a surprised Kyla and on up the stairs to the library. There, he released her arm and shut the door solidly behind them.

Sheridan sank down on a sofa, all the fight going out of her. Too tired to hold back the tears, she stared down at her folded hands on her lap.

Jeremy sat down beside her and covered her hands with one of his own. "Are you truly unharmed?" he asked gently.

She nodded slowly, knowing it would only be seconds before he saw her swollen, bruised lips. With his free hand, he carefully tipped her face up toward his.

"Oh, love." His voice was filled with tenderness, anguish and regret. He took a handkerchief from his pocket and dried her cheeks with extreme care.

"Did he hurt you in any other way, Sher? Please, I've got to know."

She looked at him then, and her heart turned over in her breast. His face was an open book, every feeling a printed line, clear and uncluttered for her to see and understand. Tenderness and concern softened his expression; a mixture of love and fear glimmered in his eyes. What frightened him—her answer or his own vulnerability?

"He only kissed me. I may have a few bruises on my arms. His grip was terribly strong, but he did nothing more."

He dropped his hand and looked away. "I should have shot him."

"When?"

"When we picked you up. Patrick and I rode over with Albert and the guards. We'd only been there a few minutes when you came running out the door. I wish we had gotten there sooner."

"It wouldn't have mattered. The evening was quite uneventful until the last few minutes. I was so upset that I didn't even see you." She leaned her forehead against his jaw. "Thank you for being there."

He put his arms around her and held her close. "Tell me what happened tonight. Where were the other guests?"

"There weren't any."

"What?" His arms tightened.

Sheridan related the evening's events, explaining about the lack of guests, the pleasant dinner, how he had taken her in to see her mother's picture and then had kissed her. She could feel Jeremy growing more tense with every word, so she left out many details, as well as Macveagh's plan to keep her at his castle to force her to marry him. She was afraid of what the American might do if he thought she was still in danger.

"Why did you stay when you found out no one else was there?" He kept his voice even, but she could sense his wariness. She considered her words carefully.

"First of all, I felt an obligation to thank him after what happened this morning. Also, I sought peace with my neighbor. I realize it was foolish, but I wanted to end the ill feelings between my family and him."

"It seems your uncle was right to dislike him."

"Yes, although I think I can understand why Macveagh acted as he did. He worships my mother."

"Even now?" Jeremy frowned.

"He keeps her picture in a room by itself. There is no furniture, no other paintings, nothing but candles. It's like a shrine."

"Stay away from him." He leaned back to look down at her. "Promise me you'll stay away from him. I don't want you near him or his land."

"You don't need to worry. I'll keep my distance." She grew silent and thoughtful, pondering how to bring up what had happened on the hillside that afternoon. Surely, he didn't truly find her contemptible, not with the way one hand held her close and the other slowly caressed her arm. Still, she felt she needed to apologize for her behavior.

He kissed her forehead and asked softly, "Will you forgive me for the way I acted this afternoon?"

She pulled away and looked at him, bewildered. "Forgive you? But Jeremy, it's you who should forgive me. I behaved like a wanton. I practically threw myself into your arms. I forgot everything I ever learned about what is upright and moral. Instead I almost . . . almost—"

"Gave in to my seduction? I was the one in the wrong, love. I should never have let our passion get out of hand. You almost gave me a very precious gift this afternoon, one I yearn for and would greatly treasure, but the time and place were wrong."

She suddenly realized he had called her "love" for the second time.

"It's a gift meant for a big feather bed and a wedding night." At her gasp, he cradled her jaw in his hand. "I love you, Sher, and want you to be my wife."

Instead of the joy he hoped to see on her face, confusion and fear lit her eyes. He lowered his head quickly, and the kiss he had intended to be sweet became one of tender desperation.

He pulled away slowly and dropped his hand. She looked down at her lap, avoiding eye contact.

"I don't know what to say," she whispered.

"How about, 'I love you, too.' " He winced, realizing he had left himself wide open for a complete setdown.

"I want to love you, but something holds me back." She looked up, her eyes begging him to understand and to help her understand. "There's been so much pain in the past . . . ." Her voice trailed off, and she reached across the small space between them, taking his hand. "I would marry you anyway."

He shook his head and smiled sadly. "No, sweet. I promised myself a wife who will love me in my old age, not just when I'm a braw young man."

Sheridan smiled faintly and clutched his hand tighter. "Will you teach me to love you? Even if . . . if it takes a while?"

Jeremy looked down into her beseeching face and was forever lost. He might hold out a month or even two, but he knew eventually he would take whatever terms she offered. Life without her wouldn't be worth living. He reached up and brushed a wayward curl from her cheek.

"Yes," he said softly. *Even if it takes forever.*

Chapter 7

"I'm happy you and Patrick decided to ride with us this morning, Kyla." Sheridan placed the last package in the small cart. "You need to get out of the house, and it won't hurt your father to do without your presence for a morning."

"I think he'll be glad to be rid of me for a while," Kyla said lightly. "He says I'll make him a lunatic with all my fussin', so he must be gettin' well."

"Albert, we'll leave as soon as the gentlemen arrive."

"Aye, mum. I'll saddle up yer horses and bring them around front in a few minutes." He left the horse and cart where they stood, the horse contentedly eating from a bag of feed hung over his nose.

As the women climbed the front steps, the sound of an approaching carriage reached their ears. Turning, they watched in surprise as an ornate coach with four riders came up the lane. Sheridan's temper began to rise when she recognized the four guards and the coach from the night before.

The carriage drew to a halt, and the footman scurried around to open the door and place the steps in position. Sheridan suspected that the elegantly dressed lady who gracefully stepped down from the conveyance was Lady Grant. Melissa waited a moment, whispering instructions to the footman, who turned and removed a long, gray cloak from the seat. He followed along behind her as she glided toward the manor door.

"Good morning, Lady Sinclair. I am Lady Melissa Grant, a friend of Lord Cameron Macveagh."

"Good morning, Lady Grant. Won't you come in?" Sheridan fought hard to be civil. The last thing she wanted was to invite anyone connected to Macveagh into her home.

"Thank you, my dear." She reached around and took Sheridan's cloak from the footman, handing it to her. "I'm returning your wrap, since it was left behind in your haste last evening."

Sheridan passed the cloak on to Kyla when they walked into the entry hall. Leading the way into the great hall, she said, "I am grateful for its return; however, couldn't a servant have done the chore just as well? It's kind of you to take your time. I was under the impression you were out of town."

Sitting down on the dark blue velvet settee, Melissa replied, "I decided not to stay at my cousin's after all. I returned late last night to find Cameron distraught over his actions. He asked me to return the cloak to you, knowing you would never consent to see him. He has asked me to convey his sincerest apologies for his behavior and begs your forgiveness. He sent along a small token as a peace offering." She handed Sheridan a small velvet case.

Opening the case, she found a pair of exquisite sapphire earrings. "They are beautiful, but I cannot accept them. I do not make it a habit of accepting expensive gifts from men, especially men I have just met. You may thank his lordship for his consideration, but please return them to him." She closed the case and passed it back to Melissa.

She accepted it with a sigh. "You must try to understand, Lady Sinclair. Cameron has loved your mother all these years, and when you appeared on the scene, that love was transferred to you. It seems strange, I know, but what he feels for you is genuine. As an artist, he has an extremely passionate nature. There is no middle ground for him, nor does he have any patience. He is a man of action," she said, smiling kindly at Sheridan, "perhaps sometimes of too much action. He truly meant you no harm. His love for you is all consuming, overshadowing everything else. I truly hope you can forgive him."

Sheridan kept her voice calm and low by the sheer force of her will. "I can never forgive him. I am not a simple milk maid to be commanded about and forced to yield to any man's will. What he tried to do last night was the most despicable thing I have ever seen. I had hoped to end the animosity between him and my family, but it does not appear it will be possible. If Lord Macveagh continues in his current manner, there can never be anything but bad feelings between us. I appreciate your efforts, and I do not doubt his sincerity. However, since he has such a passionate nature, I can only surmise that it is best if I see him as little as possible."

Melissa's gaze slowly measured the young lady sitting across from her. "I'm going to give you some advice. I know Cameron Macveagh better than anyone."

No doubt you do, thought Sheridan.

"When he sets his mind to something, he will no' be deterred. He can be very gentle and very loving if only given the chance. By the same token, he can be cruel and hard, relentless in his goal. If you are wise, you will think about his love for you and make up your mind to at least give him time to win your heart. He will no' turn away from you. As I said before, he is consumed by you and will no' stop until you are his—one way or another."

Sheridan sprang to her feet. Sparks of rage shot from her eyes. "Are you trying to threaten me, Lady Grant? Were those his instructions?"

"No, he did no' tell me what to say. It is no' meant as a threat, only as a warning. He is no' a person one deals with lightly."

"I told him last night I cannot love him. I tried to explain it to him kindly, but he wouldn't listen."

"It is just that point which I've been trying to make."

Neither woman had noticed Jeremy when he quietly stepped into the room. He wanted to get the drift of the conversation before interrupting it.

"You may tell Macveagh that if he bothers Sheridan again, he will have to answer to me, and I assure you it will not be to his liking to do so."

Both women whirled around to stare at the owner of the steel-coated voice. Sheridan did not miss the widening of Melissa's eyes or the sensuous look that rapidly replaced her surprise. "And, who may I say is Lady Sinclair's protector, sir?" she cooed.

Jeremy raised an eyebrow at the innuendo suggesting Sheridan was his mistress. "I am Jeremy Mackenzie, of Boston, madam. Lady Maclaren is my aunt." His gaze moved to Sheridan, warming considerably as it did so. "Sheridan is very dear to me, and I value her safety and happiness most highly.''

''Jeremy,'' said Sheridan, ''this is Lady Melissa Grant. Unfortunately, she was just leaving.''

Melissa smiled mockingly at Sheridan as she rose and moved smoothly toward the door, her scarlet satin gown swaying gently. She stopped directly in front of Jeremy, giving him a provocative smile, her body only inches from his.

Placing a hand on his chest, she flashed him a look of pure invitation. ''Welcome to our little area of the country, Mr. Mackenzie. We're no' often honored to have so handsome a guest in our neighborhood. You must come to visit at the castle and tell me all about your America. Surely you can take time out from acting as bodyguard to this child for a visit to a lonely woman. There are so few gentlemen who are free to pass a quiet evening these days.''

Jeremy reached down and pointedly removed her hand, then dropped it so it fell to her side. ''I'm afraid I will have no time for a visit with you, Lady Grant. I'm much too preoccupied elsewhere. I'm certain you have no trouble finding men to pass an evening with you; as to whether they are gentlemen or not, I cannot say.''

Melissa stepped back from him as if she had been struck. Muttering a crudity about a ''rude Colonial,'' she swept from the room. Her ire rose when she noticed Albert standing in the hall, the front door open wide, ready for her exit.

Jeremy shook his head and chuckled as he crossed the floor to Sheridan. ''It would seem, my love, Macveagh's friends are as unprincipled as he is. I've never been quite so publicly mauled by a so-called lady in my life.''

Sheridan tried to force a smile, but failed. '' 'Tis a good thing you gave her the cut, or I'd have clawed her eyes out! The nerve of her. Acting like a—a harlot in my own house.''

"Why, Sheridan, I do believe your eyes are turning green.''

She looked up into his twinkling eyes and smiling face. "Yes," she said, slowly returning his smile, "I am jealous. Terribly so, in fact.''

He leaned toward her and whispered against her lips, "Good.''

A polite cough made him lift his head and turn in irritation toward the door. "Excuse me, m'lady, Mr. Mackenzie, but Kyla and Mr. Hagen are waitin' for ye out front.'' Albert shuffled his feet in embarrassment. It was improper for a lady of quality to be kissing a gentleman, especially where someone might happen upon them, but the old servant wasn't quite sure how much propriety he could force on his young mistress.

Sheridan gave Jeremy a wink. "Thank you. We'll join them right away. I'll just put on my hat.'' She picked up the cocked chip hat and fastened it to her hair. Flicking a loose thread from her dark gray riding habit, she looped her arm through his. "Mr. Mackenzie, will you join me in a ride around my property?''

"I'd be delighted to, my lady.''

When everyone was mounted, the small procession started out, walking the horses at a slow pace to allow discussion. Albert followed along behind in a two-wheeled cart loaded with gifts for the tenants. Two armed guards rode behind him, constantly keeping an eye on the surrounding countryside.

They made their stop at each cottage. The tenants came out from the huts or in from the fields to greet their new landlady. They were surprised and pleased at her gifts, noting with affection how the young mistress had grown into such a beautiful and thoughtful woman. Curious glances were discreetly cast at the attractive gentleman who accompanied their lady, noting his pleasure as he watched her dealing with her tenants. His affection was most openly displayed when she took time to speak to each of the children on the estate.

The Daniels's home was the last on their route. Mr. Daniels waved at the entourage and unhooked his team from the plow, heading toward the cottage from the field. Millie and her three little ones were in the front yard, the older children playing while the mother took time out from the washing to nurse her new baby. When the riders were a short distance from them, she turned her back, removed the baby from her breast and straightened her clothing.

"Good day, Millie. How are you and the baby doing?" asked Sheridan, sliding down from her mount into Jeremy's waiting hands.

"We're fine, m'lady. He's a hungry wee lad, but sleeps most of the night, now. 'Tis such a pleasure to see ye, mum, but we were so sorry to hear about his lordship. He was a mighty fine man, and we miss him. He always treated us fairly, that he did."

"I miss him, too, Millie, and I hope I will treat you just as fairly. I've brought you some presents. Here's a special gift for the baby." She handed Millie the package while Albert took the other gifts from the cart. "May I hold your baby while you open them?"

Millie beamed at the grand lady holding out her arms to her little tyke. "Of course, m'lady, but be careful he doesna' wet on ye; he just ate, so the other will be followin' soon."

Sheridan laughed when she took the infant in her arms. "I'll keep a sharp eye on his nappy." Jeremy stepped up beside her and held out a finger to the baby, who grabbed it in his tiny hand and tried to stick it in his mouth. Sheridan smiled up at him. "You have a way with children, Jeremy."

"One this small would grab on to anything and try to put it in his mouth," he joked. "But I do like children and hope to have several of my own someday." He raised his eyes from the cooing child to stare deeply into hers. "You'll make a good mother, my love," he said softly for her ears alone.

Her heart pounding wildly, Sheridan broke away from his gaze and looked back at the child just in time to see a growing wet spot on his nappy. She held him away from her gown quickly.

With a broad grin, Millie took the child and disappeared into the hut as Mr. Daniels tied up the horses and came over to stand beside them. "Good day, m'lady. Ye looked pretty as could be holdin' the babe in yer arms."

"Thank you, Mr. Daniels. He is a lovely child. I want to thank you, too, for the fine job you've done in draining the swamp near your field. Were you able to bring in the lime as I suggested?"

They walked slowly toward the newly reclaimed field, Sheridan talking with her tenant, and Jeremy following along a few paces behind.

"Aye, m'lady. I brought in the lime. Do ye really think it will help?"

"According to everything I've read, it should. Tests have been run showing most of the soil in Scotland devoid or severely lacking in lime, and it is important for the growth of healthy crops. I suppose only time will tell. What do you think of the new plow I sent up?"

" 'Twas a blessin' to work with it, mum. My work went much faster and easier than with the old one. It did a better job. The furrows are deeper and with only two horses to contend with, they're straighter, too."

"Good, I'm glad it was a help. We'll experiment for the next few years to find what will grow best. I'm asking each of my leaseholders to plant part of their land in turnips for winter fodder and part in oats. It would be wise, I believe, if you put up part of your land in potatoes, too."

She looked up at the heather-covered hills surrounding the glen. "The demand for our Scottish cattle is increasing in England, and we should take every advantage of the need. I will be purchasing some more cattle and see how they fare. However, I intend to follow my neighbors' example and raise more sheep on the moors. Sheep do better here than most anything. I will not displace you or any of the other tenants, Mr. Daniels. You have been loyal, even when times were not the best, and I can use your help with the stock."

"Thank ye, m'lady. We dunna' want to leave. Me and Millie have lived here ever since we got married."

"If you ever have any suggestions or complaints, please come to me immediately. I'm determined to make my lands productive, and I will do what I can to accomplish the goal. One other thing. Since you're so willing to experiment with me, and we don't know for certain how these things will work out, I'm suspending your rent for this year. What monies you have already paid will be returned to you, and no further amounts will be charged for the remainder of the year. After we see how successful we are, we'll renegotiate the matter of rents for the coming year."

Daniels's reaction was the same as that of all the other renters. He stopped in his tracks and looked at her in astonishment, his eyes wide. After a minute, he blinked hard and shook his head. "Ye are too kind to us, m'lady. Ye'll lose all yer money if we have a bad year."

"I appreciate your concern, Mr. Daniels, but I assure you, I have more than enough funds to operate in this manner. I feel 'tis only fair to have the fact up front, so you won't be worrying about how to pay the rents should the crops fail." She smiled at him sweetly. "Of course, if we weren't beginning a grand new scheme, I wouldn't be so generous."

She turned her back on the field and again looped her arm in Jeremy's as they walked with her tenant back to his home. "If I am not at home, bring any problems or suggestions to Andrew. He's going to help me oversee matters around the estate." Seeing Mr. Daniels's frown, she continued, "I know he is young, but he has a sharp mind, and he cares a great deal about the land and for those who live here. He will deal fairly with you, I'm certain."

"Ach, yer right, m'lady. I be forgettin' he is grown up now. I still picture him as a mischievous lad tryin' to steal me apples."

"If he handles himself well, he'll soon have apples of his own," she replied merrily.

They made their farewells and mounted up, joining Patrick and Kyla as they rode across the moor. "Albert," Sheridan called, "do you still have the picnic basket, or did we give it away, too?"

Albert chuckled, urging his old mare to pull the cart a little faster. "I still have it, m'lady. Would ye be gettin' hungry after handin' out all them sweets to the wee ones?"

"That I am. I almost grabbed a shortbread from the last package before we gave it to Mrs. Daniels." She glanced at Jeremy and then flushed, knowing full well he remembered the events of the last afternoon as vividly as she did.

"Why don't we eat under those willows down by the

loch?'' suggested Kyla.

"A good idea," answered Sheridan, suddenly feeling like a young girl on a lark. She kicked her horse to a gallop, calling over her shoulder, "The first one there chooses the spot." Taking everyone by surprise with her impulsiveness, she made good her lead and was the first to arrive at the clump of trees standing by the water's edge. Jeremy was only a half a length behind her when she reined in her mare, her face flushed with exertion and happy excitement.

"You cheated," he growled, fighting the grin that gradually overtook his face. He swung down from his horse and moved to her side, holding up his hands to help her down. The horse was between them and the others, who had now arrived and were occupied in dismounting also. He lifted her from the saddle, letting her slide down against him. He held her there. "You like head starts, minx."

"I'm sorry," she said, still a little out of breath from the ride. "Suddenly, I felt so free to be away from the city, I just couldn't resist." She looked up at him to find him watching her in adoration, a tiny smile dancing on his lips.

"You weren't meant to be cooped up in the city. Incredibly, you've grown even more beautiful these last few days. Your newfound freedom agrees with you."

"I've always been happier here." She smiled a little, thinking how much his presence added to her joy. Her gaze dropped to his lips, then flickered back up to look him in the eye, recklessly inviting his kiss.

"Later," he whispered, brushing her lower lip with the side of his thumb. He moved his hand back down to her side, his eyes sparkling in amusement as his fingers spread across her rib cage and spanned her tiny waist. "You've found another liberty, one of which I certainly approve.''

Her slight confusion seemed to raise his humor a bit more as she noticed a twitch at the corner of his lip. ''What?'' she asked.

He leaned back slightly, surveying the soft, gentle curves of her body. ''Freedom from your armor, m'lady.'' He slowly caressed her midsection, his smile spreading across his face like a ray of sunshine. He lowered his head near hers to whisper in her ear. ''You have no idea how pleasant it is to touch you and feel your body soft and warm beneath my hand instead of the stiff, hard bone of a corset. I much prefer you smooth and unbound, my love.''

Her flush rose from her toes, she was sure. On impulse, she had worn a loose unboned bodice instead of her corset, knowing her riding habit fit just as well without it, but it wasn't the sort of thing to be discussed openly between the sexes.

Suddenly, her embarrassment seemed ridiculous. He was, after all, a man of the world and had certainly not spent all of his time on board ship. He probably had a fair knowledge of ladies' corsets and such. In all likelihood, his opinion was shared by most men, even though they seemed to like the slender waist and fuller bosoms that stays often provided. Too, hadn't he paid her a high compliment, indicating her figure was lovely enough in its natural state?

She smiled and said shyly, ''I'm glad it pleases you, Jeremy. Although I've always worn my stays loosely, you have no idea how wonderful it is to be free of them, nor how marvelous it is just to take a deep breath.''

Jeremy threw back his head in a hearty laugh before grabbing her in a giant hug. ''You're delightful. 'Tis so nice to find an honest woman.'' He moved back a step, his hands resting lightly on her shoulders. His smile faded slowly. "Always be honest with me, Sheridan. Never be afraid to share your thoughts and opinions with me."

"What if I disagree adamantly with you on something? Will you not be like other men and think me a simpleminded female?"

"No, I don't think I could ever consider you simpleminded. If we disagree, then we will disagree openly and perhaps even angrily, but we will not lie to each other." The twinkle returned to his eyes. "Besides, just think of all the fun we could have making up after a fight."

"Thank you, Jeremy, for being willing to listen to my opinions. I consider it a great honor and will do my best to always be truthful to you." She smiled softly and reached up to take his hand. "I'm starved. Let's go eat." With that they ambled over to the picnic Kyla had spread out under the trees.

The meal passed in quiet, peaceful conversation as the fresh spring air stirred softly around them. At last Albert packed the remainder of the luncheon in the basket and loaded it into the cart.

"I'll be on my way, now, m'lady. Will ye be stayin' out for a while?"

"Aye, Albert. We'll relax a bit here and then go for a ride, I think." She leaned back against the tree trunk and glanced first at Jeremy, then at the watchful guards sitting a short distance away. "We'll be safe enough."

"Very well, m'lady. Have a bonnie afternoon." Albert climbed into the cart and made his way across the moor, whistling a cheerful tune.

Once the older man was out of sight, Jeremy stretched out on the grass next to Sheridan and put his head on her lap. Shading his eyes against the filtered sunlight, he smiled up at her. "You don't mind if I take a nap, do you? You make a very nice pillow."

"Just behave yourself," she warned, threatening his nose with a blade of grass.

"Yes, ma'am." He grinned up at her and closed his eyes, folding his hands sedately across his midsection.

Sheridan gazed down at him from beneath lowered lashes, admiring his handsome face. She decided she liked this arrangement very much. It gave her the chance to study him at her leisure. In a few moments, her gaze wandered down to his shoulders, his chest and down his long legs to the tips of his shiny boots. She didn't think she had ever seen a more manly figure.

"Patrick and I are goin' down to feed the ducks." Sheridan's gaze flew to Kyla's smiling face. Kyla gave her a wink and picked up a chunk of bread she had saved for the birds. "We'll be back in a little while."

"Take your time," murmured Jeremy.

"We will," said Patrick with a chuckle. He leaned over toward Jeremy and said softly, "But don't forget you've got two chaperones."

"I could send them with you."

"Don't you dare," growled Patrick. He pushed himself to his feet and offered Kyla a hand. "We'll give a shout if there's trouble." He pulled her up beside him, and they walked down toward the loch, arms around each other.

Once they dropped out of sight of the others, Patrick pulled his love into his arms and kissed her thoroughly. "I've been wanting to do that all day," he whispered against Kyla's lips. "I love you, little one, and I'm dying without you." He captured her lips with a scorching, hungry kiss, and the bread tumbled to the ground.

A little later, after retrieving the ducks' treat, they settled down on a large grassy area next to the loch. Tearing off bits of bread, Kyla tossed them to the ducks as they waddled ashore. She and Patrick laughed at the older birds' greedy antics while the fluffy little ducklings watched shyly from the water's edge.

"We're leaving in a few days for Loch Maree. Jeremy has to tend to his father's business. We'll be gone for two weeks." He spoke in the deep rumble she knew signaled strong emotion. Patrick waited until the birds quit honking and headed back toward the water. He looked down at Kyla, gazing at her intently. "Will you marry me when we get back?"

She smiled up at him, secure in his love, sure of her own. "Yes, as long as Papa continues to improve. He should be strong enough by then that he will no' need my care."

"The day after we get back?"

"Aye, love. I'll give you two weeks of freedom. You'd better enjoy it while you can, because I'll be a jealous wife."

"You can keep me under lock and key, as long as you're there with me." Patrick drew her into his embrace, kissing her with all the love and tenderness he possessed. Then he scooped her up in his arms and spun around on the grass, ending his little dance with a ferocious Indian war cry.

Jeremy sprang to his feet at the sound of the blood-curdling yell and raced down the brae toward the water with the guards several steps behind. Sheridan scrambled to her feet and followed, running as fast as her cumbersome skirt would allow.

"Patrick, where are you? What's wrong?"

"We're over here. There's nothing—" Patrick gaped openmouthed as Jeremy skidded down the hill. The soft dirt crumbled beneath his feet, loosening a small avalanche of pebbles and soil. He flew over the embankment and into the loch with a loud yell and a huge splash. He came up sputtering.

"—wrong." Patrick scratched the back of his head, a sheepish expression spreading over his red face.

"Nothing wrong!" Jeremy glared at his friend and pushed through the shoulder-high water toward a low place to come ashore. He lost his footing on the slippery bottom and went under again. When he came up this time, his teeth were chattering. "There is now."

Patrick met him at the water's edge and offered him a hand, pulling him up the embankment. Jeremy shrugged out of his wet coat and wrung the water out of it.

"What the devil's all the hollering about?"

Patrick took off his coat and draped it around Jeremy's shaking shoulders. "Kyla agreed to marry me. I guess I got a little carried away."

Jeremy grinned and slapped his partner on the back. "Well, why didn't you say so? Congratulations. You'll have to watch him, Kyla. He gets carried away like that every once in a while."

"Thanks for the warnin'. I'm no' sure my ears will ever be the same." Kyla smiled up at her fiance and shook her head.

Sheridan and the guards waited a few steps up the hill and joined the trio as they came back up.

"I heard." She hugged Kyla, wishing her and Patrick well. "When is the wedding?"

"As soon as Patrick gets back."

"You're going somewhere?" Sheridan frowned up at Jeremy.

"I have to tend to my father's business. We leave day after tomorrow for Loch Maree."

"How long will you be gone?"

"Two weeks." Jeremy noted her bemused expression. "What's wrong?"

"I'm going to miss you," she said softly, looking

down at the ground. They stopped as the others went on up the brae out of sight. "A lot, I think."

"I hope so." He leaned over and kissed her, touching her only with his lips, but surrounding her in love and sweetness. He raised his head and looked deeply into her eyes. "I truly hope so."

Chapter 8

Sheridan roamed impatiently around the drawing room, ventured into the library for a moment, glanced at the filled shelves with disinterest and headed for the stairway. Jeremy had been gone for a little over two weeks and had sent word he would be home late in the evening. She was a little surprised by how much she missed him and waited anxiously for his return. She had kept busy every other day, but today she could keep her mind on nothing.

Finally, she stalked through the kitchen, grabbing a piece of freshly baked bread on her way out. "I'm going for a walk," she called over her shoulder to Kyla and Waverly, who sat at the table. "I won't be gone long." Once outside, she crept around behind the bushes and made it through the gate in the wall without the guards seeing her. She simply didn't want any company for a while.

She walked across the moor without seeing the

countryside around her, her thoughts on Jeremy, and wondered if he had missed her half as much as she missed him.

Sheridan wandered aimlessly through the glen and partway up another hillside before noticing she was in an area of the estate she had never visited before. Her uncle had always forbidden her to come to this part of the property, saying the ground was craggy and prone to give way under one's feet. She stopped and looked around in surprise. There was no crevasse, and the soil was firm and rich, held in place by thick undergrowth and trees.

Bewildered, Sheridan looked behind her to get her bearings before pushing her way through the dense undergrowth. In a few minutes, she broke through the tangled brush into what had once been a large clearing, covered over now with weeds and unkept shrubs—not just the natural heather and grasses, but huge over-grown rhododendrons and hydrangeas. She was certain that in all her time on the estate she had never been here, but there was something vaguely familiar about the scenery before her. Tiny shards of fear raced up and down her spine, but she was compelled forward by a force she could not deny.

A building loomed just ahead of her to the right. It was covered over with trailing ivy, and appeared to have been left to slowly deteriorate. Upon nearing it, she realized it was the remains of what had once been a large coach house. Stumbling through the twisted mat of vines, Sheridan stepped through an opening in the trees and followed the overgrown lane up the hill. The fear spread from her spine to cover her with its coldness, yet her feet moved automatically up the long forgotten roadway. Images of a grand house skittered across her memory just beyond her grasp.

The birch branches crowded out the sky, forming a

dense roof above her head, allowing only tiny pinnacles of light to shine through. She felt as if she were in a tunnel without end or beginning, trapped forever in a shadowy world. She ran forward, soon free of the leafy umbrella, and emerged from the woods to stand in front of a burned ruin.

Rooted to the spot, Sheridan could only stare at the charred remains before her. Waves of terror crashed over her, suffocating her as she tried to draw a choking breath. Memories fought to rise from the deepest caverns of her mind, but were forcefully pushed back to remain hidden.

"Sheridan, you should no' be here." Macveagh's voice was soft and gentle. When he saw that she could not move her eyes from the blackened walls, he stepped to her side and tenderly put his arm around her shoulders. "Come, my dearest, you must move away from here."

Forcing her mind to obey, Sheridan resisted the instinct to shut herself off from her surroundings. "Cameron?" she whispered, using all her concentration simply to look at him. She pleaded silently for his help, and he understood. When he carefully lifted her in his arms, she buried her face against his shoulder, trying to block out the image she had just seen. He carried her down another drive in the opposite direction from the way she had come.

Macveagh moved some distance from the ruins to where the trees blocked the area from view, before gently placing her on the ground. Sitting down beside her in the afternoon sunshine, he took her in his arms. The shock left her cold, and she trembled violently from the combination of her terror and the chill. Cameron's hand stroked her back and arms in an effort to warm and soothe her. Very slowly the trembling ceased, but she still clung to him like a terrified child.

His lips brushed her forehead, then her closed eyelids. "Sheridan, will you talk to me?" he asked softly.

She opened her eyes and was astounded by the flow of love and concern she saw upon his face. There was no passion in his eyes now, nor anger and torment, only overwhelming tenderness.

"It was my home once, wasn't it?" she whispered.

"Aye. You have no memory of it?"

"No."

"Then you dunna' remember the fire?"

"No."

"Thank God you dunna' have to live with that memory."

From the anguish in his voice, she knew it was a memory he lived with constantly. In the last few minutes, she had glimpsed the man her family had once called a friend, and her heart went out to him in his despair. She touched his cheek with her hand, trying to soothe the pain as he had eased hers only moments before.

"You were here that night?" she questioned quietly. When he nodded, she said, "Tell me what happened, please. What torments you so, Cameron?"

He probed the dark pools of her eyes with his own, begging her for understanding. Her hand slid weakly from his cheek to rest against his chest. He turned his face from her and stared over the open moors.

Drawing a ragged breath, he began. "I loved your mother, Sheridan, with a love beyond anything I have ever known. She cared for me, too, but would no' break her marriage vows. I tried to live with it, tried to accept her feelings for what they were, but I could no'." The shudder of his sigh gently shook them both.

"The night of the fire, I had too much to drink and decided to settle it with her. I came here to beg her, knowing your father was at the mayor's house for a meeting. I pleaded with her to leave him and come away with me, but she refused.''

He closed his eyes for a long moment, his grip tightening minutely. ''At that point Kenyon came in. He demanded I leave and threatened me if I ever bothered his wife again. I was so drunk, I challenged him, and we fought. During the scuffle, a candlestand was knocked over, setting fire to the draperies.''

He brushed a wisp of hair back from her forehead. ''Your mother ran upstairs to get you and took you out of the house, while we continued to fight. We fell, and I suppose your father hit his head; I never really knew. I passed out from the drink, and when I came to, the room was full of smoke. I couldna' even see your father. I crawled out of the house, choking on the smoke, and collapsed on the grass. I later learned Albert dragged me to safety.'' He paused, taking a deep breath and exhaling slowly.

''In the confusion, it was a few minutes before anyone realized Alyson had gone back into the burning house to find Kenyon.'' Choking, he waited a moment, then cleared his throat, only to have it tighten again with emotion. ''Waverly and Galvin found them before the flames reached them, but they were already dead from the smoke.''

Tears poured down his face as he looked at Sheridan in utter despair. ''Your mother had pulled him as far as the entry before she collapsed. I killed her, Sheridan, as if I had intentionally set the fire. How I wish it had been me who died instead!''

For a few minutes, she could not speak for her own tears and sorrow. At last, when she could, she lifted her hand to caress his face. No matter how she should hate him for the deaths of her parents, she could not, for he dwelt in a living hell. She shuddered at the thought of what he had lived with all these years.

"Cameron, I cannot blame you for their deaths, and you must not blame yourself. It was an accident, not something you wanted to happen."

He stared at her in disbelief, then his arms tightened around her and his cheek rested against hers. Whether it was for the man she had glimpsed earlier, a man of tenderness and compassion, or whether it was simply to take away his torment for a moment, she didn't know, but she didn't move away.

His breath was warm against her cheek, softly blowing the wispy tendrils curling about her ear. "When you're in my arms, I dunna' feel the pain," he said softly.

Exhausted from the long walk and the shock of seeing the burned-out manse, Sheridan was so numb she didn't feel his lips touch her cheek in a sweet caress. She found comfort in his embrace and felt no need to turn away when he raised his head and studied her face.

Dazed and resting pliantly in his arms, her eyelids fluttered closed. He brushed each lid with a gentle kiss, taking her off guard when his lips suddenly covered hers. All gentleness vanished with his growing passion as his hand moved over her possessively. Trembling anew, Sheridan pushed against him, but her meager efforts were futile. Her fear grew, knowing if he should try to take her now, she wouldn't be able to fight him, neither physically nor emotionally.

He raised his head and gazed at her, a triumphant gleam flickering in his eyes.

Her fear was mirrored in her face. "Cameron, please don't," she whispered.

His hand moved down to rest against her ribs. "I'll stop for now, but as I can no' stop loving you, I can no' stop trying to make you mine. Only you can give me peace, Sheridan; only in your arms am I free from torture." A sad smile played upon his mouth. "You do no' hate my touch as much as you wanted to believe. It is possible you will grow to love me yet.''

"No, 'tis impossible. I don't want to hurt you, but I can't return your love. I don't think I can truly love anyone." I can't even fall in love with Jeremy, she thought miserably.

A closed look fell over his face, and the anguish returned to his eyes. Carefully, he moved her away from him and stood up, drawing her up beside him. "I'll take you home."

Calling his horse to him, he lifted her up on the mount, then swung up behind her, his arms going about her in support. They had reached the bottom of the brae when Andrew galloped up from across the moor.

He glared at Macveagh, noting the way Sheridan sagged limply against him. "Countess?" he asked, his anger, as well as his concern, evident in his voice.

"I'm only tired, Andrew."

"Your mistress wandered upon the old burned manse. I'm afraid the site was a great shock to her. Since you seem bent on playing the hero, lad, I'll let you take her back home." Macveagh urged his horse forward and lifted Sheridan into Andrew's waiting arms. He smiled wryly as the young man's arms tightened around her protectively. "You seem to have smitten us all, my dear." Then his smile faded, and his eyes took on a hard glint. "I will never give you up, Sheridan. You belong to me."

She raised her head from where it rested against Andrew's shoulder. "I will never belong to you, Cameron," she said with quiet conviction.

Anger contorted his features. "If I canno' have you, no one will!" He spun his horse around to gallop at full speed through the heather, jumping the animal in a fluid movement over the hedge fence that separated their properties.

Andrew flicked the horse's reins, prodding it to move forward at a slow pace. He held Sheridan firmly, letting her rest tiredly against him. He was painfully aware of the leaves tangled in her long hair and of a large tear in her skirt. They had gone a short distance before he asked in a tight voice, "Did he hurt you, m'lady?"

At his question, Sheridan realized how she looked. "No, Andrew. I look a mess, but 'tis my own fault. I must have ripped my skirt in the underbrush when I was trying to get to the top of the hill. I suppose I would have fainted if he had not come along. He saw me walking toward the old house and rode there to see to my welfare. This time he was kind, but I cannot say how he will be the next time we meet."

His arms tightened unconsciously, and he kicked the horse to a gallop. "We must make sure ye are never alone with him," he muttered under his breath.

Kyla came running out when she saw them galloping across the glen. "Sheridan, what happened?"

Andrew swung down and dropped to the ground. With tender care, he lifted his mistress from the saddle. "Can ye walk, m'lady?"

Andrew turned away and led his horse to the stable as Kyla put her arm around Sheridan's waist. They walked toward the back door, and Kyla asked, "Sher, are you hurt?"

"Only here." Her hand rested over her heart. "I came across my parents' home. I know Uncle Galvin meant well in not allowing me to ever go there, but the shock of stumbling upon it was almost more than I could bear. I don't know what would have happened if Cameron hadn't come along."

"Macveagh was there?"

"Apparently he was out riding and saw me walking across the glen toward the hill. By the time he made his way around, I had found the charred ruins and was standing there in shock." The tears began to roll down her cheeks as Kyla helped her up the stairs to her bedroom. "It was so awful, Ky. I couldn't move. I felt as though I were choking and couldn't get my breath. I could almost feel the smoke stinging my throat and eyes. Images flashed across my mind—of a beautiful white mansion with lots of flowers out front."

Kyla eased her onto the bed and pulled off her slippers. Eyeing her disheveled state, she asked in a quiet, soothing voice, "How did Macveagh help you?"

"I couldn't move; I simply stood there staring at the blackness. I was terrified! It was as if I were a little girl again and feeling all the horror I must have felt then. When Macveagh spoke to me, I barely had the strength to turn my head away. He picked me up and carried me to a spot hidden from the ruins."

She caught Kyla's skeptical glance at her hair as she helped her out of the torn gown. "He was kind, Kyla, and did nothing to harm me. I know I look terrible, but it was my own fault. The bushes were so thick that they caught my hair and tore my skirt when I pushed through them."

Kyla pulled the covers up around her friend before sitting down beside her on the bed.

"He told me what happened that night."

"What did he say? As far as I know, only your uncle was ever told what happened, and of course, it was Macveagh who told him."

Sheridan related the story before adding, "I feel sorry for him. He is so miserable."

Kyla looked thoughtfully across the room and out the window at the bright afternoon sunshine. "Dunna' mistake the sympathy you feel for somethin' else, Sheridan. You said he was kind and tender to you. Do you think he will leave you alone now?"

Sheridan shook her head. "No, in fact, he swore he

wouldn't. For a few minutes there was peace between us. I suspect I saw a side of him few people know.'' She stared across the room thoughtfully. ''But I fear I have become his ruling passion. His need of me goes beyond mere desire. I sat there under the tree with his arms around me and saw the agony in his eyes disappear. For some strange reason, the only time he is at peace is when I'm with him, and it's frightening. When he suggested someday I might learn to love him, I told him I could not, that I am not capable of loving anyone.'' She picked nervously at a loose thread on the quilt.

''What did he say?''

''He didn't say anything then, except to offer to take me home. After we met Andrew and he turned me over to him, he said he would never give me up. He said I belonged to him.''

''Oh, Sher, what did you do?''

''I told him as quietly and calmly as I could that I would never belong to him. I've never seen a man grow so angry. He declared that if he could not have me, then no one would.'' Her eyes met Kyla's troubled gaze. ''He turned his horse and rode away as if the fires of hell were licking at his heels.''

''They probably were. Do no' trust Macveagh to stay away from you.'' Kyla rose and pulled the window curtain closed. ''Try to sleep for a while; perhaps our men will be back when you wake up.'' She paused at the door and gave Sheridan a tiny smile. ''I've missed Patrick terribly these weeks. I still can no' believe I'll be getting married tomorrow. You'd be wise to do the same.''

''All he has to do is ask. Jeremy, I mean, not Patrick.'' Sheridan smiled sleepily and closed her eyes, snuggling down in the covers.

Patrick and Jeremy exchanged a weary look as they

trudged along the roadway at a snail's pace. Lord Maclaren smiled to himself, continuing his long narrative of a historical battle in which neither man was the least bit interested. At the end of his story, his lordship chuckled and said, "Jeremy, why dunna' you two go on ahead. Bradley and I can make the trip by ourselves. We've done it many a time before. You can tell your aunt will we be home a few hours after you so she can have the cook prepare dinner." His round belly shook with laughter. "No doubt, you'll have to send one of Sheridan's servants to tell her since you'll be making straight away for your sweethearts."

Jeremy sat a little straighter in the saddle, his face breaking out in a grin. "You're sure you don't mind if we go on?"

"Of course no', lad. Though I'm no' young, I'm always anxious to get back to your aunt. Unfortunately, nowadays a fast ride takes its toll on me. You two run along and give each of your pretty ladies a kiss for me."

"We'll have to force ourselves to give them that kiss, Uncle," Jeremy joked. "I'll let Aunt Genna know you're on your way. Thanks."

"Thank you, sir," called Patrick, urging his steed to catch up with Jeremy, who was already racing his stallion as fast as he dared on the rutted dirt road.

In a little over an hour, they pulled the lathered animals up before Sheridan's door. Andrew opened the entry and made his way quickly down the steps to take the reins, leading the horses away to the stable, where they could be cooled down and cared for.

Albert stood beside the open door. "Good evenin', gentlemen. The ladies are in the kitchen. Do ye wish me to announce yer arrival, sir?" Albert allowed a tiny smile to twitch at the corner of his lips, knowing what Jeremy's answer would be.

Jeremy grinned. "No, I'd like to surprise her. After

all, I've seen her in the kitchen before. I hope you haven't let her spend all her time there while I've been gone. She'll get fat if she keeps sampling Cook's baking.''

Albert smiled affectionately at the young Americans. "Nay, sir, she hasna' spent too much time eatin'. Indeed, she has eaten little since ye've been gone.''

Jeremy pushed open the kitchen door, bending low so Patrick could lean over him. The two men stuck their heads through the opening at the same time. "Would ye bonnie lassies be willin' to spare a plate of food for two starvin' travelers?'' he asked.

Sheridan and Kyla looked toward the door and exclaimed in unison, "Of course!'' They jumped up from the table and ran across the room to meet their beaus when they came through the doorway.

Kyla reached Patrick first, and he swept her up in a giant bear hug. "How are you, little one?'' he asked softly.

"Happy, now that you're back,'' she answered, oblivious to the fact that her feet were dangling in midair. She welcomed his kiss and waited until he put her back down on the floor to ask about the trip.

Jeremy spotted Sheridan's pale face the moment he came into the room. Instead of swinging her up in the air as he had intended, he drew her gently to him. "Ah, my love,'' he said quietly, resting his cheek in her hair. "I missed you so.'' She raised her face, her eyes brimming with unshed tears, and he tenderly kissed her quivering lips. "Are you ill, Sheridan? You're so pale.''

"No, not really. I just had a very bad day. I'll tell you about it later, after you've eaten.''

She clung to his arm as they moved across the room. Maisie placed two heaping plates of steaming food on the table, clearing away the dirty dishes from the meal the others had just completed. Sheridan scooted her chair over next to Jeremy so their legs touched beneath the table and his arm rubbed against her shoulder as he ate.

Her afternoon rest had been plagued with bad dreams, leaving her even more emotionally drained and badly in need of having others around her. She had slipped into a comfortable thigh-length muslin jacket and petticoat and taken refuge in the kitchen.

The conversation was casual during the meal, with the men reciting the highlights of their trip and some of the more interesting details.

When Andrew came into the kitchen, Sheridan smiled warmly at him, saying, "I saw you talking with Mr. Daniels this afternoon from my window. What does he think of the new sheep?"

Andrew smiled in return. "He thinks they'll improve the flock. All the tenants are impressed with the things ye've done, m'lady."

Jeremy was startled by the look of tenderness on the young man's face, and he frowned thoughtfully as he eyed the servant. There was a new air of intensity in Andrew's attitude toward Sheridan, a deeper level of protectiveness than had been there before. He wondered even further at what had happened to cause her to look so drawn and tired.

"Excuse me, Mr. Mackenzie, but would ye be needin' to send a message to yer aunt or anythin'? Yer horses had quite a run, and I know Lord Maclaren doesna' like to travel fast. I'd be happy to take a message to her if ye need it."

"Thank you, Andrew. Indeed, I did promise to tell her he will be along in a few hours. I'd greatly appreciate it if you would advise her."

"I'll be off then." Andrew walked to the back door, but stopped upon reaching it and turned around to face the others. " 'Tis good ye're back, Mr. Mackenzie. Yer lady has need of ye here." He looked at Sheridan, his expression demanding that she tell Jeremy what had happened. When she nodded slightly, he turned abruptly and walked out the door.

"Sheridan, I think it's time you let me know what has been going on."

"After you've finished your pie, we can go into the library. I'll explain then."

Jeremy and Patrick polished off the last few bites of dessert and left the kitchen in the company of the ladies. Kyla took Patrick's arm, directing him into the drawing room, and Sheridan led Jeremy into the library. He was surprised when she closed the door behind them, but said nothing. He stopped beside a high-backed chair, turning to lean slightly against it. She slowly crossed the room and stood trembling before him, her white face streaked with flowing tears.

"Hold me, Jeremy."

His arms went around her, molding her tightly to him, wrapping her in his love. After a few moments, he picked her up and carried her to a couch in the corner of the room. He sat down, holding her on his lap, her head resting against his shoulder.

"Tell me what happened, my love."

"I went for a long walk today in an area of the estate I had never been to before. Uncle Galvin had always told me the area was dangerous and I should never go there. I didn't plan to go in that direction; I was just walking and wound up there." She sat back so she could look up at him. "Anyway, the land wasn't crumbly and unsteady as uncle had said. Something drew me through the trees and up the hill until I came to a clearing." A shudder rippled through her, and she took a long, shaky breath.

"I found my parents' home. It's just a charred ruin

now, but I knew what it was the moment I stumbled onto it. Memories kept flashing through my mind, but I couldn't grasp any of them. I was so terrified. I couldn't move and felt as though I were choking. I don't know how long I would have stood there if Macveagh hadn't come along."

Jeremy stiffened. "What was he doing there?"

"He saw me walking toward the ruins and came to check on me. It's all right, Jeremy. He was kind and did nothing to hurt me. He carried me away so I couldn't see the clearing and stayed with me until I got control of myself. Then he brought me back toward the house. We met Andrew, who had come looking for me, and he brought me the rest of the way home."

"Where were the guards? They were supposed to stay with you anytime you left the house." His fingers curled into a fist. "I'll have their hides for this."

"Don't blame them." She shook her head slightly, her curls brushing against his chin. "I wanted to be alone, so I slipped past them."

"Of all the idiotic things to do." His breath came out in a huff.

She raised her head to look at him. "Yes it was. I even knew it at the time, but I was sick of having someone with me constantly. I missed being out on the moor by myself, and since we hadn't seen Macveagh or anyone else around the whole time you had been gone, I decided we were being overly cautious. I fear I let impulsiveness overrule what little good sense I have."

She dropped her gaze and fingered his lapel. Funny, she mused, it didn't seem improper to be alone with him in the library or even to be sitting on his lap. Her trembling ceased because of his presence and his strength. He gave her comfort and peace of mind; much, she supposed, as she did for Cameron.

Still looking down at his cravat, she related the things

Cameron had told her about the night of the fire and her parents' death.

"You sound doubtful. Do you remember something that makes you think things happened differently?"

"Not anything I can pinpoint. After I returned here, I tried to rest, but I kept having nightmares. I can't recall what most were about, but when I woke up, I had the definite feeling something is wrong with his tale. If I could just remember what happened. I try and try to search my memory, but everything is a muddle."

"Possibly in time it will become clear to you. Maybe it's best you don't remember." He looked down thoughtfully and tipped her chin up with the crook of his finger so she met his gaze. "You haven't told me everything, have you? Before, you were mostly angry with Macveagh. Now you seem terrified of him. What did he do, Sheridan?"

"I didn't realize before how—how determined he is. I knew he had the strange idea I could take my mother's place, but I thought it was just a whim. Now I realize it's something he believes with almost fanatical zeal. He is beyond reason. He declared that I belong to him, but when I told him I could never love him, he became enraged. He said if he couldn't have me, no one would."

Jeremy's face was grim. A tiny muscle worked in his jaw, and his eyes sparkled with a sharp glint of stubbornness. "That settles it. I want you right where I can protect you night and day. Marry me, Sher, right away. Tomorrow."

"I thought you had . . . well, some reservations."

"Those were ramblings of a foolish mind. I want you with me, and not only to protect you. I have enough love for both of us, and I'll willingly take whatever you can give me for now." He grinned down at her upturned face. "Think how much easier it will be to fall in love with me once I show you what you're missing." His expression grew tender and wistful. "It will be very special for us, I think. Something akin to heaven."

"How can I turn down heaven?" she whispered, reaching up to draw him down for her kiss. Even if she had not said the words, he would have felt the answer in her touch.

When Jeremy broke off the kiss, he gave her a bear hug, buried his face against her neck and mumbled a faint, "Ya-hoo."

"Is that the best you can do?" Sheridan laughed, wiggling away from his rough beard.

"Plug your ears." She obliged, and he cut loose with a yell loud enough to bring the house down.

Patrick and Kyla rushed into the room to find Sheridan still sitting on Jeremy's lap. He was beaming and grinning from ear to ear; she was pink cheeked and giggling.

"Did all that noise mean what I think it means?" asked Patrick with a twinkle in his eye.

"Would you mind having a double wedding?" Though it seemed impossible, Jeremy's grin spread a little wider.

"Of course not! It would be wonderful!" cried Kyla. She bent over, threw her arms around their necks and gave them an exuberant hug. When she straightened, Patrick shook hands with Jeremy and pounded him on the back enthusiastically.

"Congratulations to both of you. Now maybe Jeremy'll be fit to live with. He's had his nose out of joint ever since we left for Loch Maree. If I even mentioned my wedding while we were gone, he snarled at me." Patrick slipped his arm around Kyla's waist and pulled her firmly to his side.

Kyla smiled up at him. "Come on, love. Let's go tell Papa the good news and find Andrew so he can tell Rev.

Ainsley about the change in plans. I think these two want to be alone.''

Patrick let her lead him out into the hallway, where he stopped abruptly and pulled her into his arms. "Let them go spread the news. They're not the only ones who need to be alone right now." He kissed her deeply before grudgingly easing his lips away from hers. "Ah, my tiny flower, you're sweet fragrance to my senses. I'll grow drunk from your kisses."

"It better be all that makes you drunk, my braw American," Kyla teased, thumping her finger lightly on his wide, hard chest. Overcome by his aura of manliness and power, she spread her hand across his chest in a caress. "You are no' the only one who is drunk from our love, Patrick," she whispered.

Patrick brushed her lips with his once again before catching her hand and going off to see Waverly.

Closing the library door, Sheridan smiled at the little love scene, hiding the sudden twinge of envy that pricked her. Oh, to be so sure of herself and her feelings!

Jeremy opened his arms, and she stepped into his embrace, content to be held gently, his chin nuzzling her hair. "I should ride over and give Aunt Genna the good news, but I'll come back. Have Maisie prepare two guest rooms. Patrick and I will stay here tonight as an added precaution. I'll have the guards post a double watch tonight and tomorrow. If Macveagh gets wind of our marriage, he might try something."

"I'll feel better having you here." She slid her arms around his trim waist and frowned up at him. "Be very careful, Jeremy. Even though Macveagh is tormented by my mother's death, he doesn't seem to be bothered in the least by my father's. You might be the one to suffer his wrath instead of me."

He looked down at her worried face, still pale with

dark smudges beneath the tear-reddened eyes. Even the star bursts seemed dulled from her exhaustion. "I'll keep a sharp lookout for trouble. Why don't you go on up to bed, love. I'll ride over and back as quickly as I can. I'll check in on you when I return."

She shook her head. "No, I'll wait up until you're back. I don't think I could sleep until then. I'll check with Cook and Maisie on the preparations. I'm sure they've heard the news by now."

He opened the library door, and they walked across the drawing room arm in arm. Kyla and Patrick were standing near the fireplace stealing little kisses. They reluctantly pulled apart when Jeremy and Sheridan in stopped front of them.

"I think we should stay here tonight—in the guest rooms," Jeremy added, noting the twinkling in Patrick's eyes. "The ladies need more protection." He chuckled and added, "However, I may have trouble making you two remember that the wedding is not until tomorrow."

Patrick bowed gallantly toward Kyla. "I will do nothing to tarnish the lady's honor, sir." Kyla laughed, a flush of pink softly spreading up her neck and cheeks, making her even more beautiful to her betrothed. He grinned at her mischievously before turning his attention to Jeremy. "Do you intend to advise your aunt tonight?"

"Yes, I'm going there now. They would be worried if we simply didn't show up tonight. Besides, our ladies might appreciate it if we had something to wear tomorrow other than dust-covered, travel-wrinkled clothes. Tell me what you want to wear, and I'll pick it up. Uncle Balfour's man can pack up the rest and bring it over tomorrow." He glanced over at Sheridan before turning to Kyla. "Take care of my girl and try to get her to rest. I'll be back soon."

Patrick accompanied Jeremy to the stables, while the women went into the kitchen. The servants sipped their final cup of tea for the evening, excitement running high over the news of their lady's wedding. A few minutes later Andrew left again, this time to tell the minister about the double wedding. Cookie and Maisie went over the last-minute details with the brides.

Sheridan only half listened as they discussed various dishes and seating arrangements. Patrick came in the back door to join Kyla in approving the final plans while Sheridan toyed with her teacup, her thoughts miles away. Only when Jeremy returned, did she relax. A short time later, he coaxed her into going to bed, personally escorting her up to her room.

He stopped at the door, taking both her hands in his and bringing them tenderly to his lips. "I'll be just across the hall, Sheridan. If you need anything, just call out, and I'll come to you."

She smiled up into his eyes. "It seems you told me something along that line once before."

"Yes, I did, and even though I had only just met you, I meant it as much than as I do now."

"Thank you, Jeremy. I'm sure I'll sleep better knowing you're near."

"I love you, Sheridan." Still holding her hands, he kissed her gently. "Good night, sweet. Dream of me."

"Always," she whispered truthfully as he released her hands.

His heart soared. When she stepped into the room, he pulled the door closed and retired to his own room. Restless, he paced quietly back and forth in the shadowed darkness, tired from the journey, but too aware of Sheridan's nearness to sleep.

He was anxious for the wedding to take place, not just for the passionate lovemaking, which he was sure would soon follow, but for the strength and protection marriage would allow him to give to his wife. It was the right decision; it had to be. Even now, he longed to be at her side, simply to let her rest peacefully in his arms. He smiled ruefully at the thought. She might rest peacefully if he were with her, but he, no doubt, would get no sleep at all.

Chapter 9

Sheridan sighed softly and snuggled farther into the comfort of her down-filled bed. Her fingers twitched on the soft muslin sheet, while in her dream her mother took hold of her hand, and they raced across a beautiful green lawn surrounded by bright, colorful flowers. A large black and white house stood proudly in back of them, with brilliant red roses climbing up a trellis just to the side of a wide window. A little dog scampered along beside them as they slowed their pace to a walk and ambled down a long sunlit lane. At the far end of the lane, a horse galloped toward them; a tall blond man sat straight in the saddle.

The horse stopped in front of them, and Sheridan's father leaped off to sweep her mother up in his arms. Sheridan jumped up and down in excitement, the little puppy barking animatedly at her side.

"My turn, Papa, my turn. Swing me high and dunna' ever let me come down."

"Ach, Alyson, who's this wee lass who keeps pestering me? Do I know this tyke from someplace? Surely, 'tis no' wee Sheridan, for, if so, she has grown a foot since I but saw her a month ago." He bent down in front of the little girl. "Let me see your face, lass." She dutifully tipped up her little chin to give him a good view. "Ach, it must be my own wee daughter, for she is the image of her mother, and there is no other as bonnie."

He picked up the child and swung her high in the air, around and around, until she thought she could fly. Slowly, he quit twirling around, giving her a big hug and kiss before setting her on the ground. The family walked slowly up the lane, hand in hand, the puppy running ahead of them and the horse trailing along behind.

Suddenly, the dream changed. The sunlit sky grew dark from the heavy growth of trees overhead. A grown-up Sheridan tried to run through the thick weeds and escape the endless tunnel in which she was trapped. A scream tore from her throat as a dark, menacing figure towered over her. Strong viselike hands reached out and grabbed her arms, halting her endless flight.

"You're mine," growled Macveagh, his face looming gigantically before her.

"No," she sobbed, "I belong to Jeremy."

"Nay. You've come back from the grave to be mine, Alyson. You'll never belong to another. I'll kill him first, and then you'll love me." Wicked laughter echoed around her. Then, she was a child again, being carried through thick, black, billowing smoke. She coughed and choked and fought to be put down, to be free from the arms that now pushed her toward the smoke instead of away from it.

"Sheridan, don't fight me, love. 'Tis me, Jeremy. Don't be afraid. Come on, sweet, wake up. 'Tis only a dream. You're safe. I'm here, and I won't let anyone hurt you.''

Jeremy's crooning voice slowly penetrated the nightmare, and he felt her relax in his arms. In the darkness of the room, she whispered, ''Is it really you, Jeremy? 'Tis not just another dream, is it?''

''No, my love. I'm here. I'll pinch you, if you'd like.''

In the blackness, she knew he was smiling, and she silently thanked him for that smile. ''I'd rather you kissed me.''

''Easily arranged, my dear.''

His touch was gentle as he moved his mouth over hers. He moved his large hand to slowly caress her back, while cradling her against him with the other. ''Are you better, now?''

''Yes.'' She kissed him in return before saying softly, ''Jeremy, stay with me. I need to feel your arms around me. I need to be safe.''

''Slide over.''

Sheridan obeyed, expecting him to crawl beneath the sheet beside her. She had no doubts where such action would lead, but her need of his closeness was so great, she was willing to pay the consequences.

''Jeremy?'' she asked, when she felt him lie down on top of the covers.

He slipped his arm beneath her neck and drew her against his shoulder, wrapping his other arm around her. ''Go to sleep, love. You need to be rested for your wedding day.''

''Oh.''

She felt his shoulder shake when he chuckled. ''You sound disappointed. Is there anything wrong?''

''Well, no. That is . . . I thought you'd crawl under the covers. Won't you be cold without a blanket?'' She was thankful he couldn't see her burning face in the darkness.

A soft, deep masculine laugh spread to the corners of the room. "There's no chill likely with you in my arms. I'm still dressed, so I'll not be cold."

"Oh. Well, good night. Sleep well."

" 'Tis not likely."

After a long pause, Sheridan whispered, "Jeremy, do you want to make love to me?"

"Of course, I do, you little twit." Again, she knew that he was smiling by the sound of his voice. "But I'm not going to, as difficult as it may be for me. When I make you mine, I want to take my time and love you the way you deserve to be loved. Knowing how protective your friends are of you, I expect someone to walk in at any minute to check on you. It would prove highly embarrassing for us if we were found naked in your bed."

"I suppose you're right." She yawned and wiggled closer to him.

Jeremy stifled a groan. "Sleep well, love."

"I will. I won't have bad dreams as long as you're here. You get some sleep, too," she said drowsily.

"I'll do my best."

Standing silently in the hallway, Kyla gently closed Sheridan's door. Patrick stepped out of the shadows and walked down the hall with her until they reached her bedroom.

"That was quite a scream," he whispered.

"She'll be fine, now. Jeremy's there. I think he plans to stay with her."

Patrick slipped his arms around her and drew her close. "Good." He brushed his lips against her forehead. "Are you afraid of the dark?"

"No." She smiled up at him and rested her hands on his shoulders.

"Too bad. I thought I could stay close by so you wouldn't be scared."

"How close?"

"Very, very close. In bed with you would be just about right."

"You'd think me a loose woman."

"Never." He leaned down to nibble at the side of her neck.

"What kind of example would I be for Sheridan?" she asked in a ragged whisper.

"If Jeremy's in bed with her, she doesn't need an example."

"He's on the bed, she's in it."

"There's a difference?" He shifted to the other side of her neck.

"Aye, there's a difference." The wind picked up, swirling about the castle with a mournful howl. A loud clap of thunder crashed overhead, and rain lashed against the windows.

"Are you afraid of storms?" He gently nipped her shoulder through her robe, then glanced up at her face.

"No, Patrick." Kyla laughed softly. "Now, off to your room, you rake." She touched his cheek with the back of her fingers. "It would break my father's heart if I did no' do what is right."

"Aye, little one, I understand. I can wait one more day."

"I love you."

"I love you, too." He hugged her tight and kissed her deeply. "Now get to bed, woman."

A slender ray of early morning sunlight stretched across the pillow to nudge Sheridan into wakefulness. Eyes closed, she came to an awareness of Jeremy's arms still encompassing her and the gentle warmth of his steady breathing as it rustled her hair. She moved her head from his shoulder to turn and look at his peaceful face. He murmured in his sleep at her movement, and his arms tightened about her. It seemed so right to awaken in his arms. The blanket still separated them, and even though the thought made her blush, she longed for the moment when they would lie together without the barrier.

Reaching up with a hand warmed from resting against his chest, she traced the line of his jaw down to his full, sensuous lips. She brushed her fingers gently over the spot where her lips longed to be, and she was rewarded by a gentle kiss on her fingertips.

"Good morning, Countess."

"Good morning, milord. Were you really asleep, or were you just pretending?"

Strong masculine muscles stretched lazily as he flexed his arms and legs. He closed his arms around her again, drawing her even closer. "Asleep. I honestly didn't think I'd be able to sleep with you in my arms, but surprisingly, I did. You were sleeping peacefully, and I found myself to be so content that I got almost a full night's rest. I'm beginning to understand this thing called love. As much as I desire you, I can still be happy in giving you security and comfort when needed, heedless of my wants."

He smiled wryly down into the sparkling sapphire eyes. "A man would have to be touched in the head to be able to spend the night with you and do nothing more than put his arms around you and steal a few kisses." He promptly stole another kiss, then kissed her on the tip of her nose.

"Now, my beautiful, tempting morsel, I'll leave you before our tranquillity is disturbed. I shall sneak back to my own bed so as not to cause a scandal among the servants."

Her bottom lip stuck out in a pout when he pulled

away from her and stood up. "You can do no wrong in any of the servants' eyes."

He kissed her playfully, nibbling on her lower lip, teasing away the pout. "All except Andrew. He's so in love with you, he might challenge me to a duel if he found me here this morning."

"Jeremy, he's just a friend." She sat up in bed, pulling the sheet up self-consciously even though her sleeping jacket covered the décolletage of her nightgown from Jeremy's eager gaze.

With a sigh, he straightened, knowing that before he slept again, her lovely body would belong to him. "A friend, yes, but he loves you, too, dear Sheridan. The lad would give his life for you if the need arose, just as I would."

She frowned thoughtfully. "Have I been unkind in seeking his friendship? I have encouraged him in no other way, Jeremy, but I don't want to hurt him. He is a fine man, and I earnestly value him as a friend."

Jeremy smiled at her, pleased with her kindness and concern for others. Most beautiful women he had encountered cared nothing for anyone else, but only about their own welfare. She reminded him of his mother, always looking out for others and mindful of their needs.

"The only unkindness would have been in rejecting his fellowship and service. As you said, he is a fine young man and highly intelligent. Some young lass will catch his fancy soon, and he, too, will settle down and get married."

He strode swiftly to her wardrobe and threw open the doors. "Which of these lovely gowns will you wear today, my sweet? I do not intend for you to be married in black, you know."

She slid off the bed and hastily pulled on her deep pink silk robe and slippers before crossing the room to stand beside him. Before she could answer him, he kissed her tenderly on the cheek and rubbed the lace collar of her sleeping jacket between his fingers.

"I'll not tolerate such foolishness after we are married, madam. You will not be embarrassed for me to see your body, nor will you try to hide your riches under high-collared fluff such as this. If you have nothing more tantalizing to wear, my dear, then wear nothing at all."

Sheridan smiled timidly and said meekly, "Yes, milord. I will strive to please you." Thinking of the extremely low neckline of her fashionable sleepwear, she blushed. "I believe most of my nightgowns will meet with your satisfaction." Her smile deepened, and her eyes sparkled as she gazed up at him. "And if they do not meet with your approval, you may shower me with gifts to your heart's content."

He hugged her, burying his face in her hair to smother his laughter. "I'll do just as you ask, my love. Anything you require or wish for need only be requested, and it shall be yours. If you don't tell me of your preferences, then I'll bestow upon you mine."

"Such generosity." She grinned up at him and pointed at the closet. "Do you find a preference here for my wedding gown, or shall I be allowed to choose?"

He touched a curved forefinger and thumb to his chin and pursed his lips thoughtfully, his gaze racing swiftly over her wardrobe. In quick succession, he touched three of the gowns hanging there. "Personally, I would choose one of these three—the blue silk, the silver, or the blue one with the white lace. However, it is your wedding day, and I think most appropriate for you to choose your own gown." Smiling down at her, he closed the wardrobe doors. "Actually, I have no choice, other than it not be black. From the clothing I have seen you wear before, you have excellent taste. Now, I must get out of here before someone comes barging in.''

He stopped at the door and turned to speak once more. ''I realize it is customary for the groom not to see the bride on their wedding day until the ceremony, but since we've already broken the tradition, I'd like a word with you in private later today. There is a matter I wish to discuss with you before we actually say our vows.''

''We can meet after breakfast, if you wish. I don't intend to stay in my room but will be downstairs right in the thick of it, seeing to the preparations. I feel much better than I did yesterday, and it won't be fair if I let Kyla handle all the last minute details.''

Jeremy pulled open the door, taking a cautious peek down the hall before tiptoeing across to his room. He grimaced as the door squeaked upon opening and stepped through it quickly.

Sheridan stifled a giggle and closed her door soundlessly. She washed her face in the cold water left in the pitcher the night before and brushed her hair until it gleamed. She looked at her glowing reflection in the mirror and smiled. It had been a long time since she felt so happy. She did not try to analyze her feelings; she simply wanted to enjoy them.

She dressed in an apple green lutestring gown, buttoned from the modest falling collar down the fitted bodice and long, full skirt to the hem. She was tying the wide sash at the small of her back when Kyla came in. At her smile, Sheridan said, ''I promised Jeremy no more black. Help me decide what I should wear this afternoon.'' She pointed to the three gowns Jeremy had chosen. ''The silver is best for a wedding, I think.''

''Aye, it will be perfect.''

They rushed downstairs to find the men waiting for them in the dining room. Their breakfast finished, they were discussing the day's coming events over a second cup of coffee. Sheridan served herself from the sideboard and sat down next to Jeremy. Before she could ask, he reached for the tea pot and poured her a cup.

"I've never seen you drink coffee, so I assumed you wanted tea." At her affirmative nod, he continued, "Now, don't eat so fast. You'll make yourself sick, and I'll not have my bride holding up the wedding because she has a stomach ache."

She smiled and slowed her pace. Between bites, she said, "I was only hurrying because you want to talk to me, and I didn't want to keep you waiting."

"There's no real hurry. I arranged with Bradley to pack our things and bring them over this morning. We will dress here. Take your time, while I simply enjoy looking at you."

She complied, and after she had a second cup of tea, Jeremy took her hand and led her up the stairs to the library. Closing the door behind them, he reached into his coat pocket and pulled out a document.

"Sheridan, I had this contract drawn up while I was at my father's estate. His solicitor was there from Perth to go over the estate business. It is legal and binding, requiring only our signatures and those of two witnesses. It states that all of the property you bring into this marriage, both land and movable properties such as the ship, shall remain solely yours. I have no need of a dowry from you, dear heart, and it is not your property that concerns me. I will offer counsel when asked, but otherwise the handling of your estates and your investments will be left up to you."

She looked at him in surprise. "You had reconsidered marrying me, even before you returned?"

"I missed you very much," he said gently, "enough that I knew I couldn't last much longer without you. I like to plan ahead, so I talked to the solicitor while we were there."

"Were you so certain I would agree?"

"No, but you had said you were willing to marry me even though you weren't sure of your feelings. I could only hope you still felt the same."

"I have to admire a man who comes prepared." She grinned impishly at him.

He smiled back. "I was uncertain how the laws of the various countries involved would affect your inheritance since you have property in both England and Scotland. Each has different laws concerning what a wife forfeits whenever she marries. At any rate, I was promised this would be the simplest way of assuring the government, and you, that the true ownership of all your current possessions would stay in your hands."

"I don't know what to say. I had assumed the Scottish laws would apply, and you would obtain possession of my movable property. I really wouldn't mind if you did, you know. However, I can see how this would make everything simpler." She took the paper from his hand and skimmed it quickly, knowing he expected her to sign nothing until she had read it. Looking up at him with a smile on her face, she said softly, "Thank you, Jeremy. I'm grateful you trust me to handle my affairs, although there will be many times when I will seek your wisdom and advice."

"On the ships, yes, but heaven help you if you ask me anything about farming. I'm liable to tell you to harvest the lettuce in the middle of winter."

She laughed and moved to her desk, dipping the pen in the ink, then signing the document. "There," she said, blowing on the ink gently to hasten the drying. "Now all you have to do is sign it and have it witnessed." He came across the room and leaned over the desk also. She gave his arm a gentle squeeze. "I'll go and ask Patrick and Kyla to sign, too."

After the contract had been legally witnessed, Lord

Maclaren's servant arrived with Jeremy and Patrick's clothes. They went upstairs to pick out something to wear for the wedding. With the help of two village girls, the castle had been cleaned and polished until it shone. Kyla and Sheridan picked and arranged fresh flowers while Maisie and Cook were occupied in the kitchen.

In the early afternoon, Kyla took Sheridan by the arm and directed her up the stairs to her room, where a steaming tub of water awaited her. She soaked in the scented water, relaxing for several minutes before bathing and washing her hair. Kyla was unusually quiet as she helped Sheridan from the tub, drying her with the towel and gently rubbing fragrant lotion onto her smooth skin. She brushed her hair carefully until the silken locks sparkled. Leaving it hanging down her back, Kyla pulled the dark curls away from Sheridan's face with a shimmering silver ribbon.

Sheridan sat silently watching her friend's ministrations, her calm outward appearance hiding her inward anticipation and nervousness. Aware of her ignorance as to what actually happened between a man and a woman when they made love, she was beginning to fear she would be found lacking and not please her new husband.

Kyla's sharp eyes watched her in the mirror. When Sheridan frowned, her friend asked, "What's wrong, Sher? Is there somethin' troublin' you?"

Sheridan smiled uncertainly before dropping her head for a moment to hide the flush of her cheeks. She took a deep breath and looked up at Kyla, who lowered her hand, the brush still held in it, to her side. "Kyla, I'm afraid I won't know what to do or won't like what happens. What if I disappoint him?"

Kyla smiled reassuringly and took her hand. Leading her over to the bed, she sat down and curled her legs up beneath her. Sheridan followed suit, sitting in the same manner as they had often talked when she was a young girl. Kyla spoke softly, matter-of-factly telling Sheridan what to expect.

In conclusion, she said, "Sheridan, I dunna' think there is anythin' you could do to displease Jeremy. He is a very gentle and patient man who loves you very much. He will be a good teacher in the art of love. Just relax and do what comes naturally. The Good Lord gave us the instincts, it's up to us to use them."

Sheridan hugged her friend and blinked hard as tears came to her eyes. Her life would be very different from now on. Kyla would remain her friend forever, and to some extent her confidant, but somehow she knew after today, Jeremy would be the one to share her secrets and her dreams. He would be the one to first share her joys, sorrows, and problems, instead of this dear friend who had always been available for such a long time.

The rumbling of a carriage drew their attention, and Kyla hurried to the window to check on the arrival. " 'Tis the Reverend and Mrs. Ainsley." She flew to the wardrobe, snatching up the silver gown, and held it out for Sheridan to step into. Less than ten minutes later, someone tapped on her door.

"Sheridan, 'tis Mrs. Ainsley. May I come in?"

Sheridan gave Kyla a knowing smile and replied, "Yes, of course, madam."

Mrs. Ainsley opened the door and carefully negotiated her rotund figure across the room to Sheridan. "My dear, how lovely you are." She hugged her gently before taking the chair Kyla pulled over for her. "You'll make such a beautiful bride." Her gaze narrowed as she watched Sheridan fasten the clasp of her pearls. The necklace rested against her bare skin above the straight neckline of her silver lace tucker.

"We were rather surprised when Andrew rode in to see us last evenin'. Mr. Ainsley wanted me to check with you, dear. He is concerned about the hastiness of this marriage.''

Sheridan smiled sweetly, knowing the minister and his wife were truly concerned about her welfare. Unlike some men of the cloth, Mr. Ainsley genuinely cared about his flock, particularly looking after the widows, orphans and the poor.

"I know 'tis hasty, and may appear disrespectful to marry so soon after my uncle's death, and I was concerned about it. But Jeremy is a good man, and he will be a good husband. So much has happened these past months, I cannot bear to be alone anymore." She looked down at her clasped hands, then back up to meet the older woman's eye. "Please try to understand, Mrs. Ainsley, and don't judge me too harshly. I need the strength and love that only Jeremy can give to me."

To Sheridan's surprise, the reverend's wife wiped a tear from her eye with a small lace handkerchief. "We know you've had a heavy load to carry since your return, child, and we dunna' begrudge you your happiness. We stopped on our way here and talked with Lord Maclaren. We have his lordship's assurance that Mr. Mackenzie is a fine man. We talked with him briefly after our arrival. We both believe he is of good character and loves you very much." She pushed her large frame from the small chair, wincing at the creaking of the wood as she did so.

" 'Tis my belief the Good Lord sent him to you, Sheridan, to ease your pain and give you love as only he could. God takes care of His children, and He'll take care of you through your fine young American."

Sheridan placed a small kiss on the older lady's cheek. "Your words have blessed me, madam, and I thank you for them."

The older lady meandered to the door. "We'll be waitin' downstairs, my dear. Maisie has promised us some tea and her delicious cakes. Take your time, for the Maclarens are no' here yet.''

After their guest left the room, Kyla smiled. ''Now I'll make a mad dash across the hall and change my clothes. I see the Maclarens coming up the lane, so I'll be quick.''

A few minutes later, Sheridan rested her forehead against the cool windowpane, watching her friends' arrival at the front door. Jeremy came out to greet them. He glanced up at the window and waved before blowing her a kiss. She raised her hand to him in greeting and debated about going on downstairs. Having made up her mind to go greet her guests, she paused at the mirror once more and ran a hand over her hair to smooth it.

She was only a few steps from the door when someone knocked. Opening it, she found Kyla and Waverly waiting for her. He held out his arm for her hand.

''M'lady, may I have the honor of escortin' ye lassies down to the weddin'?''

Taking his arm, she answered, '' 'Tis I who am honored, Waverly. I'm thankful you're able to move around well enough to give the brides away.'' She secretly worried about his strength, for she could feel him tremble by the time they reached the bottom of the stairs.

Sheridan was about to question him when Jeremy stepped into the corridor from the great hall. Her breath caught in her throat at the sight of him. Dressed in a rich brown brocade coat and gold embroidered waistcoat, his hair flamed with golden-red glints matched only by the sparkle in his deep amber eyes. His gaze caught hers and held it while he crossed the floor to stop in front of her.

''God's blessin' on ye both,'' Waverly said softly,

slipping his arm from beneath her hand. With Kyla still at his side, he escorted her into the great hall to join Patrick. There, he repeated his heartfelt blessing, lifted Kyla's hand from his arm and placed it in Patrick's large palm. Then he clasped both hands in his and kissed his daughter's cheek.

Jeremy and Sheridan stood outside the room, lost in the haze of the moment.

"You've never looked more beautiful," murmured Jeremy.

"Nor you so handsome."

"The others await. We should not keep them."

Later, Sheridan couldn't remember walking into the great hall with Jeremy; in fact, she was barely aware of any of the ceremony. As they took their vows, Jeremy's voice was deep and strong. He held her hand firmly in his, pressing it gently at the end of his pledge. When Sheridan repeated the minister's words, her voice, though clear, was so soft the others had to strain to hear her. At the end of the ceremony, Jeremy's kiss was tender, almost reverent.

Having traveled this road before, Kyla's responses were strong and clear. Happiness added another note to her lilting Scots. Patrick's voice was deep and rumbling, strong and clear.

There was a lot of hugging and hand shaking after the wedding, until Maisie announced the meal was ready. Laughing and discussing whether they should live in Scotland or America, the newlyweds and their guests moved into the dining room.

Sheridan was impressed by the wonderful meal Maisie and Cookie had prepared. A minted leg of lamb served as the centerpiece, with wild duck in wine sauce, poached salmon, a variety of vegetables and fruits, whole meal bread, potato scones, and buttery rowies scattered around it. Dundee cake, served at

Christenings, weddings and Christmas, completed the feast.

When Sheridan saw the dessert, she looked at Maisie in surprise, knowing the special fruitcake was usually aged for a while before using. "Maisie, when did you make the cake?"

The housekeeper grinned at her mistress and winked boldly at Jeremy. "Shortly after ye returned home, m'lady, after ye came out of your deep sleep. I could feel it in my bones that a weddin'—or two—wouldna' be too far away." Sheridan smiled and Jeremy chuckled, while the rest of the guests had a hearty laugh.

Sheridan was too excited to eat much of the food placed in front of her, and noticed that Jeremy did not eat his usual double portions and only sipped at his wine. Everyone else, however, ate heartily, filling the room with lively and happy conversation.

The guests retired to the drawing room for a short time after dinner before the minister and his wife announced their departure. The Maclarens followed afterward, leaving both newlywed couples waving from the front entry.

"Come, Sher, let me play the lady's maid one last time."

Sheridan cast a swift glance to Jeremy, her heart skipping a beat at the look of possession and hunger on his face. Turning quickly, she entered the castle, Kyla at her heels.

Chapter 10

Sheridan glanced down uneasily at her white linen nightshift. The billowy sleeves were edged with a lace ruffle below her elbow. Lace also bordered the floor-length hem. But it wasn't the sleeves or the hem that made her uncomfortable. It was the narrow filigree at the top of the very low-cut gown. She chewed on the inside of her lip, wishing the edging were several inches wider. The delicate openwork barely covered her breasts, yet at the time of purchase, it had seemed modest. Some of the nightshifts had been cut in such a way that the bosom was not covered at all.

"Oh, Ky, do I look indecent?" She turned anxiously to her friend and absently dabbed a bit of rose scent on her wrist.

"You look lovely. Now quit your worryin'. Everythin' will be just fine as long as you relax and trust him." Kyla handed Sheridan her blue satin robe, smiling at her relieved expression as she slipped on the garment.

A knock sounded at the door. When it swung open, Jeremy stepped inside and halted, his eyes fixed upon his bride. He had removed his cravat, leaving it with his coats in the other bedroom. A robe was thrown casually over one shoulder.

Sheridan set the bottle of perfume on the vanity and turned to face her new husband. She smiled nervously and forced her hands to remain relaxed at her sides.

"Blessin's, peace and joy to you both." Kyla slipped from the room, closing the door quietly behind her.

Jeremy tossed the robe across a chair. His dark skin was rich against the cream color of his shirt, the fine mat of chest hair gleaming golden in the open triangle at his throat. He crossed the room slowly, soundlessly, even though he still wore his high-topped boots.

Gently brushing her cheek with the back of his hand, he spoke softly. "Good evening, wife." She felt his hand tremble slightly against her cheek. He kissed her tenderly before drawing back to gaze into the brightly shining eyes looking up at him.

" 'Wife'—that has a nice ring to it." He again brushed her lips with his, resting his hands lightly on her shoulders, gently caressing the sides of her neck with his thumbs.

He raised his head and caressed her face with his gaze. "Don't be afraid, Sher."

"I'm not," she whispered, then gave him an uncertain smile. "Well, not too much." For a long moment he feared she might pull away, then she self-consciously slid her arms around his neck. Taking a shaky breath, she looked him in the eye. "Truly make me your wife, Jeremy. Please."

"Yes, my love, yes." This time there was no guilt or uncertainty; there would be no shame, no regrets.

Slowly, so very slowly, he traced the soft inner skin of her lips with the tip of his tongue. Go slowly, caution warned. Be gentle, this is unknown to her.

He tried to hold back, but the wanting was too intense; it had been a constant companion too long. He ran his hands up and down her back, drawing her against him until he could feel the pounding of her heart against his chest. He took her mouth with a kiss of raw, untamed desire.

Her lips parted eagerly beneath his as he proclaimed without words his love and need of her. She met him kiss for kiss, need for need and with a wild abandon that delighted him.

Gradually, he regained control, lessening the intensity of their embrace. His lips left hers to feather molten kisses along her cheek and down her throat, only to come back once more to her waiting mouth in a touch of gentleness.

"Let me look at you," he whispered. His fingers fumbled at the ties of her robe, but he took a deep, steadying breath and concentrated on pulling the right ribbon. The bow slid loose. He moved his hands to rest lightly on her shoulders and searched her face for signs of fear. In a few minutes, she would belong to him completely, and he was determined to make that surrender as pleasant and painless for her as possible.

He held her gaze with his and slowly slipped the robe from her shoulders, easing it carefully down her arms. The billowing, blue cloud drifted to the floor unnoticed. He kissed her softly, then straightened.

When his gaze dipped to the décolletage of her gown, he sucked in his breath sharply and held it. Lowering his head, he brushed her collarbone with his lips, then bestowed a whisper of a kiss on her lace-covered flesh.

Sheridan gasped softly and closed her eyes.

Jeremy straightened, looking back up at her face. He

gently gathered the nightshift in both hands and pulled upward. Keeping her eyes lowered, Sheridan raised her arms so he could pull it off over her head. Without glancing away, he tossed it on the stool by the vanity, then took a step back and looked upon his love, his Circe.

How beautiful she was! And he would be the first—the first to run his hands along her creamy skin, the first to taste its silkiness with his lips, the first to teach her the joys of being a woman. It would be his name she would cry out at that moment of ecstasy, his chest she would cuddle against in sleep, his child she would cradle in her arms. He took another deep breath and let it out slowly, wondering how a man could love so much.

"Do . . . do I please you, Jeremy?"

He didn't have to look at her face to know of the uncertainty there, but he tore his eyes away from all the places he wanted to touch, and met her wavering gaze.

"Yes, my love, you please me very much." He rested his fingers on her shoulders and let his thumb graze the upper curve of her breast, enjoying a spark of pure male satisfaction from the crescendo of her thudding pulse. "I've lain awake for weeks, wondering what you'd be like, trying not to let my imagination conjure up perfection so I wouldn't be disappointed." He kissed her softly. "I'm not at all disappointed."

She rested her forehead against his chin. "I'm so glad. I was afraid you might be."

Sheridan lifted her hands and silently began to undo the last buttons on his shirt. Tugging the garment from the top of his breeches, she pushed it from his shoulders and down his arms until it, too, fell silently to the floor.

Eyes aglow, she reached out to touch the hard, bulging muscle of his upper arm. "Oh, Jeremy," she whispered, "you're the one who's perfect."

His chest swelled with pride.

She moved her fingers in a gentle pattern up his arm to his shoulder, lingering there to tenderly touch an old scar.

"A memento from the revolution," he said softly.

She dropped a kiss on the pale, taut scar, following with tiny kisses across the wide expanse of his furry chest. The curly, crisp hair tickled her skin, and she pulled back with a smile and twitch of her nose. Inquisitive, she traced the broad muscles of his chest, journeying down his side to rest her hands at his slim waist.

Sensing her hesitation, he smiled tenderly, picked her up and placed her reverently on the bed. Swiftly, his clothes fell in a heap, tossed carelessly aside. Her arms opened to him, and he slid onto the bed beside her, gently drawing her fully against him.

Sheridan trembled from the impact of skin touching skin, of the sheer beauty of lying beside him. He kissed her eyelids gently, then her cheek, coming at last to her waiting, expectant lips. Jeremy worshiped her with his hands and his lips, arousing feelings she never knew existed. A sense of joy and belonging swept over her, an emotion so intense it almost stole her breath away.

Jeremy watched her face for a time as he caressed her, a face filled with wonder as her world became one of touch and pleasure. With a knowing smile, he lowered his head to spread lingering kisses all across her creamy skin.

Soon, it was not enough just to have him touch her; she felt a compelling need to touch him, to give him pleasure in return. Sheridan timidly ran her hand along his shoulder and down to his chest. At his quick intake of breath, her gaze flew to his face, but his closed eyes and pleased, sensual smile told her he liked her hands on him. Her courage grew, and she let her fingers trail

along the side of his ribs, down past his slim waist to the
hard muscle of his hip.

Jeremy groaned and captured her mouth in a blazing
kiss. "No more, love. I can't wait." In spite of his need,
Jeremy joined with her gently, holding back until he felt
her relax. He kissed her tenderly, slowly building the
passion until she moved eagerly beneath him. Then, he
took her to heaven.

Later, limbs entwined, Jeremy's head resting on her
breast, Sheridan said quietly, "I never thought it would
be like this, Jeremy. Is it always so?"

"No, but it will be for us." His countenance sobered,
and his gaze touched her soul. "I love you, Sheridan."

Her eyes grew wide, then filled with tears, and she
turned her face away. His words brought her tre-
mendous joy, yet filled her with despair. His love was
the greatest gift anyone had ever given her, but she
could not return the gift full measure. She knew her very
silence hurt him, but she could not lie to him. Perhaps
someday the words would flow easily from her lips, but
for now they were only taking root in her heart.

With painful tenderness, he drew her face around
toward him. "I can wait. When you tell me you love me,
I'll know 'tis true."

"I don't want to hurt you."

"I know." He brushed away a tear as it trickled down
her cheek. "It would hurt me more if you lied to me. It
will come, love, it will come."

He smiled and kissed her gently, tucking the blanket
about her shoulders. Fingering the bedding, his smile
spread into a grin. "Now this is the way a blanket is
supposed to be used."

Sheridan giggled and snuggled closer. Contented,
they drifted off into a dreamless sleep.

She awoke to the normal early morning sounds,
except this morning Andrew's whistle somehow

sounded happier as he tended the horses, and Dora's usually off-key singing was perfect as she crossed the courtyard to milk the cow. Sheridan lay cuddled against Jeremy, his arm a pillow for her head, her leg thrown across his thighs. His breathing, deep and even, softly stirred tiny wisps of hair on her forehead, and she closed her eyes for a moment in memory of last night's pleasure.

Shifting slightly, she raised up on one elbow to look at her husband, her lover, her friend. A lock of hair fell across his forehead carelessly, and sleep softened his features. The first rays of sunshine peeked through the open shutter, draping him in a golden light. Her gaze moved over him with admiration, contentment filled her soul.

Unable to resist, she cautiously rested her hand on his chest. Slowly, she moved it across the deep, firm muscles, memorizing the contours of his body. She followed the fine line of golden hair down across his belly to his waist. Even in sleep, his stomach was hard from vigorous exercise, and she marveled at him, wondering how he managed to stay so fit.

When she inched her hand lower, Jeremy drew a sharp breath. Sheridan's eyes flew to his face to meet his burning gaze. With a small cry, she moved into his embrace, their love savage and untamed, hungry and impatient. They came together with a heat that forged their souls into one, rivaling the now fully risen sun in its brilliance.

Sated, they curled together, Sheridan's back against Jeremy's chest, his knees tucked beneath hers. He nuzzled the nape of her neck, pushing aside her tangled hair with his lips. "Ah, madam, you do please me. In the presence of others, you are a grand lady, beautiful, courteous and regal. But in my bed, you're a tigress, a temptress whose passions inflame my own. 'Tis a very pleasing combination.''

He chuckled when her stomach rumbled in a very unregal manner beneath his hand. She smiled, twisting around to look at him. ''Alas, my lord, even a tigress must eat. I'm ravenous.''

''And well ye should be, lass. 'Tis a great deal of exercise ye've had this night, and if I have my way, 'twill be a great deal more of the same before the day is out. Now, out of bed, wench, before I change my mind and force ye to stay here with me.''

Giggling, Sheridan leaped out of bed, playfully dodging his hand as he reached for her, and slipped on her robe. Tossing Jeremy his robe, she pulled the rope to ring for Dora, who was now her attendant.

In a few minutes, the young girl knocked softly on the door, coming in when told to do so. ''Mama sent ye up some breakfast, m'lady,'' she said, placing a large tray on the table. ''She said ye probably would be of a mind to eat here instead of comin' downstairs.'' She glanced shyly at the two lovers, their hair still disheveled, their faces flushed from lovemaking. Her own face began to grow pink, and she hastily added, ''If ye be needin' anythin' else, just ring for me, mum.''

Choking back a giggle, Sheridan said, ''Thank you, Dora. The breakfast looks wonderful. Please thank Maisie for her thoughtfulness. I'll ring for you to bring up some bath water later.''

Dropping a quick curtsy, the girl fled the room.

The door closed behind her as Sheridan and Jeremy pounced on the food. Laughing, they fed each other bites of cheese, smoked meat, fresh hot bread slathered with butter and bowls of stewed dried fruit, washing everything down with mugs of cold milk just brought in from the spring house. Sheridan licked the white milk film from Jeremy's upper lip, then nibbled on his mouth.

"Will you share my bath, my pirate captain?"

"With pleasure, madam." He leaned forward, running a light finger along her collarbone. "Have you ever made love in a bathtub?"

"Of course not. Have you?"

He grinned. "Tried it once. I about drowned the wench and got a kink in my back. Couldn't stand up straight for a week."

"Serves you right." Tossing him a scornful look, she crossed the room and rang for the bath water.

A short time later, Jeremy returned from the room across the hall just as Sheridan stepped into a steaming tub of water, her hair piled on top of her head and secured with a ribbon. Frowning, he placed a change of clothes on the bed and removed his robe, easing himself down across from her in the large tub.

"Why the frown? Don't you relish the idea of taking a bath with me?" she asked. She partially rose from the tub, so he could straighten out his legs. When he was settled, she stretched out on top of him, her hands resting on his shoulders, her body brushing temptingly against his.

Pulling her fully against him, he took her bottom lip between his teeth and nipped it gently. "Vixen. Of course, I relish being in the tub with you." He glanced around at the tub. "Especially one this big. Gives me ideas." He smiled suggestively.

"Keep your ideas up here." She tapped him on the forehead. "I don't want you hobbling around for a week. Now, why were you frowning?"

"I was irritated because I wasted valuable time crossing the hall to fetch my things. Time I could have more appreciably spent in watching my lovely wife disrobe. I do not intend to keep separate bedrooms, my love, nor, I would hope, do you."

She picked up a bar of soap and began to wash his

chest and arms. "I would much prefer to share your bedroom, Jeremy. I have no desire to have a room of my own where I can lie in wait each night, hoping I have not displeased you and that you will share my bed. I want to lie peacefully in your arms every night, secure and wanted."

"As you command, Countess. I will never give you cause to doubt my love. You could never displease me so much that I would turn away from your bed."

He took the soap from her hands and lazily washed her back and arms, writing messages with the soapy bubbles, rewarding her with a kiss each time she deciphered a letter correctly. They were jolted out of their idle play by a sharp knock at the door.

"I'm sorry to disturb you, Sheridan," called Kyla, "but Lord Balfour and Mr. Biggs are downstairs. His lordship says he has some news about your uncle. He wishes to speak with you right away. Shall I tell them to wait?"

"Yes, please. We'll be down in a few minutes."

Jeremy kissed the tip of her nose and rinsed the soap from her back. He put his hands to her waist in gentle support as she climbed from the tub. She grabbed a towel from a nearby bench and briskly rubbed her skin. Jeremy followed suit, but never let his gaze move away from her.

Flashing him a radiant smile, Sheridan opened the wardrobe and drew out a sky blue muslin gown. By the time she had on her chemise, undercoat and stockings, Jeremy was reaching for his boots. He jerked them on as she buttoned up her gown and tied the sash in a quick, lopsided bow in back.

She snatched the ribbon from her hair, and the rich brown mass fell about her shoulders. Grabbing a hairbrush from the dresser, she attacked her hair, yanking in frustration at the tangled mass of curls.

"They'll wait. Give me the brush before you tear your hair out." Jeremy firmly took the brush from her hand and carefully worked through the tangles. In a few minutes, her hair fell in soft curls down her back.

"Thank you."

"Anytime." He opened the door with a slight bow, following as she scurried past. Covering the stairs in record time, they hurried into the great hall moments later to find the visitors sharing a pot of tea and scones with Kyla and Patrick.

"Good morning, Jeremy, Sheridan," said Lord Maclaren. "I'm sorry to disturb you so early, but Biggs has just come from the magistrate's office in Lochearnhead. One of the men who robbed your uncle was arrested late last night." He shook his head.

"He's a bit slow witted, that one. He stopped in at The Bell and was into his cups when he began bragging about robbing some rich lord a short while back. Biggs was sitting right there, and after he heard enough to be sure he was his man, he took him into custody." Reaching into his pocket, he pulled out a large ruby ring and handed it to her. "He even had this in his possession. I believe 'tis Galvin's ring. Am I correct, lass?"

Sheridan turned the ring over in her hand to stare at it. In a reflex motion, she gripped it tightly. "Yes, it was Uncle Galvin's. Grandmother and I gave it to him for Christmas when I was fourteen. He was quite pleased with our gift." Jeremy touched her shoulder, and she reached up to cover his fingers with her own.

Lord Maclaren sighed. "Just as I thought. He always wore the ring. I could no' ever remember seeing him without it." He was quiet for a moment, gazing at the floor, remembering his friend.

Sheridan turned her attention to Biggs. "Did the robber say anything about the others?"

"From what I have been able to learn from the prisoner, he was with a band of highwaymen that roam the border country. He never questioned why they came so far north. He finally remembered some talk after the robbery that indicates they had been brought up here specifically to rob and kill Lord Sinclair. Evidently, no one but the leader of the band knew the reason they came here or who hired them. The rest simply came along because he ordered them to. They committed the deed and fled back to the south."

"How is it this man came back?" asked Jeremy.

Biggs couldn't keep back his smile. "He wanted to see a young wench he met before. Poor lad, in the few weeks since he bedded her, she married a hulking blacksmith and would have nothing to do with him. He stopped at The Bell to drown his sorrows."

"Is there any way to catch these other men, particularly the captain?" asked Jeremy.

"I've sent messages to every magistrate from here to the border requesting their help," said Lord Maclaren. "The few I've heard from have promised to advise us of any leads or if the man is caught. From what I can gather, he is a slippery fellow. He's wanted for many crimes, but has never been captured. I've also spread the word around the county, so if anyone new shows up in the area, I'll know about it."

"Do you think I'm in danger from him?"

"We have no way of knowing, Sheridan, but you must no' take any chances. These men were hired for the expressed purpose of killing your uncle. Since we do no' know who hired them, we have no way of knowing if he might want you harmed, too. After all, there was an attempt on your life, so it would be a logical assumption that the same men are involved."

"She won't go anywhere without a proper guard, I can assure you." Jeremy gripped her fingers tightly, evoking a nod of agreement from her.

Lord Maclaren abruptly stood up. "I'll no' be keeping you any longer. I have much work to do, and you have much better things to do than to stand here talking to me." He grinned at Sheridan and winked at Jeremy. "You should take the lass for a walk in the sunshine, lad. The fresh air will do her good."

"My thoughts exactly," Jeremy replied. "Why don't you take the ring upstairs, love, and I'll see our guests out."

Sheridan stood up. "Thank you again, milord, and you also, Mr. Biggs. Please excuse me."

As she climbed the stairs, Sheridan was heedless of the gentlemen walking to the front door, her thoughts spinning. Why would the murderers have been hired to come all this way to kill her uncle? Who would do such a thing?

She placed the ring in her jewelry case and moved to stare out the window. Although she did not hear the door open, she sensed Jeremy's presence and leaned back against his chest when he stepped up behind her. His arms went around her, holding her tightly.

"Do you want to talk?"

"Who would have killed him, Jeremy? There just has to be another reason besides the land. The estate is not enough, but for the life of me, I can't think of anyone he ever wronged. He was a kind and loving man, too easygoing for his own good, according to my grandmother." She released a shuddering sigh. "I want to get away from this place."

"Uncle Balfour and Aunt Genna are going to Edinburgh next week. Why don't we go along? They won't mind."

"Yes, I would like to go. I have a ship coming into port in the next week or so. I had forgotten about it with the wedding and all. Will you inspect it for me?"

"Of course. Now, come, my bonny lass, let's stroll through the garden and dance in the sunshine." For the next several hours, Jeremy entertained his wife, teasing her, making her laugh, and for a little while making her forget the pain of her uncle's death.

Chapter 11

On their third day in Edinburgh, the new Mr. and Mrs. Mackenzie threaded their way through the crowded, winding streets of Old Town, pausing now and then to visit a shop that caught their fancy. They arrived at Mr. Smithson's office at the appropriate time, climbing the dingy staircase to the second floor. At Jeremy's sharp knock, the door was opened to reveal a small, wizened man staring at them over his spectacles.

"Come in, Lady Sinclair. You are as punctual as your dear uncle always was." He stepped aside, opened the door and gave Jeremy a scrutinizing appraisal when he entered the room.

"Mr. Smithson, I'd like you to meet my husband, Jeremy Mackenzie."

"I'm pleased to meet you, sir, although I was under the impression Countess Sinclair was no' married." He picked up the letter Sheridan had written him upon her arrival in Scotland and waved it absently in the air. "You did not mention it in your letter."

"Sheridan and I were married a few days ago, Mr. Smithson; however, all of her holdings are still in her name and are her property." He reached in his coat pocket and drew out the marriage contract. "I had this drawn up before we were married. I believe everything is in order, but please feel free to inspect it. I am here only in an advisory capacity to my wife."

Looking at him thoughtfully, the elderly man took the document from Jeremy and held it near the lamp to read it carefully. "You are correct, young man. Though 'tis none of my business, I'm happy to see the lady dinna' marry a man after her inheritance." Again, he studied him closely. "American?"

"Yes."

"Are any of your kin still in Scotland?"

"Lady Grenna Maclaren is my aunt."

Mr. Smithson nodded curtly, as if that settled any questions he might have concerning Jeremy. Turning briskly toward Sheridan, he handed the paper to her.

"I have posted a notice of your uncle's death, advising his creditors to get in touch with me. So far, no one has informed me of any outstanding debts. He usually paid for his purchases at the time he made them, so I doubt if there will be any."

"Thank you, Mr. Smithson. You have been very thorough. What about the vessel my uncle was having built? Is it in port?"

"Yes, m'lady, *The Alyson* is docked at Leith."

"He named it after my mother?"

"It would appear so, m'lady."

"How long will the ship be in port, Mr. Smithson?" asked Jeremy, to cover Sheridan's surprise.

"Captain Tripp said he planned to leave at the end of the week, sir. He is taking on cargo before heading to the Continent and then on to the United States.''

"I see," said Sheridan. "Then we must make a visit to the ship soon. Is there any paperwork I need to attend to, Mr. Smithson?"

"I only need a signature on this receipt, m'lady. It is merely for my records, to indicate I have given you all the proper deeds and titles to the estate." He picked up a stack of papers and handed them across the desk to her.

"Your uncle's will was very clear, m'lady. He left everything to you with the exception of twenty-five thousand pounds, which is to be disbursed to your servants. I have drawn up drafts from the bank in their names. Here is a list of the amounts."

He handed her the list, which she looked over carefully. Her uncle had left ten thousand pounds to Waverly, ten thousand to Maisie and Albert, and twenty-five hundred each to Andrew and Dora.

Sheridan smiled sadly. "They were much like family to him. I am sure they will appreciate his kindness. If you wish to send the drafts with me, I will be happy to deliver them for you. They can either cash them or put the money in the bank in Kingshouse."

"Thank you, m'lady. It will save me a trip to the country. I believe everything else is in order. The deeds have been recorded, as well as the change in title to the property."

Standing, Jeremy offered the solicitor his hand. "If you have nothing else to discuss with my wife, sir, I feel we should be going. This whole affair has taken its toll on her, and I would like to see her rest this afternoon."

Mr. Smithson gave Jeremy's hand somewhat of a shallow shake, then bowed to Sheridan. "I believe our business is concluded, m'lady. Please accept my condolences on the death of Lord Sinclair. He was a fine gentleman."

Sheridan rose to stand beside Jeremy, thankful when his arm gently slipped around her waist. The discussion had been more of an emotional strain than she had anticipated, and she again turned to Jeremy as an unspoken source of strength.

"Thank you for all the work you've done, sir. I shall contact you if I have any further questions regarding the estate."

They walked across the room to the door, leaving Mr. Smithson standing in front of his desk. Upon reaching the doorway, Sheridan stopped and turned thoughtfully toward the solicitor. "Mr. Smithson, can you think of anyone who hated my uncle, anyone who might have wished him dead?"

Startled, the gentleman almost dropped the spectacles he was polishing with a clean white handkerchief. Trembling noticeably, he replaced the eyeglasses on his nose, fumbling as he hooked the earpieces behind his ears. "Why, no, Lady Sinclair. I . . . I can think of no one who would want to harm your uncle."

Sheridan pressed the matter further. "You can't think of anyone who did business with him who might have somehow felt my uncle was less than honest or fair? Any dealings in the past that might have caused such hard feelings?"

Regaining his composure, the elderly man replied, "No, m'lady. Lord Sinclair was held in the highest regard by all those he dealt with. Surely, you are aware of his reputation and what kind of man he was."

"Of course, I am, sir. I am simply trying to determine if there is any reason someone might have wanted my uncle dead."

"It was my understanding it was a simple robbery. Unfortunately, it happens often that the highwaymen kill those they rob, many times brutalizing their victims before they actually kill them. 'Tis only fortunate, m'lady, you were no' already in the country and visiting your uncle. I would hate to think what those villains would have done to a fair lass like you.''

Jeremy pressed his arm gently against Sheridan's side in warning, hoping she sensed something was amiss, as he did.

Taking his cue, she replied with a brilliant smile, ''Yes, of course, I'm sure you're right, Mr. Smithson. I'm certain it was just a case of robbery. I simply find it hard to account for so senseless a death and fear my imagination runs away from me at times. Thank you again for your assistance.''

They took their leave from the lawyer and made their way back down the murky staircase, thankful when they stepped out into the light of the street. The air was filled with a variety of smells coming from the various shops around them. The fragrance of freshly baked bread mingled with the pungent aroma of fish from the North Sea, and sweet bouquets of fresh flowers from a walking street vendor's basket rivaled the foul-smelling garbage strewn along the streets and alleyways.

Jeremy purchased a nosegay of roses for his lady, presenting it to her with such a flourish that the other less fortunate women around them stopped their work and gaped at the young couple.

''Ye must be keepin' him happy, lass,'' called a fishwife.

Jeremy smiled at the woman, bowing slightly in agreement with her observation, and Sheridan colored mildly.

''There ain't a man alive who'd no' be happy with her about,'' said a nearby baker, smiling at Sheridan with an appreciative eye.

''Lookin' to take his place, are ye?'' said the fishwife with a laugh. ''Ye'd have to take off ten years and lose a stone or two to give that handsome lad a run for his money.''

Sheridan laughed and tipped up her chin to look at her husband, an action that was promptly rewarded by a very public and lingering kiss amid the cheers of those around them.

When Jeremy straightened, she lowered her eyes to the ground, her color deepening furiously. "Why did you do that?" she gasped.

He tucked his finger beneath her chin and gently lifted it, forcing her to look at the wicked gleam in his eye. "I'm just a crass American, my dear. I simply wanted to make sure every man around here knows you belong to me. Now come, love. We've given them enough to talk about for today."

Taking her arm gently, he smiled at the onlookers, giving the fishwife a wink, and escorted his still blushing wife down the street.

Before turning the corner, Sheridan glanced up at Mr. Smithson's window to find him watching them. After they stepped from his view, she said, "I have the impression Mr. Smithson knows something about Uncle Galvin's death. Did you notice how nervous he became when I questioned him?"

"Indeed, I did. I thought he was going to have some kind of fit right then. He recovered himself quickly enough. I'm given to believe he was warning you in a thinly disguised manner. That old man knows more than he is letting on, and I intend to see what we can find out."

"Will you have Biggs look into it?"

"Yes, he seems efficient. It will be interesting to learn with whom Smithson has dealings. In the meantime, my love, we must be especially careful of your safety, and from now on, you must keep your questions very low-key."

"I thought I was being low-key today."

"You did well enough." He guided her around a crumbled part of the uneven cobblestone walk. "We must use the utmost caution, since your uncle's enemies seem to be turning up in the most unlikely places."

"I can't imagine Uncle Galvin having anything to do with something illegal. He was the most honest man I've ever known."

"Unquestionably. Lord Maclaren has said the same thing many times. But what if he somehow stumbled onto someone else's illegal intentions, or perhaps the crime itself?" Jeremy glanced down, his gaze meeting hers as she looked up.

"Surely, he would have gone to the magistrate immediately."

"Perhaps, unless he was uncertain of all his facts and decided to wait until further evidence turned up or might be delivered to him. From what you've told me, he doesn't strike me as a man who would accuse someone unjustly."

"No," said Sheridan with a frown. "He would go to great lengths to try to prove he was wrong before he would run the risk of hurting someone, especially if it was a friend."

He nodded grimly. "Or if such person were an employee, possibly a solicitor."

"Somehow I can't imagine Mr. Smithson having someone killed. I suppose because he's such a shriveled-up little man, I simply can't fathom him having the courage to do such a thing."

"My feelings run the same, and I've learned over the years to trust my gut instincts—pardon my language, madam. However, there is no question in my mind that he is involved in some way." They paused at the edge of the street, waiting for an approaching carriage to pass by. "Well, let's head back to the townhouse and rest up for the evening."

They stepped across the street to where two of Lord Maclaren's men waited for them in the carriage. Jeremy helped his bride inside the coach and gave instructions to the driver before seating himself comfortably beside her.

"Are you certain you won't come to the ball tonight? It will be a meddlesome bore without having you there."

"I simply can't go, Jeremy. I've thought it through and know I just couldn't handle it. This may not be London, but people still frown if you observe a period of mourning for too short a time. I know I've given up black, but I've not given up mourning for my uncle, and to attend a ball would be too disrespectful. You go ahead and be certain to extend my best wishes to the Thortons. The viscount assured me last evening at dinner he would not feel it amiss if I failed to attend."

"Very well, love. I'll go with my aunt and uncle, but will leave as soon as I possibly can and still maintain an acceptable level of courtesy." His eyes glittered devilishly. "I shall sneak back to my uncle's balcony and dance with you to my heart's content."

He slid his arm around her shoulders and pulled her close to him on the seat. Leaning her head back against his arm, she parted her lips slightly as his mouth lowered to hers. "Or better yet, I'll take you to the bedroom, open the windows to hear the music and twirl you around in that delightfully meager thing you call a nightshift."

" 'Tis a nightshift."

"I'm not complaining."

"Good, now give me a kiss."

Being a dutiful husband, Jeremy complied and found riding in a closed carriage with his wife a rather pleasant way to travel.

In the evening, Sheridan sat on the bed, watching her

husband as he finished dressing. Her eyes flitted longingly to the lovely deep rose-pink ball gown Kyla had persuaded her to bring with them to Edinburgh.

"Won't you come, love?" Jeremy kissed her forehead tenderly. "I have a yearning to see you dressed in your finery. We could leave anytime you wish."

She shook her head. "No, 'tis best I stay here, but hurry back as soon as you can. As for my finery, well, what I have on will have to do. It would be unkind to rumple my rose gown by merely wearing it around here. It would make a great deal of extra work for Dora to press it again."

Jeremy appraised her slowly. The dark burgundy of her gown lent a deeper color to her eyes, turning them almost violet. The neckline was fairly modest, so she had put aside her neckerchief, leaving a pleasant swell of bosom for his appreciation.

His gaze wandered on down to her waist, and he found himself wondering if she would still have such a tiny waist after bearing his children. A tender smile touched his face at the thought—his children. What a pleasant ring those words had! He raised his eyes to find her watching him wistfully.

"Your gown is more than satisfactory, my love. Indeed, it only serves to enchance your beauty." He kissed her sweetly. "I shall return as soon as I possibly can," he said, brushing her lips with his fingertips.

"Don't have such a good time that you forget about me. Mind who you dance with, Jeremy Mackenzie."

"Only matrons and dowagers, I promise. Nice tottering old ladies."

She accompanied him downstairs, where he joined Lord and Lady Maclaren and left for the party along with Patrick and Kyla. Since the event was being held next door, the group walked the short distance.

Sheridan drifted into the library and searched the

shelves until she found something she hoped would take her mind off her loneliness. Even the servants had gone off to their various tasks, leaving her entirely by herself. The book was relaxing but not engrossing, and it was not long before it fell to the floor when she dozed off to sleep.

Cameron Macveagh stood near the doorway of the viscount's townhouse, listening absently to the rambling of one of Edinburgh's more prominent citizens. He noted every person who came through the entry, his gaze searching for one young lady in particular.

The butler had announced their arrival, and the Maclarens and their guests were promptly greeted by their host. "Welcome, Balfour, Lady Maclaren. Mr. Mackenzie, it would appear your wife held to her decision no' to come?"

"Yes, my lord. Sheridan believes it would be disrespectful to her uncle to appear socially so soon after the tragedy."

Cameron's face contorted with rage at the words he had overheard. He fought to control himself while he watched Jeremy and the rest of his party slowly begin to circulate about the room.

"Cameron, what is amiss?" asked Melissa, taking his arm and leading him toward the open doors of the terrace. "Calm yourself, my dear. You look as if you could kill someone."

He took great gulps of the fresh evening air after they walked onto the terrace, slowing bringing his wrath in check. "Aye, I'd like to kill him," he rasped. "I'd like to carve him up inch by inch."

"Ah, Mackenzie must have arrived." She peeked back into the ballroom, spotting Jeremy in a crowd of people. With a little purr of appreciation, she turned back to Cameron. "Do no' carve him up, dear, he's much too handsome.'' She craned her neck and looked back into the room. ''I do no' see Sheridan? Dinna' she come?''

Cameron shook his head. ''Nay, she's taking her mourning to heart. She stayed behind.'' He looked down at Melissa, his eyes full of pain. Suddenly, the hurt was replaced by pure venom. He looked out across the lantern-lit gardens, his stance rigid, his fingers clenched. ''She has married him. She betrayed me just as her mother did.''

''But, Cam, she never gave you reason to think she loved you. She never encouraged you the way her mother did.''

''No! She did encourage me. The day I took her away from the ruins, she lay in my arms willingly. She welcomed my kisses and my touch.''

He turned to his friend, and she glimpsed a spark of madness in him. She feared he would indeed go insane if he were rejected again.

With a sigh, she took his hand in hers. ''We'll go on with the plan, dear. It might even be simpler without her here. When I give you the sign, you make your way over to the Maclaren townhouse. No doubt, she will stroll out onto the terrace eventually. The music will draw her. Leave the rest up to me. And remember, be sweet and persuasive. She's no' the kind of woman to respond to force or anger.''

Jeremy made his rounds throughout the evening, greeting those he had already met during the stay and making acquaintances of many others at the introduction of his uncle. As he had promised, he danced only with the older married ladies or the dowagers.

Thinking he had been in attendance long enough, he made his way in the direction of the terrace to take his leave and slip back to his bride. Moments before reaching the doorway, Melissa stepped into his path and placed a lightly restraining hand upon his arm.

"Mr. Mackenzie, you have done me a great disservice this evening."

"How so, m'lady?"

"You have graciously danced with every widow and married woman here but me. Am I so unattractive, sir, that you would snub me in this way?"

His gaze flicked over her, from the pile of flaming curls to the soft lavender of her gown, a gown cut so provocatively, he wondered absently what kept it in place. When his gaze came back to her face, he found her lips puckered in a pout, her eyes revealing a look of hurt.

"The snub was entirely unintentional, m'lady. I simply made a promise to my wife that I would dance only with the elderly ladies this evening, and you hardly fall into such a category."

She gave a musical laugh and tucked her arm through his. "I can understand Sheridan's jealousy. If I were married, or a partner in some way to a man such as yourself, I'd be jealous, too. But whether the slight was intentional or no', you still must make amends by dancing with me, sir."

At Jeremy's hesitation, she said, "Mr. Mackenzie, I am a woman who knows what she wants, and right now I want to dance with you. I am no' used to having my wishes denied, sir. If you seek to insult me further, I will make such a scene that you will no' be able to show your face around here for years."

He slid his arm around her waist and took her hand in his free one, stepping into line with the other dancers. With a forced smile, he tolerated her flirtatious looks.

"You are a marvelous dancer, Mr. Mackenzie. I thought Americans were practically barbarians and certainly no' so refined. Of course, your aunt would no' let you be remiss in the social graces."

The smile faded, and with effort, Jeremy kept his annoyance from being obvious. "My parents instructed me in the social graces, m'lady. They are not so different in America as they are here. You forget, many Americans come from some of the finest families in England and Scotland. Just because they chose to settle a rugged wilderness does not mean they lack culture. While it is true that on the frontier life is hard and not as luxurious as you might wish, the more settled regions are as civilized as England or Scotland."

She chuckled. "I'm no' sure if you are paying your country a compliment, sir. There are parts of Scotland that are very uncivilized."

"Quite true." Jeremy wondered what his barbarian mother would think of Lady Grant's lack of subtlety. Her open flirtation had not been missed by those around them, and Jeremy groaned inwardly at the speculative glances and whispers.

The song ended, and Jeremy abruptly dropped his arm from her waist, released her hand and took a step backward. "There, m'lady, you have had your chance. Now, if you will excuse me, I intend to spend the rest of the evening with my wife."

"I shall accompany you for a brief walk through the garden, Jeremy. Dancing with you has left me breathless."

She slipped her arm through his before he could protest. He could not escape without attracting further attention, so with a grim expression on his face, he guided the lady toward the terrace doors. He caught Patrick's eye, and with a barely discernible movement of his head, asked him to follow as they stepped out into the cool, evening air.

As Melissa predicted, the music had drawn Sheridan out onto the terrace. The gate between the two estates squeaked on its hinges, and Sheridan raced down the steps.

"Jeremy," she cried softly. "I thought you'd never come."

"Very touching, my dear. Unfortunately, 'tis no' your beloved husband," said Cameron. "The last time I saw him, he was renewing his acquaintance with Melissa. They were dancing quite well together, and he seemed to be enjoying himself immensely."

Sheridan came to a sudden halt a few feet away from her unwelcome guest. She started to turn away, but he reached out quickly and gripped both of her arms firmly.

"What are you doing here? Jeremy will be along any minute, and he will be furious to find you here."

Remembering Melissa's words of admonition, Cameron relaxed his grip on her arms. Placing a hand gently on her back, he nudged her toward the upper portion of the terrace.

"I dinna' come to make you or your American angry, love. I simply came to see you, to check on your welfare and to feast upon your beauty for a few moments. I was very disappointed to learn of your marriage, Sheridan, and am concerned for your happiness. I dunna' believe Mackenzie will be a good husband to you.

"I had hoped to spend some time with you this evening at the ball, but I see that was a foolish thought. If you had been at the party, Mackenzie would probably have hovered nearby. If he had no' been in constant attendance, then you would have only been shamed by his fliration with Melissa." He looked at her kindly. " 'Tis good you were no' there after all. They are quite the talk of the party."

She stepped away from him to the edge of the terrace, stopping when she reached the stone ledge surrounding it. He moved behind her but did not touch her. "So you came rushing over to make sure I heard about their supposed flirtation? I doubt if one even exists.''

He slid his arms about her and pulled her back against his chest. She tried to jerk away from him, but he held her fast, planting tiny kisses along the nape of her neck and nuzzling her ear.

''Ach, lass, it would seem you dunna' know the kind of man he really is. He and Melissa left the dance floor together. At this moment, he is in the garden with her, applying his talents at seduction.''

Sheridan stood rigid, repulsed by his touch. She fought hard to keep from crying out, suspecting that if Jeremy heard her, he might challenge Macveagh to a duel. ''If anyone is attempting seduction, it would be Melissa. She practically mauled him in my own living room. Now take your hands off me, Macveagh.''

Instead of complying with her terse command, he pulled her further back into the shadows. She struggled against him, fearful of what he intended.

''Be still, Sheridan. I will no' hurt you. Look and listen, sweet. See how faithful your American is to you.''

It took a moment to realize the reason he had drawn her back into the darkness. Down in the garden, across the fence but easily viewed from the higher terrace, were Jeremy and Melissa.

Jeremy moved his arm, effectively releasing it from Melissa' grasp. Turning to face her and take his leave, he was startled when she took a step forward and pressed her body against his.

''Jeremy,'' she cried, ''I want to feel your arms around me again and feel your lips against mine.'' She grabbed his hand and pulled it up to her breast. ''I'm a woman who knows how to please a man, Jeremy, and I ache for your touch. Make love to me again. Take me here, like before in the woods.''

Standing on tiptoe, she tried to pull his head down to her kiss, but he firmly resisted her. Jerking his hand away from her bosom as if it had touched a hot iron, he seized her other hand in a viselike grip and removed it from behind his neck. He glanced to the Maclaren terrace and was visibly relieved when he did not see Sheridan there. He took a step backward and glared at Melissa in the light of a nearby lamp.

"I do not know what you're about, madam," he said in a low, angry tone, "but I want no part of you this night or any other night. I have a wife who pleases me above all others, and I will do nothing to hurt her or my marriage. I suggest you return to the ballroom as quickly as possible. There might be those about who would happily fill your needs this night, but I'm not one of them.''

"How dare you insult me? I shall tear my gown and say you attacked me. Where will you be then, Mr. Jeremy Mackenzie?''

"I have no doubts most people here would think you got what you asked for. Your open flirtation during our dance was not missed by those around us, madam. In any event, there are witnesses almost upon us who would see that your drama would be staged by you alone. Look down the path. Others have strolled out to enjoy the evening air, also.''

A small group of guests, including Patrick and Kyla, were making their way toward them, admiring the gardens, but easily within range to see that Jeremy was standing several feet away from her, his hands down at his sides. When he was certain the others were watching, he turned swiftly and made his way to the garden gate.

Sheridan, who had heard only Melissa's words, turned to the man hovering behind her. "Get out of here before I call every servant on the place to throw you out.'' Her voice shook with emotion. "I never want to see you again, Cameron Macveagh. Leave me alone.''

Cameron decided a confrontation with Jeremy at this point wouldn't help his cause and quickly faded into the darkness, going through the doorway just as Jeremy came through the gate. He moved quickly down the hall and let himself out the front door, unseen by anyone.

Jeremy ran up the steps, anxious to be with Sheridan, but he stopped short when he saw her angry face.

"I will speak with you in private," she said, her voice low and quivering with anger. Avoiding his hand when he reached out to her, Sheridan spun around and ran up the stairs.

Jeremy muttered an oath under his breath and followed after her, growing angrier with each step. He slammed the bedroom door behind them as Sheridan whirled around to face him.

"How dare you parade your harlot before me! Did you think I wouldn't overhear or see you in the garden with her?''

"Sheridan—''

"Don't you growl at me, Jeremy Mackenzie. I'll not be made a fool of. Wasn't it enough to make love to her? Did you have to dance with her and stroll in the garden, flaunting your affair in front of me and half of Edinburgh?''

"Sheridan, I have never made love to that woman.''

"No, I don't suppose you would call it love. Lust is the more appropriate word. Did you go to her the day we almost made love in the woods? Did it make it easier to send me away because you had someone else to take my place? Someone who knew how to please a man?''

Jeremy paced across the room, stopped briefly in front of the fireplace, then moved back to stand in front of her. "Sheridan, I have never touched that woman."

"You were touching her tonight."

"It was her doing, not mine." Jeremy released a sigh. "Sheridan, why won't you believe me? You know I can't stand her. Do you trust me so little as to believe I would go to her when I could have had you?"

She turned away from his penetrating gaze, hurt and confusion replacing her anger. "I . . . I don't know. She's so beautiful and so . . . so experienced." She took a shaky breath and rushed on, feeling childish but unable to stop herself. "You promised you would only dance with the matrons tonight, yet you danced with her, and from what I am told, enjoyed yourself immensely."

"She threatened to make a scene if I didn't dance with her." His eyes narrowed, his brow creasing into a deeper frown. "Whoever told you I enjoyed it is a liar. Who was here?"

"Macveagh," she said softly.

"You must repeat yourself, madam. I don't believe I heard you correctly."

Sheridan raised her head and looked at him, the cold steel of his voice piercing her heart. "Macveagh told me."

Jeremy's face flushed, and a muscle tightened in his jaw as he clenched his teeth in an effort to control his anger. "I left instructions with the servants that he was not to be admitted to this house. Did you override my directions?"

"No, he came through the gate from the Thorntons', just as you did."

"And you welcomed him."

"No, of course not."

"Why didn't you call the servants? Surely, they could have forced him to leave."

"There was no need. There really wasn't time. He

was only here for a few minutes.''

"Time enough for a few stolen kisses, perhaps? For a secret caress or two in the darkness?''

"Of course not!''

He slammed the table with his fist, rattling the porcelain lamp. "Or was there only enough time to spy on me?'' he cried, his temper flaring. "How was it I did not see you on the terrace, wife? Were you lurking in the shadows with your lover? Did you restrain your passions simply to watch Melissa play out her little charade?''

"Jeremy, you know it wasn't like that. You know I detest him.''

"Yet you didn't even call for help.''

"I didn't want to make a scene. I was afraid you two would fight if you found him here. He . . . he didn't even try to kiss me.'' She turned away again, blushing slightly.

"I don't believe you. He can't keep his hands off of you whenever you're near. Was he simply content to caress you? The shadows on the terrace aren't too deep. You must have been very close to him for me not to see either of you.''

He stepped up behind her and spoke quietly, his voice flat and grim. "Did he run his hands over you, Sheridan? Did he touch you where only I have the right? Did he nibble at your delicious neck and whisper lies in your lovely ear?''

Sheridan looked over her shoulder at him, her eyes wide with surprise because his words so closely resembled what had happened. "N—no,'' she stammered.

Jeremy sighed, running his fingers through his hair. He moved across the room to stop in front of the door. His hand on the doorknob, he looked back at Sheridan, pain clearly etched on his face. "Am I to believe you?"

"Yes." She glanced at his hand as he turned the knob, sick with the fear that he might actually leave.

"Because I trust you?"

"Yes," she whispered, tears filling her eyes and spilling over the brim.

"Trust is a two-way bridge, Sheridan," he said, his voice empty.

"Jeremy, don't go," she whispered.

"I need time to think."

"Will you come back?"

The haunting pain in his eyes tore at her heart. "I don't know."

Jeremy left the townhouse, walking the streets of Edinburgh until the wee hours of the morning. Drained and feeling lifeless, he turned back to the townhouse. He entered the garden through a small gate near the front of the house. Finding a bench near the back door, he sat down, one leg resting on the bench, his arm thrown across his bent knee.

He shook his head sadly, remembering his harsh words and accusations. He had accused her of being unfaithful, yet they hadn't been apart long enough since their marriage for any secret meetings with Macveagh, and she had been a virgin when they married.

Now that the heat of anger had passed, he knew she had not welcomed Macveagh nor his advances. His mind unfurled the image of her stricken face when he had returned from Loch Maree. No, there was no way Macveagh was her lover—unless he forced her. The thought struck him cold. Would she give him her body out of fear? Did he have some hold over her, something no one else knew anything about?

Had Macveagh truly been there for only a few minutes, or had he met her secretly in the garden earlier in the evening? Had he done more than just touch her?

Jeremy slammed the bench with his fist, wishing the man were around to be the recipient of his frustrations, and cursing him for planting seeds of suspicion in his mind.

He entered the house quietly and made his way to their bedroom. As he undressed, he watched Sheridan toss fitfully in her sleep. Her eyes were swollen from crying, and the bedclothes were rumpled. He smoothed the sheet of his side of the bed and crawled in beside her. The instant his cool body touched hers, she turned into his arms.

"Oh, Jeremy," she whispered sleepily, clinging to him. "I made such a muddle of things."

"No more than I." He kissed her forehead and held her close. "Sher, there's nothing between Melissa Grant and me. I've not been with another woman since I met you."

"I know." She buried her head against his neck, muffling her words. "I was jealous. She's so worldly, so experienced. I know so little about pleasing you. Sometimes I feel so inept."

"You aren't inept," he crooned. "You please me very much, more than any woman ever has." He leaned back so he could look down at her face. "I'm glad you're jealous."

"You are?" Her swollen eyes opened a fraction wider.

"Yes, because it shows you care for me, at least a little."

"More than a little." She paused and searched his face in the light before dawn. "I'm beginning to realize how much I care. Jeremy, I don't want Macveagh. I hate it when he touches me. It's only your touch I want, only you I need."

She drew his head down for her kiss. Her heart tried to speak to him through that kiss and tell him the secrets locked inside, the secrets she could not yet believe, nor give voice to.

Very gently, he caressed and kissed, tenderly making love to his wife and showing her how much she pleased him. But he couldn't hear her heart's song. A tiny suspicion blocked out its message, an ugly sore that would be slow to heal. He told himself it was only a matter of wording, but some devil in his mind would not let it pass. She had not actually said Macveagh was *not* her lover.

Chapter 12

Although Sheridan and Jeremy ate breakfast late the next morning, they did so alone since Lord and Lady Maclaren rested from the previous night's festivities. Patrick and Kyla had just joined them when the butler stepped up beside Jeremy's chair.

"I beg your pardon, Mr. Mackenzie, but there is a gentleman by the name of Biggs here to see ye, sir. Shall I have him wait in the drawin' room?"

"No, please send him in here. I'm anxious to hear what he has to say."

Moments later, the tall, burly man entered the dining room. With quiet confidence, he quickly scanned the room, pausing to gaze at Sheridan for a long moment before speaking to Jeremy.

"Thank you for seeing me, Mr. Mackenzie. I'm sorry to disturb your breakfast."

"No problem. Will you join us?"

"No, thank you, milord."

"What do you have for us? You may speak freely."

"The bird has flown, sir. I went to his office shortly after we talked yesterday afternoon, but it was locked up. I found the landlord and was advised Smithson had closed his office and gone to the Continent. He turned over his clients to another solicitor down the street, saying he had urgent business in France. I checked at his townhouse and found it for sale. The agent said much the same thing. He had urgent business on the Continent and instructed him to sell the house and everything in it. He left no address where he could be reached, advising he would contact the agent in a few months regarding the sale of his home."

"Thank you, Biggs. It would appear we frightened Mr. Smithson even more than I realized. I didn't think he would flee so soon. Tell me, is it possible to find out who his other clients were? Possibly there is a connection somewhere."

'I can try, sir, but these legal-types are pretty tight-lipped about who they represent."

"True. Do you have any contacts in France who might be able to help us?"

"I'm acquainted with some who might give us assistance."

"Very well. Were you able to find out on which ship he sailed?"

"Yes, sir. I have the record of the ship and its destination."

"You know your job well, Biggs. You do what you can with your contacts. I also have some acquaintances in France who might be able to help us. I am curious to find out why the little man ran so quickly. Check in with me whenever you have anything. If we aren't here, send word to us at Sinclair Castle."

"Aye, sir, that I will. Good day to ye, sir, ladies." He

nodded to Patrick and the women and walked to the doorway with Jeremy, advising him of the ship's name and destination.

Jeremy and Sheridan had planned a visit to her ship that day, but the excursion was delayed for a few minutes while Jeremy dashed off a letter to the Marquis de Lafayette. He requested help in finding Smithson, as well as permission to visit his old friend in Paris. The letter was dispatched by messenger before Jeremy and Sheridan took his uncle's phaeton and made the journey to Leith to inspect her new vessel. Jeremy drove the team with ease, and both occupants of the open carriage enjoyed the fresh air and sunshine.

Having sent word of their plans to Capt. Tripp the previous day, they were not surprised when the man walked briskly down the gangplank to meet them.

"It is an honor to meet you, Lady Sinclair," he said with a bow. "And you as well, Mr. Mackenzie," he added, extending his hand.

"May we come aboard, Capt. Tripp? My husband is also a seaman, and I am anxious to have his opinion of my new ship."

"Permission granted happily, m'lady." He stepped aside to allow them to walk up the ramp before him.

The flurry of activity aboard the vessel came to an abrupt halt as every man stopped to gaze at the beautiful woman. Every one of them envied the man who took her arm protectively as she stepped aboard. Few of these ruddy sailors had ever seen such a lady up close and were stunned by the sight. Her bright blue silk gown highlighted her gentle curves. Resting atop a cluster of curls, her white bonnet only served to draw the viewer's gaze back to her face and her beautiful sapphire eyes.

One by one, the men glanced at the stern expression

of the man accompanying her and drifted back to the job at hand. Most of those on board were experienced sailors, and one look told them this gentleman was very much at home aboard ship. There was no doubt in their minds that he commanded his own vessel, nor would he tolerate any hint of disrespect for his lady.

The visitors moved about the ship, and at Jeremy's request, Capt. Tripp explained the various items that Sheridan found interesting. They moved from bow to stern as the captain recited the ship's merits to its new owner. All the while, Jeremy carefully noted the workmanship of the vessel and the manner in which it was being maintained.

At last, they retired to the captain's quarters for a cup of tea. "Well, Mr. Mackenzie, what do you think of the vessel?" asked Capt. Tripp.

Jeremy smiled over his teacup at the captain. "She is a fine vessel, a quality example of British craftsmanship. No better than our own American craftsmanship, to be sure, but on equal footing nonetheless."

The captain was having a difficult time keeping his eyes off Sheridan and mentally shook himself as he turned again to Jeremy, noting the displeasure in the man's eyes.

"Do you find everything else in order, sir? Do you feel she is being well maintained?"

"Aye, Captain, it would appear things are in good hands. You have a good reputation here in the harbor, and from all appearances, it is justified."

"I thank you, sir."

"Where is your destination when you depart Leith, Captain?" asked Sheridan quietly.

The man's blood warmed at the softness of her voice, and he answered with equal softness, his eyes raking over her boldly when Jeremy turned to pour himself another cup of tea.

"We sail first to London, m'lady, to deliver approximately a third of our goods. There we will take on further cargo and head for the Continent, then on to America with New York as our final destination on this particular journey. We will return with our holds full of lumber, furs, and anything else the new country has to offer. I daresay, we shall make a tidy profit for you on the journey."

Sheridan blushed under the captain's heated gaze, much to his delight, until he noticed the scowl on Jeremy's face. Realizing he had tread on thin ice, the captain turned swiftly to his desk and brought forth a ledger.

"Perhaps you would like to see the ship's manifest, m'lady."

"Thank you, Capt. Tripp," she answered coolly. Jeremy moved to stand behind her chair as they both looked over the list of cargo.

"It would seem everything is in order. Do you agree, Jeremy?"

"It's a good cargo and should bring a good profit. I find no fault in that area, Captain."

There was no doubt in the captain's mind in what area Jeremy did find fault, and the man suddenly became very uncomfortable. He broke away from Jeremy's steady gaze and rose swiftly to his feet. "If you have no further questions, or need of me, m'lady, I should see to the running of my ship. Please feel free to look about as much as you like."

"Thank you, sir," said Jeremy. "By the way, do you have a full crew? It appears there aren't as many men aboard as there should be."

"Aye, you have a captain's eye, sir. I am short-handed. I plan to hire four or five more lads in the next few days."

"Very well. I'm certain you will take great care with

the vessel. I believe we will be going now, unless you have anything further you wish to ask, Sheridan.''

"No, I believe all my concerns have been satisfied. Thank you for your time, Captain. When do you leave?''

"We should be shipping out within the week, m'lady.''

"Then I wish you a safe journey, sir.''

"Thank you, m'lady.'' He followed them up the stairs to the deck, where he stood watching while they left the ship and climbed into the phaeton. "I shall find a way for us to meet again, fair lady, without your over-protective husband around,'' he whispered to himself.

Jeremy clucked to the horses, slapping their backs gently with the reins, urging them to move into the flow of traffic along the waterfront.

"What did you think of Capt. Tripp?'' asked Sheridan.

"He comes highly recommended; however, I distinctly felt we couldn't trust him. I can't pinpoint exactly what it is, but there is something in his manner that bothers me. I certainly didn't like the way he looked at you, but I guess I'll have to get used to men leering at my beautiful wife.''

"He was rather bold, wasn't he.'' She shifted her weight toward him on the seat, absently resting her hand upon his thigh. "I agree something is amiss. I don't know what it is either, but something about him bothers me, and it's not just the way he looks at me.''

Jeremy glanced down at her hand and smiled to himself. He shifted his weight in the seat so her shoulder rested against his arm. His thoughts briefly strayed to other more pleasant matters before returning to the problem at hand. "I'll have Biggs check him out, too. It might be wise to have someone keep him under close scrutiny for a while.'' They drove back to the townhouse, stopping for a short time to watch workmen constructing other new homes in the area.

After lunch, Jeremy walked out to the waiting carriage with Sheridan. ''Enjoy your shopping spree, love, and pray don't spend all of your money.''

''I shan't be too extravagant. Kyla will be my watchdog.'' Her friend laughed and shook her head, indicating she had no say in the matter. ''What are your plans for the afternoon?''

''Patrick and I are going back down to the port. Our own vessel should be arriving this afternoon. I don't know when we'll return, probably after you.'' He kissed her briefly and helped her into the coach. He stepped back as the carriage and the two outriders pulled away, then gave her a jaunty wave.

''You didn't tell her you were going to see Macveagh?'' asked Patrick.

Jeremy turned to his friend, all traces of merriment gone. ''No, I saw no need to worry her. I don't intend to challenge the man to a duel, although I will if it comes down to it. I want this settled.''

''Do you want me to come with you?''

''No, I have to handle this one on my own.''

A short time later, Jeremy was shown into the Macveagh drawing room. He was not pleased to find Melissa there.

''Why, Mr. Mackenzie, have you come to apologize for your rudeness last evening?''

''No, madam, I have not.'' Jeremy's face was stern, and he did not try to hide his dislike of the lady. He did not even bother to take her hand as she held it out to him. ''I have come to discuss a very grave matter with Macveagh. I wish to speak with him in private.''

''Well, I see your manners have not improved since

last night. Cameron is in his study. No doubt he will talk
with you there.'' She rose and walked across the room
to the open terrace doors. "I believe I'll take my little
Moppsie for a walk. His company is so much more
pleasant than yours.'' She called her little dog to her,
and with a haughty toss of her head, strolled out into
the garden.

"Lord Macveagh will see ye in the library, Mr.
Mackenzie.'' The butler turned crisply on his heel to
lead Jeremy down the hall, disapproval evident in his
every movement.

"So, we finally meet,'' said Macveagh, when Jeremy
stepped into the library. "I had thought you would
come sooner, Mackenzie.''

"I have often considered calling your hand. I only
refrained out of respect for Sheridan and the desire not
to cause her further distress.''

Jeremy stepped in front of the desk, placing one hand
on a stack of books resting there, and looked Macveagh
straight in the eye. "You went too far with last night's
fiasco. Much too far. Sheridan is my wife. She belongs
to me and me alone. I will not tolerate you bothering her
again.''

Macveagh slowly crossed the room and picked up a
decanter of brandy. He poured a small amount into a
glass and offered it to Jeremy, who shook his head
resolutely. Macveagh took a sip and savored the taste in
his mouth, all the while watching Jeremy out of the
corner of his eye. At last he turned to face him, the
drink in his hand.

"You expect me to walk away, to simply turn her
over to you without fighting for her?''

"I do. Sheridan is a married woman, a woman of
integrity and honor. She could not forsake her marriage
vows for an illicit affair.''

"I wanted to marry her, not make her my mistress!" Anger turned Macveagh's gray eyes to molten steel. "I offered her marriage."

"No, you declared she would be your wife," Jeremy said quietly. "You threatened and frightened her. She would never come to you, Macveagh, even if she weren't already married."

A look of surprise passed over Macveagh's face. "I frightened her?"

"Aye, and last night's little drama hurt her."

Macveagh cocked his head to one side, his expression changing to one of bewilderment. "I do no' want to hurt her. I love her."

"Then leave her alone. If you truly care for her, you will not want to bring her disgrace. Doing so would only cause her more hurt."

Macveagh rubbed his forehead, obviously in pain. Jeremy frowned, a little unnerved by the other man's fluctuating emotions.

"I want your word that you will not come near Sheridan again." He spoke quietly, but with commanding authority.

Macveagh dropped his hand and looked him in the eye. "Surely, even you must realize our paths will cross. Do you expect me to be so uncivil as no' to speak with her when we meet?"

"I want your word that you will not seek to be alone with her, nor will you touch her except in the most formal of greetings."

Near panic flickered over Macveagh's face.

"I want your promise, Macveagh."

The Scot ran his finger around the rim of the glass, staring into the amber liquid, a faraway look in his eye. "I take it you intend to take your bride back to America."

"Eventually, but our future is not your concern, Macveagh."

"To no' talk to her or touch her," the troubled man murmured. He sighed and rubbed his forehead once again. "To only admire her from afar—nay, 'tis too much to ask." He looked back up at Jeremy.

"But I do no' want to hurt her. I'll have to remove myself from temptation's path, Mackenzie. I have an estate on the North Coast. 'Tis time for a long visit to that ruggedly beautiful place." From his expression, Jeremy could see his mind drifted. "I could paint something for her . . . ." Macveagh shook his head slightly and focused his eyes on Jeremy.

"I love Sheridan as much as you, perhaps more. I have always loved her, you see. I can no' give you my word that I would no' be driven to try to see her. Send word to me when you leave for America. I'll stay away from Loch Earn until then."

Jeremy measured the man carefully. He wasn't sure if he believed him. "Do I have your word as a gentleman that you will stay away?"

"Aye. 'Tis the only way to keep the devils at bay." He laughed a mirthless, bitter laugh. "You have my word I will stay away until you leave the country." His expression changed then, mellowing into a sad, haunting smile, his gaze fixed on some distant point beyond Jeremy's shoulder. "I have loved her for so long, so very long. I only want her to be happy. There is but one thing I would ask. Tell her I will always love her. I'll always want her for my bride. I'll wait until it's my time." He turned away, seeming to forget Jeremy's presence, and pressed a small square on the ornate mahogany wall. A panel in front of him slid to the side.

Seeing the beautiful picture in front of him, Jeremy took a step forward before he could stop himself. A pain-wracked moment passed before he realized the portrait wasn't of Sheridan. So much the same, yet different; the hair was a little too dark and the smile a little more petulant, the womanly curves beneath the thin gown a little fuller. Had Sheridan's mother really posed so seductively, or was the painting a product of Macveagh's tortured mind?

Macveagh stared at the picture, continuing to speak softly. "I have been so patient. So very patient. You are his, yet you are mine. You turn to him, but your eyes search for me. You smile for him, but your laughter is for me. You go to him, but your longing, ah, your longing is for me. You are his, but he shall not live forever. When he is gone, I'll still be waiting. And then, then you will be mine, only mine."

Unnoticed, Jeremy moved to the door and left the room quietly. He was even more concerned than before he came. Macveagh was besotted to the point of madness. How could he trust the word of a madman?

He sent a message to Biggs to have someone follow Macveagh as well, breathing easier two days later when the detective reported that his lordship was on his way to the North Coast, and from all indications, planned a long stay.

Sheridan awoke to something tickling her nose, which she promptly twitched, trying to go back to sleep. The tickling came again. This time she rubbed the offended part of her face with the back of her hand, and with a grumbled "Umph," turned over on her side, pulling the covers up under her chin. There was a long pause, almost long enough to allow her to go back to sleep, before the tickling came again.

Sheridan opened one eye to find a hand poised in front of her face, a feather from the pillow protruding between the thumb and index finger. She turned her head to find Jeremy peering down at her, his eyes holding a bright glimmer of mischief.

"Good morning, Mrs. Mackenzie." He smiled down at her frown. "You're certainly hard to wake up this morning. I've been lying here for hours waiting for you to rouse. My, but aren't we grumpy today." He moved the feather toward her face a fraction.

Sheridan shifted hastily to her back to stare up at him belligerently. "There are nicer ways to wake up, you know."

"Ah, yes, but those methods tend to lead to a longer stay in bed. Unlike some people, I have things to do today. Tell me, wife, are you going to spend the whole day shopping as has been your habit of late?"

"I hadn't given it much thought. I suppose I could go to the milliner's today. I do need a new hat to go with the red dress I ordered yesterday. Then I could go look at some new pans and linens."

Jeremy groaned and fell back on the bed. "Woman, I'm glad you're rich, otherwise I'd soon be a poor man."

"I didn't know I married such a miserly husband. You could always become a pirate again."

"Privateer, not pirate. Speaking of ships—"

"Was I speaking of ships?"

"No, but I am. If you can tear yourself away from your shopping expedition, I'd like to take you down to my ship, the *Golden Eagle*, today. Patrick and I have arranged for you ladies to tour the ship and have luncheon aboard—that is, if you can spare a few hours of your time."

"I don't know." She yawned and stretched her arms above her head. "I was just down to the docks but a few days ago. I'm not sure I'm interested in looking at another old boat.''

''Wench. Ship, not boat. And she's not old. She happens to be one of the finest vessels to sail the seas, and you, madam, are going to act duly impressed.''

Sheridan stared at the ceiling thoughtfully, her hand resting beneath her pillow. ''Why do men always refer to their ships in the feminine gender?''

''When she skims over the waves, she moves with the grace of a beautiful, sensual woman. If a man takes proper care of her and treats her with an adequate measure of affection, she'll do anything he asks.'' He looked at her out of the corner of his eye and smiled seductively.

Sheridan raised up to lean on one elbow, turning on her side to rest against her husband provocatively. She carefully brought her hand around to his chest, hiding the feather she had meticulously worked from her pillow.

''If I agree to go visit your vessel, will you promise never to tickle my nose again?''

''Well . . . I don't think I can make such a vow. You looked so sweet twitching your pretty little nose. I think I'll save that particular torture for special moments.''

She moved against him in a most intriguing way, dropping little kisses across his cheek and down his neck. When his eyes closed in anticipation, she quickly brought the feather to his nose, administering the same persecution he had previously bestowed upon her.

His eyes flew open, and his large hand grabbed her small one, holding the offending instrument at bay. ''Imp,'' he cried with a laugh. ''I surrender. I promise never to tickle your nose with a pillow feather.''

''Or anything else.''

''Nay, I'll not make so rash a promise, my sweet.'' By now, he had forced her hand open and removed the feather. "A blade of grass, a peacock's feather, a flower; all will do just as well."

"But not so easy to have within reach."

"True. I'll have to plan my tactics ahead of time."

He gave her a quick kiss and her bottom a gentle pinch before hopping out of bed. He threw the covers off of her and held out his hand. "Come, love, we have work to do today. I look forward to spending the whole day with you. After we pay our visit to Capt. Driscoll, I will graciously accompany you wherever you wish to go, since I have such a generous nature."

"Even to the milliner's?"

Jeremy grimaced. "I'm not sure I'm that generous. Aye, a promise is a promise. Even there, although I can think of more interesting things to do."

"So can I. Would you like simply to walk through the new park on Princess Street and enjoy the sunshine?"

"Much more to my liking, I assure you."

After a light breakfast, the two couples chatted casually in the carriage as Robert, one of Lord Maclaren's men, drove the vehicle to the docks of Leith. When he stopped the coach on the waterfront, Jeremy jumped out and turned to assist Sheridan down. She paused on the steps when she spied the magnificent vessel in front of her. *The Alyson* was a fine ship, and one of which she could be proud, but the *Golden Eagle* was truly something to behold.

"Oh, Jeremy," she cried softly, "she's beautiful." She lifted her gaze to the top of the highest of the three masts, gasping as she watched a small sailor climb about on the rigging.

Jeremy tugged gently on her arm to move her out of the way so the others might disembark the coach. "I told you that you'd be impressed." He beamed proudly as she scanned the length and breadth of his possession.

Without question the ship was the finest vessel in port as well as the largest. He chuckled when he heard Kyla's exclamation behind him, and turned toward his partner with a grin. "Shall we take the two bonniest lassies in all of Scotland aboard, Patrick?"

Patrick grinned back. "I'm not too sure the men can handle it." He motioned toward the ship, and when Jeremy turned, he found the sailors had stopped their work and moved over to the rail to stare at the beauties before them.

Capt. Driscoll waved at them from atop the gangplank.

"Permission to come aboard, Captain?" called Patrick.

"Permission granted, sir."

Sheridan hung onto Jeremy's arm as they moved up the steep ramp. She clung more tightly after glancing down and seeing how high they were above the rippling waters of the harbor. Jeremy could feel her apprehension and took her hand in his left one, slipping his right arm about her waist.

When they reached the main deck, the captain shook hands with both men and bowed slightly to the ladies. Silver-gray eyes sparkled in a wrinkled, sun-worn face as he gave first Sheridan and then Kyla a long appraising look.

"You've done yourselves proud, lads," he said at last. "I couldn't have picked two finer ladies for you if I had done the choosing myself."

"Which is what you've been trying to do for the past four years," chuckled Patrick.

"I just didn't want you to wait as long as I did to discover the joys of having a wife at your side."

"You mean your wife sails with you?" asked Kyla, disbelief tinting her soft voice.

"Aye, m'lady, she did for a while, but now we have two tiny tots at home, and there's no place for them on a ship. I've a mind to give up the sea after this voyage; I miss my Clara."

"Mrs. Driscoll and her mother were passengers on a voyage five years ago. By the time the journey ended, the good captain and the young lady were very much in love and were married within a week after the ship touched shore."

"Are all Americans so impetuous when it comes to choosing a mate?" whispered Sheridan, as they followed the captain around the ship.

"Only the slightly insane ones," replied Jeremy, jumping back to avoid being punched by a delicate fist.

Their first impression of the vessel was born out throughout the tour. Even to Sheridan's untrained eye, it was obvious this was one of the finest ships afloat and that its owners and captain kept it in excellent condition.

After being shown two smaller cabins used by Jeremy and Patrick when they sailed, they shared lunch with the captain in his quarters. Capt. Driscoll was a lively story-teller and carried the load of the conversation by relating adventures of his own as well as tales about the escapades of his employers.

"Thank you for the lovely tour and lunch, Captain," said Sheridan as they stood up to leave. "Your cook does as well as many of London's prized chefs."

"I will forward your compliments, m'lady. Why, we have men fighting each other just to sail with us—for his cooking, of course."

Sheridan chuckled at his twinkling eyes. "I could almost believe it."

After a short consultation regarding the status of the cargo, the party made its way ashore. With a last wave to the captain, Sheridan climbed into the waiting carriage after Kyla, scooting next to her husband when he sat down beside her.

He thumped the top of the coach with his fist, and Robert started up the team. The inside of the coach was silent, the occupants watching the busy activity along the wharf. Sailors hurried about carrying large barrels hoisted on their shoulders, moving steadily on and off the ships along the quay. Large stacks of cargo lined the docks: lumber for buildings and sailing vessels, bundles of wool, kegs of rum and bales of cotton from America.

Kyla stretched contentedly in the seat. "I think I be ready for a nap." She glanced coyly up at Patrick. "Some people forget a bed is for sleepin'."

Patrick grinned back at her. "Now, love, you know a bed is for—"

A loud explosion rocked the carriage, stopping Patrick in midsentence. Another blast filled the air, and Jeremy swung the door open to look out. Ahead of them loomed a blazing inferno as barrels of gunpowder exploded, sending fiery missiles into a large stack of nearby cotton. One warehouse was already in flames, and the fire raced haphazardly along the waterfront.

The driver fought to control his frightened team, and Jeremy jumped from the coach to help him, followed by Patrick.

In back of them, pandemonium broke out as others tried to flee the approaching fire. Carriages overturned when the drivers desperately tried to turn them around. In haste, the freight wagons tipped and lost their cargo. People ran wildly down the wharf toward the only avenue of escape, a narrow, winding road leading up the hill and on to Edinburgh.

"I think I can get the horses out, Mr. Mackenzie," called Robert over the din of the screaming people and the roaring fire, "but the carriage is hopeless."

At his words, the women scrambled from the coach, stunned by the sight that met their eyes.

Jeremy seized Sheridan's arm and yelled in her ear to be heard. "Get to the ship."

"What about you? I'm not leaving you."

"We'll be right along. Now run, woman!"

Sheridan obeyed his command, jerking Kyla's arm so she would follow. Glancing over her shoulder, she saw Jeremy and Patrick unharnessing the horses. Robert lithely hopped astride one of them, taking the other's reins firmly in hand.

"Try to get the horses out, but if you can't, set them free and take care of yourself," called Jeremy. "Don't risk your neck, man."

Robert nodded and swung the horses around, picking his way carefully, but speedily, through the throng of fleeing people. His mount wasn't accustomed to carrying a rider, and it took every bit of skill the young man possessed to keep the frightened animal under control.

Sheridan and Kyla ran along the wharf, jostled from side to side as brawny seamen and frantic lords and ladies crowded the cluttered waterfront. Out of the corner of her eye, Kyla saw someone fall and grabbed Sheridan's hand to pull her over to an old flower vendor they had smiled at only moments before. Shielding the woman with their own bodies as best they could, they helped her to her feet. Between them, they half carried, half dragged the woman toward the ship.

"Capt. Driscoll!" screamed Sheridan when she saw the gangplank being hauled aboard.

The man somehow heard her cry above the noise and motioned for the ramp to be lowered again, though the ship strained at its moorings, the sails catching the wind and billowing out majestically.

Kyla helped the old lady up the ramp, while Sheridan ran to assist a bewildered young woman standing by an overturned vegetable wagon. The woman's leg was cut and bleeding, but a quick glance at the crying baby in her arms assured Sheridan the child was only frightened and not hurt.

Unable to talk above the racket, Sheridan slipped her arm around the woman's waist and guided her to the waiting boat. As she went up the gangplank, she searched desperately for Jeremy and Patrick. She breathed a prayer of thanks when she saw them racing through the crowd, both men carrying a child under each arm. Upon reaching the deck, she caught a better view of them through the billowing smoke. The children were some of the dozen little urchins they had seen playing on the waterfront earlier, and she wondered what had happened to the rest of them.

The deck was already crowded with people. Those unable to keep up with the panicky swarm had been herded onto the vessel by the first mate, a man named Brannigan. Jeremy and Patrick reached the bottom of the gangplank and put the children down to send them scurrying up the ramp. Just as they were to follow, the bulk of the crowd passed by, drawing their attention to an elegantly dressed lady pulling wildly at an overturned phaeton. With one look, both men turned and ran several feet back down the dock to come to a halt by the vehicle. The driver lay beside it, his neck obviously broken.

"My children," the lady sobbed, "my children are trapped underneath."

Patrick peeked through an opening and smiled. "I see them. They look all right, just stuck."

"Get on board the ship," yelled Jeremy, pointing her

in the direction of the vessel. "We'll get your children." He glanced up at the rapidly approaching fire and commanded, "Hurry!"

The woman followed his command and struggled up the ramp, collapsing on deck, finally overcome from a hard blow she had received to her head. A seaman picked her up and carried her over to where Sheridan and Kyla were attempting to help the injured and calm the frightened children.

Sheridan looked up to see the gangplank being raised and the moorings being tossed ashore. Jumping to her feet, she pushed her way through the throng to the railing, searching for Jeremy. The bundles of wool directly across from them burst into flames as the *Golden Eagle* moved slowly away from the wharf.

"Jeremy!"

At her anguished cry, Branningan strode swiftly toward her, shouldering his way through the crowd. He reached her side in time to see Jeremy and Patrick dive into the murky water, each with a child clinging to his back. With powerful strokes, the men swam toward the ship.

Brannigan calmly threw three lines overboard and pulled off his boots and shirt. As he climbed up on the railing, he flashed Sheridan a wide grin. "They do like to make a grand entrance." With a roguish wink, he dove overboard, breaking back up through the surface of the water seconds before the two men reached the hull of the boat.

Brannigan tied the ropes around his friends' waists. Jeremy and Patrick began the climb up the side of the ship, the children hanging on for dear life. Brannigan grasped the third rope and trailed along behind the now rapidly moving ship.

When they reached the railing, strong sailors hauled

the children over to safety as others reached out to help the men past the final hurdle. When the others were safely aboard, Brannigan quickly scaled the side of the ship.

Kyla appeared at her husband's side, tossing both him and Jeremy blankets. She handed another to Sheridan to wrap around one of the children while she took care of the other.

When Brannigan was pulled over the railing, Jeremy thrust a blanket at him and gave him a big smile. "Thanks, my friend. I was beginning to get tired."

"I couldn't let you two get all the glory now, could I?"

A sailor took the children away to their mother, who lay on a makeshift bed nearby. Some of the color returned to her face as she held them close, crying softly, "We're all safe. We'll be fine now."

Sheridan wrapped her arms around Jeremy, blanket and all, trying not to cry from sheer relief. Kyla hugged Patrick, then stepped back, hands on hips, and gave him a piece of her mind.

"Patrick Hagen, if you ever try anythin' so foolish again, I'll stop speakin' to you."

"Is that a promise?" He smiled wearily at his little love, admiring her trim figure and the sparks flying from her eyes. Her mouth tightened into a grim line, and he gave her a quick kiss. "You know we couldn't leave the children there, little one."

"Of course, you could no' leave the children, but did you have to be so slow about gettin' them out? If you'd speeded it up, you would have been able to walk up the gangplank like an ordinary man."

Sheridan giggled nervously. "Brannigan did say you liked to make a grand entrance."

Brannigan shrugged and looked innocent.

"Nothing to it. Just a sailor's typical day," commented Jeremy with a slight chuckle. His face sobered as he looked over Sheridan's head to the roaring flames. She turned silently to watch at his side, shifting closer to him when he slipped a blanket-covered arm around her.

Capt. Driscoll maneuvered the ship out into the deep channel of the firth, heading upstream in the general direction of Falkirk, but stopping near a small harbor. The sea-going vessel was too large to enter the small port, so he gave the command to drop anchor when they had moved out of the main portion of the channel.

By the time the ship was anchored, Patrick and Jeremy had changed into dry clothes, which they kept on board. The injured were attended to, and the cook set out a meal for all those aboard. Sailors, beggars, peddlers and grand ladies sat on barrels and boxes side by side, thankful for the meat, cheese and bread the cook brought them.

The two aristocratic children who had been pulled from the overturned phaeton sat huddled in blankets along with the other children who had been rescued from the fire. For the moment, class did not exist as the children became fast friends, comparing stories of their rescue.

Although they had moved farther up the river Forth, the flaming waterfront was still visible in the distance, the bright red blaze licking at the black, smoke-filled sky. Sheridan stood transfixed at the railing, staring at the sight, feeling somehow transported to another place and time.

Jeremy slid his arms around her and pulled her back against his chest. She leaned her head against his shoulder and took a deep breath, saying a silent prayer of thanksgiving for their safety.

"Did Robert make it up the hill?" asked Jeremy.

"I think so. I caught a glimpse of him as he started up the narrowest part of the street. I'm surprised no one pulled him off and tried to ride."

"The horses were so frightened that I don't think anyone else could have handled them. I suspect most people were afraid of them."

"What happens now?" she asked, weariness creeping into her voice.

"We'll row everyone ashore since it's too shallow for the *Eagle* to get any closer. It'll take a while since we have only two small boats aboard. Patrick and I will go in the first boat and arrange transportation back to Edinburgh for the others." He shook his head. "Some have lost their livelihood, such as the old flower lady. The young woman with the baby lost her cart and a week's supply of vegetables; it will take more than she has to replace the cart."

"Can't we help them?"

"I intend to. The flower lady has agreed to take the children back to their families. She knows them and where they live, and they are more than willing to go peacefully with her."

"What happened to the other children?" She thought of the others they had seen earlier, and her voice cracked at the thought of them dying in the blaze.

"One of the boys said they left earlier, had a disagreement with the ones remaining and stormed off in a huff."

"Thank goodness."

"Aye, we couldn't have gotten them all out, I fear, although the older ones might have been able to run fast enough to keep up."

It took three trips with each boat to ferry everyone to shore. The sun was low in the sky when Jeremy and

Patrick returned to the ship. "Do you want to go back to Edinburgh or stay on board for the night, sweet?" asked Jeremy, his gaze running over his exhausted wife, taking in the soot-covered gown and the dark smudges on her face and arms.

"What I want is to crawl into bed and stay there for a week, but first I want a long, hot bath. Can you arrange such a wonderful treat on your magical ship?"

"Aye, but it wouldn't be as nice as being in the large tub back at the townhouse. The bed's not nearly so comfortable either."

"Then let's be off. It shouldn't take too long to get there."

He took Sheridan's arm, and they walked over to thank Capt. Driscoll. "You did a good job today, Tom," said Jeremy. "I thank you for handling the situation so expertly. Without a doubt, many lives were saved by you and the crew, as well as our ship and much of the cargo."

"You did your share, lads. Now take these lovely ladies home and let them rest. I'll wait here until I receive your instructions regarding the rest of our cargo."

To Sheridan, the journey back to Edinburgh seemed to take no time at all because she fell asleep in Jeremy's arms inside the hired hack. When they arrived at their destination, he gently shook her to wake her up. She was too tired to function properly, so she didn't protest when Jeremy swung her up in his arms and carried her inside the building.

Robert raced down the hall to meet them as they came through the front portal. "Is she hurt, Mr. Mackenzie?" he asked anxiously.

"No, lad, just tired. None of us was injured. And yourself?"

"The team and I were able to get through without any damage, sir."

"You did a good job. I'm proud of you. Now, if you'll get one of the maids to ask Dora to bring hot water, my wife would like a bath."

With a nod of his head, the young man scurried back down the hall, stopping only for a moment to greet Patrick and Kyla.

Jeremy and Sheridan reached the bedroom, and he set his wife gently on her feet. "Can you undress, or do you need some help?"

"I can manage. I'm sure you're as tired as I am. It's too bad the tub isn't as big as the one at home. Then we could share it."

"I can wait." He eased himself down in a comfortable chair, pulled off his boots and stretched his legs out before him. With a sigh, he leaned his head back against the chair and closed his eyes. When he opened them again, Sheridan was stepping from the tub, all traces of smoke and soot gone.

"You can bathe now," she murmured against his lips, stopping beside his chair and bending to kiss him tenderly. "Do you want fresh water?"

"Is it still hot?"

"Fairly so. I didn't linger."

"I'll use what is here. I washed all the smoke off when I dove in the harbor. Now, all I need is to get rid of the salt."

She kissed him on the neck and made a face. "Aye, you taste a little like salt pork."

"Such loving compliments."

She grinned and motioned for him to get into the tub, watching affectionately as he removed his clothing and climbed in the water.

"Warm enough to do the job," he gurgled, sinking

beneath the water only to surface a moment later and run his hands over his eyes to wipe way the soapy water. He burst into laughter.

"What's so funny?"

"I forgot about your wonderful soap. Now I will bear the distinctly unmasculine smell of a rose garden. On you, it's irresistible, but on me, well—"

"I won't complain." Sheridan pulled a soft white nightshift over her head and curled up in the middle of the bed to dry her wet hair with a towel. When it was almost dry, she brushed it carefully, working the tangles out slowly.

Jeremy rose from the tub when the water began to cool, and dried his body briskly. After roughly drying his hair, he crawled up on the bed beside his wife, tossing the towel near the tub. He took the brush from her hand and slowly, lovingly brushed the thick locks, admiring their shine. When her hair was brushed smooth, he placed the brush on the night table and took her in his arms.

She entwined her arms around his neck and welcomed his kiss. He moved his hands over her body, gently caressing, reassuring as he drew her down on the bed.

"When I saw you still standing on the dock, I thought I had lost you," she said quietly. Her grip tightened, and she pressed her forehead against his cheek. "I don't want to lose you," she whispered fervently.

His heart leaped with joy.

"Nothing, or no one, can take me from you, nor you from me." He sought to lighten her dark mood. "We'll both die in about fifty years in our bed—from passion."

"Think so?"

"Know so. Now get rid of that shift and cuddle up

close, wife. I may be tired, but I need very much to love you."

It was one order Sheridan had absolutely no trouble obeying.

Chapter 13

In the middle of the night, Jeremy stirred, awakening to find Sheridan crying softly in her sleep. He pulled her into his arms, trying to comfort her and gently wake her, but she remained asleep, startling him when she cried out in a small, childlike voice.

"Mama, dunna' yell at Uncle Cameron. I dunna' like it when you yell. I dunna' want to go back to bed. Please promise you willna' fight anymore. Aye, Mama, I'll go to sleep. You promised. Tell Uncle Cam to go home. I dunna' want him here. He makes Papa angry and makes you cry."

She coughed and gasped for air, clutching Jeremy's arms as he tried to soothe her. "Mama, the house is on fire! The smoke, I canna' breathe. Papa, get out! Stop fighting! Get out! Make them stop, Mama."

She gave a small, anguished cry, squeezing Jeremy's arm until her nails dug into his flesh. "Papa's hurt," she sobbed. "Uncle Cam hurt him. Make him get up,

Mama. Please make him get up.''

She coughed again, then her breathing became easier. When she spoke, her voice was strangely hushed. "Mama, dunna' go in the fire. Dunna' leave me. Please, Mama, dunna' leave me.''

Her whispered words gave way to shuddering sobs, and Jeremy realized she was awake. He drew her more fully against him, holding her tightly, stroking her hair and whispering words of comfort.

At last, Sheridan lay quietly in his arms. He raised up to lean on his forearm and looked down at her face, trying to see her expression in the dim moonlight. She met his gaze, her eyes full of agony.

"Papa's death wasn't an accident. Cameron killed him. He hit him in the head with the fireplace poker.'' She squeezed her eyes shut and breathed a shuddering sigh. "Mother was carrying me out, and I watched them over her shoulder. They were fighting, and Papa tripped. When he fell to his knees, Macveagh grabbed the poker and hit him. He hit him again as he fell over.'' She opened her eyes and looked up at Jeremy, full of despair. His eyes grew misty, and he blinked hard, tightening his grip on her arm.

"I tried to tell the others she had gone back in the house, but there was so much confusion, they wouldn't listen. I should have tried harder. I should have made them understand.''

He brushed her cheek with his fingers, then cradled her jaw in his palm. "You can't blame yourself, love. You were only five years old. It's Macveagh who is to blame. He's the one who should be punished. We'll go see the magistrate tomorrow and tell him what happened.''

"No, I can't!" She shook her head frantically, her eyes wide and fearful.

"Why not? He killed your father and caused your

mother's death. He's put you through a lifetime of pain. He should go to the gallows, or at least to prison."

"He's been in his own prison all these years. Maybe that's punishment enough."

Jeremy had not forgotten Macveagh's visit to the Edinburgh townhouse. Sometimes, it seemed as if the man held some strange power over Sheridan. She had tried to play down his visit, and now it was almost as if she wanted to protect him. Jeremy groaned inwardly as his heart was seared with pain. Had he been wrong? Did Sheridan care more for Macveagh than she would admit? Was she like her mother, married to one, yet somehow needing the other? Was she so starved for love that she needed the love of both men?

A storm of rage swept over Jeremy, and he gripped her shoulder painfully, shaking her slightly. "Why do you protect him?"

"I don't know! I have to!" she cried in a voice bordering on hysteria. Tears poured from her eyes, and her breath came in jerky gasps. She clung to him, her nails digging into his side. "Don't hate me, Jeremy," she sobbed. "I couldn't bear it if you hated me."

He eased his grip and laid his head back down on the pillow, holding her close, forcing himself to calm down. He took a deep breath, then let the air out slowly. He could tell Sheridan fought to regain control as she flattened her hand out against his side, trying with her fingers to smooth out the indentations left by her nails.

"You don't have to go to the magistrate tomorrow, Sher, but you must tell him what you know."

"I was only a child. He won't believe me after all these years."

"He might." She lay silently in his arms for a long time, so long that he thought she had fallen asleep.

"I'll go," she whispered, "but not now. Let me decide the time. I can't bear to bring it all up again now, but I promise I'll talk to him.''

He tried to push aside his doubts, chiding himself for having an overactive imagination, but he could not rid himself completely of the nagging fear. Macveagh had some kind of hold over her, but what?

She kissed his chin and whispered, ''Thank you for not pressing me.'' She nestled in her refuge, unaware of the thoughts plaguing her husband or of the reassurance he needed. She eventually slept, though it was not a restful sleep. She tossed and turned and more than once cried out in the darkness.

In the following days, Sheridan and Jeremy spent their time almost constantly together. They went for walks, rode about the estate, talked and laughed and grew to know each other better.

It was at these times that memories would sometimes haunt her. A teasing moment might splash a picture across her mind—her mother smiling impishly up at Macveagh. Jeremy's laugh would evoke whispers of another laugh from long ago. Once, when he ran his fingers down her arm, she remembered seeing Macveagh's similar caress before he pulled Alyson into his arms for a fiery kiss and very intimate embrace. Even the little girl, who had hidden behind the bushes and watched, had known it wasn't right for Mama to kiss Uncle Cam that way. In her child's heart, she had known Mama liked Uncle Cam better than she liked Papa.

Sheridan tried to push the thoughts from her mind, and willfully did not dwell on them. She wanted to enjoy her time with Jeremy and was determined not to let things long past affect her marriage and her deepening affection for him.

One afternoon they returned from checking on the crops and decided on a stroll in the rose garden. ''I haven't seen Macveagh around. Do you think he's gone on a trip?'' She clipped several deep red roses from an overflowing bush before he answered.

"He's gone to the North Coast.''

"Did you see him before he left?'' She dropped the roses in a brown basket and straightened, looking up at him.

"Yes."

"When?"

"The afternoon following the Thortons' ball.''

"I was wondering how long you would wait before you confronted him." She smiled. "Will you tell me what happened?''

Jeremy looked uneasy, picked up the basket and guided her hand through the crook of his arm. They walked down the path until the came to a bench beneath a shady oak and sat down. He sat stiffly, toying with the basket handle.

"I went prepared to call him out.''

"Oh, Jeremy, you wouldn't!'' She grabbed his arm, her eyes pleading with him to deny it.

"I would if it were necessary, but it wasn't. I ordered him to stay away from you and demanded his word that he would. He said he was afraid he could not stay away from you if he remained here. He decided to go up to the coast until we leave the country. He gave his word he would stay away.''

"I had not thought my marriage would be much of a deterrent to him.''

"I should have mentioned it. It would have set your mind at rest to know he was gone. You wouldn't have felt threatened by him these past few weeks.''

"I haven't felt threatened by him." She noted Jeremy's frown and smiled. "How could he hurt me when I've been with you almost constantly?'' She kissed away his doubtful look. "Few damsels in distress are protected by so gallant and handsome a knight.''

Jeremy forced a smile. Why did she brush Macveagh's threat aside so easily? His smile quickly faded, and he looked across the garden, avoiding her gaze. "Do you regret his absence?"

"Good heavens, no. Why would I regret it?"

Jeremy shifted on the bench, stood up and walked across the path to clip a delicate pink rose from the bush. "I thought you might miss him."

"I certanly don't miss his harassment."

Jeremy picked another rose, still avoiding her gaze. "I thought perhaps his attentions were more in the line of seduction."

"He might think so, but I don't. Jeremy, look at me."

Kneeling down to pick several roses from the bottom of the bush, Jeremy looked up at her.

"Just as I thought. Your eyes are green today."

"My eyes are never green; they're amber."

"But you are seeing things through a jealous haze, my dear." She stepped close to him when he stood up. "I'm glad Macveagh's gone; I don't have to worry about you fighting with him. I am not afraid of him as long as I have you nearby, Jeremy. I don't care to see him again, and the only person I care to be seduced by is you."

Jeremy grinned and propelled her toward the back stairway. "I'm troubled about one thing, Sher. When are you going to see the magistrate about your father's death?"

She stumbled, and he caught her arm, bringing them to a halt.

"I'll go see him tomorrow if you'll come with me. It will be hard, I think, but I know I must. I haven't wanted to bring it all up again. It's bound to be painful, and my life has been so pleasant lately, I hate to stir things up."

"I'll go with you, love. You know I'll stand by you." He slid his arm around her shoulders in a warm hug.

"I know." She rested her head against his shoulder, wishing she could totally quell her uneasiness about talking to the magistrate. It was the logical, right thing to do. Then why did she feel as though she was being torn in half—one part declaring it was only avenging her parents; the other condemning her for speaking against Macveagh? She wished she could put all of it behind her. She looked up at him wistfully.

"I wish we could go somewhere else for a while."

"How would you like to go to Paris next week?"

"You heard from Lafayette?"

"Aye, this morning. I was going to surprise you tonight at dinner."

"Will Patrick and Kyla go, too?"

"Of course."

"Wonderful! I'd better start planning what to take." She raced up the stairs, grinning at Jeremy over her shoulder. He was only a few steps behind when she reached the bedroom.

"Just a minute, young lady." He pulled her into his arms. "You were saying something about seduction down in the gardens."

Sheridan fluttered her eyelashes outrageously. "Why, Mr. Mackenzie, would you indulge in such a pastime in the middle of the afternoon?"

"In the middle of the afternoon, in the morning, in the dark of night, anytime the mood strikes and the lady is willing."

Sheridan looked indignant. "Will any willing lady do, my lord?"

"Well, she does have to be my wife."

"That rather limits your choices, sir."

"Exactly what I intended, madam." Jeremy ran his hands over her; his kiss was long and sweet. He caressed her through her dress until she moaned against his lips, her breath coming quickly. Slowly pulling up her skirt, he slipped his fingers beneath the hem of her garments, sliding them smoothly up her thigh to caress her bare hip. He brushed lightly with his fingertips, then cupped her bottom with his fingers, kneading gently.

"Jeremy," whispered Sheridan, pulling at his shirt, "I hope you're in the mood because your wife is very willing."

He chuckled thickly. "That, too, is what I intended, madam." And he lowered her to the bed.

A week and a half later, Sheridan stood on the steps of the Paris home of the Marquis de Lafayette. "Will you return before evening?" she asked, after receiving a warm kiss from her husband.

"It appears doubtful. There is so much disorder and disruption at the Assembly, it takes all day to debate anything, and often even that discussion is useless."

Sheridan wrinkled her nose at Jeremy, but grinned as he kissed the tip of it.

Her look of annoyance, although small, did not go unnoticed by Gilbert du Motier, the Marquis. With an absentminded peck on his wife's cheek, the tall, red-headed man turned toward Sheridan, his wide hazel eyes gazing at her intently.

"It would seem, Sheridan, you do not approve of my monopolizing your husband. Please accept my apologies. It has given me such pleasure to have my old friends here with me that I have indeed been selfish."

" 'Tis I who am selfish, Gilbert. I have had his undivided attention for the last month." A soft smile washed over her face. "I will have a lifetime to enjoy his company, sir. You have only a few more weeks. I do not begrudge you his companionship."

"My thanks, madame. I do place a high value upon both Patrick and Jeremy's friendship and their advice to me. Circumstances here are very precarious, and I need their wise counsel."

The men climbed into the waiting coach for their ride

across Paris to the National Assembly, which met in the Riding School of the Tuilleries. Lafayette stuck his head out the window and called to his wife. She moved rapidly down the steps to stand by the carriage window.

"You have made the arrangements for this evening?"

"Yes, Gilbert. Everything will be ready for the dinner. How many do you expect?"

"I don't know. Perhaps fifteen or twenty. Who is to say?"

"We will be prepared."

"Thank you, Adrienne. You are very valuable to me in these matters." He reached out to squeeze his wife's hand, which rested on the window edge. When she raised her head in surprise, he withdrew his hand and tossed a wave to Kyla and Sheridan.

Adrienne stood still, watching the coach disappear down the street, before hastily rejoining her guests on the porch. "Would you like a walk in the garden? It's especially beautiful at this time of morning."

"I'd love one. Do you have time to join us, or are you preparing another feast for this evening?" Sheridan smiled at her new friend as they turned down the corridor toward the gardens.

"I'm planning another dinner, but I have time to walk with you. I've already talked with the cook and the other servants." She smiled, and sparkles lit up her eyes, giving life to an otherwise plain face. "They are used to it by now. We've been having dinners like this several nights a week for the last two years. First, it was in an effort to gain voting rights for the Third Estate; now it is for the club to decide how to vote."

"You must get tired of it."

"No, not really. For the first time in our married life, I am able to contribute something to my husband's work. Always before, there has been no place for me to help him, thus I never saw him. He was always gone, either to America or off somewhere to a meeting or to his country estate.''

"You don't really see him very often now," Sheridan said, thinking how many times he had rushed off at all hours to settle some emergency. Her comment was softened by a smile.

"No, but it is more than ever before." Adrienne pursed her lips and frowned thoughtfully. "These dinners are a way in which I can show him my love and respect.''

"You care for him very much, don't you?"

"Yes, I do. Strange, I know. Usually an arranged marriage is devoid of love, sometimes even filled with hate. But we are fortunate; he cares somewhat for me, and I for him.''

"I think you do more than care just a little for him. No, don't look so surprised. You don't display your love for him openly. In fact, I doubt if he is even aware of it. I see it on your face after he leaves, especially when there is a crisis.''

Adrienne blushed and leaned over to smell a bright pink carnation in a nearby pot. "We were married very young. Gilbert was sixteen and I was fourteen. It had been decided by his guardian—''

"He was an orphan?"

"Yes, his father was killed fighting the English when Gilbert was only two. His mother died when he was thirteen, and his grandfather died only two weeks later. He inherited the estate from his mother and wealth from his grandfather.''

"He must have been very lonely." They strolled along the path, stopping now and then to admire the violets, pansies and carnations.

"I think he was, and his life was somewhat dismal. When he was younger, all the women in his home wore black. He lived with his widowed mother, a spinster and two other widows. He would escape to the kitchen or to the village, where he would find companionship with the villagers of Chavaniac. They adored him, even though he was their lord. And he adored them." Adrienne looked over at Sheridan.

"It was there he discovered the first inklings of every man's need to be his own man. It is something that has stayed with him all his life."

"You said you were only fourteen when you married. Had you met him before?"

"Oh, yes. When his guardian and my parents decided on a wedding to unite our families, they couldn't make up their minds whether to marry him to me or my sister, Louise. They were in quite a quandary for a while."

"From the twinkle in your eye, there's more to the story," Kyla guessed merrily. Adrienne joined in her laughter.

"There is. My sister, Louise, is quite lovely. Just when they had about decided to match her with Gilbert, Louie XV met her. He was quite taken with her and sought to make her his mistress. In order to protect her from the king's advances, she was quickly cloistered in a convent. She stayed there until he lost interest." She stopped and broke off a long-stemmed red carnation for each of them.

"And long enough for the families to decide to have you marry Gilbert," said Sheridan.

"Yes. We were only children when the betrothal was announced. My mother invited him to come and live with our family for two years before the wedding actually took place. It gave us time to become friends and for him to develop a certain affection for me."

"And you?" asked Sheridan quietly, sensing a subtle change in her hostess's expression.

Adrienne stared silently across the garden, glancing down at the clusters of violets at their feet before lifting her eyes to meet Sheridan's. "He became my world, my reason for existence."

"And he doesn't know." Sheridan thought of the exchanges she had witnessed between Lafayette and his wife. During the time she had been a guest at their home in Paris, she had never seen any indication of love given by him to his wife. Other than this morning, she corrected herself silently. The peck on the cheek had appeared to be a reflex action, a thing to do simply because Patrick and Jeremy had kissed their wives on their departure. But the unexpected caress at the carriage had been genuine. She smiled at the thought. Maybe Jeremy's open affection was rubbing off on the Marquis.

"There has never been an opportunity to tell him. I do not wish to distress him in any way. Someday when the time is right, I will tell him of my love. For now, I will simply try to help him in any manner I can. He cares for me in his own way. It is enough." She smiled suddenly. "Enough serious talk. Let us finish our walk. It will soon be time to leave to see my mother. There, we will discuss nothing but frivolous matters, for today at least."

That evening, Sheridan adjusted the white lace tippet over her shoulders before slipping her diamond earrings onto her earlobes. A diamond pendant nestled against her exposed skin at the point where the folds of the lace scarf met at the top curves of her bosom. She turned to check the back of her red silk dinner dress in the mirror, and met Jeremy's gaze as he stood behind her.

He automatically completed the tying of his cravat, letting his gaze roam over his wife in open approval. "You'll cause the men to forget why they are gathered here this evening, my love."

She smiled at him in the mirror before turning around to face him. She unfurled her fan and lifted it to her face, hiding all from him except her eyes. Her lashes fluttered coyly before she lowered the fan and closed it with a snap of her wrist.

"Nothing will make these gentlemen forget their purpose, sir. How can they forget when they are caught up daily in the workings of the revolution?"

"Do I sense disapproval?"

"No. I just sometimes wish we were back in Scotland." Her lips puckered into a seductive pout. "I miss having you at my beck and call."

"Countess Sinclair, if I didn't know better, I'd say you were bored."

"Shhh, don't let anyone hear you. You're right. I've grown used to running an estate, not traipsing around looking at museums or going to visit duchesses for lunch or tea. I wouldn't hurt the Lafayettes' feelings for the world, but I can only handle so much idleness."

"Gilbert was worrying that perhaps you were disappointed not to be going to court and participating in the social life there."

"Please assure him I'm not the least bit disappointed. I find these evening dinners quite interesting and enlightening. In fact—" she grinned mischievously "—I'm gaining a better understanding of my husband and his country."

"The United States isn't much like France."

"No, but the desires of Lafayette and the others are the same. They want all the people to have the same opportunities and freedoms. In many ways, the plight of the common man in France was much worse than in England or Scotland, but I'm not blind to the inequality found there."

Jeremy took her arm and escorted her down to the dining room, which was filling rapidly with people. In addition to the sixteen guests from the Assembly who had already arrived, Lafayette's three children took their places at the dinner table. Eight-year-old Virginie sat next to Sheridan, while eleven-year-old Georges sat across from them between Patrick and one of the assemblymen. Anastasie, age fourteen, sat next to Jeremy and Kyla.

"I've been meaning to ask you, Virginie," said Sheridan, "have you always eaten your meals with your parents when they have guests? You all seem so at ease with adults and never cease to amaze me when you answer in whatever language you are spoken to."

Virginie assumed a very mature air, sitting up straight in her chair and answering in perfect English. "We have been taught both French and English from the beginning. When we reached the age of four, we were allowed to dine with Papa and Mama. It was expected of us to be able to talk with those around us whether they spoke French or English. Papa always says one is never too young to learn about liberty."

"Your Papa is right."

The little girl's eyes widened slightly, and she nodded her head emphatically, her curls bouncing up and down upon her shoulders. "Papa is always right," she said solemnly.

Sheridan smiled at this innocent adoration and turned her attention to the conversation between Lafayette and one of the assemblymen.

Lafayette shook his head in response to a remark she didn't hear. "It seems I am always in the middle. As Commander of the National Guard, I must try to keep the peace and protect the king and queen. As Vice-President of the Assembly, I must work to promote the ideals of the republic. Now the differing factions grow stronger, and I fear there will be further bloodshed. If only Marie Antoinette did not have such influence over Louis, this revolution might have ended by now."

"You should have let the crowd have her, eh?"

"No, I couldn't do that. I have sworn to protect them, and I must keep my oath."

The assemblyman turned to Sheridan and smiled, pleased she was listening to their conversation. He noticed her interest and continued. "It is unfortunate she is so ungrateful to you. If you could but influence her, our cause might be more easily won."

Lafayette smiled, shaking his head when a servant offered him more partridge pâté. He took a helping of turkey with truffles before answering his compatriot. "She has never made a pretense of even liking me. She is at least honest in her open contempt of me. I think she would have almost preferred the mob to take her than to be rescued by me."

The assemblyman looked at Sheridan and motioned his head toward Lafayette. "Have you heard how our friend dragged the queen onto the balcony in her night-clothes?" At Sheridan's look of surprise, he smiled, took a sip of wine and said, "Then I shall tell you the tale."

"You make me sound like a rogue, Andre," joked Lafayette. "Truly, Lady Sinclair, I am not the person my friend makes me out to be." Tolerantly, he continued eating while Andre proceeded with his story.

"Last October, there was much controversy over whether the Assembly should allow the king to have the right of veto. Through the unending efforts of Lafayette, a compromise was reached, and the proposal was presented to the king. At the same time, the more vocal factions against the right of veto began a propaganda campaign." He paused for another sip of wine.

"Marat and the Duke d'Orleans were behind it. The duke's agents warned people all over Paris that the king would use the veto, and people would have no bread. Now, madame, to a Frenchman, to have no bread is the greatest disaster of all."

"What was the compromise presented to the king?" asked Sheridan, curious to hear about the balcony scene but not wishing to appear so.

"It was decided to give the king the right to veto, but not to dissolve the Assembly. The Assembly also kept the upper hand with the ability to refuse him funds whenever they wished to bring him to terms. It appeared to be the best solution all the way around."

"You speak as if the goal were not accomplished. What was the king's reaction?"

Andre smiled again, obviously enjoying the attention of the lovely Scot. He shot a glance at Lafayette to reassure himself he was not offending his friend with the story. He hesitated for a moment as Lafayette put down his fork and toyed with his wine goblet, but when he did not speak, the assemblyman continued.

"The king refused to ratify the Declaration of Rights. The propaganda of Marat and Orleans over the veto threat might have been nullified had it not been for the king's idiocy. There were a variety of rumors flying about. Supposedly, flour was being horded at Versailles; the king would veto and there would be no bread; and the queen had trampled on the tricolor, our symbol of freedom."

By this time, the other conversations at the table had grown quiet, and all attention was focused on the lone speaker. Most of those present knew the story, but since all were friends of Lafayette, they relished the hearing of it over and over again.

"The instigators triggered the street crowds. They decided to march off to Versailles to capture the flour and butcher the queen. They truly hated her. They also intended to get rid of the Assembly president, for the Assembly met at Versailles at that time. The motives of those in the crowd varied, but they all agreed on one thing.''

"And what was that?"

"They agreed to force Commander Lafayette to accompany them. He claimed to be for the people. This would be his opportunity to prove his loyalty to their cause. They began congregating at the National Guard headquarters early in the morning. All day long our Commander argued with them, but they would not be deterred. Even his own guardsmen took the people's side. Work that had taken months to accomplish hung in the balance.''

Andre turned to Lafayette, who sat tensely in his chair. "I think, my friend, it would be better if you finished the story," he said softly.

Lafayette relaxed, stared thoughtfully at his wine glass and then smiled a somewhat bitter smile. "The mob grew even angrier. I could do nothing to dissuade them. At last, they called for me to go to Versailles or be strung up." At Sheridan's gasp, he smiled and lifted his eyes to meet hers. "I didn't fear the hanging; it would have been preferable to be hung than to be butchered in the streets as some have been. What I did fear was the destruction of our work, the destruction of the positive outcome of so many labors. Once before the crowd had not listened to me, and two men had been cruelly butchered. At that time, I had resigned as Commander, but I was asked to return to the job. I did so on the condition that the people swear an oath of loyalty to maintain justice and public order.

"They had become frightened, so they took the oath. Now, they found it hard to keep. I compromised with them. I agreed to go with them to Versailles if they would give an oath of allegiance to the throne.''

"Did you really believe they would keep their promise?"

"No, I seriously doubted it, but it was better for me to go with them than for them to go alone. There was always a slim chance I would be able to restrain them. When we arrived at Versailles, to my surprise they gave me complete freedom of action. I quickly assured the Assembly president that my guardsmen and I would protect the king and queen and the process of law. The crowd milled around outside the palace while I went inside and spoke with the king."

He leaned forward in his chair, resting his elbows and forearms on the table. All motion at the table had ceased, forks and glasses remained still. All were caught up in the unfolding drama.

"It was before dawn. We had argued and then marched from Paris to Versailles, the whole of it taking almost a full day's time. The king was persuaded to dismiss most of his foreign bodyguards, whom the people detested. He would not dismiss them all, but I managed to replace many of them with the National Guard." His voice grew sad, heavy with emotion.

"The mob fired on those that remained. Two were killed, and others were injured. A screaming mass moved into the courtyard, the guards making only a feeble attempt to hold them back." He took a deep breath and smiled at Sheridan and the others.

"At five in the morning, I knocked on the queen's chamber door. Oh, how she hated being waked up at that hour. I'm certain she was already awake, but she pretended it was I who had roused her. No one could sleep with the crowd screaming as they were." He shook his head at the memory. "They were verbally dissecting her, and she knew they would be doing it physically before long. When she opened her bedroom door, a robe thrown over her nightshift, I grabbed her arm and led her toward the balcony. I do admit she protested such an action, but one doesn't drag the Queen of France anywhere.''

The knowing smile on his face and the delighted sparkle in his eyes told his listeners that drag her was exactly what he had done. A ripple of laughter spread around the table.

''When we reached the balcony, an angry roar rose from the crowd. The queen has taken no pains to endear herself to our people. In fact, she has gone out of her way to do the opposite, generally being haughty and disdainful.''

''How could she face those screamin' people knowin' they wanted to tear her apart?'' asked Kyla. ''I dunna' know if I could have done it.''

''Even queens know fear, Kyla. She was ready to flee back inside. I warned her not to shrink. She drew upon her arrogance and stood still while I bowed low and kissed her hand.''

''What happened?'' prodded Sheridan, when he paused as if he might not go on.

''The mob hushed at the sight. They knew I wanted their freedom, but that I believed in orderly change, not undisciplined impulses. There was a murmur that first rippled, then swelled to a shout. '*Vive le general! Vive la reine!*' Long live the general! Long live the queen!''

''Surely, she expressed her gratitude for saving her life.''

''She almost choked,'' said Lafayette with a laugh. ''I'm not sure which infuriated her more, my kissing her hand with her standing there in her nightclothes, or the crowd shouting my salute before hers. I have never been her favorite person, and the incident did not greatly endear me to her.''

''Well, at least now you know how to aggravate Her Majesty—send Lafayette to her rescue,'' Jeremy teased fondly.

The others joined in the laughter, easing the tension in the room, and the diners continued their meal with more pleasant conversation. The children were urged to finish their dinner quickly, and just as quickly were put to bed.

After the others left, the Lafayettes and their house-guests sat in the salon for a long while. The two Americans and the Frenchman exchanged stories of their adventures together during the American Revolution, but they kept the mood light, only telling tales meant to amuse their ladies.

Sheridan was struck by the aloofness with which Gilbert treated Adrienne. It was obvious he respected her and admired her virtues, but there was no great warmth between them even after so many years of marriage.

When they retired to the bedroom for the night, Sheridan had grown pensive and thoughtful. As she began to unfasten her clothing, she wondered if she would grow like Gilbert in the years to come. Would she be cool and reserved toward Jeremy, wounding him daily by the very absence of her love?

She turned to watch him disrobe, and a warm glow spread from her middle down to her toes and to her fingertips. No, she doubted she would ever be cool and reserved toward Jeremy. The very sight of that magnificent body set her pulse racing.

He looked up and flashed her a grin that said, "I'm glad you like what you see." Then he glanced down at her stilled hands and raised an eyebrow.

Sheridan laughed and returned to the task at hand. Once she had stripped down to her shift, she moved to stand by the open window. It had been hot ever since they arrived in Paris, hot and sultry. Once again she longed for home.

Home—it meant so much more now that Jeremy was a part of it. In fact, life meant so much more since Jeremy was a part of it. He gave her strength when she needed it, encouragement when she sought it, laughter when she least expected it. And the things he could make her feel simply by a look! He had sent one of those looks across the room tonight, crowded as it had been with fervent, talkative revolutionaries. The others had faded into the wallpaper as her insides turned to mush. Then, he'd pulled a funny face and made her laugh.

Her thoughts returned to Sinclair Castle, and she suddenly realized it would be only a cold, stone building without Jeremy there. He was the warmth, the heart of it—the heart of her. *I love him. No, don't even think it. I can't.* She looked back at him as he crossed the room toward her. *Is it true? I'm not sure, not yet. Just a little longer. I mustn't say anything until I'm sure.*

Jeremy stepped behind her and pulled her into his arms, dropping tiny kisses across her shoulder, stopping to nibble at a special spot at the nape of her neck that drove her wild.

"Mmmmm, you taste good. I've been wanting to taste your neck since dinner."

"Didn't you get enough to eat?"

"Main courses, yes, but I saved you for dessert." He kissed his way up the side of her neck and nipped her earlobe before raising his head. He slid the top edge of her chemise off her shoulders, exposing a goodly portion of her bosom for his appreciative gaze.

"I wish I were an artist," he murmured. "I'd paint you like this, seductive and full of fire." He chuckled wryly, easing the chemise farther down on her arms. "We'd never make it past the first brush strokes."

An image from long ago made Sheridan gasp. She covered her mouth with her fingers as her mind played out the scene, vivid and clear as a theater drama.

"Sher, what's wrong?" Jeremy's warm hands clasped her upper arms.

She looked up at him over her shoulder, her sapphire eyes filled with a strange mixture of bewilderment and understanding. "She was his lover."

"What?" Jeremy frowned, turning her gently to face him.

"Mother was Macveagh's lover. I wandered into the studio once when he was painting her portrait."

The picture in Macveagh's study, thought Jeremy.

"At least, he was supposed to be painting her portrait. When I came in, they were lying together on a sheepskin in front of the fire. They still had their clothes on—well, partly on—and, of course, I was too little to understand what was happening." She stopped and took a deep breath, unsettled by the memory. Jeremy took her hand and led her over to sit on the edge of the bed.

"But I'm not too little now to understand. They were making love right there in the studio. Papa had gone somewhere, to Edinburgh, I think. When they saw me, Macveagh jumped up and turned away from me. Mama straightened her clothes and looked up at him anxiously." She toyed with his finger, staring down at their clasped hands.

"She called me over to sit in her lap. She hugged me and said she and Uncle Cam had been playing a little game. She didn't want me to tell anyone about it because it might get them into trouble with Papa. She said Papa would be very angry and would send her away. She said I mustn't ever say anything bad about Uncle Cam to anyone or she would have to go away and could never come back." Her voice cracked. "She made me promise."

"That's why you didn't want to go to the

magistrate." Jeremy smoothed her hair. "A part of you was afraid to break your promise."

"I . . . suppose so."

"Oh, love, I'm so sorry." He gathered her close, resting his chin in her hair and holding her firmly.

"I can accept it, Jeremy. Now I understand why I felt as though I had to protect Macveagh. It wasn't a decent promise so I'm not bound by it." She pushed lightly against his chest, and he loosened his arms so she could sit up straight. She gave him a wobbly smile. "I feel strangely relieved."

"And well you should."

"A lot of things make more sense to me." She smiled up at him, feeling free, and ran her hand up his arm. "Make love to me, Jeremy. I need your love right now."

"Yes, ma'am." He eased her back on the bed, pulling away only to blow out the candle. He kissed and caressed her gently, lovingly, intending to prolong his lovemaking to give her pleasure after pleasure. But moments after he began, a flame was struck, igniting their passion as never before.

Gentle kisses gave way to hard, driving ones. Sheridan whispered her need, begging him to come to her, and when he did, they both cried out from the sheer power of their joining.

Afterwards, they curled together, exhausted and complete. Sleepily, Jeremy kissed her brow and closed his eyes.

Moments later, he was staring up at the ceiling, listening to the even breathing of his wife. *I love you, Jeremy.* His heart was racing, and his mind along with it.

"Was I dreaming?" he whispered to himself.

"No," came the soft reply, too soft for him to hear.

Chapter 14

The following morning Kyla and Sheridan relaxed in the back garden, trying to find some respite from the heat. The men had left early, long before Sheridan or Kyla had risen, and Adrienne was busy conferring with her staff. A slight breeze ruffled the leaves, doing little to stir the sultry air.

Sheridan took a long sip of lime punch, then stared at the pale green liquid. She regretted waiting to tell Jeremy of her love. Last night would have been the perfect time. She frowned, chewing her lip thoughtfully. In fact, she thought she had told him, but either she dreamed it or he hadn't heard, because she was sure he would have had some kind of reaction to such a statement.

"Sheridan, will you listen to me?"

Sheridan looked up, meeting Kyla's irritated gaze. "I'm sorry. I wasn't attending."

"Humph! Here I am, about to burst with my news,

and you're off wool gatherin'.'' Kyla sniffed disdainfully and tossed her head.

"I'm sorry, dear. What is your news?" She leaned forward in anticipation, having a strong suspicion of what her friend's answer would be.

"I'm goin' to have a baby," Kyla said, her face beaming and eyes sparkling.

"Congratulations!" Sheridan jumped up from her chair to hug Kyla. "Have you told Patrick?"

"Aye, last night. I was no' sure until just a few days ago."

Sheridan frowned slightly. "You look a little pale."

"I'm doin' fairly well. Early mornin' has its moments, but otherwise I dunna' feel sick at all. Of course, Patrick would have me carried around on a pillow if I'd let him. I think he'll be hard put to let me lift a finger."

"Well, you should be careful. You are small, and, of course, your advanced years are a concern."

"Advanced years! I'm plenty young to have this one and several more, thank you." Kyla joined in when Sheridan burst out laughing. "Let's walk a bit. Mayhap we can find a spot that gets more of the breeze."

They strolled toward the back wall as Kyla told Sheridan about Patrick's tender reaction to her pregnancy. "I thought he was goin' to cry. After he calmed down a bit, we spent half an hour discussin' names. If 'tis a boy, he wants to combine our fathers' names, and call him Robert Waverly. 'Tis good I like it, since he will no' hear of anythin' else."

"What about a girl? Has he something in mind?"

"Nothin' in particular. He wants somethin' unusual, even exotic." Kyla looked up at Sheridan, her eyes twinkling. "Can you imagine my big bear of a husband bouncin' a tiny girl on his knee and callin' her Vespera?"

Sheridan took a breath to reply, but at that moment, two men jumped out from behind some large shrubs directly in their path. There was no time to react before one of the men struck Kyla across the cheek. Her head jerked to the side, and she crumpled to the ground.

Sheridan choked out a stifled scream, but before she could gather her wits and breath and scream in earnest, another man clamped a grimy hand over her mouth from behind, and grabbing her around the waist, pulled her tightly against him.

"The laird will be sendin' ye some instructions soon. This be a warnin' as to what'll happen if ye dunna' do as yer told," the man growled in her ear.

Sheridan watched in horror as the other man pulled a knife from his belt and ran it along Kyla's upper arm. Though stunned from the blow, Kyla moaned with pain. Sheridan struggled as blood began to flow from the gash, but her captor squeezed her midsection so tight she couldn't move.

"There'll be one more warnin' before ye get yer message. If ye dunna' do as the laird says, they will no' get off so easy next time." He squeezed again, forcing all the air out of her lungs, then threw her to the ground. The two men scaled the back wall before Sheridan could call out.

"Guard, help, guard!" Sheridan screamed. Tearing off the sash from around her waist, she tied it around Kyla's bleeding arm. Seconds later, two of the guards on duty at the front of the Hotel de Lafayette tore down the path.

"They went over the wall," she called. "There were two of them."

As the guardsmen took a running jump and swung over the top of the wall, two footmen raced down the path. Adrienne and several servants hurried along behind. Adrienne took immediate command of the situation, sending one of the servants for a doctor and directing one of the footmen to carry Kyla to her room. A maid skilled in treating wounds accompanied him.

As the footman picked the tiny woman up and started toward the house, Adrienne helped Sheridan to her feet. "Are you injured?"

"No."

"How many were there?"

"Two."

Adrienne took Sheridan's arm and nudged her toward the house. She watched her face carefully, looking for signs of shock. "Did they try to rob you or molest you?" she asked quietly, keeping up a steady pace to the back door.

"No." Sheridan shook her head, breathed deeply and composed herself. "They weren't after money. Only one of them spoke, but he was a Scot."

"A Scot!" Adrienne ushered her to a couch in a back parlor. Moments later, she handed her a small glass of brandy. "Drink this, *mon ami*, it will warm you and hold off the shock."

Sheridan drank a few sips of the brandy before jumping up from the couch and moving toward the door. "I have to see Kyla."

"Wait, Sheridan." Adrienne crossed the room and laid a detaining hand gently on her arm. "Before I send for Gilbert, I must know what happened."

Sheridan described the incident. "He said this was a warning so I'd know what would happen if I didn't follow instructions."

"Whose instructions? What are you supposed to do?"

"I don't know, but I can guess. The man said the instructions would come from 'the laird.' I'd be willing to wager my estate that Cameron Macveagh is behind all of this.''

''Who is this Macveagh?''

''A neighbor.'' Sheridan hesitated, wishing she didn't have to tell the rest. It all seemed so distasteful. ''He was my mother's lover years ago, before she died. Now he has decided he is in love with me. I thought Jeremy had convinced him to leave me alone, but it seems the man's word is no good.'' She folded her arms in front of her and shivered. ''He believes I can take her place.''

Adrienne pursed her lips. ''Could he be your papa?''

''No, thank goodness! According to my housekeeper, I was born a month or two before Mother met Macveagh.'' A fearful look spread over her face as she remembered the next part of the assailant's warning. ''Adrienne, we must send word to Jeremy quickly. The man said there would be another warning before my instructions came. They could be in danger.''

''I will send the message immediately. Unfortunately, I don't know where they are right now. Gilbert had several meetings planned today, and I've already heard of one disturbance he probably had to calm.'' She nibbled on the tip of her forefinger. ''Nevertheless, we must try to find them. I'll send messages to every place he might be. In the meantime, I'll ask the guard to post extra men around the hotel, including the back court-yard. Now run on up to see Kyla. I thought I heard the doctor come in a few minutes ago. I'll be up as soon as I dispatch the messengers.''

Sheridan went upstairs to find a young doctor stitching up Kyla's arm. He had given her a liberal dose of laudanum before he began the procedure, so she was not in a great deal of pain. He finished stitching quickly and bound up the wound.

''Madame will be uncomfortable for several days, but

you must use care with the laudanum. I do not believe it is good for the baby if we drug the mama.'' He patted her hand and left the bedside, turning to Sheridan. ''Try to keep her comfortable without the medicine. I did not have the heart to sew her up without it. The wound will heal. Her face will be bruised, but she suffered no other damage. She will mend.''

''Thank you, Doctor, for coming so quickly.''

''Ah, madame, I would have been a fool not to hurry when Madame Lafayette called. I will come back tomorrow and check on our little patient.''

The doctor let himself out of the room, and Sheridan tiptoed over to stand beside the bed. Kyla was sound asleep, though at times she would move her hands with little jerky motions. The tiniest movement of her left arm would cause her to moan softly.

''I'll stay with her, madame.'' The maid looked at Sheridan anxiously. ''You should try to rest.''

Rest! How could she even think of rest when Jeremy might be in danger? Or could it be Patrick or Gilbert or even Adrienne or one of the children who might be used for the next warning? Sheridan shuddered. *Please, God, don't let anyone else be hurt.*

''I'll go to my room. Please call if you need any help or if she needs me.'' Sheridan left the room quickly, guilt pricking her every time she thought of the white bandage on her friend's arm.

She retired to her room but barely paused to sit down. Instead, she paced back and forth, then changed her pattern and went around the room in circles. Her frustration mounted as the clock on the table ticked off minute after minute, then hour after hour with no sign of Jeremy.

Jeremy relaxed in the carriage seat, happy that they were at last going back to the Hotel de Lafayette. The day had been spent literally flitting from one place to the next, talking with various groups in an effort to defeat legislation that Lafayette strongly opposed. There had also been a confrontation with some of the citizens that resulted in the National Guard being called out to settle the dispute, with Lafayette in the lead.

He watched Patrick and Gilbert as they wearily discussed the day's events, trying to get a feel for how the vote would go on the following day. Jeremy's thoughts strayed to his wife, and he smiled at the warmth that filled him simply from thinking of her. He would almost swear she had told him she loved him the night before, but it was possible his mind was playing tricks on him. He wanted her love so badly, perhaps he had been dreaming after all. He mused about several delicious ways he might entice such a declaration out of her, and smiled to himself again.

He was ready to go back to Scotland, ready to get away from the blasted heat and throngs of people. He was fed up with the frustration of arguing with stubborn men who held out greedily for legislation that would put money in their pockets. There was an uneasiness all over France, but especially in Paris. Tension ran high as the revolutionaries sought more freedoms by alternately negotiating with the king and threatening him.

A nasty mob could form in minutes, almost as if some wizard were standing on a high hill and waving a magic wand. And, it seemed no matter what the grievance, it took the power and authoritative charisma of Lafayette to calm them.

Jeremy didn't like exposing Sheridan to this type of danger. So far, Lafayette was in control, but what would happen if one day he lost control and a mob decided to storm the Hotel de Lafayette? There were guards there, to be sure, but that handful of men could not hold out long against several hundred. He decided to remain with his friend one more week. Lafayette would understand his reasons for leaving.

Jeremy's gaze strayed to the street outside the carriage as people rushed home from their day's work and others hocked their wares to those who dashed by. Something seemed out of place with the scene, but he couldn't put his finger on what was amiss. Abruptly, his vision focused on a wizened little man making his way through the throngs of people a block or so down the street. In an instant his senses were tuned, keenly alert. He tapped Lafayette on the sleeve.

"Smithson." He pointed over the front edge of the carriage as Gilbert called out for the driver to stop. Jeremy swung open the carriage door and leaped to the ground, pushing his way through the crowd in the direction of the old man.

Traffic in their direction had snarled a short way in front of them as two carriages locked wheels when one tried to pass the other. Patrick and Gilbert stood, watching over the driver's seat as Jeremy pushed ahead.

"He's a lot quicker than I. He shouldn't have any trouble catching that old man," said Patrick.

The bespectacled little man suddenly looked over his shoulder to see Jeremy perhaps half a block behind. A look of dismay spread over his face, to be replaced rapidly by one of total fear. He broke into a run, pushing and shoving, darting through the crowd.

"Smithson, come back," Jeremy called, still running after him. "I only want to talk to you."

Smithson glanced back over his shoulder and ran blindly into the street, directly into the path of an approaching mail wagon. Jeremy called to him, but it was too late. The horses hit him, knocking him to the ground. He rolled to the side of the road, avoiding the wagon wheels, but when Jeremy reached him, he was struggling to breathe.

Jeremy knelt down on the brick street and lifted the old man's head. He pressed his handkerchief to a bloody wound on Smithson's temple.

Smithson opened his eyes, making a great effort to focus his blurred vision on Jeremy's face. He raised a trembling hand to clutch at Jeremy's arm.

"Dinna'   mean   for . . . Sinclair   to   die. Letter . . . only wanted money . . . no' dead."

"What letter, Mr. Smithson?" Jeremy asked quietly. "Who wrote the letter? What was it about?"

"Servant wrote . . . old murder." His eyes grew wide, and he gripped Jeremy's arm with a force that surprised him. "Your   wife . . . danger . . . Macveagh . . ." The last word was barely a whisper as his fingers loosened and fell from Jeremy's arm.

Macveagh. Did he mean Sheridan was in danger here in France from Macveagh or just while they had been in Scotland? Jeremy stared thoughtfully at the old man, closed his eyelids gently with his fingertips and lowered his head to the ground. He had to get back to Sheridan.

"He killed the old man," a voice called in French. "The aristocrat killed the citizen!"

As Jeremy started to stand, someone hit him over the head, sending him to his knees. A terrible pain shot through his skull, followed by one in his face as a hard blow struck his jaw. Fighting to maintain consciousness, he dragged his hands up to cover his face and head.

"Death to the aristocrat!" Jeremy had the vaguest impression the French words were spoken with a Scottish brogue, but at that moment, he was kicked in the side. Others, Frenchmen, took up the shout. Someone kicked him again and he keeled over, unconscious.

"They're beating him!" cried Patrick, bolting over the side of the carriage as it stopped again half a block away from Jeremy. Lafayette followed right behind him. With a mighty yell, Patrick charged into the crowd like an angry bull. Onlookers scattered left and right, but by the time Patrick and Lafayette reached Jeremy, the instigators had disappeared into the crowd. Patrick swung around in a circle with a ferocious growl, but, of course, no one would admit they had had any part in the attack.

Patrick bent down over Jeremy and checked for a pulse. "He's still alive." His voice broke with pain and guilt. He touched Jeremy's head where the blood was already beginning to clot. "I should have come with you."

Lafayette squeezed his shoulder. "Put him in the carriage, *mon ami*. We'll get him home quickly." As Patrick lifted his limp burden into the carriage, Lafayette addressed the crowd in French.

"I am Lafayette." There was a hum of murmurs as this fact was confirmed. "This man is my friend. If any of you saw who started this, I want you to tell one of the National Guard. Name the culprits, if you can. Give us a description. My friend is an American." He paused as whispers once again went round. "He has been here working for your freedom. You owe him."

The crowd was silent as Lafayette turned and gave instructions to one of several National Guardsmen who usually travelled with him. "Question everyone. Leave no lead unchecked. I want the men who did this." His face flamed with such anger that several bystanders gasped. The calm, diplomatic Lafayette barely held his rage in check.

When the men returned to Hotel de Lafayette, Sheridan raced out the front door to meet them, planning to be the first one to tell Patrick about Kyla. Halfway down the steps, she spotted Jeremy's limp body leaning against Patrick.

"Oh, no!" She commanded her legs to carry her down the steps and across the walk to the carriage. Lafayette hopped down and held the door for Patrick. "He's not dead, is he?" she whispered.

"No, my dear." Gilbert put his arm around her shoulders. "He was badly beaten and is unconscious. I have sent for a doctor."

Sheridan stared at her husband's pale face. One jaw was swollen and turning black and blue. There was a bloody, purple lump on the back of his head with streaks of blood matted in his hair. His coat and shirt were grimy. She shuddered. His shirt bore the imprint of a boot across his ribs.

Patrick lifted Jeremy over the side of the carriage and walked into the house, heading directly upstairs.

" 'Tis my fault," whispered Sheridan, looking up at Gilbert, tears trickling down her cheeks.

"No, no. How can you be the cause of this?"

Adrienne stepped up beside them, taking Sheridan's hands in hers. "You go to your husband. I'll explain everything to Gilbert."

Sheridan smiled her thanks, wiped her face with the heel of her hand and ran after Patrick.

The doctor declared Jeremy had a concussion and possibly a cracked rib. He was sure it wasn't broken, but from the swelling and discoloration in the area, he suspected it was cracked. With Gilbert's help, he tightly bound his ribs. The doctor departed a short while later, leaving instructions for someone to watch over Jeremy for the next several days and a bottle of laudanum to use after he regained consciousness.

Jeremy woke up shortly after the doctor left. When he groggily opened his eyes, Sheridan knelt beside the bed so he could see her face.

"You're going to get well, love. The doctor said

you'll heal." There was no holding back the tears that filled her eyes—relief, joy, guilt, heartache were not to be denied. "Stay awake for a few minutes, Jeremy. Then I can give you something for the pain."

Jeremy tried to say something, but couldn't make his voice work. It was too hard to think. He needed sleep. He tried to shift his position, but a stabbing pain in his side took his breath away. Added to his throbbing head, it was almost more than he could stand.

"I'll help you, love. Which way do you want to go?"

He pointed with his finger, and she helped him roll over on his side. He gasped in agony, and the gasp brought still more torture. But drawing in a deep breath was worse, in fact impossible. She was saying something . . . what?

"You were hit on the back of the head, and in the jaw and the ribs. At least both your sore jaw and ribs are on the left side, so you can lie on the other one."

Her cheeks were shiny and wet. *Rain. No, silly, not rain. Tears.* He worked to think, to stay awake in spite of the pain.

"Here, darling, here's the medicine." She held his head and slipped the spoon into his mouth when he opened it. He couldn't hold back the groan when she eased his head back down on the pillow.

"Jeremy, there's something I have to tell you." She gripped his hand in both of hers and looked directly into his eyes.

Stay awake. This is important. He blinked slowly a few times, but managed to focus on her face.

"I love you, Jeremy."

He smiled faintly and squeezed her hand, giving in to the drug, letting sleep come. *I'm the luckiest man alive.*

Chapter 15

"Sheridan, you should try to rest more. You are much too pale." Adrienne studied her friend closely. "We should not have allowed you to stay up with Jeremy all night. It is impossible for one who is not used to this heat to sleep during the day."

"I couldn't have slept anyway. Now that he is resting more quietly, I'll let one of the servants watch over him tonght as you suggested. I can catch up on my sleep then."

She stared at her teacup, her thoughts drifting to the conversation with Gilbert and Patrick the evening before. She had been afraid Patrick would hold her responsible for the attacks on Jeremy and Kyla, but his kind heart could hold no malice toward her.

Both men had been adamant in their concern for her welfare, insisting she must not give in to Macveagh's demands whatever they turned out to be. Finally, in exhaustion, she had agreed she should seek their counsel before she carried out any of his instructions. She was careful, however, in how she phrased her capitulation, admitting only that she *should* tell them, not promising she *would* tell them. She knew in her heart she would do anything within her power to protect Jeremy, whether she had Patrick and Gilbert's approval or not.

"Excuse me, madame." The butler stood rigidly beside Sheridan's chair. "There is a Capt. Tripp here to see you. I told him you were not receiving, but he said it was most urgent he speak with you. He said you would know him."

Sheridan looked up, startled. "Tripp is here? I thought he would be on the way to America by now. Yes, I'll see him. Please show him into the front saloon." She stood, looking over at Adrienne. "Will you excuse me for a few minutes? The gentleman is captain of my ship." At Adrienne's nod, she walked briskly from the small sitting room.

Moments later, she joined Tripp in the saloon. "Good afternoon, Captain. Is there a problem with *The Alyson*?"

"Good afternoon, Lady Sinclair. You are looking as lovely as ever." Tripp's eyes narrowed as he took in her pale face. "I am happy to report everything is shipshape with *The Alyson*."

Sheridan sat down in a gold brocade chair and looked directly at him. "Then why are you here and not on your way to America?"

"A mutual acquaintance sent me." Tripp watched her pale face grow white and her eyes widen in comprehension. He pulled a chair over next to hers and sat down, keeping his voice low. "I trust your husband and Mrs. Hagen are mending from their unfortunate accidents?"

"Accidents!" she hissed. "You know very well they

weren't accidents. If Patrick hadn't intervened when he did, Jeremy would be dead.''

''His lordship did not intend for him to be killed this time. However, if you don't do exactly as he says, Mr. Mackenzie won't live long enough to get out of his sickbed. If you still persist in resisting Lord Macveagh's command, Mrs. Hagen will follow your husband to an early grave. Then everyone else you care about will follow them, one by one.''

Sheridan gasped and covered her mouth with her hand. Squeezing her eyes shut, she tried to block out the agonizing thought of causing anyone's death. ''What must I do?'' she whispered.

''You will slip out the side gate in the garden at ten o'clock tonight. A carriage will be waiting to take you to your destination. You may bring a bag, but pack light. You will only need clothes for three to four days. Afterwards, his lordship will buy whatever you desire.''

''I would rather go half naked than have him buy me anything.''

''That situation would be very pleasant for me and my companions, but I doubt if you would find it very comfortable, m'lady.''

Sheridan's face flooded with color as she shied away from his leering gaze.

''No one must follow you or try to stop my men. They will be killed if they do. I trust you will do as his lordship says and not cause all manner of problems. I fear his patience has been stretched to the limit.''

''You promise Jeremy and Kyla will not be harmed if I come with you?''

''I can make no promises, m'lady. All I know is what Lord Macveagh told me. If you want to keep them safe, you will do as he asks.''

Sheridan shivered at the thought of doing Macveagh's

bidding. "Do you know what he intends to do with me?"

"I believe he plans to take you on a long trip. He fully expects your husband to divorce you. Even though you are very beautiful, no man would want a wife who has run off with another."

"He will know I had no choice. He knows I detest Macveagh."

"Perhaps, but will he want you after you have shared his lordship's bed? He will know Macveagh does not intend for you to sleep alone."

"I will never yield to Macveagh willingly, and Jeremy knows it." Her eyes flamed with feeling. "Our love is strong enough to defy even the devil himself, and, in the end, it will be Macveagh who falls. He will pay for his sins, all of them."

Tripp sat back, startled by the strong conviction sketched so plainly on her face. He envied her husband. Few men were loved and trusted so deeply.

"Be ready at ten o'clock, if you value his life," he said curtly, standing up. "Once I turn you over to Macveagh, my job is finished. It won't matter one whit to me what he does with you." He looked down at her, trailing a finger along the smooth skin of her jaw. "Still, it'll be a while before he joins us. Mayhap you'll learn to like my company." He chuckled when Sheridan jerked her head away, gritting her teeth to hold back a shudder. "Until tonight, my lovely lady." Tripp left the room and the townhouse quietly.

Sheridan remained in the saloon for several minutes, trying to collect her wits. There was no choice but to follow Macveagh's orders. She had known it from the moment the assailant ground out his warning in the garden. She would give her life to protect Jeremy, even if the sentence meant living with Macveagh instead of death.

When she finally felt composed, she returned to the sitting room, forcing a smile when Adrienne looked up from her embroidery.

"Is there a problem with your vessel, dear?"

Sheridan thought frantically. She had forgotten Tripp was supposedly there on business. "It's repaired now. There was some problem with the rudder. Capt. Tripp was concerned I would hear he was still in port and draw the wrong conclusions. I believe he plans to ship out tomorrow."

"Well, good, I'm glad it wasn't anything serious. Now, *mon ami*, why don't you go up and lie down for a while. You look wilted."

"I think I will go up. In fact, would you mind if I took a tray in my room at dinnertime? I don't think I could even smile tonight, much less carry on a decent conversation."

"I was just about to recommend it myself. Jeremy wouldn't even know you were in his room now with all the laudanum. Regain your strength. You'll need it much more in a few days when he no longer needs the sleeping draught, but still has to stay in bed. I don't think he'll be an easy man to keep down."

"Yes, you're right. Thank you, Adrienne." Sheridan turned away quickly and made for the door. *Will I see you again? Will I ever see any of you again?*

By the time Sheridan reached her room, she was trembling from sheer nervous exhaustion. She collapsed on the bed, falling asleep instantly. When she awoke some four hours later, she was much more in control of her mind and emotions.

"I brought up yer tray, m'lady," said Dora, setting it on a small table near the open window. "Shall I bring up water for a bath?"

Sheridan glanced at a clock on the bedside table. "No, I'll wait and take one in the morning. I think I'll just eat and go straight to bed.''

"Aye, m'lady, that'll be the best thing for ye. I wish me mum were here. She'd give ye some o' her special tea and have ye sleepin' like a wee bairn.''

"I'll do fine without her tea, Dora. As long as someone is watching over Jeremy, I'll do fine.'' Sheridan ate, surprised to find she was hungry. After Dora helped her undress and change into her nightshift, she dismissed the girl for the evening. She found it hard not to hug the young maid when she curtsied good night.

Clad in only a nightshift and robe, Sheridan took her pen and ink and composed a letter to Kyla. "My dearest friend, I must say farewell for now. Macveagh bids me come to him, and I must go. If I do not, he threatens to kill Jeremy in his sickbed. If I still remained, you would be next. I know not how; but please keep a careful watch over Jeremy and yourself. I do not trust Macveagh to keep his word. He may try to harm you further anyway, but I know with full conviction he would try to kill you if I did not yield to his command.

"Tripp was his emissary. I do not know how he came to be mixed up with Macveagh, but he is in his pocket now. I suppose they intend to use my ship as a means of escape, but again I cannot know for sure. He told me nothing except I am to steal out the garden at ten o'clock tonight. I shall try to send word somehow of where I am. I hope, when he is stronger, Jeremy will want to find me. I love him so. Help him to understand. Your friend, Sheridan.''

She read the letter over as she gently blew on the ink. Then she picked up another piece of the delicate stationary. Her hand shook, rattling the parchment. How could she convince him of her love in a letter? With a heartfelt prayer, she began.

"My darling Jeremy, I love you with all my heart. I

never thought I was capable of loving someone so deeply as I love you. I find I would give my life to keep you safe, and that is what I have been called to do. By now, I'm sure Patrick has told you I have gone to Macveagh. I have no choice, my love. If I do not, you will die, and others may, too. If you weren't hurt, I would not leave, for you are a worthy opponent for Macveagh. I know Patrick and Gilbert would stand with me, but it is not the same as having you at my side. You are in such a weak condition, it would not take much to send you over death's edge. I dare not take the risk.

"Please know, Jeremy, that I love you with all my heart and soul. I will belong to you, and only you, until the day I die. Cling to that knowledge, my love, no matter what happens. I pray you will forgive me, for I fear I will be forced to be his harlot. He may claim my body, but he will never touch my heart, for it is yours.

"I will try to send word where I am. I hope you will come for me when you are well, and with God's grace we can begin anew. Please forgive me. Yours forever, Sheridan."

Angry, bitter tears welled up in her eyes, a few dropping to stain the parchment in her hand. Why now? This awareness of her love was too new, too profound to be dirtied by Macveagh. For one brief instant, she longed for that old numbness, wishing it could cloak her in protective darkness. But she rebelled against the thought, knowing she had to be strong. Jeremy's life was in her hands.

She folded the letters, addressed them, melted a dab of wax to seal each one and pressed her signet ring in the warm wax. Planting a tender kiss upon Jeremy's letter, she propped both up on her vanity where Dora would find them in the morning.

Sheridan checked the clock and found she had less than an hour before she was to meet Tripp. Pulling a small bag from the wardrobe, she quickly filled it with a few dresses and petticoats, a hairbrush and small hand mirror. She took her plainest, most comfortable dresses, knowing it would taunt Macveagh a little because she chose not to dress extravagantly for him. She also slipped a tiny cloth bag of gold pieces into a hidden pouch in the bag. It was not a lot of money, but it might be enough to bribe someone to help her get word to Jeremy.

The clock chimed at half past nine. Sheridan flung off her nightgown and shrugged into her chemise and undercoat. From a box on her vanity, she took a small Scottish house pistol. Her uncle had often carried it, either tucked into his boot or in the sporran when he wore his kilt. She ran her fingers along the pearl grip and gold inlay, tracing the pattern of the meticulous engraving, and thought of him.

Giving herself a shake, she quickly took out a soft kid leather belt with two pouches hanging from it, and tied it around her waist. She had gotten the idea from the style of old-fashioned lady's pockets which were worn underneath the gown. Her dresses, however, were not made with the slit in the side for access to the pockets, so she had made the pockets to rest just above her knee.

She leaned over and tied them securely to the outside of each thigh with the attached leather strip. Into one, she slipped the pistol, a few cartridges and a small bag of priming powder. The other pouch had been stitched to form the perfect holder for a small dagger and sheath. She had carried the dagger and a similar pistol in her knotting-bag for years, but had never had call to use them.

"I could kill him. Then he couldn't hurt anyone,' she whispered. "I've killed before. I could do it again." *And you'd be no better than he.* She shook her head, knowing she could only use the weapons if her life were in danger. She left the other pistol in her purse, certain Tripp would search it, and hoped he would end his search when he found the firearm.

She pulled a comfortable traveling dress over her head and fastened it up, her fingers trembling. As the time neared to leave, she feared her courage would fail. Sheridan paused and took several slow, deep breaths. "Calm down or you'll give yourself away," she scolded softly.

She slid her feet into her slippers as the clock struck a quarter to ten. Picking up her bag, she started for the door, only to hurry back across the room to the wardrobe. There was no telling where Macveagh would take her, so she grabbed a cloak and draped it over her arm.

Holding the bag and cloak behind the door, she opened it slowly, wishing her thundering pulse would calm down. With her heart pounding so loudly, how in the world would she hear if anyone were coming? She peeked out the door carefully. The hallway was empty.

Tiptoeing down the long stretch of carpet, she paused for a minute outside Jeremy's room. She longed to see him one more time and stretched out her hand, touching the doorknob. The brass handle was cold to her fingers, surprising her. That tiny shock seemed to clear her mind. She dared not even look in on him. There would be someone with him, and she could not risk questions.

"Good-bye, my love," she whispered. With a swift glance behind her, she hurried down the hall to the servants' stairs. She crept down the stairs, praying with each step that she would not meet anyone. At the top of the last flight, two servants walked by below, and Sheridan shrank back in the shadows. It seemed an eternity before their voices trailed away and she could continue her descent.

She rushed to the back door, easing it open. After checking for anyone in the garden, she slipped through the door and pulled it quietly shut behind her. How much time had passed? She chewed on her bottom lip, fearful that she was late. The garden was dark, and there was only a half-moon shining through a partly cloudy sky.

A loud crack echoed through the night when she stepped on a small broken branch. Sheridan froze. No one responded to the sound, and she made her way to the side wall. It was difficult to find the gate in the dark. Though a walk led to it, there were numerous other walkways that led to small alcoves with benches for sitting. She turned into three of these before finally reaching her destination.

Sheridan leaned her head against the wrought iron railing and took a deep breath. Her nerves were frayed. Drawing her watch from her pocket, she strained to see the time by the moonlight, but the light was too dim. The gate opened with a small squeak. She held her breath, standing perfectly still. After a few seconds, she ventured a peek beyond the wall.

Two guards paced along the walkway, coming to within twenty feet of her before doing an about-face and walking away in opposite directions. The soft clop of horses hooves drew her attention to a carriage coming down the street. It stopped directly in front of her. The door swung open, and a man jumped out and lowered the steps. With an exaggerated flourish, he bowed in her direction.

Sheridan stepped through the gate, automatically shutting it behind her, and rushed to the carriage.

"Good evenin', m'lady. So good o' ye to join us." It was the same man who had restrained her in the garden. Sheridan recognized his gravelly voice even before she met his mocking gaze.

"Where's Capt. Tripp?"

"He'll meet us soon. Now, get in." He jerked the

cloak and bag from her hand, and threw them in the coach. Sheridan scrambled in when it appeared he wanted to throw her in after them.

The coachman spoke softly to the horses, and the carriage began to move slowly down the Rue de Bourbon. They drove past one of the guards. He didn't even look their way.

"You bribed the guards?"

"Aye, they're young and eager for pocket money. They're used to seein' fancy ladies sneak off in the night to meet their lovers."

Sheridan shuddered, fearful that there was more truth in the statement than the man realized. In those young men's eyes, she was probably just another unfaithful wife.

They passed the Square of the Palais Bourbon and several outriders joined them. It was pitch dark inside the coach, but occasionally they passed through a light shining from one of the large mansions along the street. At those times, Sheridan's gaze was drawn to the brute with the gravelly voice. He sat across from her, keeping his eyes on her, and a pistol pointed at her midsection. The coach was old and musty, and her companion probably hadn't bathed in six months. The springs were broken, having given up the ability to cushion the ride long ago. She gritted her teeth; it would be a torturous journey.

They followed the streets along the Seine for a mile or two, then turned southeast. After several minutes, they turned again and stopped. Sheridan chanced a look out the window and recognized the Boulevard St. Germain.

Her captor threw open the door and jumped out, lowering the steps. "Get out."

Hiding her surprise, Sheridan obeyed. Another carriage pulled up behind them, and Capt. Tripp stepped down, smiling broadly. He no longer appeared the seafaring captain, but every inch the prosperous gentleman, wearing an elegant striped frock coat, satin waistcoat and silk breeches.

"Come, come, Lady Sinclair. Surely, you didn't think we intended to travel in that rattletrap." He closed the small distance between them and took hold of her elbow, propelling her toward the newer coach. "Unfortunately, it was deemed best not to have a perfectly new conveyance, but I believe this one will prove adequately comfortable." He helped her up the steps and climbed in after her.

The outside lanterns illuminated the interior, revealing plush, thickly padded red velvet cushions and highly polished wood. A thick blanket and fluffy pillow lay in one corner of the seat.

"You see, my dear, I've tried to anticipate your needs," said Tripp, climbing in after her. "Here's a pillow so you can sleep and a blanket in case it gets chilly." He pointed at a basket near his feet. "There is food and wine, even some tea so that you may have a cup when we stop along the way. You'll find the coach well sprung and quiet. His lordship spared no expense for your comfort. However, I must inspect your handbag." He held out his hand.

Sheridan pretended to look alarmed, then gave it over to him with a resigned sigh. Seconds later he held up the pistol.

"Tut-tut, m'lady. How silly of you."

"It was worth a try."

"I would have thought you more original." He watched her keenly.

Sheridan quelled a real stab of panic. To her surprise, her eyes grew damp, and she felt herself losing control. She twisted a strand of hair around her finger. "I haven't been able to think straight since this all began," she muttered, her voice wavering.

"No, I suppose not. Calm yourself, m'lady. There is no need to fall apart on me now." Tripp leaned out the door and glared at the brute with the gravelly voice as he threw Sheridan's bag and cloak into the back of the coach. "Have a care, Sims. You are to treat the lady and her belongings with the utmost courtesy."

Sims muttered something unintelligible and climbed up to the top of the carriage. Moments later they were on their way, the vehicle traveling over the cobblestones with a smoothness that rivaled the best of carrriages.

"Is Macveagh waiting for us?"

"No, he'll join us later. He said he had some business to attend to first, a transaction he hadn't been able to complete."

Tripp leaned back in the seat, stretching his legs out in front of him. " 'Tis a pity I can't see you more clearly; however, the outer lantern does cast you in an intriguing light." His voice dropped low and silky. "I suspect it is much as you would appear with only one candle on the nightstand. Soft and vulnerable, anxious, yet a little excited." He released a small sigh. "You do evoke the most delectable fantasies, Lady Sinclair."

"You touch me and I'll claw your eyes out."

He chuckled. "I like a woman with fire, and I'll wager you have lots of it." He said nothing more, but watched her closely, taking in her every move.

As Sheridan shifted in the squabs, the dagger pressed against her leg. She resisted the urge to try it on Tripp. She knew how, having been trained in its use by both Waverly and her uncle. But even if, by some miracle, she killed Tripp, the others would deliver her to Macveagh. And, of all the men she had seen so far, Tripp was probably the safest one to be with. He liked power and he liked taunting her, much as a cat teases with a mouse. Yet she didn't think he would force her, not because he was a gentleman, but because he feared

Macveagh. He knew the Scot would kill him if he hurt her.

When they neared the outer wall of the city, Tripp commanded softly, "Lie down on the seat, my dear, and pretend to be asleep. Do not try to speak to the guard, or we will be forced to kill him."

Sheridan glared at him, but picked up the blanket and fluffed up the pillow. As she lowered her torso to the seat and her head to the pillow, Tripp plucked the blanket from her hand. Surprising her with his swiftness, he grabbed her ankles and swung her legs up onto the seat.

"Allow me, m'lady," he said with a leering grin as he unfurled the blanket with a flick of his wrists and spread it over her. Very carefully, he pulled it up so her face wasn't visible.

The coach stopped. Sheridan could hear a few exchanges in French between the driver and the guard at the gate. She understood enough of the language to ascertain they were supposed to be an English couple, Lord and Lady Heathcoat. They were on their way to Basel, Switzerland.

The door opened quietly, and the guard looked inside. Sheridan kept her lids lowered, appearing to be asleep. She could make out Tripp raising his finger to his lips as a signal to the guard that she slept. The man nodded and closed the door, waving them on their way. Once past the wall, Sheridan started to sit up.

"Nay, m'lady." Tripp dropped his hand on her shoulder and gently pushed her back down onto the seat. "You might as well sleep. It will be several hours before we stop. You won't be disturbed, I assure you."

She eyed him warily. "I prefer to sit up." He removed his hand, and she pushed herself to an upright position.

"As you wish, m'lady."

In spite of her determination to stay awake, Sheridan dozed off in an hour or so, waking a little later to find Tripp leaning over her. With a gasp, she looked up at him, wide-eyed.

"Don't be afraid. I was only getting the pillow for you." He tucked the pillow between her head and the side of the coach. He drew the blanket over her and said softly, "Go back to sleep, fair lady."

Sheridan leaned against the pillow and closed her eyes, but it was a very long time before she fell asleep again.

Chapter 16

"She's gone! She's gone!" Dora burst into Adrienne's private sitting room. "Kyla, Mr. Hagen, Lady Sinclair's gone!"

"What do you mean, she's gone?" boomed Patrick, jumping to his feet.

Dora, beside herself with worry for her mistress, fought back tears. " 'Tis gettin' late, and with Mr. Mackenzie feelin' better, I thought I'd best go up and wake m'lady. But the bed's no' been slept in, and her small bag and some o' her clothes are gone." She started to cry. "I found these on the vanity." She held out the letters to Patrick.

He glanced at the names and handed Kyla's to her, sitting down beside her on the couch. Adrienne went to comfort the sobbing Dora and sent a footman for Gilbert. Kyla tore the seal on the letter. Moments later, she looked up at Patrick, her eyes wide and full of alarm.

"She's gone to Macveagh."

"What?" he whispered.

"Here, you read it, I can no'—" Choking back a sob, she handed him the letter.

Patrick read it, then slowly handed it back to Kyla. Absently, he put an arm around her, cradling her head against his shoulder. "We'll find her, little one."

"How, Patrick? She could be anywhere. For the love of heaven, she's already been gone twelve hours."

"Aye, it will be hard to trace her." He looked out the sitting room window, not focusing on the garden outside or the Square of the Palais Bourbon beyond. "What I have to figure out, is how to tell Jeremy."

"What has happened?" Gilbert came rushing into the room from his study. "The footman said I was needed immediately."

"Sheridan has gone to meet Macveagh," said Patrick. "According to the note she left Kyla, she went to Macveagh because he threatened to kill Jeremy and Kyla."

Gilbert frowned, taking the note from Patrick and reading it carefully. "Forgive me, my friend, but I must ask. Is there a chance Sheridan has a *tendre* for this Macveagh?"

"No!" cried Kyla. "She canna' stand him. She is terrified of him. Gilbert, she saw him kill her father when she was just a child. The memory was long buried until recently, but now 'tis fresh and clear. She knows he is capable of murder. She will do anythin' to protect Jeremy." Patrick looked at her strangely, and she knew he was questioning Sheridan's feelings for Jeremy. "She loves him," she said softly.

"I'll check with the watch at the city gates," said Lafayette. "They will know if a carriage left Paris last night. It is possible he will try to keep her here, but not very likely. I suspect they left the city straight away. If he is an intelligent man, he will expect me to check on all departing travelers.

"I'll also question the guards who were on duty here last night. They should have reported her leaving to me." He glanced at the clock. "Jeremy will be wondering why she does not visit him. Do you want me to come with you, Patrick?"

"No, it'll be better if I talk to him alone. He's still weak, and it will be a hard blow." He looked down at the letter in his hand. "I hope this will give him something to hang onto."

A few minutes later, Patrick stepped quietly into Jeremy's temporary bedroom. He was propped up on several pillows stacked against the headboard of the bed. His hair was combed, but the three-day stubble of his beard only accentuated the bruises on his battered face. His left jaw was swollen and vibrant purple, the swelling fading to a light blue puffiness around his eye. He frowned at Patrick.

"I thought you'd be Sheridan," Jeremy said irritably, trying to limit the movement of his jaw. "I keep waiting for her to come in and see me, but she hasn't showed up. She never sleeps this late." His gaze narrowed. "Is she sick? Is that why she hasn't been in this morning?"

Patrick sat down on the chair beside the bed, resting his forearms on his knees. He stared down at the floor for a few seconds before working up the courage to look at Jeremy. When he did, he couldn't hide the pain he felt for his friend.

"What's wrong with her? Why didn't anybody tell me she was sick?" Jeremy made a move to get out of bed, but dropped back on the pillow with a groan, clenching his side.

"She's not sick, Jeremy. She's gone."

"Gone? Gone where?"

"To Macveagh."

Jeremy's sharp intake of breath brought him agony, but it was nothing compared to the ripping apart of his heart. He squeezed his eyes shut to hide his tears. He wanted to die. All his hopes, all those soft words he thought she had whispered had been a dream. She didn't love him. He had lost after all.

"She didn't go because she wanted to."

Jeremy opened his eyes. He listened quietly as Patrick related the events of the past few days and was filled with a bewildering mixture of relief, pain and fear.

"We have to find her, Patrick."

"Lafayette is doing everything that can be done for now. She left this for you." He handed him the letter, rose from the chair and walked over to the window, where he stared out at the lush green garden below.

With shaking hands, Jeremy broke the seal on her letter. Before unfolding the paper, he eased the covers down. Sweat broke out on his upper lip. He drew in as deep a breath as he could without making himself hurt, then leaned back on the pillow, waiting for the hot flash to pass. He wiped his upper lip gingerly with one hand and raised the letter up with the other.

"My darling Jeremy, I love you with all my heart." He closed his eyes, letting his hand drop to the sheet. *I love you with all my heart*. In his mind's eye, he could picture her last night—or was it two nights ago?—softly telling him of her love. He smiled and swiped at his right cheek with his fingers, absently wiping the moisture on the sheet. Picking up the letter, he continued, alternately smiling and being stabbed with heartache. He read the letter through, then closed his eyes again and let his hand relax against his chest.

Tears flowed freely down his face as he went over her words in his mind. ". . . I love you with all my heart and soul. I will belong to you, and only you, until the day I die . . . . I would give my life to keep you

safe . . . . Come for me . . . . please forgive . . .'' He
felt so helpless, so useless. His heart lurched in his chest;
he thought he would explode with rage. *If he hurts
you . . . if he . . .*

"Don't even think about what he might do," he
whispered softly. "Don't give up, Sheridan. No matter
what he does, love, you're forgiven."

Patrick turned from the window and walked over to
the bed. Placing a big hand on Jeremy's shoulder, he
squeezed gently. "We'll find her. Somehow, we'll find
her. You stay there and get stronger. Everything's being
done that can be right now."

Jeremy nodded and looked away, unable to let his
friend see his tears. Patrick left the room quietly as
Jeremy picked up the letter to read it one more time.

Patrick returned to Jeremy's room about two hours
later with Gilbert. Jeremy had fallen asleep, but roused
quickly when they quietly entered the room.

"I talked to the guards who were patrolling outside
the house last night," said Gilbert. "The two on duty
when Sheridan left were young and inexperienced. They
said they were told the lady wanted to sneak out to meet
a lover, a common occurrence among my peers, unfortunately. They were paid to ignore the carriage when it
came their way." He noted Jeremy's grimace. "I'm
sorry, my friend. They will be disciplined." He smiled.
"However, one of them didn't ignore the coach. He
described it as old and outdated. He said it creaked and
groaned like an old woman."

Jeremy frowned. "It doesn't seem like Macveagh to
haul her off in something of that caliber. What about
the guards at the city gates. Did they have anything to
report?"

"Macveagh is a very clever man. Ten carriages, all
fairly new and well sprung, left the city last night
between ten-fifteen and ten-thirty. They left from

different gates, taking the different roads that lead out of Paris in every direction. The passengers in each were supposedly an English couple, Lord and Lady Heathcoat. Each time, the lady was curled up on the seat, pretending to sleep. I assume all the ladies had dark hair, though not every guard was able to see well enough to tell.''

Jeremy let out a low whistle. "I underestimated him."

"I've dispatched patrols after each carriage, but they have a fourteen hour lead on us. They could be anywhere.''

"Sheridan didn't go empty-handed,'' said Patrick. "Kyla checked her room and found she had taken a small Scottish house pistol and her dagger. Kyla says she had a pouch to wear under her skirts to carry them. I think she took some gold, too. Kyla said she couldn't find the small bag of coins Sheridan keeps for pocket money.''

"Well, that's something at least. I just hope she doesn't get hurt by trying to protect herself.'' The other men nodded in agreement. "I guess all we can do now is wait.'' Jeremy muttered a soft oath. "Help me out of this bed. I'm getting weak as a kitten lying here.''

Patrick and Gilbert eased his feet over the side of the bed and steadied him when he stood. The room spun, and he waited a minute for his head to clear before taking four wobbly steps to a chair. His face glistened with a damp sheen as he collapsed into the chair.

"Whew!'' Jeremy leaned back, groaning. His rib felt as though it had grown spikes and each one jabbed him. And he could have sworn someone was standing on his head and pounding it with a hammer. He sat there, panting short, shallow breaths for what seemed like an hour. "Gilbert, give me something better than broth for dinner. I've got to get my strength back.''

"I'll arrange something special and filling. Don't sit

up too long, *mon ami*, you mustn't overdo." He shook his head and smiled sadly, looking at Jeremy's purple, swollen jaw. "You look as though a horse kicked you."

Jeremy nodded, then winced at the small movement. "Whatever it was, I didn't see it coming."

"We questioned those around there at the time, but didn't turn up much. All they could say was the man was Scottish and had a gravelly voice," said Patrick. "I've been trying to figure out why Tripp is involved in all this."

"Me, too. I even wondered if he was behind it instead of Macveagh, but I decided against it. He might lust after my wife, but he doesn't have the funds to set up an operation like this." Jeremy motioned feebly for Patrick to come to his side. "Come on, my friend, help me get back in bed. I don't like to admit it, but I'm worn out."

Patrick and Gilbert helped him into bed, making a great show of fluffing his pillows and smoothing out the sheets. They even managed to get him to smile once or twice with their antics, though it made his jaw hurt.

Sheridan wiggled in her seat and stretched her legs out in front of her. They had been on the road for almost fourteen hours. Though she'd slept part of the night, she was exhausted. Their pace had been quick, yet not grueling, for Tripp had stopped for breakfast at the first decent inn they spotted after dawn. He had appeared the most proper of gentlemen, and rapidly secured a private parlor. The only time she had been alone was to use the convenience, and then he had waited a few steps away, not allowing her the opportunity to speak to anyone.

They had travelled across the chalky plain of Champagne most of the morning. Earlier, the landscape had been covered with grape vineyards, but as the plain gave way to gently rolling hills, the vineyards, too, disappeared.

As she bent her neck slowly from side to side, Tripp smiled at her kindly. "We're almost to Troyes."

"Will we stop?"

"Aye. We'll wait for Lord Macveagh there. It's a lovely city. Of course, you can't get out and enjoy the scenery, but you'll have a good look before we arrive at the house we've rented."

She studied him for a long minute. "Why are you doing this?"

"Money."

"He's paid you well?"

"Aye, m'lady. When you have been safely delivered to his lordship, I'll be a very rich man." His face hardened slightly. "Rich enough to buy my own ships instead of risking my life so someone else can make the profit."

"But why you?"

He shrugged. "Macveagh and I go back a long time. I worked for him a few years ago with his tobacco imports. He knew I was weary of seafaring and knew, too, that I wouldn't harm you. He needed someone he could trust to keep you safe. And I needed the money." He grinned at her. "It all boils down to greed, pure and simple. I want to live a life of luxury, and that is impossible on what a ship's captain earns."

"Where is my ship?"

"It's safely tucked away in a small harbor in case our plans go awry and we need to escape. It would be ironic, wouldn't it, if we used your vessel to spirit you off to some distant land." He chuckled at her disgusted look. "Of course, if we don't need to sail away to China, it will become the first vessel in my fleet."

"It belongs to me."

"For the moment, but there are ways of juggling the

legal terms to effect a simple transfer of ownership to me. All we would need is a signature. Forgeries are easily obtained. Smithson has your signature on a letter, so it will be a simple matter to have the documents signed in your lovely hand. It's quite a thorough plan, actually. To the world, all will appear legal and tidy.''

Thoughts and uncertainties lurked in the back of her mind. *Did I do the right thing? Was this really my only choice, or have I been a fool? Oh, why didn't I ask Patrick and Lafayette to help?* She turned her head away from the gloating man and looked out the window, trying to calm her fears.

They reached the outskirts of the city. Tiny streets wound past lovely gabled half-timbered houses. Narrow walkways ran adjacent to the streets.

Sheridan's eyes widened in surprise when an opening suddenly appeared in a wall as they passed by. A baker stepped through the previously hidden door, tossed her a jaunty grin and went on his way. As she craned her neck around to watch, the door slowly slid back into place, and the seemingly solid wall reappeared.

"The city is full of secret passages and hidden doorways. I find it quite intriguing," said Tripp. "It burned in the 1500's, but there was a school of sculpture here, so when they rebuilt, they turned it into a masterpiece. Look out the other side of the carriage, my dear, and you'll see a magnificent cathedral."

Sheridan obeyed and was rewarded by the beautiful sight of over a hundred stained glass windows. "Oh, please, could we stop and go in?" She turned her pleading gaze to Tripp.

The captain stared down into those beautiful sapphire eyes and steeled himself. She would be hard one to deny.

"Please," she whispered, driven by the thought of taking something fresh and beautiful with her into her prison.

Tripp ran a finger lightly along her jaw. "Such a small request, how can I deny it?" He thumped the roof, and the carriage slowly drew to a halt.

He helped her down and called up to the driver. "Wait here. We'll only be a few minutes."

Sheridan withdrew a lacy scarf from her knotting-bag and draped it over her head before they went inside. A few people knelt in prayer, and a priest sat with an elderly man near the front of the church. He looked up and smiled, but remained where he was, draping an arm across the old man's shoulders as he wept quietly.

Sunlight blazed through the stained glass, giving life to those forever enshrined therein. She gazed from one scene to the next, saying a silent prayer for Jeremy's recovery and her own deliverance. She needed solace and reassurance and the peace only her beloved Highlands could bring.

It was so subtle, she didn't notice its beginning, but slowly, as she absorbed each picture, she was gradually filled with the tranquillity found in the house of God. She knew a peace unlike any she had ever known and an assurance so deep it shook her very core. *All will be well.* She could have sworn she heard a soft voice whisper the words, but there was no one nearby.

Before Tripp could prod her to leave, Sheridan turned to him with a quiet, self-assured smile. "Thank you, Captain. I'm ready to go."

Tripp's eyes narrowed, but he took her arm and escorted her from the building to the waiting carriage. They traveled for about ten minutes when the coach stopped again.

"Come, m'lady, we have reached our destination." Tripp pushed open the door after the steps had been lowered and climbed down to the cobblestone street. Sims waited beside the carriage, holding Sheridan's bag, her cloak thrown over one arm.

Tripp took Sheridan's hand as she disembarked, and tucked it through the crook of his arm. "We shall walk a little way." He guided her down a long, narrow alley whose entrance was completely hidden from the street by the carriage. When they had walked about fifty feet into the alley, Tripp stopped.

Sheridan looked around, but there was no doorway or walkway to be seen, only the back portion of a timbered house. Tripp pushed a board to the side, and reached in the small box it concealed, pulling on a short cord. In the distance, Sheridan heard the tinkle of a bell. A few moments later, a door made to look like the regular boards of the house, opened. A man stepped aside, and Tripp nudged Sheridan through the doorway.

The narrow passage, lit by barely enough tapers to light the way, followed along the back wall of the house before dropping down about ten steps. They passed beneath a cross wall and what might have been a street before going under another wall and coming up in the basement of another building. After they climbed another flight of stairs, a door swung open in front of them. Sheridan came face to face with a man she had known as Jeremy's friend, his first mate, Brannigan.

Chapter 17

It took Brannigan a second or two to hide his astonishment at seeing Sheridan. Unsure of why she was in Troyes and why she was with Tripp, Brannigan held his breath, waiting for her to give him away. She recognized him; he could see it in her eyes, but when she made no comment, he took the initiative.

"Gor, Captain, where'd ye pick up this bit o' fluff?"

"Mind your manners, Brannigan. Even a scoundrel like you should know the difference between a lady and a piece of muslin. Lady Sinclair is going to be visiting with us for a few days. You are to do nothing to make her uncomfortable. Understand?"

"Aye, Captain, I understand." He glanced over at the pretty young maid, Yvette, who paused at the foot of the stairs. "I've got plenty to keep me busy anyways." His grin spread across his handsome face, and the girl smiled back saucily.

"Ah, lad," Tripp said with a chuckle, "I can see

you've been adding to your reputation. You'd best keep your hands to yourself where Countess Sinclair is concerned, or Lord Macveagh will run you through when he gets here.''

Brannigan managed to keep the grin on his face, but the sparkle faded from his eyes. So, that's what this was all about. He wondered if she was here because she wanted to be, or had she somehow been forced?

Sheridan glanced around. They were standing in a back parlor. There was a music room off to the left and the dining room on the right. Down the hall, toward the front of the building, were two other doors, evidently leading to the front parlor and possibly a library. The rooms were well maintained, furnished with heavy, polished mahogany furniture of a different era. The carpet was worn, but clean, and a vase of fresh flowers brightened every table she could see.

''Mayhap, the lady would like to rest up?'' asked Brannigan. ''My pardon for saying so, m'lady, but ye look a bit done in.''

''I am tired. Would you show me to my room, Captain?'' Sheridan glanced at Brannigan, but didn't try to hold his gaze. She was sure he had been afraid she would give him away, and that could only mean Tripp did not know about his connection to Jeremy.

''I'll let Brannigan do the honors. I need to give the rest of the men their instructions. Your bedroom and sitting room are on the second floor. I will expect you to join me here in the dining room for meals. You may move about in the back part of the house as much as you wish, but you are not to go to the front of the building, nor, of course, are you to try to leave. Do I make myself clear, m'lady?''

''Yes, Captain. I suppose I should be thankful you are not locking me in my room.''

''Be warned, Lady Sinclair. If you try to charm any

of my men into trying to help you escape, I'll do just that.''

With a majestic lift to her chin, Sheridan turned gracefully and left the room, waiting for Brannigan at the stairs. He took her bag and cloak from Sims and joined her. Once out of the others' sight, she looked up at him.

"You've taken up with very poor company," she whispered.

"Aye, but it was at Jeremy's request." He put his hand to the small of her back and urged her up the stairs. "He thought Tripp might be up to something, so I hired on *The Alyson*. I rescued Tripp from a few brawls, so he took a liking to me." Brannigan grinned at her as they reached the second floor. "Of course, he never realized I was the one who provoked the fights."

She smiled and stepped into the doorway he indicated, a bedroom in the back part of the house. "Does Jeremy know you're here?"

"I don't think so. We left the ship at Calais and came here. Tripp rented this house and told me and Hodgkins to stay here until he got back from Paris. I had Yvette mail a letter to Jeremy, but since he hasn't sent any word back, I doubt if it got through. I think he would have tried to contact me."

"He's been badly hurt. That's why I came. Macveagh threatened to kill him if I didn't. I was afraid he couldn't stand any other kind of wound."

"How was he hurt?"

Sheridan quickly related the events and Jeremy's condition.

"He's strong, m'lady. He'll be up and about in no time. You didn't happen to bring any money, did you? I might be able to send a messenger to Paris. I have some money, but not too much."

Sheridan quickly opened her case and pulled the small

bag of gold coins from its hiding place. "This might help." She handed it to him, holding onto his hand for a minute. "I'm so glad you're here, Brannigan."

He squeezed her hand, then slipped the bag of money into his loose-fitting shirt. "I'll help if I can, m'lady, but it doesn't look too good. You may have to go with Macveagh if Jeremy or Patrick don't come in time."

Sheridan grimaced. "I know. Don't try anything foolish, please. I don't want you getting killed because of me."

He grinned down at her. "I hadn't planned on it. I'd better go. Tripp'll be wondering what I'm doing up here."

Brannigan hurried from the room. To his eternal thanks, he met Yvette coming down the staircase. He pulled her into his arms, kissing her breathless. "Meet me tonight after dinner in our secret place," he whispered in her ear.

"*Oui, cheri.*" She brought her lips back to his and pressed her willing body tightly against him. When his response was not as fiery as usual, she drew back. "What is wrong? You prefer the English woman to Yvette?"

"No, lass, no, but I had to talk to her. She's my friend's wife, and I had to find out what she's doing here. Now, I'm in trouble and I'll need your help."

"Anything you need, I will do."

"If anybody asks, I didn't go into Lady Sinclair's room. I was here in the hall with you all this time."

"Oui, you did not go in. You were here making sweet love to Yvette."

"Mmm, yes, sweet love." He heard someone coming up the stairs and dipped his head to plant a hard kiss on the side of her neck.

"Brannigan!" Tripp climbed the remaining stairs,

coming into sight. "Have you been out here all the time?"

Brannigan raised his head, the picture of surprise. He grinned sheepishly. "Aye, Captain. Yvette came by 'bout the time 'er ladyship and I reached 'er room. I put the bag on the bed and come right out. And, well, this little French chickie was 'ere waitin'. Sorry, Captain."

Tripp opened his mouth to spit out a reprimand, but the little maid smiled up at him seductively, turning so he was given the most advantageous view of her abundant charms. Instead of scolding his man, the captain grinned. "Hard to resist, eh, Brannigan?"

"Nigh impossible, sir." Brannigan shook his head mournfully.

"Does she pass her favors around?"

"No, sir. She's a one-bloke woman—at least one at a time. Her cousin works a few houses down, though. Pretty little thing, too. I think she'd be quite taken with ye, Captain."

Tripp glanced at Sheridan's door. "I'll keep her in mind."

His look told Brannigan that only a closed door kept him from the one he really wanted. He knew he would have to get word to Jeremy as soon as possible. He could handle Sims and Hodgkins, and probably even Tripp if it came down to it, but several outriders had arrived with Tripp, and there was no way he could take on them all.

That evening, Sheridan dined with Tripp. Brannigan waited in the back parlor, ostensibly reading as he strained to hear every word from the dining room across the hall. Tripp did his utmost to be gracious and charming; Sheridan remained cool and distant. After dinner, the captain escorted her into the parlor.

Brannigan stood immediately and bowed slightly to the

lady. "Good evenin', m'lady."

Sheridan gave him a curt nod in return, acting as if she had only met him that afternoon.

Brannigan studied her as Tripp showed her to a chair and she sat down. He could see her calm self-assurance was beginning to annoy the captain. He had never heard of Tripp getting rough with a woman, but he'd have to keep his eyes and ears open.

"Captain, I think I'll go out and get a breath o' air. Take a turn around the area and make sure everythin' looks like it should."

"Good idea. I don't imagine we were followed, but we need to be on the lookout just in case. Take your time. The lady and I are simply going to sit and talk for a while."

Brannigan went out the front door, stopping to talk briefly with Hodgkins, who stood guard. He walked down the street, crossing to the other side, and turned the corner. At the back of the first house was another narrow street. He turned there and walked quickly past two houses until he reached a vacant building directly across from the one Tripp had rented.

After checking to make sure no one was around, he pushed aside a specific brick on the wall, and a small door clicked open a crack. He pushed his way through, entering another passage known only to him and Yvette. Steep stone stairs immediately took him underground. Minutes later, he had crossed beneath the street to a hidden portion of Tripp's basement. Yvette was waiting for him in a small room off the passageway.

"Ah, at last," she murmured.

"No time for sweet lovin' tonight, lass."

She looked up at him, her lips rounded in a pout. He gave her a quick kiss, but pulled back before she could wrap her arms around him.

"Yvette, is there anyone you can trust to take a message to Paris?"

The French woman studied his face in the candlelight. Her own expression grew serious, and she dropped her hands from his shoulders. "Only my brother, Henri. I think he would go, but he will want money."

"I have some, and when he gets to Lafayette's, I'm sure he'll be given more."

Yvette mouthed a silent "Oh," and her eyes widened. "The Marquis de Lafayette?"

"Yes, he is a friend of Countess Sinclair's husband. I need to get word to him that she is here."

"But someone is coming for her. Perhaps she does not wish to go back to her husband."

"Yes, she does. She doesn't want to go with Macveagh, but her husband has been hurt, and to keep Macveagh from killing him, she agreed to meet him here. If I can get word to Lafayette, he will send men to help us. I can't do much by myself."

"We will help you."

"You're an angel." He hugged her tightly, then pushed her gently aside. "I need paper, pen and ink. Can you get them for me?"

"Oui. Wait here." She disappeared down a corridor that led upstairs to the library. Moments later she returned with the necessary writing tools.

Brannigan sat down on the bed and pushed the candle over to the edge of the table. There was barely enough room on the small table for the paper, ink and pen.

"Is there another entrance to Lady Sinclair's room?"

"No, only one in the captain's. The passageway goes on up from the library. The one in the lady's room was boarded up about ten years ago by the owner." She grinned down at him as he spread out the paper. "He liked to keep his young wife at home."

"Too bad. It would have made it easier to get her away." Brannigan wrote quickly, telling Jeremy where they were and the situation. He paused and looked over at Yvette as she sat down on the bed beside him. "Will your brother come back to show them the way?"

"If you pay him enough."

"Jeremy will pay whatever it takes to get Sheridan back." He added a line to the letter about the money and the instructions to come back with Henri. Then he sealed the letter with a small dab of wax. Since common thugs didn't wear signet rings, he scrawled his initials in the wax.

"There, now all we can do is hope they get here in time." He addressed the letter to Jeremy Mackenzie at the Hotel de Lafayette on Rue de Bourbon. He added Patrick and Lafayette's names as an afterthought.

Pulling the bag of gold from beneath his shirt, he pressed it into her hand along with the letter. "This is all I have. Tell your brother Mackenzie will pay him more when he gets to Paris. Tell him, also, that Mr. Mackenzie has been hurt, so if he is unable to accept the letter, he can give it to Lafayette or a man named Patrick Hagen." He frowned down at her. "Are you sure he will go?"

"If he does not, I will." Giving him a quick kiss, she scurried down the passageway and disappeared before he could stop her.

The next morning, her cousin showed up for work in her stead, telling Tripp that Yvette was ill. She later confided to Brannigan that the maid had indeed gone off to Paris to deliver his message. When he asked why her brother didn't go, the cousin gave a blank look and informed him that Yvette didn't have a brother.

Yvette arrived in Paris late the next afternoon, exhausted, yet at the same time exhilarated at being in the city. It had taken some time to find a horse she could purchase with the funds Brannigan gave her. Convincing her cousin to take her place at the rented house hadn't been hard; persuading her not to tell her uncle about Yvette's mad scheme had cost most of the remaining gold coins.

As was her nightly custom, she had taken a small basket of leftover food from Tripp's, only this time she had added a little extra and a small flask of wine. She had "borrowed" her uncle's saddle, as well as a pair of breeches and shirt left out to dry. Wearing his shirt over hers, she had tied his breeches up with a rope, and covered her hair with an old kerchief. She had rolled up her skirt and put it in with the food, tying the basket to the saddle.

It had been almost two o'clock in the morning when she set off, galloping down the road by the light of a full moon. The horse wasn't fast, but did have good stamina. Yvette was not an experienced rider, but she was used to hard work and long hours of tedium. She hung on and waited to rest until the animal seemed to need it. In later years, she would look back on her adventure and admit that it was the most grueling day of her life.

When she reached the outskirts of Paris, she hid behind some shrubs and changed her clothes. Stopping for a drink at a sparkling stream, she washed her face, smoothed her hair and smiled at her horse. "I may be tired and in need of a bath, but at least my face and clothes will be clean when I meet the famous Lafayette."

All it took was her quick smile to obtain the directions she needed; still, it was almost six o'clock in the evening when she turned down the Rue de Bourbon. The poor horse plodded the last steps, but Yvette did not mind. She had worked in some of the nicest homes in Troyes, but none could begin to compare with the luxurious mansions in this area.

A short distance from the Hotel de Lafayette, she met an ornate carriage driving slowly down the street. The gentleman inside was striking—black hair with a touch of gray at the temples, icy gray eyes that held her gaze. Suddenly, he smiled, his eyes sparkling. He plucked a rose from his lapel and tossed it out the coach window to land at her feet.

"I've won," he said quietly as the carriage rolled slowly past. "He's dead, and she's mine." Then he threw back his head and laughed. The coach picked up speed, but the sound of his laughter drifted back to her—triumphant, hysterical laughter.

Yvette shivered and kicked her horse forward. Moments later, they stopped in front of Layafette's home. Guards paced back and forth in front of the mansion, turning away all who stopped at the front courtyard gate. She peered over the throng of people milling around in the street. Black mourning crepe was draped across the door.

Yvette slid to the ground and questioned a man nearby. "Has something happened to Lafayette?"

"No, thank God. But one of the American guests has died. The poor fellow was beaten by a mob a few days ago and died this morning of his wounds." He craned his neck, trying to see past the gate.

Yvette reeled. She was too late! She leaned her forehead against the horse and whispered to herself, "I came for Brannigan. They will still want to try to save him and the lady."

Leading her horse, the young woman pushed her way through the crowd and stopped one of the soldiers. "I have a message for Lafayette."

The soldier looked at her skeptically before glancing down at the letter.

"It is about Mr. Mackenzie's wife," she said quietly. The guardsman reached for the letter, but Yvette drew back her hand. "I am to deliver it personally."

"Come." The guard took her arm and barked a curt order to another to open the gate. Other guards rushed out the opened gate to keep the crowd from flowing inside the courtyard as Yvette, her horse and the guard moved through. A short while later, she stood waiting in the most elegant salon she had ever seen.

"I understand you have a message for me, *mademoiselle*?"

Yvette turned, her gaze sweeping up to meet the hazel eyes of her hero. For a moment, she was too stunned to speak. "*Oui, monsieur.*" She held out the letter. "I have brought a message from Brannigan."

"Brannigan!" Patrick snatched the letter from her fingers.

She opened her mouth to protest, but shut it again when the man held the letter so Lafayette could read it, too. He had to be Patrick Hagen, she thought, and wondered how she had missed him when he had come into the room.

"Thank God! I'll take this right up to Jeremy," said Patrick.

"I'll alert the men to prepare to ride and then be right up."

Both men turned away and headed for the door, leaving Yvette standing in the middle of the room.

"Pardon me, *monsieur*, but where should I wait?"

Lafayette stopped and swung back around. "My pardon, *mademoiselle*!" He held out his arm. "Come, I'll take you to my wife, and she'll see to your needs. We were so relieved by your news and anxious to tell Mr. Mackenzie that I fear we were quite rude."

"He's not dead?" Yvette gingerly placed her hand on Lafayette's arm and looked up at him in confusion.

"But the crowd outside and the mourning crepe . . ."

"A ruse, my dear." He escorted her down a long hallway toward Adrienne's private sitting room. "One of my servants came to me last night saying a man had hired her to poison Mr. Mackenzie's food. She is very loyal and had never intended to carry out the plan, but thought it best to agree to it. We decided it might be to our advantage to let Macveagh think he had been successful in killing Jeremy. Perhaps he will not be so careful in hiding his trail if he thinks he is dead." They reached the door of the sitting room. "However, I must ask you not to discuss this with any of the servants. There are very few who are aware that he is alive. It is a precaution we must take in these times."

"*Oui, monsieur*, I understand."

They walked into the sitting room where Adrienne was busy with her accounts. She rose immediately and came to meet them.

"Adrienne, this young woman has brought us good news of Sheridan. She is . . ." Lafayette smiled and looked down at the young maid. "I'm sorry, my dear, I do not know your name."

"I am Yvette."

"Well, I knew you certainly weren't Henri. Did he come with you?"

"No, I came by myself." She blushed and looked down at her feet. "There is no Henri, *monsieur*. I lied to Brannigan. I did not know anyone who would make the trip, so I pretended I had a brother." She lifted her chin definately. "I could not sit by and simply let him be killed, and he will if he tries to get her away by himself." Her impish grin spread across her face. "Besides, it might be my only chance to see to Paris."

Lafayette laughed. "Yvette, this is my wife, Madame Lafayette. Now I must leave you in her capable hands. Patrick will be wanting to ride as soon as possible. I assume you intend to return with us?''

"Yes, *monsieur*. I need to show you the way once we reach Troyes. Are you taking a coach?''

Lafayette hid a smile at the hopefulness in her voice. "Of course. Lady Sinclair will need it for the return trip, and you are far too tired to make the journey again on horseback. Did someone take your horse to the stables?''

"*Oui, monsieur*. You will need to sell him, I think. I have no need of a horse and only bought him last night. I do need to take the saddle back to my uncle.''

"It will be in the carriage. Now, please excuse me.''

Adrienne rang for a servant, then invited Yvette to sit down. "I am dying to hear your news. How is Sheridan? How did you get here? And, who is Brannigan?''

Yvette answered all of her questions, telling her everything she knew of the situation in Troyes. By the time her story was finished, a servant had brought a tray. Adrienne insisted she eat right there in her sitting room. Within the hour, Lafayette himself came to escort her to the stables and the waiting carriage.

Yvette glanced at his attire. "You are not going, *monsieur*?''

Again, Gilbert hid his smile. The tone of her voice indicated they could not possibly obtain their goal without his leadership. Hero worship by such a lovely young woman was pleasantly flattering.

"I fear I cannot. Tensions are too high in Paris for me to leave. I must stay here in case I am needed. A calm word at the right time does much to avoid a riot.''

"It has been an honor to meet you. I will remember it all my life.'' They stopped at the open door of the coach.

"It is I who am honored, Yvette. I shall not forget your courage in helping us.'' He lifted her hand to his lips and placed a polite kiss on her knuckle.

In a daze, she climbed into the coach, wondering if she could avoid washing that particular spot for the rest of her life. Once settled in her seat, Yvette looked up to find not only Patrick in the coach, but Jeremy as well.

"Mr. Mackenzie?" she asked politely, though the purple bruise on his jaw confirmed his identity.

"Yes, alive but not kicking." He smiled and tossed her the biggest bag of gold she had ever seen. "My thanks, Henri. Your breeches are with your uncle's saddle."

"Oh, I forgot about them. My uncle will be furious because I took them." She hefted the gold in her hand, thinking she had not come because of the money but knowing how much her family could use it. "Thank you, Mr. Mackenzie, both for the money and the breeches."

The carriage rolled out of the stables and onto the street. Lafayette's fine coach with his family crest emblazoned on the door and the squad of National Guardsmen riding beside it formed quite a sight. Pedestrians turned to gawk, and other carriages and riders seemed to melt out of their way.

Yvette knew that once out of Paris she would give in to her tiredness, and rest would be necessary. But for the moment, she looked this way and that, trying to soak up every sight, smell and noise of the city. Jeremy and Patrick talked quietly, wondering what Macveagh's next move would be. Something in their conversation tickled her memory.

Drawing back from the window, she frowned and nibbled on her fingernail. Suddenly, it came to her. The man in the carriage near the Hotel de Lafayette had sounded like a Scotsman.

"Excuse me, but does this Macveagh have dark hair and strange gray eyes?"

"Yes. Have you seen him?" Jeremy leaned forward, wincing as he did so.

"*Oui*. He drove past the Hotel de Lafayette minutes before I got there. I remember him, because he looked right at me and said something about winning. I could not understand him too well. But the way he laughed—I felt as though death walked beside me."

"Which way was he going?"

"Out of the city. Right after his coach passed me, it speeded up."

"Hounds of hell! He's ahead of us." Jeremy leaned back in the seat and closed his eyes as the carriage passed through the city gate and picked up speed. "God help her."

Chapter 18

Sheridan came downstairs early in the morning to find Macveagh waiting for her. Dressed to perfection, his hair still damp from a bath, he greeted her as if it were the most natural thing in the world to join him for breakfast.

"Good morning, my dear. I trust you slept well?" He rose unhurriedly from the table and pulled out a chair for her. Once she was seated, he leaned over and brushed her cheek with his lips.

Sheridan gripped the edge of the table to keep from wiping her cheek. "I slept very well, thank you. Of course, I didn't know you were here, so I had no cause for concern." In truth, she had barely slept at all.

Cameron watched her closely, sitting down beside her. "Tripp gave you no problem?"

Sheridan hesitated, remembering the captain's amorous persistence of the previous evening. Up until then, he had acted, for the most part, like a gentleman.

But last night, his patience seemed to snap. She had gone upstairs shortly after dinner, taking along a book to read. Two hours later, long after she had changed into her nightshift and curled up on the bed with her book, Tripp simply walked into her bedroom.

He tried to seduce her, and when she did not respond as he wished, he tried to force her. Only the reminder of Macveagh's jealousy had stopped him.

"No, he didn't bother me."

Cameron grabbed her hand, squeezing so tightly it brought tears to her eyes. "You lie!"

"Cameron, you're hurting me!" He immediately eased his grip and brought her hand to his lips, gently kissing her palm.

"What did he do?" he murmured, his head still bent over her hand. He raised his head and impaled her with his gaze. "Tell me everything."

"He . . . he didn't do anything until last night. He came to my room." The sudden flare in his eyes and the tightening of his hand around hers filled her with trepidation. "I didn't invite him, Cameron; he just walked in. I told him to leave, but he didn't. Instead, he tried to charm his way into my bed. When I wouldn't cooperate, he grabbed me and kissed me."

His fingers tightened, but not to the point of pain. "And?"

"Cameron, please, I don't want to talk about it." She glanced at Sims, who stood silently by the door, staring at the floor. "Nothing serious happened."

His fingers squeezed a fraction harder. "What else did he do?"

"He . . . he tore my sleeping jacket." Her face flamed as she bowed her head and whispered, "He pulled my shift down and touched me."

His fingers clamped down on hers, and she bit her lip to keep from crying out.

"It all happened so fast. When I gathered my wits, I reminded him how angry you'd be. It was enough. He let go of me and stormed out of the room."

Macveagh loosened his grip and began to massage her numb fingers. He looked up at Sims, who met his gaze directly. "Kill him." Sims turned abruptly and left the room.

"Cameron, no! Send him away, but please, don't kill him because of me!"

He looked at her strangely, as if she were some child who didn't understand a well-known truth. "He touched you. I'll kill any man who touches you, my dear."

Sheridan shuddered, both at his words and at the flicker of triumph in his eyes.

"Now eat your breakfast," he said matter-of-factly, heaping food on her plate.

Sheridan played with the food, choking down a few small bites, waiting for the shot that would end the captain's life. In a few minutes, Sims meandered back down the stairs and stuck his head in the dining room.

"Job done, milord. All nice and tidy like."

Sheridan put her hand to her mouth, fighting the bile that rose in her throat. She could not force it down and grabbed a napkin when her stomach heaved.

Cameron handed her another napkin and put his arm around her. A few moments later, he pulled her close. "There, there, lass, no need to be upset. The man tried to rape you; he only got what he deserved."

Sheridan closed her eyes and took a slow, deep breath. When she had regained control, she looked up into Macveagh's icy gray eyes. "What about you, Cameron? Will you try to hurt me, too? What will you do when I don't yield to your seduction?"

"But you will, my dear. You have no choice. The Fates sent you to me. You were given to me to replace what I lost when your mother died. You will be willing, even hungry for me, as she was.''

Sheridan was a little unnerved by his incredulous expression. He fully believed every word. ''Cameron, how can I come to you when I love my husband?''

''No! You don't love him!'' His rage suddenly evaporated, and he grinned at her. ''No wife loves her husband. She marries for money and stature, and then takes the man she truly wants as her lover. 'Tis the way it is done in our society, my dear.''

''Then why did you kill my father?'' she asked quietly.

''Did your memory return or did you see the letter?'' He turned his face away, his voice heavy, weary, and slid his hand from her shoulder to the back of the chair.

''We were at the docks in Leith when the fire broke out. It was enough to jog my memory. I remember seeing you pick up the poker and hit Father with it. I was watching you over Mother's shoulder as she carried me out.''

''He would no' set her free. She should have been my wife, not his. She was made for me. It was I she longed for, me she loved.'' He looked back at her, anger turning his eyes to molten silver. ''But Kenyon was too proud. He would no' disgrace his mighty family honor by going through a divorce. He forbade me to see her again. I could no' live without seeing her. He had no right to demand it.''

''She was his wife.''

''Nay, she was his possession. He did no' love her. He would leave her for weeks at a time. She was only a beautiful trinket to come back to, like his fine house and his grand ships. She had married the aristocratic way—for money, not love.'' His lips curled in a snarl.

His face suddenly changed, a wistful, longing expression softening the harsh lines. ''But she loved me.

I can still hear her voice go soft and liquid when she whispered my name. I can still feel her body pressed against mine, soft and fluid, filled with desire for me, no' for him. Never for him.''

The anger returned, contorting his face. "Honor— honor demanded she stay with him and you. If it had no' been for you, she might have left him, but he swore he would never let her take you. Because of you, I lost her.''

The anger faded, and a smile lit his face. "So, to set things right, you were sent to me. After all my torment, the Fates have smiled on me. My punishment is over, and you are my comfort. I'll live out the rest of my days with the woman I love.'' He ran a finger down her cheek. "Soon—very soon, I'll hear your voice go soft and liquid in the night.''

God have mercy, her mind screamed, he truly is mad! Am I to pay for my mother's sin? Panic gripped her, chilling her through and through. Only her trust in Jeremy and the belief that he would come kept her from reaching underneath her skirt and drawing the pistol. She had kept it loaded ever since their arrival in Troyes, priming the pan with fresh powder each morning. But she would have only one shot, and even if she managed to kill Macveagh, there would still be all his men to contend with.

Sheridan placed a trembling hand upon his arm. "Let me go, Cameron. Don't compound your crime with another.''

"I can no'.'' His tone was almost apologetic. "Too much has happened. If I let you go, you will tell the authorities about your father, and I would go to prison. I could no' survive shut up in a cell. No, you will stay with me, so I can control you. You would no' be able to convince anyone that I killed your father after you left your husband and came to me.''

"The magistrate already knows I saw you kill Father. My memory is not enough to convict you of the murder, Cameron. I was a child when it happened, and even though I know it to be the truth, no court would simply take my word for it."

"I can no' take the chance. Too much has happened." He looked away from her, toying with a spoon. "If there had no' been the letter . . ." His voice trailed off, and he turned the spoon over, spinning it slowly round and round on the tablecloth.

"What letter?" Her voice was soft, soothing. "What was in the letter? Did someone else see you strike my father?"

He watched the spoon in fascination, twirling it ever faster with his finger and thumb each time it slowed. "Alyson's maid came down the stairs right after you, but disappeared after the fire. No one ever heard from her until a few months ago."

"She sent a letter to Uncle Galvin?"

"Aye, she was ill and afraid she was dying, so she wrote to your uncle to clear her conscience."

"Uncle Galvin must have shown the letter to Smithson for his advice, and he told you about it, for a price."

He nodded. "I had Galvin's castle searched, but my man could no' find it. Sims was so careful, Galvin did no' even know he had been there."

"So when you couldn't find the letter, you had Uncle Galvin murdered," she said, still speaking quietly.

He twisted his fingers with a snap, and the spoon whirled off the table. "The woman died. Galvin and Smithson were the only ones who knew, and I already had Smithson under my thumb." He shook his head ruefully. "I had forgotten you were there that night. In fact, I had forgotten all about you."

"But you remembered later, and hired someone to

kill me, too." Sheridan couldn't quite keep the bitterness out of her voice.

"Nay, lass. I dinna' know anything about you until I met you that day in Lochearnhead. Sims heard of your return and took it upon himself to try to kill you. He thought it would help me if you were dead; he was afraid you would find the letter. I did no' hear of the attempt until after my arrival home, after I met you in Lochearnhead."

Cameron shook his head, as if to clear his mind, and quickly stood. He took hold of her arm and pulled her up, also. "Come, my dear, I brought presents for you." He smiled down at her and nodded toward the front parlor. "I took the liberty of visiting your mantuamaker in Edinburgh. We came up with some gowns that will look exquisite on you, Alyson. I want you to look your best when we reach Vienna."

Sheridan looked at him sharply, but didn't resist as he guided her down the hall. She knew she would have to tread carefully; he was wavering in and out of reality. "Will we go straight to Vienna?"

"Yes, although we can take a few days to enjoy Switzerland. 'Tis beautiful this time of year." They arrived at the front parlor. "Here we are. This is a small taste of the things I will buy for you, love. I've worked hard and invested well so you can have anything you desire."

Sheridan gasped at the sight before her. Beautiful, costly gowns were draped over every chair and sofa save one, and on it, spread out like a royal robe, was the most beautiful sable cloak she had ever seen. The tables were covered by hats and gloves, perfumes and parasols. Diamonds, emeralds and sapphires seemed to be everywhere. Broaches and earrings were tucked in the hats and gloves, and an open parasol dripped with necklaces and bracelets.

"If there is anything else you want, you need only ask," he said softly, sliding his arm around her waist.

"Let me go. Let me go back to Jeremy." She turned her head, gazing up at him with beseeching eyes.

"Never." He spat out the word with cold finality. Seconds later, he turned toward her, settling her body snugly against his. "You do no' want to leave," he said softly. His gaze roamed over her face lovingly. "I'll make love to you as I used to, and in ways you've never dreamed of. We're together at last, and no one will ever tear us apart." He spread his hand across the back of her head and held her immobile. His breath blew softly against her lips as he lowered his head.

Yvette opened the door to the secret passage across the street. "This leads under the street and up to the first floor library. There is a peephole, so you can see if anyone is in the library."

Jeremy nodded. "We'll wait in there until I hear Patrick and the others downstairs."

"*Oui*. Be careful, *monsieur*. The steps are sometimes damp and slick."

Yvette hurried out of the abandoned house, meeting Patrick and four guardsmen at the corner. Other National Guardsmen were scattered around the block, ready to stop anyone who tried to get away, and to take out Macveagh's man at the front door when the action started.

Patrick and his men followed along a distance behind her, waiting around the corner when she went up the alley to go in the back entrance of the house.

Yvette pushed aside the board and pulled the bell cord. Its faint tones were barely audible, but a few minutes later, Brannigan edged open the door. When he saw her, he threw it wide and jerked her inside.

"You little minx, I've been worried sick about you."

Before she could say a word, he pulled her into his arms and gave her a hard, swift kiss. "You lied to me."

"I had to, Brannigan. I knew of no one who would go to Paris. It is so beautiful! Of course, I only saw a little on my way to Lafayette's, but it is a sight I'll remember all my life." She pushed against his chest, stepped back and whispered, "Is the way clear? Mr. Hagen and some guardsmen wait in the alley."

"Yes, everyone else is upstairs." He stepped to the door and stuck his head around the doorjamb. When he spotted Patrick peeking around the corner, he waved for him to come.

Patrick and the others trotted down the alley and slipped inside the door. Brannigan slapped Patrick lightly on the back and grinned from ear to ear.

"What is the situation? How's Sheridan?"

"I saw her about a quarter hour ago, and she looked fine. Macveagh's arrived, though, so you got here just in time. Where's Jeremy? Was he hurt too bad to come?"

"He shouldn't have made the trip," said Patrick, "but he did. He's as battered and bruised as the time that wave threw him against the mast, concussion and cracked rib. But he should be upstairs in the library by now."

"I'll go on in so I can send my cousin out of the house," said Yvette. "I don't want her to get hurt."

Brannigan looked down at her and dropped an arm across her shoulders. "Go ahead. We'll wait until you two come down in the basement, but you're to go with her." He smiled slightly at the militant expression on her face. "We don't need to worry about one of Macveagh's men using you for cover."

"*Oui.*" She nodded her head in resignation.

They made their way down the passage until they neared the basement. Yvette went on ahead, crossed the basement and went upstairs. She found her cousin clearing off the breakfast table.

"You're back!" she whispered, her eyes glowing with happiness and excitement.

"*Oui*, and we must get out of the house. There is going to be shooting any minute," she whispered back. The maid took her cousin's arm and walked down the hall toward the back door, speaking in a normal tone. "I'm feeling much better now, so you can run along home. Mm. Dupree will be back tomorrow, so you should give yourself the afternoon for a holiday."

When they stepped through the door leading down into the basement, the young women raced down the stairs. Brannigan and Patrick were waiting in the shadows.

"There are two men in the back parlor and one in the kitchen," said the cousin. "A black-haired man arrived this morning. He is in the front parlor with the lady."

"Good. Now you two get out of here." Brannigan could tell Yvette didn't have the slightest intention of leaving. "I said get out of here. I don't want my woman to get hurt."

She blinked at him in surprise before a saucy grin spread slowly across her face. "Your woman, eh?"

"That's what I said, didn't I? Now go on, you're wasting time." He sighed heartily when they turned and ran down the passageway toward the alley. Patrick and the guardsmen had already started up the basement stairs. Brannigan hurried after them.

Cameron's kiss surprised Sheridan with its tenderness. His fingers tightened in her hair when she tried to pull away, but his lips moved gently, lovingly across hers. He lifted his head slightly, trailing kisses across her jaw and down the curve of her neck.

"I love you, sweet Alyson, more than life." He

placed his mouth back on hers, this time demanding and full of passion.

Sheridan fought against him, straining her neck as she pushed her head against his hand. She kicked and flayed at him with closed fists. Finally, she bit his lip—hard.

Macveagh thrust her away, wiping his bloody lip with the back of his hand. "What's wrong with you? Why are you fighting me?" Anger flared in his eyes, and his face flamed. A muscle worked in his jaw as he took a step toward her.

"Keep away from me! I don't want you to touch me!"

Macveagh stopped and relaxed, an evil smile lighting up his eyes. "Oh, I'll touch you all right, lass. And when I do, you'll forget all about that husband of yours."

"Never! You can never make me forget him. You'll never make me stop loving him." Sheridan edged away from him as he slowly came toward her. His arrogant expression taunted her until anger overrode her common sense. "No matter how many times you take me, Macveagh, I'll never want you. No matter how much you try to pretend, I'll never love you. I'll love Jeremy for the rest of my life, and someday he'll come for me. And when he does, he'll kill you."

Macveagh stopped stalking her and laughed. Shaking his head, he smiled at her, looking as if he were about to let her in on a private joke.

"But, my love, he can no' kill me—I've already killed him."

"What?" The blood rushed from Sheridan's face, making her dizzy. She grabbed hold of the back of the chair, willing her wobbly legs to stand. "What are you talking about?"

"Why do you think I stayed in Paris, lass? I hired someone to poison him." He chuckled, obviously well pleased with his game. "I bought out one of Lafayette's own servants. I waited a couple of days until your precious husband was doing better. I wanted him to feel well enough to know he had been poisoned, to know he had lost." He threw back his head and laughed. "I can just picture it. In those few minutes from the time his stomach began to burn until he breathed that last gasping breath, he realized I had killed him and that you would be mine forever."

He looked at her thoughtfully. "I wonder if he had time to think about us? Do you suppose he pictured you in my arms? I hope so, I truly do."

Sheridan's stomach lurched, and the room spun around crazily. She dropped her gaze and stared at the brocade chair seat. *No, he can't be dead! He can't! You lie!* She struggled for breath, but the heartache was too intense. The familiar blackness began to close in, but she fought it. *All will be well.* Those soft words passed gently through her mind, giving her an anchor to hold onto.

When she looked at up Macveagh, an overwhelming rage swept through her. "You lie!" she screamed.

Throwing the chair aside, Sheridan flew at Macveagh, raking his face with her fingernails. He blocked her hands as she tried to come at him again, then slapped her and shoved her away from him. Sheridan stumbled for several steps before falling to the floor.

The door burst open, crashing back against the wall. Jeremy stood in the doorway, his pistol aimed at the Scot.

"I told you if you ever hurt her, Macveagh, I'd kill you."

"You!" Macveagh looked stunned. "But you're dead!"

"No, fortunately for me, Lafayette's servants are

loyal. We decided to let you believe otherwise.'' He lifted the gun a little higher, in line with Macveagh's chest, and glanced over at Sheridan.

Macveagh dropped to one knee and reached inside his boot for a pistol.

Jeremy lowered the barrel of his gun at Macveagh and automatically took a deep breath before squeezing the trigger. A familiar sharp pain shot through his ribcage, causing him to jerk as he fired the round.

He missed.

Macveagh smiled and slowly stood, bringing the small Scottish house pistol up with exaggerated slowness until it pointed directly at Jeremy's chest.

A wave of dizziness poured over Jeremy. *Not now. Not now.* He blinked his eyes, trying to make the room stop spinning, and groped in his jacket with his left hand for the other pistol.

"This is even better than poison, Mackenzie. Think how it will be when you're dead. She'll be mine, all mine."

Jeremy fought down another wave of dizziness. His head was throbbing with an almost blinding pain. *Where is that blasted pistol?* Shots came from somewhere else in the house. *They're too far away. Patrick, get here.* Jeremy squinted at Macveagh and told himself to concentrate on what he was saying.

"Picture her in my arms. Think about her kissing me, making love to me, loving me."

"Never!" Sheridan's soft voice drew Macveagh's gaze to her. She silently prayed for dry powder and squeezed the trigger of her little pistol. The room reverberated with the thunderous crack as the gun fired.

Macveagh gave her surprised look, then crumpled to the floor as a deep red stain unfurled beneath him.

Sheridan stared at him, stunned.

Jeremy took a few weaving steps toward her before Patrick burst through the doorway, knocking two surprised National Guardsmen out of the way. As Jeremy's legs buckled, Patrick was at his side with a strong arm around his waist.

"By Sher," Jeremy mumbled as his friend half-carried him to a nearby couch.

"I'll get her." Patrick swept some dresses to the floor and eased him down on the couch before walking over to kneel beside Sheridan. He took the gun from her limp fingers and stuffed it in his pocket. "It's over, Sheridan. They've all been taken care of." He took her hand and squeezed gently. "There's a man over here who could sure use some attention."

Sheridan came out of her stupor and looked over at Jeremy, then up at Patrick. "How is he?"

"Mending, but he needs a lot more rest." He stood and helped her to her feet. He glanced over at Macveagh and cleared his throat. "Looks like you saved Jeremy's life."

"I was saving mine, too. I don't know how I ever thought I could go with Macveagh. I would have died a little every day."

They walked over to the couch where Jeremy sat resting the right side of his head against the cushioned back. His eyes were closed, but he reached out for Sheridan. She took his hand and sat down beside him.

"Thanks, Countess."

"You're welcome." She paused, blinking back tears. "Jeremy, forgive me for leaving you. I didn't know what else to do." Her voice cracked, and she swallowed hard as he opened his eyes to look at her face. "I love you," she whispered brokenly.

"I know, love, and I know that's why you came to meet Macveagh. There's nothing to forgive. You thought you were doing the right thing. I love you, too.'' His eyes drifted closed again.

"Are you in great pain, Jeremy?" she asked softly, kissing his blue, still swollen cheek. "You look terrible."

He opened one eye and smiled a little. "Nice compliment. If you really want to know, I feel terrible. I'd like to kiss you, but everything hurts too much."

"We'll have plenty of time for kisses later. Why don't we get you upstairs to bed?"

Jeremy nodded and mumbled something about her joining him there, but she only smiled and helped Patrick carry him up the stairs.

They paused outside Sheridan's bedroom door as Brannigan carried Tripp by. There wasn't a mark on him.

"Somebody suffocated him, probably with the pillow, long before you lads showed up," said Brannigan. "I was wondering why he hadn't come down for breakfast."

Jeremy noticed the sick expression on Sheridan's face and nudged her chin with his knuckle. "Sher?"

She looked up at him, guilt filling her eyes. "Macveagh had his man Sims kill him early this morning. He . . . made advances to me last night, so Cameron killed him."

"He didn't . . ." Jeremy couldn't bring himself to say the words, but his expression said what he was thinking clearly enough.

"No. Neither of them did. I'm fine, Jeremy. In much better shape than you. Now, come on and get some rest."

After they got Jeremy settled, Patrick went back downstairs to check on his men. He was thankful to learn none of the National Guardsmen had been injured, since they had taken Macveagh's men by surprise. They gathered up Sims and his henchmen to take to Paris for trial.

Brannigan took Tripp's body down to the basement, along with several other ones. When Brannigan walked back upstairs, Yvette was waiting for him.

He took her hand and led her down the hall to the library, shutting the door after them.

"Are you my woman?" he asked, drawing her into his arms.

"For as long as you want me, *cheri*."

"How about for always?"

She looked at his chin, avoiding his probing gaze. He kissed her forehead, closing his eyes, cherishing her.

"When you went to Paris, I called you every name I could think of. I couldn't understand at first why I was so angry. I figured it was because I didn't like trusting such a job to you, that too many things could happen to keep you from getting to Jeremy. But then I realized that wasn't my main reason for worrying about what happened to you. I'm in love with you, Yvette. I want you to be my wife."

She looked up at him and smiled sadly. "I'm not the kind of woman a man asks to be his wife, Brannigan. You know there have been others."

"So? I've had lots of women before, too, but I intend to be a one-woman man in the future." He looked away and swore softly. "I'm not the kind of man a woman wants for a husband, either."

"Then we should make quite a pair, eh?"

"Does that mean yes?"

"*Oui*, but you'll have to take me to America."

"I will; I'll take you all over the world." He kissed her deeply, edging her toward the passageway door.

"How?"

"I'm first mate on a fine sailing vessel, and I'll make captain soon. Then I can take my wife with me."

Yvette's answer was to give him that special saucy smile and lead him down the passageway to their secret boudoir.

Jeremy and Sheridan rented another house in Troyes for the next month. It was peaceful in the town, and Jeremy needed to heal before making the journey back to Paris, let alone back to Scotland. Sheridan's nerves and emotions needed a rest, too.

One afternoon, two weeks after Patrick and the others had returned to Paris, Sheridan tiptoed into the bedroom and curled up beside her husband. Though growing stronger day by day, Jeremy still rested for a while most afternoons. This particular day was a good day for being inside, since a summer storm drenched the countryside with a downpour.

Jeremy turned over to face her and opened one eye. "What are you up to, minx?"

"Just waiting for you to wake up. We got a letter from Kyla."

"Are they doing well?"

"Yes, her wound has healed." Sheridan giggled. "I think Patrick is driving her half mad with all his attention. He won't let her lift a finger. She's not used to such pampering."

"Every woman deserves to be pampered occasionally." He began to make tiny circles on her stomach with his finger, frowning as she didn't seem to notice.

"Brannigan and Yvette stopped by Lafayette's a few days ago. Kyla said she was dressed like a queen." She paused, thinking that the woman had probably worn some of the clothes Macveagh had brought from Edinburgh. Sheridan certainly hadn't wanted them, so as a thank you for her help, she had given Brannigan's new wife all the clothes and the jewels, even the sable cloak. To her surprise, the dresses fit Yvette, even though her curves were somewhat fuller than her own.

"Jeremy, do you think Mother was a little bigger than I?"

He stopped moving his fingers across her belly and glanced up at her face. The picture of her mother in Macveagh's study blazed across his mind. "Possibly. Why do you ask?"

"I just wondered why the gowns fit Yvette so well. I lost a little weight after you were hurt, but not that much." She looked down at him thoughtfully. "I think Macveagh must have told the dressmaker the wrong measurements. Oh, well. At least Yvette is getting some good out of them."

Jeremy smiled to himself. For the first time since his death, mentioning Macveagh didn't seem to bother her. It was a welcome sign.

"Did Kyla say when Brannigan is going to take over *The Alyson*?" He ran his fingers lightly up her arm, and she snuggled closer.

"They were leaving the next day. Gilbert and Adrienne send their love. The debates continue at the Assembly, and Paris is calm for the moment. Kyla's not as sick in the morning as she was for a while. She thinks she'll be feeling well enough to sail to Scotland soon after we return to Gilbert's."

Jeremy ran his finger along her collarbone, and Sheridan let the letter slip through her fingers to the floor. He began unbuttoning her dress.

"Jeremy, it's the middle of the afternoon."

"Mmm, more like late afternoon." He kissed her soft, creamy shoulder.

"But, what about the servants?" A few more kisses and she wouldn't give a hang about the servants.

"No need to worry. They're French." He raised his head and grinned. "Besides, I gave them the rest of the day off. Told them to get lost until tomorrow morning."

"Clever fellow."

"Must be why you married me." He interrupted her answer with a long, delicious kiss.

"Well, it was one reason." She grinned mischievously.

"There are others?" He raised up on one elbow and leaned his head on his hand. "Well? I'm listening."

"Oh, no. You only get one compliment a day. You'll get another one tomorrow."

"And every day—if I'm nice?" He smiled lazily.

"Yes," she said softly with a twinkle in her eye.

His smile faded, and he gazed down at her with aching tenderness. "Forever?"

Her eyes grew misty, but her face was radiant. She reached up and caressed his cheek gently with her fingertips. "Forever, my love."